FLESH
AND
BLOOD

Flesh and Blood

Emma Salisbury

AUTHOR NOTES

The Care Quality Commission is the independent regulator of health and social care in England. At the time of writing (March 2019) 935 homes registered with it were rated as good and 57 were rated as outstanding, 328 required improvements and 87 were rated as inadequate.

Some heavy lifting reading was required to get a better understanding of the issues facing the sector: Winterbourne View – A Time For Change (2014), a report by the Transforming Care and Commissioning Steering Group. At the time of the Winterbourne View scandal there were 3400 vulnerable people in specialist hospitals. Currently 2300 vulnerable people remain in them.

Source: NHS Digital April 2019

ACKNOWLEDGEMENTS

Although as a writer of fiction I tend to make things up as I go along, there are times when facts are required. The websites and reports referred to in my Author notes were particularly helpful, and I found myself returning to a particular book when writing the post mortem scene: **Sue Black**, *All That Remains,* (London: Penguin Random House, 2018). Even though it tackled a difficult subject matter, it was so fascinating I found it hard to put down.

I am enormously indebted to my early readers, in particular Lynn Osborne, whose feedback is always invaluable. Thank you for being so generous with your time.

As ever, thank you to my family and friends for putting up with my overactive imagination, which has been known to seep into reality at the most inopportune times. And, thanks, of course, to Stephen.

FRIDAY NIGHT

CHAPTER ONE

He was stark bollock naked. Like the day he was born. And cold. The wind whipped over him as he bolted down the street like a streaker at a cup final. The reaction from the folk he passed depended on whether drink had been taken; a cheer or whooping noise came from those half cut, while the sober ones tutted and looked away. A group of teenagers followed him, Forrest Gump style, filming and sharing his antics online. Startled by the sound of tyres screeching and car horns blaring as he ran across the road, he sought shelter in an off licence. The customers inside pointed and stared while Shafiq Ahmed, the off licence owner, phoned the police. 'A car is on its way,' Mr Ahmed said to no one in particular as he draped a blanket over the young man who had hunkered down in front of the counter. The teenagers that had followed him stood in the shop doorway holding their phones aloft until Mr Ahmed picked up a sweeping brush and chased them away.

Custody Suite, Salford Precinct Station

The custody suite rang out with the sound of screaming as the young man was given a pair of threadbare jogging bottoms and a sweatshirt which he refused to put on, tightening the grip on Mr Ahmed's blanket as though suddenly overcome with modesty. A doctor had been summoned who informed the custody sergeant that it was unlikely the young man shivering and babbling in front of him was high on drugs or off his face on booze as they'd first thought, but was on some sort of spectrum; the severity was hard to tell at this stage given the distress he was in and the unfamiliar surroundings. A sandwich and a mild sedative were prescribed. It was agreed that he'd be kept in the cells until the PCs who'd brought him in found out his name, together with an address they could deliver him back to.

His shouts could be heard from behind his cell door, a series of words, albeit hard to make out. Each cell had CCTV in it and they'd shown him how to use the bright red panic strip but to be safe it was agreed to place him on fifteen minute obs. Friday nights were the worst of the week but a few well-chosen words from the custody sergeant encouraged the noisy ones to keep the volume down. He made his way over to the young man's cell and opened the viewing hatch in the door. 'Keep the racket down, mate,' he said in the voice he normally saved for when he got home. 'You're disturbing my other guests.' The young man fell quiet almost immediately, began tracing shapes on the wall with his finger instead.

The custody sergeant closed the hatch and turned to the A4 sized whiteboard mounted next to the cell door. He'd written 'Indecent exposure' on the board when its occupant had first been brought in; he now removed his marker pen from his top pocket and added 'Query special needs.' He glanced down the corridor at the other closed cell doors and the whiteboards beside them. Two assaults, one shoplifter, an attempted murder, one breach of bail conditions and several no shows at court, rounded up and awaiting to appear before the magistrate on Monday morning. He moved to the next cell and clicked down the viewing hatch; might as well since he was down here. The occupant was a young lad he'd not come across before, arrested for breach of the peace, though that covered a multitude of sins. It did no harm to offer a bit of reassurance, their bravado often slipped when they were separated from their mates. 'You alright son?' he called into the void.

'I fucked your mum,' the lad called out when their eyes met; getting to his feet and dropping his joggers around his ankles, he turned his back on the door and bent over, hands parting his bony backside. 'Right up the bum.' Sighing, the officer clicked up the hatch and pulled out his pen, scribbling the word 'Gobshite,' on the board before returning to his desk.

*

It should have been the night shift's shout but the duty sergeant had gone home sick with Tonsillitis and DCI Mallender had a seminar in Bristol to attend the next morning. 'I need someone experienced on this from the get-go,' he'd said when he'd made the call, but they both knew he was offering him a lifeline. With a Professional Standards hearing looming he needed all the brownie points he could get.

Detective Sergeant Kevin Coupland pocketed his mobile before handing the smelly bundle he'd been cradling back to his daughter. 'Saved by the bell,' he grimaced before planting a kiss on Amy's forehead. 'Anyway, I never was any good with the nappy end.'

'Don't I know it,' his wife Lynn muttered as she walked into the front room carrying a tray. The floor was strewn with baby paraphernalia and a changing mat with a contraption over it that resembled a high school gym. She stepped carefully over several teddy bears and a clown that shouldn't go anywhere near a small child in Coupland's view, placed a teapot and a packet of biscuits on a coffee table that had been relegated to the corner of the room. 'You've not long finished your shift, why have you been called back in?'

Coupland pushed himself off the sofa and sighed. 'There's a fire at a care home in Pendlebury, a bad one by the sound of it, one fatality already reported so far.'

Lynn nodded. She'd stayed late at the hospital where she worked enough times to know you didn't walk away easily when your shift ended, and if you were called back in afterwards there was a damn good reason.

'Be careful, Kev,' she said, moving towards him to plant a kiss on his cheek.

'Aren't I always?' he shot back, ignoring the look his wife and daughter exchanged. 'With any luck I'll be back in time to give this one his morning bottle. Mind you if Turnbull's the crime scene manager it's more likely the next drink I give this little fella will be his first pint.'

*

The blaze could be seen for a good five minutes before Coupland arrived at Cedar Falls Residential Home. The air on the approach was thick, cloying. The immediate area had been cordoned off with cones and crime scene tape. Three fire crews were in attendance, their vehicles forming a line in front of the main building. Three more had been despatched. Coupland parked as close as he could, beside vehicles belonging to exhibits officers and fire service personnel. Stepping round to the boot of his car he retrieved a Smurf suit and overshoes, removing his jacket before slipping it on. He held his ID badge up for the uniformed constable standing beside the CSI van to see.

Coupland stepped inside the cordon, taking time to survey the scene. For him this time was crucial. To get the lie of the land, a feel for what had gone before. Even though emergency services were crawling all over the place, these were vital minutes that helped him process what he was seeing. A crowd had gathered by the cordon but they weren't there to gawp. They knew the residents of old, knew full well that the emergency services would need help shepherding them to safety. A human chain formed as figures emerged from the burning building, each resident patted and handed to the next person like a human pass the parcel. First stop the paramedics who allowed the walking wounded to be taken into the nearby sports centre where they were wrapped in blankets and given sweet tea. The kindness was met with bewildered faces, too sleepy or too medicated to understand what was going on. 'Poor little mite,' a young woman whispered to her friend as a man twice her age shuffled past.

Coupland moved behind a large white screen that had been erected. Behind it lay the body of a woman not fortunate enough to escape the fire. Her face was blackened with soot; scorched clothing looked as though it had been glued to her skin. 'Smoke inhalation,' the emergency medic blue lighted from Salford Royal told him. Coupland stared up at the flames engulfing the care home's main building, certain the coroner's office would be claiming more than this young woman by the time morning came.

The sound of sirens filled the air as the second batch of fire appliances arrived. The sight of them did little to lift Coupland's mood, he reckoned their job had turned to one of recovery, rather than rescue.

*

Amid a series of frantic shouts a fireman stumbled from the building carrying a body. A rookie by his demeanour, the sight of him caused an older colleague to run in his direction, helping him to lay the casualty behind the screen. Coupland stepped back to give them room, watching as the rookie shook his head before swiping a hand across his face. The older colleague patted his back, said something out of Coupland's earshot, though he didn't need to hear what was said to know this was the lad's first fatality. A rite of passage that he'd never forget. Something to haunt him on dark nights, replaying over and over in his head until he learned to shut it out. Coupland's jaw clenched. He was still working on *that* bit. He looked down at the body at the young man's feet and his breath quickened. 'Over here!' he shouted to the medic who'd returned to the ambulance, his services so far redundant. The medic grabbed his bag and jogged back to the screen. 'I didn't imagine it, did I?' Coupland demanded. The medic stared for a moment or two before shaking his head. He dropped to his knees to double check. There, beneath the floodlights and the melting remains of a person burnt beyond repair, the chest rose and fell.

'You did a good job, son,' Coupland said as the rookie's mouth fell open. They stood back to make room for the paramedics who swooped in now there was a live one. Morphine administered, the victim was lifted onto a stretcher and wheeled to the waiting ambulance, doors open ready to swallow them whole. Coupland patted the rookie's shoulder like a master rewarding an obedient dog. Now wasn't the time to shatter his bubble, tell him that with burns like that it was unlikely the victim would survive the journey to A&E, let alone the night. He caught the eye of the older man beside him and on this they were agreed: let the world be a hopeful place for the new kid on the block, if only for a short while.

*

DCI Mallender looked grateful when Coupland made his way over to him. His blond hair blended into the hood of his white CSI oversuit, his slim build making the regulation protective gear look classy. He'd been talking to DC Turnbull who'd been nominated Crime Scene Manager, pointing out the cordoned off area, making his hands go wide, a look of frustration across his face. Turnbull was already shaking his head. 'Pointless, Boss, the fire crews need access, the whole place will be contaminated by now anyway.'

Coupland stepped between them. 'Get uniforms to take over the human chain, and get the name and contact details of everyone in the crowd, and while you're at it take a photo of the soles of their shoes.'

Turnbull's eyes widened, 'Seriously?'

In contrast, Coupland narrowed his eyes. 'Which bit of that sounds like a joke to you?' Turnbull was a plodder, but he didn't need telling twice. He clamped his clipboard under his arm as he made his way over to a group of uniforms standing nearby. Coupland cocked a smile in the

DCI's direction. 'Managing Turnbull means telling him explicitly what you want him to do. Leave no room for interpretation. And the fewer syllables the better.' They watched as Turnbull herded a group of uniforms who'd been kicking their heels beside a police van to where the residents were being handed from one onlooker to the next. Two PCs were given the task of collecting everyone's details; the others took up positions by the cordon to receive the remaining residents, though there weren't as many being brought out as when Coupland first arrived. The flames were abating, though it would be several hours before they'd be allowed inside the building, assuming it was declared safe. 'Professor Benson is on his way, although I suspect the bulk of his job tonight will be overseeing the removal of bodies.'

Coupland couldn't disagree.

'I want you to sit on the fire chief's coat tails,' Mallender instructed. 'We need his report as soon as possible.'

'I don't need a report to tell me it's bloody arson,' Coupland muttered. 'The whole place has gone up like a tinder box.'

'No, but you need to know the paraphernalia used,' Mallender reminded him. 'Might give us somewhere to start.'

Coupland nodded, his gaze sweeping over the crowd closest to the cordon, 'Is the owner here?'

Mallender shook his head. 'He's been taken to hospital, suffered burns to his hands helping to get some of the residents out.'

'Anyone spoken to him yet?' His question was met with another shake of the head.

*

Coupland surveyed onlookers as they gave their details to the uniformed officers working their way through the crowd. Middle-aged mostly, locals who'd likely remember when Cedar Falls had been a clothing factory, before it was converted into flats during the property boom then sold on to the current owner who'd remodelled it into a care home during the social care crisis. 'These places are like gold dust, aren't they?' he said to the DCI; not that he had relatives to consider residential care for, elderly or otherwise, unless you counted an incontinent father-in-law whose only pleasure was listening to the cricket on the radio. Lynn would have had him come and live with them if she hadn't got sick, that and the fact Sonny Jim had come along and taken up the spare room.

The crowd was beginning to disperse. Two young men caught Coupland's eye. Black jogging bottoms, designer anoraks with hoods pulled up as they surveyed the action. He moved towards a CSI who was videoing the incident. 'Make sure you get a shot of rent-a-crowd before they bugger off,' he instructed, pointing in their direction. He headed towards the Watch Manager, a man close to fifty but with the build of someone ten years his junior. Coupland had attended several shouts with him over the years. ''Fraid you're lumbered with me, Mack,' he said in greeting, but the Watch Manager's reply was less convivial.

He held up his hand palm outwards. 'Whatever it is can wait,' he ordered, 'The fire has damaged the casing round the gas meter. I need you to evacuate the neighbouring homes NOW.'

Coupland scanned the crowds until he located Turnbull. The DC was using his initiative, getting the uniforms who'd finished shepherding the rescued residents into the gym to disperse the crowd back to their homes. Coupland nodded an acknowledgment. 'There's a bloody gas leak, we need to evacuate the area and push back the cordon. I'll get onto the emergency team at the council, get them to open up the primary school at the bottom of the road.'

Turnbull didn't look convinced. 'What if they won't agree?'

'Start sending everyone in that direction anyway, they'll have to open up then.'

'What about the residents we've just moved to the sports centre? I'm not sure they'll manage the walk.'

Coupland rolled his eyes. 'Come on man; help me out here. Tell 'em the place is about to go up, that'll have them shifting their arses.'

Mallender's shoulders dipped when he was updated. 'I'll stay on till morning briefing; if I leave straight after I'll make it in time for the afternoon session.'

Coupland looked around, satisfied there was nothing more he could do. 'I'll go to the hospital and get a statement from the owner of the care home. Get an update on the burns victim while I'm there.'

A task he wasn't looking forward to one little bit.

Emergency Department, Salford Royal Hospital
Coupland slowed his pace outside Salford Royal's Emergency Department to stump out his cigarette. He'd lit up the moment he'd left the scene, needed to fill his lungs with smoke that wasn't acrid with the smell of human remains. Most cops needed something to blunt the sharp edges of the job. At least Coupland's habit didn't

harm anyone else, he reasoned. He'd long since stopped listening to the passive smoking lobby. A group of youths stood close to the entrance. One of them, the oldest of the group if his bulk was anything to go by, was on his phone, the others circled him, grim faced. Nearby a man wearing a hospital gown sat in a wheelchair sucking on a roll up. He eyed Coupland's Silk Cut dimp as he dropped it into an overflowing bin. 'Got one going spare pal?'

Coupland studied the man's gaunt cheeks, wincing at his cough which resembled a death rattle. 'Should you be having that?' he asked, nodding at the cigarette in the man's trembling hand.

'Should you?' the man countered.

Coupland huffed out a breath as he reached into his pocket for his cigarette pack, put it under the man's nose to take his pick. 'Your funeral,' he shrugged.

A WPC standing in the waiting area pointed out the care home manager sitting on a plastic chair. 'His name's Alan Harkins, Sarge.' She shook her head when Coupland asked if she wanted anything from the vending machine beside the toilets. 'Drank so much tea I could pee paraffin,' she replied, her attention returning to a wall mounted TV with the sound turned down.

An advert for funeral plans flashed up on the screen. Two actors who'd seen better days standing in a conservatory looking at a brochure. Coupland grimaced; not the wisest of choices for a hospital waiting room, he reckoned. The care home manager had been watching the advert too, his attention moving to Coupland as he stepped into his line of vision. 'Mr Harkins?' Coupland asked as he drew near.

The man nodded. A wide face framed with a chiselled

beard sat atop a body with the narrowest shoulders Coupland had ever seen. His warrant card got the merest of glances; some folk were satisfied just seeing a lanyard. Harkins held up a bandaged hand. 'I wouldn't have bothered coming, just for myself,' he said, 'But I wanted to check how the others are getting on.'

'And?' Coupland prompted.

'The woman on reception said someone would come out and see me once they'd been treated. Told me to sit here and wait.'

Coupland regarded him. 'So, I understand you were a bit of a hero.' He offered what he hoped was a pleasant smile. Given the time of night and the circumstances under which they were meeting it was the best he could muster.

Harkins looked surprised, or perhaps modesty made him act it. 'What? Not really, I just did what anyone would have done, though if I hadn't been there I dread to think what could have happened... I still can't believe it.' He paused, as though replaying the incident one more time in his head. 'God knows how it started...'

'Oh, I think there's a chance a few others are in on it too,' Coupland said.

'What, you mean like arson?'

Coupland regarded Harkins. He supposed arson to some would be a relief, a vindication of sorts, that they hadn't done anything wrong. He tried hard to let it pass. Harkins furrowed his brow. 'It'll be kids most likely though, who did this I mean? Some hoodlums on a dare?'

Coupland's mouth turned down at the edges. 'Possibly,' he responded. 'Though that'd be some dare. Whatever happened to rolling a condom onto your head or throwing a shopping trolley in the canal? Happy days…'

He looked around at the sombre faces of the people waiting to be seen. Blood. Tears. Arms strapped up with homemade bandages. A man beside Harkins had a tea towel wrapped around his left hand. 'I was de-stoning an avocado,' he explained, as though Coupland gave a toss.

Harkins cocked his head as he regarded the detective. 'So you think it's something more than a prank gone wrong?'

Coupland shrugged. 'I tend not to think anything until the investigation's actually got underway, Sir. You've given my colleague a statement?' He nodded in the direction of the WPC nipping into the ladies' loo now she was surplus to requirements.

Harkins nodded. 'Yes, but there really wasn't anything I could tell her.'

Coupland cocked an eyebrow. 'I wouldn't be too sure,' he said, 'I can think of a couple of things I'd like to ask.'

'Oh yes?' He had Harkins' full attention now.

'Like why your sprinkler system wasn't working?' Coupland prompted.

Harkins jutted his chin out. 'We don't have one.'

Coupland stared at him.

'There are no regulations to say we have to have a sprinkler system installed. The law requires that we are able to demonstrate that the premises and any equipment we use is safe and properly maintained. Staff are given regular fire safety training and I personally carry out all risk assessments.'

'And look how well that turned out,' Coupland countered, his glance dropping to Harkins' hand.

Leaving the care home manager to sit and stew for

a while, his non-existent shoulders drooping even more, Coupland signalled to a passing nurse that he wanted a word. 'Tough night?' he asked when the nurse dropped his guard once he knew he wasn't speaking to a relative.

The man blew out his cheeks. 'When are they not? You here about the victims brought in from the fire at that residential home?'

Coupland nodded.

'The casualties brought in with minor burns are fine. We're keeping them on obs for a while due to smoke inhalation but they'll be good to go in a couple of hours.'

Coupland waited. 'And the last one to be brought in?' he prompted when the nurse hesitated. 'I know it's not looking good, but I'd still like to see them.' He was aware he didn't even know if the victim was a man or woman.

The nurse lowered his voice. 'We've put her in a side room,' he said, 'I'll just clear it with the consultant and I'll take you through.'

*

The name scrawled on the whiteboard above the bed said Ellie Soden. Coupland pulled out his notebook and jotted the name down. He stared at the unconscious figure lying on the bed. There wasn't a face to speak of. Melted eyelids and the cartilage of a nostril could be seen beneath an oxygen mask. The rest of the face was burned beyond recognition, an uneven landscape of blisters and pus. The consultant had made Coupland wait outside the room until the woman's condition had been stabilised. 'Pointless sending her to the burns unit,' he said when he stepped outside to speak with him, 'She isn't going to survive this. We're talking hours at most. In the meantime we're keeping her sedated.'

'Probably for the best,' Coupland found himself saying, though that's not what he meant at all. Pragmatic and thick skinned, he was fond of calling a spade a shovel yet that didn't stop him reeling at the damage one person could inflict upon another. Yesterday this woman had been going about her business and now this. A life not yet snuffed out, but slowly smothered as her organs began to fail. There was a saying, Coupland wracked his brain as he tried to remember it, 'There's no comfort to be had from soft words spoken at a safe distance.' In his line of work people didn't pass away or fall into a restful sleep, they were killed, murdered, dragged into oblivion kicking and screaming and damaged beyond repair, lives extinct before their time. The victims he dealt with knew no peace at the end. He hadn't realised the extent of it when he'd signed up for the job, was too far in now to do anything else to earn his crust. He'd learned over the years it was better to speak candidly, to let relatives know the facts as they were so they could start to process them. Even so. This would be one hell of a call to have to make. 'Have the next of kin been informed?' he asked.

'You'll have to check with one of the nurses, sorry.'

The sound of a commotion coming from along the corridor put Coupland on alert. Before the security guards hanging round the nurses' station had time to react he was running towards the waiting area in front of the reception desk. One of the young men he'd spotted by the entrance earlier was having a stand up row with the WPC. 'It's not fuckin' fair,' the bulky one said, eyes narrowed. He couldn't have looked more like a stroppy teen if he'd tried.

The WPC was having none of it. 'The receptionist has already told you she can't give out any information to anyone other than family members,' she said once more, not the least bit intimidated, sending Coupland a look that told him she had it covered, that any attempt to undermine her would not go down well at all, rank or no rank. Coupland slowed his pace, had enough blots on his copybook not to risk a complaint of sexual discrimination being added to his ever growing catalogue of misdemeanours. The WPC had as much right to get a gob full during her shift as any male officer, he knew that much. He thrust his hands in his pockets, waited long enough to see the boy and his mates stomp away, though not before one of them flicked his finger at the receptionist. Something niggled in the back of his skull as he watched the youths leave, but nothing that had the decency to make itself known at this time of night. Coupland hauled in a breath as he pushed the thought away. Right now Ellie Soden was his priority, and her time was running out.

The nurse who'd shown Coupland into the trauma unit stepped away from the bed to write something in Ellie's patient folder. He looked up when Coupland paused in the doorway. 'It's OK, you can come closer,' he said, not needing to add that that it was pointless worrying about infection under the circumstances. Coupland moved towards the bed, trying not to wrinkle his nose at the smell of burned meat.

Ellie was surrounded by tubes and monitors. The machinery beside her kept up a rhythmic beep and hum, the illuminated numbers on them told all who looked that the prognosis wasn't good. The nurse leaned in close to Coupland in case what was left of Ellie's ears might pick up what he said. 'You intending to stay around?'

Grateful for the excuse to look away Coupland turned to face him. 'Hadn't planned to,' he answered, 'Any sign of the next of kin?'

The nurse's nod was slow, 'I got her parents' details from the care home manager, managed to get through to them about twenty minutes ago. They live in Birmingham.'

'What was she doing at Cedar Falls, then?'

'Apparently it was the nearest place that could take someone with her needs. They're on their way but they'll not make it in time. I didn't tell them that obviously, nothing to be gained in adding to their agony.'

Coupland's shoulders dipped, his gaze returning to the prostrate figure on the bed. 'How old is she?'

'Eighteen.' Something cold and hard shifted in his gut. He pushed an image of Amy out of his mind. The thought of anything like this happening to his daughter… and now there was Sonny Jim to fret about… He moved towards the bed. 'How come you were able to ID her so quickly?'

'Only the top half of her body has been damaged by the fire. She has a tattoo on her left leg; the care home manager recognised it straight away.'

Coupland had heard enough. 'Don't suppose me staying on will do any harm,' he ventured, 'not as if she's spoiled for choice.'

'She's not in any pain,' the nurse said. 'We've dosed her up to the eyeballs.'

What's left of them, Coupland thought, looking on as the nurse slipped from the room.

Coupland glanced at the diamorphine drip, thanking Christ for small mercies. He forced himself to look at the burnt sphere on the pillow. Leaned in close to her face. Whether she sensed his presence or was away with the fairies was another matter. 'We'll get who did this,' Coupland promised, his throat tightening as though he'd swallowed something hard. He could have sworn for a moment that she heard him. There was a movement, albeit miniscule, a slight turn of the head in the direction of his voice. He moved until his nose was above where hers used to be. In the police dramas Lynn watched on TV Ellie would have moved then; the more far-fetched shows would have had her raising a hand to write down the culprit's name on a note pad the detective offered. But this wasn't a cop show, this was as real as it got, a young girl in resus, not even fighting for her life, just slowing drifting out of it.

He saw it then, a single tear roll out beneath the blister of an eyelid into the blackened mass that would once have been her hair. Coupland's breath quickened as another one formed. Two strides and he yanked the door open, calling for the nurse to return. 'She's responsive!' he called out. 'She's crying. Maybe she is in pain after all.' The nurse smiled at him then, the way medics do when they're trying to soften the blow. 'Her tear ducts don't work anymore, it's likely the drops I've put in to keep her eye sockets moist.'

'So she wasn't trying to tell us something?'

Like the pain was off the Richter scale.

That she was frightened.

That she didn't want to die…

The nurse shook his head. 'There are some sickos out there, I'll give you that,' he muttered. 'Preying on those who need our compassion.'

Coupland's jaw clenched. He had a word for them, alright, only sicko didn't cut it. He clenched his fists at the thought of what he'd do... then blinked the thought away. Wasn't he in enough trouble? He'd joined the force because he wanted to make a difference. Yet what difference could he make to this girl's life other than be with her when she left it, however long that took? He breathed out a sigh as he reached for his phone. Sonny Jim wouldn't know whether Coupland was there or not, he reasoned, as long as someone gave him his bottle. He dialled home.

SATURDAY

CHAPTER TWO

The incident room smelled of bonfires. Only those just starting their shift were dust free. DS Alex Moreton hadn't bothered with a suit, had decided old jeans and a shirt she wore for cleaning up would do – faint splashes where bleach had striped the colour out could be seen here and there. She'd reported for work at the crack of dawn, news of the potential gas leak had got onto social media; Salford Online had posted a photo of local residents being shepherded into a nearby school. With the fire still raging through Cedar Falls there was every chance the incident could escalate into an emergency situation.

Alex had been awake long before the news bulletins came in. Todd's sleep pattern was bordering on the non-existent; most nights would be spent with her or Carl pacing the floor with him while the other slept. She'd been scrolling through Facebook on her phone when the first report came through. Ten minutes later she was reversing her car off the drive, her grumpy baby and his grumpy dad glaring at her through an upstairs window. 'If the leak goes up it'll be a major incident,' she'd said, aware of the major incident she was leaving Carl to deal with on his own. By the time DCI Mallender returned to the station she'd run a search through the HOLMES database for anyone with a previous history of arson living within a five mile radius of Cedar Falls. Only one of the offenders who came up on the list was serving time, the others had participated in community payback orders. Alex printed off their details ready for the briefing.

Morning Briefing

DCI Mallender addressed the assembled officers from a chair he'd pulled from a desk at the front of the room. He'd been on his feet for the best part of the night and had a three hour drive to Bristol ahead of him. A brief respite was needed while he drank the coffee DC Timmins carried in on a tray. 'You do the honours, Kevin,' he said as Coupland walked in.

Coupland nodded, studying the crime scene photos that had been put onto the whiteboard: Cedar Falls' main building engulfed in flames, a photo of Catherine Fry, the first victim recovered from the scene, together with photos of three horrifically burned bodies taken in situ, prior to their removal. Someone had written 'Fatalities' down one side of the board and underlined it; four names had been written underneath. Barbara Howe, Roland Masters, Sarah Kelsey, Catherine Fry. These were the names of the residents and one staff member still unaccounted for, now presumed dead, albeit as yet only Catherine Fry was capable of identification as her injuries hadn't obliterated her appearance.

Coupland pulled the lid off a marker pen on his desk and added Ellie Soden's name to the list. Placed a tick beside it to show her identity had been confirmed.

'She didn't make it then,' Mallender observed.

Coupland shook his head. 'Was never going to,' he answered. 'She's been identified by her parents, poor buggers.' He blinked the image of Ellie Soden away. His

34

hand holding hers when her breathing became shallow, the short spell of gasps before the rattle of death. Foam appearing where her lips and nose used to be, signifying she'd run out of air. It had taken two hours for her to die.

Her parents arrived just as her body was being wheeled to the hospital mortuary. Coupland had sat with them in the relatives' room while they tried to make sense of what he told them.

'But I only spoke to her yesterday evening,' her mother kept saying as though that alone should have kept her safe. Her husband didn't speak. He'd sat down when told to do so, gripped the cup of tea a nurse placed into his hands, eyes locked onto Coupland the whole time.

'Evidence suggests the fire was started deliberately,' Coupland had said.

The information bewildered them. 'Who would do such a thing?' Ellie's mother kept asking over and over.

'Do you know where you will be staying?' he'd asked them. 'A Family Liaison Officer will be in touch…'

'Staying?' Ellie's mother looked even more confused. 'Oh… we never gave it a thought… didn't pack any clothes.'

'We won't stay,' her husband spoke up then. 'We'll go straight home, once we've made arrangements.' He caught Coupland's frown. 'For the last twelve months we've had no say in where our daughter has been living. Lack of resources, Government cuts, ring fencing, one reason after another spouted to us why she couldn't receive care in our own city. I've had enough. We came to take our daughter home, DS Coupland, albeit not in the way I imagined when we set out in the middle of the night.'

Coupland's jaw clenched as he searched for the words

to explain that Ellie's body was now the property of the coroner. That until a full post mortem had been carried out their daughter would remain in the mortuary. He'd tried to persuade them to stay, at least overnight so they could rest.

'You think I'd want to spend a night in your city after this?' Mr Soden had exploded.

Coupland had pressed his card into the man's hand as he'd walked them back to their car. 'In case you have any questions,' he offered.

'Because you've been really helpful so far,' Ellie's father had spat back.

*

One mug of coffee remained on the tray on top of DC Timmins'desk and Coupland reached for it, nodding his thanks. He circled the mug with both hands before turning to the assembled group: 'Cedar Falls is a residential home for adults with a range of complex needs. Last night someone saw fit to torch it while the patients got ready for bed. Takes balls to do something like that, eh? Whoever did this is a real credit to the community.' Several heads nodded around the room, interspersed with murmurs of agreement. Parts of Salford were infamous, no go areas, where all but the meanest men feared to tread. But at least the threat was expected, the combat open.

'Do you mean learning disabilities, Sarge? If so, what kind?' A black man with an athletic build and shorn hair shaped around chiselled features looked up, waiting for an answer. DC Ashcroft had transferred from the Met the previous year. A square peg in a round hole down south, he'd slotted into Salford Precinct's murder squad with ease. Greater Manchester Police was England's second largest force outside the Met but the difference in culture between them was like night and day. Ashcroft wasn't as defensive as when he'd first transferred, and a stint working with Coupland while Alex Moreton was on maternity leave had given him a close up and personal view of the spiky DS that many didn't see.

Coupland's eyes squinted as he pondered the question. He'd washed his face in the small sink in the toilet cubicle in the emergency department, trying to rid himself of the dust that had worked its way under his eyelids. 'Autism?' he replied, 'Downs?' he glanced at Mallender for corroboration; the DCI nodded.

'I looked Cedar Falls up online,' Alex spoke up. 'They also take residents with challenging behaviour.'

'I thought that was Tattersall,' Coupland said, referring to the inner city overspill that had developed a reputation over the previous three decades – for all the wrong reasons. A ripple of laughter went around the room.

Alex shook her head. 'Kids in care who keep running away, folk displaying violent outbursts, mental health patients refusing to take their meds, that sort of thing.'

Ashcroft nodded his thanks.

Alex slid the list of arsonists she'd compiled across her desk towards Coupland. 'Thought you'd want to check on the usual suspects.' Coupland took the list from her, scanning the names before adding them to his actions sheet.

Alex remembered something. 'I've been checking Twitter.' She held up her iPad like an exhibit in a courtroom. 'Workers from the fire station tweeted that the blaze was well established when they arrived at Cedar

Falls and that fire personnel made over thirty rescues.'

Coupland's mouth formed a thin line. He couldn't fathom the attraction of so-called social media. Did the public really need to be spoon fed their news in sound-bites? GMP were no better, every station now had a designated officer responsible for managing their Twitter account and Facebook page. At Salford Precinct it had been Alex who'd drawn the short straw, mainly for her ability to complete whole sentences without swearing.

Alex tapped the iPad a couple of times. 'The ambulance service tweeted that several people were assessed at the scene and that some were transferred to Salford Royal for further care.' More keyboard tapping. 'Salford Council has tweeted it is working in close cooperation with the emergency services—'

'—that's not quite how I remember it,' Coupland interrupted, recalling the response to his request to open up the primary school nearest to the care home to provide temporary shelter for Cedar Falls' residents. The council officer had relented, once Coupland had explained the offence of obstruction.

'I thought you'd like that.' Alex grinned. 'It goes on to say that it will be assessing the needs of the evacuated residents and arrange alternative accommodation as a priority.'

Coupland blew out his cheeks, hoped to Christ someone else from the council would be picking up *that* baton. 'Dare I ask what pearls of wisdom have we released into the ether?' he asked.

Alex ignored the jibe. Instead she tapped several more times, reading out the tweet she'd posted minutes earlier: 'The cause of the fire is currently under investigation.

The number of fatalities has not been confirmed and GMP would like to offer our sympathies to the families of those affected.'

'Blimey, the Super will be out of a job soon,' Coupland muttered. He turned to address the team. 'The whole area stank of accelerant. That this was a deliberate act is a no brainer. What we don't know at the moment is what type of accelerant was used. Our best bet while we wait for the fire officer's report is to work through DS Moreton's list and round up those we know like playing with matches. Let's shake a few trees, see what falls down.'

He handed Alex's print-out of local arsonists to DC Ashcroft. 'Work your way through that lot and see if there's anyone worth talking to.'

He turned to DC Timmins, the most junior detective in the team but what he lacked in experience he made up for in his ability to manipulate computer data. Dressed in a new slim fit suit, there was no hint of his penchant for the icing covered donuts that gave him his nickname. 'Krispy, I want you to work through the list of names uniform collected from onlookers last night. See if there was anyone there who shouldn't have been, like one of Ashcroft's arsonists observing the damage they've caused. Though Christ knows that'd make this job too bloody easy. And check the shoe sizes recorded as well, cross-match with anything picked up by the CSI team.' Krispy nodded as he made notes on his desk pad.

Coupland turned to the DCI. 'What's the situation regarding the suspected gas leak, boss?' he asked.

'Emergency repairs were completed in the early hours, enabling local residents to return home first thing,' Mallender informed him.

The WPC who'd taken the care home manager's statement at the hospital had stayed on after her shift had ended, and was now sitting on a chair at the front of the room. She was dressed in civvies, a cable knit jumper over skinny jeans, hair untied and brushed through in a hurry. She stifled a yawn as she turned in her seat to address those present. 'Alan Harkins states he was in the office when the fire alarm sounded. He ran into the adjacent building where the residents live and tried to get as many out as he could.'

'Do we know anything about him?' Coupland asked.

'Clean as a whistle. Lives on site. No partner.'

'Can anyone corroborate his whereabouts?'

'They were down to skeleton staff with it being the night shift. The only other staff members on duty were through in the residents' block.'

'What was your impression of him?'

'By the time I got to the hospital he'd been treated for minor burns he'd received evacuating the residents. He seemed genuinely concerned about his patients, and was worried about finding temporary accommodation for everyone. His behaviour didn't cause any concern.'

Coupland thanked her and said once she'd typed the statement up she could sod off home. This earned him a thumbs up sign as she grabbed her jacket, moving swiftly towards the door before anyone else had a question for her.

Coupland addressed two DCs sat nearest to him, 'Turnbull, Robinson, I want you to go and speak to Alan Harkins and his staff. Look into any disputes with business rivals, neighbours, any bugger for that matter. Who are his suppliers? Does he owe them any money? Check his finances, does he have a gambling habit? An obsession with designer clothes he can ill afford but can't resist, you know the sort of thing…'

'You think it might be an insurance job?' Turnbull asked.

'Nothing gets passed you, eh Turnbull? Well it wouldn't be beyond the realms of possibility. Just because it's the obvious motive doesn't mean it's the wrong one. He was on site, had the opportunity.'

'But to commit murder, Sarge?'

'Maybe he thought he'd be faster on his feet than it turned out. Wouldn't be the first person shocked at the speed the fire they'd started had spread. To start the fire then rescue all the residents he'd have been hailed a hero if it hadn't gone belly up.'

'He still rescued some, Sarge,' Robinson piped up. 'What does that make him?'

Coupland's mouth formed a grim line. 'That's what we need to find out.'

DCI Mallender studied the names on the whiteboard. 'What do we know about the victims?'

'Because of the extent of the burns we've yet to match a name to three of the bodies retrieved, but the owner was able to confirm the following people are missing, presumed dead: Barbara Howe, a 65 year old female care assistant; Sarah Kelsey, a 25 year old year old mother of three suffering from bi-polar disorder; Roland Masters, a 60 year old man suffering from Alzheimer's; Catherine Fry, a 30 year old woman with Down's; and now Ellie Soden, 18, who'd been referred there from a behavioural unit.' Coupland wondered what she could have done that had resulted in her being sent away from home. It had no bearing on the case necessarily, but still, loose ends bugged the hell out of him.

The DCI obviously felt the same. 'I want a full history on each victim, together with details of any other facility they've stayed in and length of time there so we can piece together anything they may have had in in common.'

'Will do, boss,' said Coupland.

Alex caught his eye. 'I can do that, and I can give you a hand with the death messages if you like, might help to get some idea of what the relatives thought of the care their loved ones were getting at the home.'

'Agreed,' Coupland nodded, before turning back to the group as he handed out further actions. 'Someone out there thinks they've got away with murder. Get your backsides out there and prove 'em wrong.'

Coupland watched the group disperse before turning to the DCI. 'I've got this under control, boss. Go before the Super realises you're still here and sends you his latest spreadsheet for updating.'

Mallender pulled a face. 'I'm beginning to wonder if it's worth going at all.'

'What's the seminar about?'

'It's more of a summit, really, a chance to share good practice with other forces about how we've dealt with organised crime. Superintendent Curtis got the invite but passed it on to me. He felt the talk would be of greater benefit to the delegates attending if it was given by someone with direct operational involvement.'

'I bet he did. More like the crowd doesn't have enough pips on their sleeves to warrant him dusting down his dress uniform.'

'Maybe.'

'So, what are you going to dazzle them with? The A-Z of Salford's gang network and why we're pissing in the wind?'

'I was aiming for something a little more positive. It's easy when you're in the thick of it not to realise what we've achieved, but huge inroads have been made, Kevin.'

Coupland raised his brows. 'In what, exactly?'

'Reduction in tit-for-tat shootings, for a start.' Gun crime had spiralled out of control in the nineties earning Manchester the title of Gunchester. Fatal shootings had been all but obliterated following the conviction of a gang a decade before. When guns were used to settle scores these days it was big news.

'I guess there'll be plenty of space at the back of the auditorium, then,' Coupland grunted.

'What for?'

'The bloody big elephant in the room, of course.'

'I don't understand.'

'I take it the Super told you to gloss over the knife crime epidemic on our doorstep?'

'Like I said, it's about sharing best practice.'

'I heard you, but wouldn't these summits be better engaged solving the problems going on in their areas rather than blowing smoke up each other's backsides?'

'It's not as simple as that, Kevin.'

'It *is* as simple as that boss, only top brass like to make it more complicated to justify their existence.'

Mallender sighed. 'If anyone should be accused of making things more complicated than they need to be it's you – have you remembered your meeting with your union rep? I bet you haven't even prepared your defence, have you?' Coupland's silence told him all he needed to know. 'The sooner you start working on your account of events the stronger your case will be. Leave it to the last minute and you could forget something that Professional Standards will pick up on.'

Coupland forced his lips into a smile, 'Yeah, I hear you, I'm all over it.'

Coupland's grin faded as he watched DCI Mallender make his way down the corridor. He felt done in. Unlike the TV show detectives who hung around waiting for each investigation to fall into their lap he already had a heavy caseload including a gang related stabbing in Higher Broughton and a hit and run outside a school near The Crescent. He was also due to give evidence in Judy Grant's trial, the woman the press had dubbed 'Medicine Woman' because of her role in doping young female migrants illegally trafficked into Salford. He'd have to prioritise; cutbacks meant there were no other teams to hand cases over to when something big hit the fan. You worked longer hours to get things done, or they simply didn't get done. He looked at his watch. Reckoned he had time to nip home for a shower and change of clothes if he was quick about it.

Alex was already on the phone to Alan Harkins, the manager of Cedar Falls Residential Home, asking for next of kin details and victim case files, together with contact numbers for any previous residential homes the victims had stayed in. Coupland signalled he was popping out, mouthing he'd be an hour, tops, if anyone needed him.

*

The conversation stopped the moment Coupland walked into the newsagents. It was his local. Not too many doors down from where he lived that he wasn't beyond walking to it in the good weather, on the rare occasion when he'd run out of fags and not had the presence of mind to stop and replenish them on the drive home. He liked to do his bit these days, carbon footprint and all that. Something wasn't right about the looks people were giving him. He was used to sidelong glances, most folk got twitchy when there was a cop in the room and the GMP logo on the lanyard he was obliged to wear these days gave his occupation away. He joined the queue, returning the glances that came his way with what he hoped was a non-threatening smile. The newsagent, anticipating his request had already placed twenty Silk Cut and a packet of chewing gum on the counter.

It was while Coupland was waiting for the woman in front to pay her paper bill that he noticed it. The headline on the pile of newspapers beside the till. He hadn't paid any attention at first; besides, the picture on the front page had been expanded so many times it was grainy and out of focus but the face was recognisable despite the bruising around the nose. Austin 'Reedsy' Smith in all his glory, beneath the headline: *My ordeal at the hands of maniac cop.'* Coupland's shoulders dipped. Someone must have taken a photograph of Reedsy while he was on remand, sold it on to the gutter press. There was a photo of Coupland too, taken when he'd nipped out of the station for a decent sandwich, given the brown paper bag in his hand and take away coffee cup. *'Long serving officer lashes out at cornered suspect,'* was the caption beneath it. Coupland snatched up a paper from the top of the pile, flicking through until he found the rest of the article. *Detective Sergeant Kevin Coupland of Salford Precinct Station lost his temper during a dawn raid, assaulting Austin Smith before he had the chance to give himself up. "I was backed into a corner," said*

45

Smith. "It wasn't like I could have gone anywhere."' Coupland scowled. Of course Reedsy wasn't going to mention the window he'd been planning to escape through, or the guns stashed behind it. No, that would have been too much to expect. *'It is understood Mr Smith has made a formal complaint to Greater Manchester Police, and a full investigation is underway.'* The sidebar to the article was a call to action: *'We pay for your stories! Call Angelica Heyworth 0161 236 2700 or email us at tips@SalfordNetwork.co.uk. We pay for videos too, simply go online and download our app'.*

Coupland dropped the newspaper onto the counter and pulled out his mobile phone, tapping the paper's name into Google's search engine. He downloaded the app when prompted. Sure enough, Reedsy's ugly mug stared up from the screen in all his technicolour glory, embedded into the online paper's front page. Several comments had been posted below the article: 'Disgusting behaviour from someone who should know better. Is this why I pay my taxes?' Followed by 'Sack the bastard,' and 'Reedsy, you fanny, you still owe me a tenner.' Another article below it showed an image of a naked man; the arrow button in the centre of the picture implied it was a video. Coupland hit 'play' and the man sprang into action, running into an off licence where he could be seen cowering by the counter. The filming stopped when an Asian man came out waving a brush handle.

'Would you like a copy?' the newsagent asked, pointing at the tabloid rag on the counter. The queue behind Coupland was growing impatient, though Austin Smith's bruised face cautioned them to keep quiet.

'Waste o' bloody money,' Coupland grunted, lifting the paper from the counter and holding it up for everyone to see. He skim read down the inside cover, found what he was looking for. The hit and run he'd been investigating was halfway down the page. 'Whatever happened to proper news?' he demanded. 'A father of two wiped out in broad daylight yet it's a paedophile's broken nose that makes the headline.' He dropped the paper once more, snatching up his cigarettes before slamming his money onto the counter top. 'You forgot your chewing gum!' the newsagent called after him.' 'No sodding point,' Coupland muttered. It would take more than juicy fruit to get rid of the sour taste in his mouth.

*

Coupland was still reeling from the newspaper article but forced it from his mind when he stuck his head round his living room door. Sonny Jim had had his morning bottle long since and was staring up at Amy while she changed him on the floor. Lynn was sat in the corner on an armchair, watching the proceedings but knowing better than to offer advice.

'This is the third set of clothes he's had on since you left last night,' Amy grumbled without looking up.

'Takes after his mother then,' Coupland shot back, winking at Lynn as he stepped into the room, tip-toeing over a cushion in the shape of a baby elephant. 'Anyway, got a name for him yet?' he asked as he plonked himself down on the sofa.

Amy's face lit up as she scooped the baby into her arms and went to join her dad. 'I was thinking about Jaxxon, with two xx's instead of the cks.' She'd been trying out different names for size since Sonny Jim had been born but there was nothing they all agreed on.

Coupland's mouth turned down at the edges as he considered this. 'You could do a lot worse than Kevin – with two vv's – if you want to stay on trend,' he suggested, enjoying the look of alarm Amy shot in his direction.

'It's not our place to decide,' Lynn reminded him. 'You can't keep poo-pooing every suggestion.'

Coupland blew out his cheeks. 'I can if I'm expected to take him to the park for a kick about when he's older. If you think I'm going to yell 'Go on Kanye!' on sports day you've got another think coming.'

Ignoring him, Lynn turned to her daughter who was patting Sonny Jim's back like a wizened old hand rather than a first time mother. 'How about Harry?' she suggested.

Coupland widened his eyes, 'Since when did you become a footie fan?'

Lynn shot him a look, 'After Prince Harry, you idiot. Anyway, it's better than Rio, or Ryan, or Eric or any of the other suggestions you've come up with so far.'

Coupland grinned at his wife, 'In your opinion, my sweet,' he muttered.

Amy smiled at her parents' banter. 'I only said Kanye the other day to wind you up, Dad!' she teased, 'Although Jaxxon does have a ring to it.'

'Like the police siren fifteen years from now,' he quipped without thinking. Amy's grin slipped as the temperature in the room became noticeably cooler. Suddenly they were on dangerous ground. The subject of Sonny Jim's father, Lee Dawson, was a No Fly Zone. A serial killer who, when nearing capture, had tried to take his own and Amy's life. Coupland had saved his daughter, leaving Dawson to slip – literally – through his fingers.

That the killer had been able to get close to Amy would always be a matter of guilt. Coupland found it hard to get his head around his grandson's paternity; he'd gone from making sly digs out of Amy's earshot, to silence out of loyalty, but his doubts were still there. The fear that flesh and blood really meant something.

The glare from Lynn had him choking on his words. His joke, though ill thought, had no ulterior meaning. 'He looks like a Harry,' she piped up in an attempt to deflect the situation.

Coupland smiled gratefully as he grabbed the lifeline she threw him. He studied Sonny Jim's bald head and hamster cheeks. 'He looks more like Al Murray,' he said finally.

'Oh, for God's sake!' Lynn muttered, as Amy carried the baby upstairs for his nap. Lynn started clearing the baby paraphernalia away, cardboard books and stuffed animals which she stowed into a basket that now lived beside the fireplace. It was funny watching the force with which she tidied them away; clearing soft toys angrily didn't have the same effect as banging down plates or slamming a door, though Coupland knew better than to let his amusement show.

'Let's not row about a stupid comment I made,' he said.

'Too right,' Lynn answered, ramming Peter Rabbit into the basket with more force than was necessary, 'I mean, we'd be rowing all the time if that's all it took.'

'Point taken.' Coupland looked around the room for something he could help clear away but Lynn's soft toy genocide had worked its magic and the room resembled once more how it had looked pre-baby days. 'I don't know why you're getting so wound up, it's not as though

Amy threw a wobbler or anything.'

'She won't though, will she?' Task completed, Lynn set the basket down and turned to face him. She looked tired, but then running around after a grandchild did that. 'She's not going to show she's upset because she doesn't want the confrontation,'

'Or to lose the free board and lodgings, not to mention on-tap babysitting if she voted with her feet.'

'Is that what you want?'

Coupland dropped his gaze. All the people he cared about were right under this roof. He couldn't think of a time he'd been happier. The feeling rattled him; he spent his days treading through families torn apart every day. 'Of course I don't,' his voice was low, as though this admission would tempt fate. They both looked up as Amy reappeared, the baby wriggling red-faced in her arms like a shoplifter avoiding arrest. 'So much for nap time,' Coupland quipped, 'Put Bargain Hunt on, that'll soon have him out for the count.'

'I thought you weren't stopping,' Lynn said.

'I'm not,' Coupland replied as he pushed himself to his feet, squeezing Amy's shoulder before making his way into the hall. 'Anyway, I've made a decision. Until you decide on something I'm going to call him Tonto.'

Both women stared at him. 'Who are you, the bloody Lone Ranger?' Lynn sniped.

'Feels like it sometimes,' he answered, eyeballing her. 'Be nice having a little sidekick about the place.'

As he climbed the stairs he could hear Amy asking Lynn if she'd mind the baby later, Lynn trying desperately to make up for his earlier faux pas by agreeing, even though she was on earlies the next day.

He was towelling himself dry when his phone rang. A number he didn't recognise. 'Yes?' he barked, hoping his tone would make the caller brief.

'DS Coupland? Sergeant Colin Ross, your union rep. We had a meeting arranged at Salford Precinct this morning. Although I seem to be the only one that's bothered to turn up.'

Coupland swore under his breath.

CHAPTER THREE

'So tell me again why you saw fit to head-butt a suspect you were trying to apprehend.'

Coupland's sigh came up from the soles of his feet. 'How many times? I've already told you. There was a risk Austin Smith was going to evade capture. I had to stop him.'

'What's wrong with the conventional methods of detention? I mean, I know it's been some years since you attended police training but even so...'

'I could say the same to you if we're playing that game...'

'And what do you mean by that?'

Coupland hissed out a breath. 'When was the last time you had to do any proper policing? I mean, it's easy for you in your high tower, having a punt at the rest of us. Finding fault, apportioning blame, picking away until the risk to our careers should someone decide to complain is so great we hold back, begin to question ourselves, hesitate that one second too long so instead of an arrest we've got a dead kid, a battered granny, an old fella knocked unconscious—'

'—OK I think we can stop it there for now.'

'Why stop now when I'm just getting started?'

The officer sat opposite him sighed. 'That's my point, DS Coupland. Which is why as your federation rep it's important I help you work through your statement, make

your responses during your interview sound a lot less…
aggressive.'

Coupland stared at Sergeant Colin Ross, an officer who,
if his demeanour was anything to go by, had never crossed
the line in his life. 'For Christ's sake man I was trying to
apprehend someone who didn't want to be arrested. How
do I do that without it becoming aggressive?'

'But the head butt, Kevin. Was it entirely necessary?'

'I suggest we call it a day there,' Superintendent Curtis
interrupted. He'd been sitting across the interview room
from them, observing, willing his fiery detective to play
nice. Roped in at the last minute because DCI Mallender
had managed to hot foot it away before Coupland
returned to the station, he sent a glare in his direction.
'We have to be seen to be following through with this, DS
Coupland. We need to reassure the public we take their
concerns very seriously.'

'The public don't give a toss, Sir. Some scrote
complains about the way he was detained after playing
a part in a little girl's death? I don't think so. At best
they'd be furious with the waste of taxpayers' money his
complaint is costing; I suspect more of them would be
cheering from the side-lines.'

'But we can't encourage that type of attitude, Sergeant.'

'I'm not. I'm just saying that the people who harm kids
are scumbags. Pure and simple. The day we have to debate
that I'll pack it all in, go and sell insurance for living.'

The Super closed his eyes. It looked for a moment as
though he was counting. He turned to Colin Ross. 'I'll
have my DCI spend some time with DS Coupland prior
to the hearing,' he offered. 'See if we can't get a little
contrition in his response.'

'I'm still here you know... Sir.' Coupland growled. 'Have you forgotten that bastard drove little kids around the city to be filmed while they were abused? You want me to act like I'm sorry for breaking his nose? He's lucky I didn't—'

'—As I said, DS Coupland, let's call it a day. You're a serving officer of Greater Manchester Police, let's try to keep it that way. The days of cattle trucks and pitchforks are long gone.'

'More's the pity...' Coupland grumbled. 'I'm joking!' he said, hands in the air when he saw the look Curtis threw at him.

'That's agreed then,' Sergeant Ross responded. 'A time to reflect and regroup.'

Coupland's jaw clenched as he got to his feet. 'Jesus wept,' he muttered once he was safely in the corridor.

*

The head teacher at Meadowvale Primary School did her best to hide her annoyance at having to turn up to school on a Saturday. 'The council has sent over emergency food packs,' she sniffed, 'But It'll be a different ball game come Monday with the best part of four hundred kids expecting to eat their lunch in here.'

'And how are the survivors of the fire doing?' Turnbull asked. 'Must be a terrible shock for them, learning some of their friends have died.'

'I wouldn't know,' she said, relenting when she saw the look that passed between the detectives. 'Look, I'm not unsympathetic, of course I'm not. But my first responsibility is to my pupils.'

Best described as a control freak, Miss Flaherty was

one of those people destined to teach. Despite her title she wore a wedding band, and there was a tummy bulge too small yet to assume was a baby, large enough to be blamed on too many cakes in the staff room.

'Our responsibility is to all members of the public,' Turnbull stated.

Miss Flaherty ignored him, turning to Robinson, 'Any idea how long this situation is expected to continue? I'd have asked the care home manager but he's barely shown his face.'

'He told us he'd meet us here once he'd finished up at the hospital,' Turnbull answered on behalf of his colleague. 'They're fine now by the way, the patients that were kept in for observation. I daresay Mr Harkins may have his hands full for the time being. Besides, I reckon your colleagues at the council are more able to help you in terms of that information. It'll depend on if any of the residential block at Cedar Falls is considered habitable, and if not, how long it will take to return it to its former state.'

'Proper little ray of sunshine, this one,' Robinson piped up at the scowl forming on the head's face. 'No good to anyone until he's had his elevenses; mind you, he has a point though, best checking with the experts...'

Miss Flaherty led them through to a large multipurpose hall with a stage at one end and tables surround by chairs filling the remainder of the room. Residents from Cedar Falls sat huddled in groups, nursing drinks in paper cups, a plate of biscuits had been left in the centre of each table. Several faces looked up when the detectives walked in. A girl with long blue hair rose to her feet to greet them. Only half her hair was blue, the other half remained its natural mousey brown as though she'd got bored half way through the colouring process. 'I'm Lucy, one of the care assistants; I guess you are the police?'

Turnbull held up his lanyard and made the introductions, when he was done Lucy moved around each table placing her hands on each person's shoulder as she gave their name.

'I want to go to my room,' a woman sat at the front of the group said. Her speech was anxious, hurried; she leaned towards the detectives, a hand pressed against her face hiding her mouth.

'Soon, Lizzy,' Lucy responded, 'we're just making the beds up.' She raised her brows at both detectives as she said this. 'We really need to get them settled somewhere,' Lucy looked pointedly at Robinson, as though she'd decided he was the one likely to get things done.

'I'm sure the council will make it a priority,' he told her, 'I don't know any more than you, I promise.'

Lucy hesitated. 'Have you any news about Barbara?' she asked, coming to stand beside the detectives. 'She shouldn't even have been working; she knocked off hours before. Is she still missing?'

'We can't say anything for certain at this stage, she hasn't been accounted for along with three of your patients, but I must warn you that four bodies have been recovered from the fire. It's looking likely that you will need to prepare yourself.'

'Oh, God…'

'One of the patients taken to hospital didn't make it,' Robinson lowered his voice as he said this, 'Ellie Soden.'

Lucy's hand flew to her mouth as though she was going to be sick.

'You here on your own love?' Turnbull asked, 'Thought you'd have had a colleague helping as well.'

'She does,' said an unshaven man with straggly hair as he held up a hand. He'd been sitting with a group clustered round a neighbouring table. Unlike Lucy he wasn't wearing a tabard; with his comfortable clothing and unkempt hair he resembled the patients sat either side of him, who were starting to fidget now strangers were in their midst. 'I'm Bernard Whyte,' he said, 'I'm technically Lucy's supervisor but as you can see she's an experienced hand.'

Lucy's smile was forced. 'They think Barbara's dead,' she informed him, forgetting they were not alone.

'I know,' said Bernard, 'but it's not been confirmed yet, stranger things have happened.'

Turnbull couldn't think of a set of circumstances he could remember where a person feared dead had turned up safe and sound but he supposed it could happen. Lucy's supervisor was trying to keep her spirits up, and with good reason. She was a lot paler than when they'd arrived ten minutes earlier. Refusing the offer of tea or coffee she turned to Robinson once more, a quizzical frown replacing her smile. 'Is it true you think it's arson?'

'Where've you heard that?'

Lucy shrugged. 'Facebook mainly.'

'Don't believe all you're reading, the investigation's only just got underway. It's early days, we're duty bound to pursue all lines of inquiry.'

'So why do you want to question me and Bernard?'

'We're going to be speaking to all the staff, just routine you understand, starting with those who were on duty. It'll help us get a better picture of what happened last night.'

'Told you they think it's an insurance job,' Bernard said. 'You can interview me first,' he added, 'I'll keep you right.'

Turnbull's initial impression of Bernard was starting to change. He decided he'd be the one to interview this prick.

'We may need to speak to some of the patients too,' Robinson told them just as a heavy-set man dressed in an inside out top pushed himself to his feet.

'I need the toilet,' he stated, his words slurred around the edges, as though he was on something.

'Good luck with that,' Bernard said under his breath as Lucy shepherded the man into the hall.

'Looks like I'll be starting with you after all,' Turnbull said to Bernard, signalling for him to join him at the far end of the dining room, away from flapping ears. 'We can take it from here,' he said to the head teacher, letting her know her presence was no longer required.

Bernard pushed his chair back, telling the group sat around his table that he wouldn't be long. He met Turnbull's gaze as he approached the table the DC had decamped to, held it longer than was necessary. Some folk did that to make a point, to show that the police didn't intimidate them regardless of whether they had anything to hide. Turnbull was used to it; his lanky build made people think they didn't have to watch their step, but policing wasn't all about brawn. His lack of bulk and quiet manner disarmed people into thinking he was no threat, the epitome of a wooden top. He was a plodder, he held his hands up to that – the world needed plodders to get the job done. But he was no one's fool.

He pulled out his notepad. 'So tell me why you're convinced this is an insurance job,' he said.

CHAPTER FOUR

Tyson Gemmell, otherwise known as UB40, was where his father had told DC Ashcroft he'd be. At the recreation park at the end of their road, keeping the hell out of his old man's way. 'You two don't get on then?' Ashcroft had asked Gemmell senior. In his late thirties, the man was a similar age to Ashcroft, but with an over-hanging gut and greasy skin that must have taken sheer effort to acquire; they had precious little else in common.

He looked Ashcroft up and down, 'You can put up with most things in small doses, can't you?' the man chimed, closing the door before the detective could ask him anything else.

The lack of surprise on UB40's face when Ashcroft turned up, together with the smartphone he was holding, told him the boy's father wasn't so hacked off with him after all. 'I take it your old man warned you I was coming?' he asked.

UB40 nodded, but there was caution in his eyes. 'He warned I should watch my Ps and Qs. Said you weren't the usual type that comes calling.'

'You mean because I support Fulham rather than City?' Ashcroft smiled.

UB40 shook his head, 'He said you were a detective. I've never had a detective come calling before.'

'Plenty of boys in blue though, I've heard.'

UB40 shrugged. 'I've had my fair share of run-ins,'

he agreed. 'But to tell you the truth I've had enough.' He reached into his jacket pocket, pulled out a vape stick. 'Given up smoking, haven't I?' he said, holding it up like a museum curator might hold a rare artefact. 'Counsellor said it would help if I didn't come into contact with any sort of fuel. '

'Is it working?'

'All that stuff's behind me, mate.'

Ashcroft nodded his approval. 'I've not worked this patch long. Why the nickname, you a fan of the group?'

UB40 looked blank. 'By the time I was twenty one I'd been up before the bench 40 times, seemed as good a name as any.' He'd certainly been a busy boy. The report Ashcroft had read stated he'd set fire to everything from litter bins in his classroom before he was expelled to bus shelters and historic monuments once he started doing community service. The local stores had a photograph of him behind their counters warning staff not to sell him matches or any incendiary paraphernalia.

A group of youths were heading away from the park, making their way towards the main road and the precinct opposite, One glanced round at Ashcroft, looked away when he caught him staring. 'Your mates didn't fancy sticking around then?'

UB40 shrugged. 'What do you think?'

'So why are you hanging round the park with that lot instead of out getting a job?'

UB40 stared at Ashcroft as though he was simple. 'Who'd employ me now? Besides, I'm still under a curfew until the end of the month and I'm hardly office job material.'

Ashcroft glanced at him sharply. 'What time's

the curfew?'

'I have to be home between 7pm at night and 7am in the morning.'

'So if I ask you what you were doing last night you're going to tell me you were at home.'

'Yeah, no choice, have I?'

'But we both know with curfews there's no guarantee that anyone will call round to check you are where you're supposed to be, and Friday nights are our busiest of the week. I reckon you'll have had a free pass for the evening.'

UB40 shrugged. 'I don't have the money for a social life. I was sat at home all night, waiting for dibble to read me a bedtime story.'

'You sure you didn't decide to take a chance and slip out later with your mates?'

A sigh. 'I didn't set fire to no care home if that's what you're asking. I was at home with me old man.'

'How do you know about the fire at the care home?'

UB40 held up his phone, 'S'all over Facebook, innit?'

'Do you know any of the staff who work there, or the patients?'

UB40 shook his head.

'You ever worked there?'

'No mate, you're not listening, I haven't worked anywhere.'

'Any idea who might have done this? Any of your mates, perhaps?'

'What? I only knock about with people who set fire to stuff? I told you, I don't know anything.'

Ashcroft decided to leave it there. UB40's alibi was non-existent. He couldn't be eliminated from the enquiry for the time being, but nothing that he'd seen so far made him think he was a suspect.

*

Darren Grey, otherwise known as Special Brew, liked a drink even though he couldn't afford it. He had a reputation in the town for 'helping folk out,' which was another way of saying he fenced stolen goods. Before he'd been re-housed, the back room of his maisonette had been used by a local gang to distil counterfeit gin that they sold on the internet as the real thing – at a knock down price of course. He was paid in hooch and it had suited him just fine, until the night he got a text from a member of the gang to say the police were on their way and he was to destroy the evidence. Instead of dismantling the network of pipes and glass that had taken over his back room he'd decided to set fire to it, the cask of gin going up like a New Year firework display. He'd been convicted of arson and served three of his six year sentence; the rest he was to serve on licence for good behaviour. He told Ashcroft he had an alibi for the night of the Cedar Falls fire, he'd had a date with a woman that he'd met online – could show Ashcroft text messages exchanged right up until he'd met her in a bar and grill in Walkden.

'And they say romance is dead,' Ashcroft muttered to himself, as he checked the table reservation voucher Special Brew handed him, a two main courses for the price of one deal through Itison.

*

It was starting to get cold. UB40 checked the time on his phone and sighed. Only 6pm but he was freezing his tits off. If he went home now his old man would be on his back about paying his way and helping his mum round the house. He tried to offer but she wouldn't hear of it, slipped him a couple of quid when his dad wasn't looking. His Universal Credit didn't stretch to luxuries like vape sticks and scratch cards. His mates hadn't bothered coming back when the detective had gone, said they had better things to do than hang around all day. It was alright for them. They had girlfriends and a cosy night watching Love Island on catch up to look forward to. He'd kill for a cigarette right now. He sighed, rummaging in his pocket for his vape stick. He trudged down Laburnum Street, making a right turn to cut through the ginnel when he became aware of footsteps behind him. It could be nothing, he reasoned. A jogger with their earphones in, unaware of the tension they were causing. He turned, ready to front it out; it never paid to show you were scared.

Two youths with hoods pulled up stared back at him.

*

Special Brew's microwave had just gone beep when the doorbell chimed. Sighing, he walked into the hallway, hoping it wasn't the bloody detective come back again. He'd told him all that he knew, which wasn't a lot since he'd been otherwise engaged last night. She was up for a rematch, then, the number of pings his phone was making. Maybe next time they could cut out the food, come straight back to his place for a night cap, Netflix and chill or whatever else they were calling leg-overs these days. He made a mental note to pick up a couple of diffusers, women seemed to like that stuff. 'Hold yer bloody horses, I'm coming!' he called out. He glanced at the baseball bat he kept in the corner, deciding you couldn't be too careful when it came to security. He opened his front door, gripping onto the bat's handle in readiness.

Two youths stood on his doorstep, their faces obscured by scarves. 'That'll do nicely,' one said as he pushed his way into the hall, relieving Special Brew of his bat in the process.

*

Warren Douglas lived with his mother in a tower block on the Tattersall estate. Six foot four with a mop of dark hair upon which he'd rammed a child size baseball cap. He scowled when he opened the front door. 'Me mam won't let coppers into the 'ouse,' he informed Ashcroft as the detective held up his warrant card. 'Says it makes the place smell of bacon.'

'You know the answer to that then,' Ashcroft replied, a smile flickering across his lips. 'Don't bring trouble to her door.'

'Move out, you mean?' Warren said without a hint of irony.

'You could try not getting into trouble in the first place,' Ashcroft offered. 'Might make your life a bit easier.'

Warren's brows knitted together, as though this was the first time this had been suggested to him.

'Let's take a walk,' Ashcroft said, raising his voice so the harridan in the back room could hear. 'Leave your mother to smoke her joint in peace. Though it'll take a damn sight longer to get rid of *that* particular smell.'

Warren shrugged but did as Ashcroft suggested, pulling the door closed behind him as he stepped out onto the tower block landing. 'We can't go far,' he said, pointing to the electronic device around his ankle. 'It'll set this bad boy off.'

Ashcroft sighed, 'When were you put on the tag?'

Warren thought about this. 'The fella came round and put it on yesterday afternoon,' he answered. 'They were going to give me community service but they've run out of charity shops that'll take me.'

'So when's the tag active?'

'Tea time until the crack of dawn,' he said, 'Got to wear it for three months, too.'

So Warren was in the clear then, for torching Cedar Falls, at least. Ashcroft had been slouching against the balcony wall; his back ached as he pushed himself upright. 'Then I guess we're done,' he said.

Warren looked surprised. 'I thought you wanted to ask me some questions?'

'Not any more,' Ashcroft answered as he turned to go. 'Seems you were otherwise engaged.'

'You fancied me for something then?' Warren laughed, 'Never thought I'd be grateful for one of these things,' he said, regarding his tag like a proud mother showing off her new-born. 'Magistrate said I'd avoided the jail by the skin of my teeth.'

Ashcroft's phone rang as he headed down the stairs; he answered it, paying no attention to the two youths going in the other direction.

*

Turnbull and Robinson were making their way out of the primary school's main entrance when they found Alan Harkins pacing the playground, a mobile phone in one hand and a Costa coffee in the other. 'I've been ringing the council's emergency line for the best part of an hour,' he moaned as the detectives approached. 'The person I've spoken to says there's not much more she can do till Monday morning.'

'Have you been told how long your place is likely to be out of action?'

Harkins shook his head. 'No, a loss adjuster is coming out early next week to inspect the damage, hopefully they'll have had their hands on the fire report by then and the rebuild can start moving.'

Turnbull hadn't dealt with many suspicious fires but he'd be willing to bet a month's salary the fire report wouldn't be ready for a while yet, though there was nothing to be gained by sharing that view. 'We need to ask you a few questions, if we may.'

'Not like I'm going anywhere,' Harkins replied, looking at the school building with the same level of contempt Miss Flaherty had shown when discussing him.

'The care assistant who died in the fire, Barbara Howe, I understand she wasn't supposed to be on shift. Have you any idea why she'd still be working?'

Harkins shifted on his feet. 'She was a kind soul. I imagine she had promised to do something for one of the patients and time ran on. It happens that way.'

'Any idea what it was?'

'Sorry?'

'What it might have been, the thing that she was doing for someone else?'

Harkins shrugged.

'So it wasn't the case that you were running the unit understaffed? That Barbara was working because no one was available to take over her shift, that she felt obliged to stay on?'

'Absolutely not! What kind of establishment do you think I am running? '

'You're aware that it's routine to look into the finances of the business owner following a suspicious fire?' Turnbull interrupted.

Harkins stopped pacing and stared at them. 'Really? I hadn't thought about it to tell you the truth. Is that necessary?'

He was trying to sound calm but Turnbull could hear the effort in his voice. 'You'd be surprised at the level of information that's flagged up,' he said.

'I've got nothing to hide.'

'Most people don't,' Turnbull told him. 'But then every now and then you come across someone who virtually leads a double life. Our job is to find out which category you fall under.'

'Unless you want to make our job easier,' Robinson offered, 'and tell us how the business was really doing. Whether you were finding it difficult to make ends meet. Whether you owed money to anyone.' It would take them the remainder of their shift to start the ball rolling as it was. The application to access Harkins' bank accounts had already been rubber stamped by DS Coupland but getting it in front of the right person at Harkins' bank depended on a number of things: how long the 24 hour helpline kept them waiting in a queue, whether the human they finally spoke to put them through the correct department first time and whether a decision maker was available to authorise the release of information given it was a weekend. Harkins' full co-operation would be a Godsend, albeit unlikely.

True to form, the care home manager's eyes widened. 'You think this is what this is?' he demanded. 'That I set fire to the place to repay a debt?'

'We're not saying that,' Turnbull reasoned. 'We're simply going through the process of eliminating you from our enquiry.'

'Look.' Harkins glared at them. 'If you want to check with my bank, fill your boots, but I'm telling you now you're barking up the wrong bloody tree.'

'We've spoken to some of your staff…'

'Ah, I see, Bernard's been bad mouthing me again.' Harkins wasn't making an effort any more. 'If there's one thing that guy excels at, it's having a pop at me.'

'I wouldn't put it like that exactly.'

'Wouldn't you? Did he tell you I was getting divorced? That I'm being taken to the cleaners so might be short of cash?'

Turnbull exchanged glances with Robinson. That had pretty much been the gist of it.

'Yeah, thought so. Well that bit's right, and it does mean I'm strapped for cash more often than not but then who isn't these days? Look, it's just sour grapes on his part because I've cut back on overtime and he's not taking home as much as he used to, though how he thinks having a go at me to the police will solve that problem I have no idea. And as for Barbara working unpaid hours, it simply isn't true. She liked spending time with the patients. She really cared about them.'

'There's an easy way to put this issue to bed,' said Turnbull.

Harkins shrugged. 'Whatever. If it'll get you off my back so you can find out who really did this then do whatever you have to,' he grumbled, finishing the dregs of his coffee before stomping into the school.

*

Back in the CID room Coupland slumped into his chair and let out a long sigh.

Alex shifted in her seat so she could eyeball him. 'How did it go?'

Coupland mulled her question over before answering. The DCs working nearby had stopped talking so they could hear what was being said. His glare sent them on their way. He turned to Alex and shrugged. 'Needs a little fine-tuning, apparently,' he remarked, 'Not saccharine enough for the rubber heelers' sensitive palates.'

Alex regarded him. 'Your federation rep is on your side, you know.'

Coupland wasn't so sure. He'd caught the irritation on the officer's face when he'd hurried into the reception area apologetically; and the look of relief as he'd packed away his things to leave after their practice session. 'I wouldn't be taking *that* to the bookies any time soon,' he said. 'I don't get it, though. I've never denied what happened,' he said after some thought. 'But I'm sure as hell not going to say I'm sorry.' He caught the look that flashed across Alex's face. 'What?'

She shook her head, deciding to keep her own counsel. 'Nothing,' it was her turn to shrug.

'He's out for the compo, Alex, he doesn't give a toss whether I'm sorry or not. If the law sees fit to award it to him who am I to object? The case against him was solid, that's all I'm bothered about.' Austin Smith, known as 'Reedsy', had been convicted for his part in the trafficking of migrants from Albania into Salford and his role in the subsequent death of a young girl he'd transported across the city for the entertainment of wealthy paedophiles. DCI Mallender had personally overseen the preparation of the evidence file against the traffickers, along with his equal number from the NCA. Coupland had insisted on being the one to drive it across the city to the CPS office in Quay Street. Reedsy wouldn't be going anywhere for a long time.

'I just think you're handing them your career on a plate if you don't play ball.'

'Since when does playing ball get you anywhere? What they want is a full blown humping session and I'm not prepared to bend over,' he growled. Officers had come and gone during his time at Salford Precinct; those adept at blowing smoke up the backsides of the powers that be were inspectors now, DCIs even, but he wondered if the job gave them any greater satisfaction, whether they enjoyed the political direction their careers had taken.

*

Alex had been about to make another call but decided against it, returning the handset to its cradle before turning to give Coupland her full attention. He was reading through messages scribbled on post it notes that had been left on his desk. He looked up to catch her studying him. 'How's Amy?' she ventured.

'Fine.'

'And the baby?'

'Also fine.'

'And Lynn?'

Coupland took out his notebook and wrote something

in it before returning her gaze. 'They're all tickety boo, Alex. Thanks for asking though.'

Alex narrowed her eyes, snatching up her phone before jabbing at the number pad. The person she was dialling didn't pick up. She sighed, left a curt message before replacing the handset with more force than was necessary. When Coupland looked up she was glaring in his direction.

'What?'

'I ask you a simple question and in return you shut me down.'

'If I recall it right you asked me three questions and I answered every one of them.'

'So everyone's fine?'

Coupland rolled his eyes, 'I know that's hard for you to believe, given the bell-end they have to live with, but what more do you want me to say?' The smile he was trying to conjure up didn't appear. 'Christ, you're turning into my work wife, do you know that, sulking if I don't respond with War and Peace every time you ask a question.'

Alex looked as though she'd bitten into something sour. 'Hardly! I just wanted to know if you and Amy had patched things up, that's all.'

Coupland's mobile rang. He picked it up and glanced at the screen, swiping and stabbing until it was silent once more. 'There was nothing to patch up, Alex. Amy hasn't done anything wrong.'

A sigh. 'I know that, but you took it hard when you found out Dawson was the baby's father. I just wondered if you've been able to put it behind you.'

Coupland knew damn well what she'd been alluding to; he just wanted to make her work for his answer. The truth was he didn't know how he felt. Holding the baby for the first time after Amy brought him home from the hospital had torn him in two. Before then, during the weeks she'd had to traipse back and forth to the neo natal unit while he put on weight, Coupland had driven her, shifts permitting, preferring to wait in the car park until she'd 'done'. 'I see tubes and monitors every time I come to this bloody place,' he'd explained to her. 'The last thing I want is to see them attached to Sonny Jim.' She'd accepted his reasoning, it had been Lynn who'd shook her head slightly the first time she'd heard his excuse. He returned Alex's stare, flashed her one of his brightest smiles, 'You can't inherit evil, if that's what you're worried about.' It was a line Lynn had trotted out to him in the early days. His tone was the right side of jovial, enough to make her return to her outbound calls, but not before she'd thrown one last worried look in his direction.

Coupland read through his emails. The DC who was doing the leg work on the hit and run case had sent him a photograph of a car found abandoned in Tattersall. A Mitsubishi Outlander. The damage on the front of the vehicle was consistent with the injuries sustained by local warehouseman James McMahon two weeks before. The vehicle had been reported stolen the night before the incident, and had now been impounded for forensic examination. It was hard being one step removed from a case, hoping the person dealing with it was just as thorough, just as committed to catching the culprit as he was. It was pompous, he supposed, to think other officers didn't share his drive for justice, his sense of outrage, his downright bloody anger. He fired back a reply thanking him for the update. Adding that if there was anything he could do to help, he mustn't hesitate to let him know. Not that he could do anything that wasn't already being done. But the offer was there.

Coupland looked up to see Alex putting a tick against something in her notepad indicating she'd completed a task, yet she looked far from satisfied. 'Problem?'

Alex shook her head, 'Not really, just not progressing as much as I'd like. I'm trying to get some back story on that care assistant. Harkins sent me through the application form she'd filled in when she applied for the job, and I've been following it up with her previous employer. Her supervisor had nothing but good things to say about her. She said Barbara's old colleagues would be devastated to hear what had happened. She'd worked there for five years apparently, no issues, then announced one day she was upping sticks and moving on. She'd kept in touch with a couple of the girls, though she didn't think they'd seen her recently, more high days and holidays, that sort of thing. Oh, and the staff file we got from Harkins doesn't have any next of kin details in it. I've left a message with him to get back to me. I'm guessing it'll be online and he just hasn't bothered keeping the paper file up to date.'

'What about the others?'

'Roland Masters had been at Cedar Falls for two years, I've spoken to his brother who lives abroad. He was single, no children, his parents are long gone.'

'When did his brother last see him?'

'Two months ago. Said he was happy, though he also said there were visits when Roland didn't recognise him. He said he was willing to help in any way he could, but, given the circumstances, the information he provided might not be reliable.'

Coupland nodded his agreement. 'What about Ellie Soden, the girl who died in hospital?'

'She was a trouble maker in her home town, or at least that's what I'm hearing from between the lines with her old school. Now she's dead folk are disinclined to say a bad word about her, but I spoke with her head teacher, who told me that officially Ellie had been diagnosed with ADHD in her early teens but by then she'd already been excluded several times. Said she'd been a handful, if the truth be told. Her guidance teacher was more sympathetic. Said she just wasn't cut out for school. If she could have left when she hit her teens and gone into a job she enjoyed she probably wouldn't have kicked off so much but by then the other kids knew which button to press to get a reaction. Her meds weren't helping to stabilize her – though she suspected she wasn't taking them, and in the end the school decided it couldn't take her back. She was placed on an outreach programme in the neighbouring town but it was still two bus rides away and in the end she stopped going. A spell in a behavioural unit followed where she assaulted a member of staff. By then the local authority had got involved and when she started running away from home they stepped in and a place was found for her at Cedar Falls.'

'So this wasn't the first time she'd been away from home?'

'No.'

'Do we know why she started running away?'

'Her parents are next on my list.'

'Tread carefully. Her dad's still bitter about not being able to take her body back with them. I'm not sure how much he'll want to engage with you, especially if their answers don't put them in a good light.'

'Would you rather make contact, if you felt you'd built up a rapport at the hospital?'

Coupland blew out his cheeks. 'Hardly. I don't think he forgives me for being with her at the end. I'll check with the liaison officer that was assigned to her locally in Birmingham. See if she can't find out for us.' Coupland was already scanning the outbound calls he'd made on his phone in the hours after Ellie had died to find the contact number for West Midlands police, hit speed dial before asking to be put through to the officer working with Ellie Soden's parents. He nodded to Alex when the call was finished. Said, 'She's on her way over there, said she'd let me know as soon as she speaks to them.'

Turnbull and Robinson walked into the CID room carrying sandwiches and takeaway coffees from the café along from the station. 'We've spoken to Alan Harkins,' Turnbull said, slumping into his chair taking a bite of what looked like hummus on brown bread. 'Told him we've requested a financial report on his bank accounts.'

'How did he take it?'

Robinson pulled a face. 'He wasn't exactly over the moon,' he answered, pulling a BLT from its triangular packaging. 'Said he'd been put through the wringer by his ex-missus but had nothing to hide.'

'We'll find out soon enough,' Coupland said.

Alex reached for her bag, slipped in her notepad and phone. 'Speak of the Devil, Alan Harkins has just emailed Sarah Kelsey's patient record across. She was only in for a fortnight's respite care, GP's orders.'

'Sometimes this job is the gift that keeps on giving,'

Coupland muttered as he got to his feet. 'You got her home address?'

'Yup.'

'No time like the present, then.'

*

Sarah Kelsey lived in a new build terraced house built on the old Willows rugby ground in Weaste two years before. The houses on Sarah's row had identical grey front doors and covered entrances, with tidy front gardens enclosed by wrought iron fencing. Rhododendron bushes planted along the pavement screened each property from the road.

Coupland rang the doorbell once, stepping back to survey the front of the house while he waited. The curtains in the downstairs window were still drawn. The sound of a television could be heard when he lifted the flap of the letterbox. 'What's the set up?' he asked Alex, when he rang the doorbell a second time and got no answer.

Alex pulled a file from her bag. 'There was no mention of a partner on the emergency contact records,' she said; skim reading a couple of pages. 'Just her mother. Maybe she's taken them out.'

'And left the telly on to put any burglars off?'

The downstairs curtain parted a fraction as a child poked its head through to peer at them before disappearing at speed, as though someone had come from behind and dragged them away. 'Think that calls for a third attempt,' Coupland stated as he reached for the doorbell, holding it down longer than necessary.

There was a sound of shuffling feet, and a bolt drawing back. The door was opened by a school age girl, primary age going by the height of her, unbrushed hair forming a cloud of frizz around her scalp. 'I'm not supposed to open the door to strangers,' she said, studying them. 'Are you going to tell me the world's about to end?'

Coupland stared at her. 'I'm not with you, love.'

'Nanna says the only people that come to the door are con men and folk selling religion. Con men never wait if you don't answer when they ring the bell, whereas folk selling religion hang around on the doorstep all day.'

Coupland leaned forward as he held out his warrant card. Watched her lips move as she read the word 'Police'. 'We're definitely not selling religion, love. But we would like to speak to your nanna or your dad if he's around?' Coupland looked behind her into the hall. 'Could you give them a shout?' he prompted when she didn't move.

The girl shook her head, 'My dad went off with a tart from the other side of the estate.' There was no malice in her words, she was merely repeating what she'd heard, no doubt from nanna. 'My mum is having a nice rest in hospital. Nanna says we can visit if we are good.' A dark look fell across the girl's face, as though she'd remembered something.

'It's OK sweetheart,' Alex soothed. 'Can we have a word with your nanna please?'

The girl's head dipped as she wrestled with her conscience. 'Nanna's at work,' she said eventually. Just then a toddler wearing a miniature City strip made his way bandy legged down the hall to join his sister. He clutched a puppet that had been made out of an old sock and looked up at Coupland, fascinated.

'Who's looking after you?' Coupland asked.

The girl lifted her chin to answer, though her voice

was less confident. 'Nanna says I'm in charge while she's at work. It's only till mummy gets better.'

'Who else is here?' Alex asked, stepping into the hallway and slipping her arms around both children's shoulders. The girl took hold of her hand, leading her into the front room, her little brother following, John Wayne style.

Coupland checked out the downstairs rooms. The kitchen was tidy, the work surfaces had been wiped down and something simmered in a slow cooker. A pasta dish had been left in front of the microwave with instructions how to reheat it written on a post-it note stuck to the microwave door. A pile of papers had been left on the counter top, a utility bill, a reminder for an outstanding catalogue payment.

'Kevin, can you come here?' Coupland followed the sound of Alex's voice into the living room. Alex inclined her head towards a doll's pram in the corner of the room, only it wasn't a doll inside it, but a baby. 'She's fine,' Alex said before he had time to ask. 'Apparently Natalie here has given her a bottle.' She raised her eyebrows as she said this.

Coupland shifted his gaze round the compact front room. A phone number had been scrawled across the top of an old issue of the radio times.

'Grandma's mobile number, apparently,' Alex told him. She moved away from the children, who had clustered round their baby sister forming a human shield. 'I'll phone Social Services,' she sighed, her voice low.

'And I'll ring granny, tell her to get her arse back here, pronto,' Coupland replied.

*

Donna Chisholm was in her late forties, skinny, overdyed hair tied back in a doughnut shape. She wore a supermarket uniform with a badge on the lapel asking *'How can I help?'* 'I'm getting my pay docked for this,' she hissed at Coupland, before turning her attention to her oldest grandchild. 'I told you not to answer the bloody door!'

'That's hardly the point, love,' Coupland chided. 'What do you think you're playing at leaving them?'

Grandma's lip curled as she eyed him. 'Oh, and you've got all the answers, have you?' she said, rounding on him. 'I told our Sarah I'd keep an eye on them but I'm a bus ride away. I took a few days off work when she first went into hospital but my supervisor wouldn't give me any more leave. I'm doing the best I can. You have no idea how hard it is trying to deal with three of them. You got kids?' Both detectives nodded. 'Imagine your daughter got knocked up by some low life,' she said, oblivious to the look Alex sent in Coupland's direction. 'Only she thinks the way to keep hold of him is to keep having more. He seemed nice enough to start with, reasonable job, company car. Our Sarah was mesmerised, all right, couldn't run up the aisle fast enough. Then it all went to pot – they came back from honeymoon not speaking – Sarah had caught him chatting up a flight attendant. None of that helped her condition, but she'd been managing it with the meds. Problem was each time she got pregnant she stopped taking it, and each setback was all the harder to recover from with her ever growing brood. To be honest, I was relieved when the slime ball buggered off.' She sighed, as though remembering she had a little audience with big ears. 'Natalie's a good kid,' she said, relenting, turning to flash her a smile, 'She wouldn't let any harm come to her brother and sister, would you love? Besides, their mum will be home at the end of the week.'

Coupland and Alex exchanged glances. 'You've not seen the news then?' Alex ventured.

Donna looked confused. 'Who has time to watch the news? My phone keeps me up to date with everything I need to know, though we have to leave them in our lockers while we're working. Why?'

'There's been a fire at the residential home where your daughter's been staying,' Coupland began.

'I'll take the kids into the kitchen,' Alex said, eyeing him as she shepherded the children into the other room, 'see if we can't find a snack.'

'There's cookies in the jar by the window,' Donna told her, her voice belying the fear in her eyes as Coupland closed the door behind them.

*

'We had to call them,' Alex said the moment she'd slammed Coupland's car door shut, keeping pace with him though for all intents and purposes she might as well have been invisible, the attention he was giving her. He'd been silent during the drive back to the station, had played Oasis tracks back to back throughout the journey and when he'd switched on the radio had listened to the news without sniping. 'It's standard procedure,' Alex reiterated. 'You know as well as I do we've to call in social services when a child has been placed at risk. They'd been left alone, for God's sake, we didn't have any choice.'

Coupland was gasping for a cigarette but if he lit up now Alex would stay and argue the toss with him and all he wanted was a smoke in peace, a chance to put his thoughts in order. 'You're right. We had no choice,' he agreed.

Alex looked up at the sky, 'Finally! So why go quiet on me all of a sudden, as though your nose was out of joint?'

'It had nothing to do with that. Well, not exactly.' Coupland shook his head, 'Just got me thinking that's all.'

'What about?'

'If anything happened to Amy we'd be left with Sonny Jim.'

Alex regarded him. 'But it's not likely is it?'

Coupland made his eyes go wide. 'None of us know that, do we? Shit happens, Alex, otherwise you and me would be out of a job.'

'I know, but you can't dwell on things that might never happen, you've got to hope for the best.'

'Thanks for that, Shirley Temple. All I was meaning was God knows who'd crawl out of the woodwork for the lad, making claims on him that for all I know could be held up in court.'

Coupland's phone bleeped indicating an incoming text. It was the FLO assigned to Ellie Soden's parents, telling him she'd spoken to them as he'd asked. 'I'll catch you up,' he said to Alex, thinking he could kill two birds with one stone, ring the FLO back while he lit up. Not quite the peaceful smoke he'd been contemplating, but better than nothing.

The FLO answered on the third ring, *'Hang on a minute Sarge,'* her voice all chirpy followed by the sound of doors closing. There was a hissing sound followed by a deep intake of breath. Seemed the FLO was thinking along the same lines as him. *'It's a sore point, obviously,'* she began, *'At the end of the day Ellie kept running away because of something her parents did but there was a reason for it.'*

'Go on.'

'She'd been prescribed medication but she hated taking it, even though it eased a lot of her symptoms. She accused her parents of tricking her into taking it.'

'And were they?'

'Yes. At first they used to trust that she'd taken them when she said she had, when they realised she was spinning them a yarn they'd watch her put the tablet in her mouth only she'd find excuses to leave the room and flush it down the loo. In desperation they admitted grinding the tablets down and putting them in her food, but that fuelled her paranoia.'

'Tough call.'

'The doc treating her at the local clinic here had told them she'd have to be hospitalised if her behaviour couldn't be controlled. Ellie didn't want to be sectioned but she wouldn't comply with the doctor's orders. She was quite adept by the sound of it. Mum and dad were pitted against each other a lot of the time. I think they were quite desperate by the time they made the call to the GP to get her admitted.'

Coupland waited a few seconds. 'How are they doing?'

The FLO paused to inhale another lungful. Her outward breath was long and slow. *'As you'd expect. They're blaming themselves, blaming each other, blaming the world and his wife… They were wondering if any of her possessions had been saved. They're desperate to find some way they can connect with her again.'*

Coupland's silence provided her with an answer. The main block, which housed the patients' rooms, had been destroyed. It was unlikely anything salvaged would recognisably be their daughter's. 'Can you get a recent photo of her from them?' he asked, 'Email it over to me

ASAP.' Although Ellie's photograph wasn't needed by the pathology lab to help with identification, it would go on the incident board, along with the others, once the relatives had handed them in. Victims' faces, looming down on the murder squad provided a focus; drove the team on when it seemed nothing more could be done. Coupland ended the call, dropping his cigarette onto the pavement, picturing the WPC he'd been talking to doing the same.

*

Coupland stared at the top of Superintendent Curtis's head while he outlined the ongoing investigation into the arson attack at Cedar Falls. The senior officer had been tapping on his iPad when he'd barked entry to Coupland's knock some twenty minutes earlier and he continued scrolling down his screen while Coupland brought him up to speed, all the while making humming and hawwing noises to indicate he was listening. He finished his tapping, said 'OK,' then leaned back in his seat, 'So you're telling me it's not an insurance job?'

Coupland's jaw clenched. High flyers like Curtis made it their business to back those lower down the rung into a corner, using phrases like 'You said,' 'You permitted,' and 'You arranged,' to cover themselves when things went wrong, yet if the outcome was successful they would bump up the part they played. Nice work if you could get it, Coupland supposed.

'I'm saying that there is no evidence to support this, Sir. That although I haven't ruled Alan Harkins out of the frame entirely, the scope of the enquiry still includes the residential home staff and his supply chain, although his business associates appear to be legit and he doesn't owe anyone any money.'

'When's the PM?'

'Professor Benson has requested the presence of a forensic anthropologist due to the extent of the burns on three of the victims. More a case of him dotting the 'I's and crossing the 'T's, but they are scheduled to be performed the day after tomorrow.'

'Sounds like you've got it all in hand,' said Curtis, closing the cover on his iPad.

Early dart for someone, Coupland suspected. The downside of DCI Mallender being away was there was no one to act as a buffer between the coal face and the powers that be. It was Coupland who had to step into the DCI's shoes, Coupland who had to stand on the other side of the Super's desk like a schoolboy summoned by the headteacher.

'Do you know what kind of accelerant was used?'

'Not yet Sir, I'm awaiting the Fire Chief's report.'

'Even so, no reason why this shouldn't be wrapped up relatively quickly,' Curtis said, his face brightening at the prospect. 'Certainly no reason to request additional resources, nothing but good old fashioned shoe leather needed to bring this one to a conclusion.' What he meant was there'd be no overtime, despite Coupland acting up in the DCI's absence and carrying out additional tasks. Might as well shove a broom up his backside while he was at it. Coupland bit back a retort that in addition to door to door enquiries his team would be searching endless CCTV tapes surrounding the area as well as studying social media, manning phones and sending countless emails to forces around the country requesting information on previous staff or patients who were sent to Cedar

Falls from out of the area, begging favours that would no doubt at some point need to be reciprocated. Bloody shoe leather. Curtis had been watching those re-runs of Heartbeat on ITV3 again.

'Getting anywhere with that hit and run?'

'I'm relying on the DC who's pretty much taken it over. Obviously I'm still being kept in the loop. A white male was seen running from the area where the vehicle was dumped but that's all witnesses are prepared to say.'

'Sensitive situation,' Curtis added, resting his elbows on his desk and making a steeple out of his fingers. 'We can't afford to lose momentum on this.'

'Which is why I thought it was best to rope someone in to assist me, given the fire is now taking up a significant amount of my time – and resources.' Christ, he was beginning to sound like the DCI.

'The press office is looking for an update; you know how these incidents attract a lot of attention.'

'I see,' said Coupland, waiting.

'I wonder if in the circumstances you should keep a closer eye on the case, be more hands on,' Curtis said. 'Might reassure everyone concerned regarding continuity, you know…'

Coupland summoned up reserves he didn't know he had, 'If that's what you want, Sir,' he said through gritted teeth.

'By the way, the monthly stats are due in at the end of the week,' Curtis added, 'be good if this could be reported as a positive outcome by then.'

Coupland had heard enough. The Super was having a laugh, surely? At times he wondered what planet he was living on. 'Salford's not like other places, Sir, we've got long standing crime families here with established firms. Tools of the trade are passed down from father to son but instead of carpentry and bookbinding skills you've got protection rackets and extortion.'

'We don't know for sure the hit and run is related to any organised criminal activity.'

'James McMahon was hit in broad daylight after walking his kids to school, yet not one witness has come forward. I think that tells us all we need to know.'

Curtis pursed his lips. 'Then all the more reason progress is needed, the public need to be reassured we are doing everything we can to bring the perpetrators to justice.' The Super had a knack of making every conversation sound like an electoral campaign, a skill that Coupland had never acquired.

He found a spot on top of the Super's head that was starting to thin. Kept on staring. 'We'll do our best, Sir,' he muttered.

Curtis's head snapped up, catching Coupland unawares. 'Everything spick and span for court next week?'

Coupland blinked. Curtis didn't normally enquire about court days but then Judy Grant's trial was the result of a high-profile collaboration between Salford Precinct Station and the National Crime Agency. The NCA had brought down the human trafficking gang, of which Austin Smith was a member; Judy Grant had supplied and administered medication bought online to make the migrants they'd smuggled in docile, which by Coupland's reckoning made her responsible for a little girl's death. 'The CPS is confident of a conviction, Sir. Her old man's already enjoying Her Majesty's hospitality; she's the last link in a very grubby chain.'

Curtis nodded, satisfied. Coupland had taken a step backwards when the Super locked eyes with him. 'Talking of evidence, how are you getting on with the preparation for your hearing, I trust you've given it your full attention?'

Coupland bared his teeth in what he hoped was a smile. 'I've had my hands full, Sir.' And now Curtis wanted him more hands on in the hit and run case.

'One of the things you need to master if you want to get on in the police service is the ability to prioritise, DS Coupland.'

'And there was me thinking it was delegation,' Coupland muttered.

'Sorry?' The Super's eyes narrowed, telling Coupland that his hearing wasn't as bad as he was prepared to make out, that Coupland was already skating on very thin ice. 'Anyway, I shall leave it in your very capable hands.' Curtis had his amenable smile on, but something behind it suggested that he knew perfectly well that the detective nodding back at him had done bugger all. 'Well, if there's anything I can do…' he said, but he was already looking beyond Coupland to the door, in case his DS had forgotten his way out.

SUNDAY

CHAPTER FIVE

Morning briefing

A low hum echoed around the perimeter of the CID room as civilian staff and officers not assigned to the fire at Cedar Falls went about their business. Those involved directly with the case sat facing Coupland, pens and notepads ready. Coupland acknowledged the core members of his team with a brief nod. 'DS Moreton has traced the histories of Ellie Soden, Sarah Kelsey and Roland Masters and has circulated the details to you.' He waited while pages were turned and skim read, salient points circled or underlined, questions jotted down. He pointed to the whiteboard beside him, where he'd placed Ellie Soden's photograph the previous evening after it had been emailed from the FLO assigned to her parents. Beside it was a picture of Sarah Kelsey, one of those mother and baby studio portraits, holding her infant while her older two children stared at the camera in coordinating outfits.

'We've still to get backgrounds on Catherine Fry and the care worker, Barbara Howe, but so far we've not uncovered any patterns between Roland, Ellie or Sarah, none of them had stayed in the same residential care homes prior to moving to Cedar Falls, nor were they known to each other. Once we've got full back histories we'll know whether that's the case for all of them. Likewise, without the care worker's full employment history we can't be certain she wasn't known to any of the residents prior to working at the home.'

Coupland looked over at Alex who was sitting closest to him. 'Barbara Howe's life prior to her previous job is sketchy. Her old boss remembers she'd been in a series of temporary jobs before going to work for her but doesn't recall what they were. I get the feeling they were cash in hand, washing dishes, bar work here and there. There's certainly no record with DWP of any national insurance payments being made. I get the impression the job was a step up in terms of commitment – and regular pay.'

'Some folk spend their lives living under the radar,' Coupland observed. 'What about family though? Friends? Someone who gives a toss she's no longer around.'

'I keep drawing a blank. She kept in touch sporadically with a woman at her previous post but she'd not heard from her in ages…' Alex didn't look happy.

'I don't get it, she's been working at Cedar Falls for the last two years yet Harkins has no emergency contact details for her. And he's been slow sending Catherine Fry's files over. What's his problem? Is he inept or a slippery sod, and if so, why?' Coupland looked around the room.

'He's never been arrested, Sarge,' said Robinson.

'Doesn't mean he's squeaky clean either,' a DC on the front row said.

'Sarge.' Coupland turned to look at Turnbull. 'We've spoken to several staff members. There's a disgruntled employee but nothing of any consequence. No serious disputes, just your typical internal grumbles, not enough overtime, always more work. No one was after him for money. The financial checks haven't flagged up any cause for concern either. No special one off payments and no direct debits to bookies or online wanking sites. He paid his bills on time by all accounts. You'll have a list of suppliers typed up and on your desk by close of play.'

Coupland nodded. 'He sounds a model member of society. Anything at all set that nose of yours twitching?'

Turnbull thought about this, 'Nothing untoward, specifically, Sarge, though there's a regular monthly payment from a company by the name of Stannis Holdings. I was going to pay him another visit, see if he couldn't shed a bit more light on it.'

Coupland looked down at his notes, added the name of the company. 'Krispy can you do the honours on that? See if what Mr Harkins tells Turnbull matches what you dig up.'

'Will do, Sarge.'

Turnbull was on a roll. 'I'll arrange to see him at Cedar Falls. The residential block might be out of action but at least we can take a look around the office.'

A DC beside him sniggered. 'What, in case he has a can of petrol hidden under his desk?'

Turnbull blinked. 'Stranger things have happened. Besides, there's a lot to be gained seeing folk in their natural habitat, isn't there, Sarge?'

Coupland raised an eyebrow. 'What, agree with you and destroy my credibility? Seriously though, you're a good 'un, Turnbull. Whoever said the IQ goes up when you leave the room needs to come and see me.'

'Cheers, Sarge. I think,' Turnbull said, his voice uncertain.

Something occurred to Coupland. 'While you're there I want you to bring back details of patients who left with an axe to grind. Were there any disgruntled relatives unhappy with the way their loved ones had been treated? They'd know their way round the place, would know the schedule the home worked to and where the most damage could be caused.'

'If it was an ex-patient wouldn't they have targeted the staff quarters? As it is that block is intact.'

'Their gripe could be with another patient. In fact it's worth looking at any internal complaints, patient against patient, rows over the remote control, that sort of thing. Anything supposed to be resolved where one party could be harbouring a grievance.'

Turnbull caught Robinson's eye. What Coupland was asking him to do was potentially open up Pandora's Box. Depending on the number of residents this line of enquiry could create dozens of trails and not all of them worthwhile, going by the care home manager's organisational skills.

'How far back do you want us to check?' Robinson asked.

'Let's start with two years. This was a callous act; I can't see it being something our killer has let fester for too long.'

Both detectives nodded.

DC Ashcroft spoke up next: 'Two of the arsonists on the list you gave me checked out. Darren Gray, A.K.A Special Brew, was on a date when the fire started and Warren Douglas is on a tag. Tyson Gemmell, A.K.A UB40, was under a curfew at the time of the fire, although no one checked on his whereabouts on the night in question so technically he could have been anywhere. His dad's backing him up, surprise, surprise, but I thought I'd pay him another visit, let his father know it's my intention to keep going round if I feel he's telling porkies.'

Coupland turned to the youngest member of the team for an update. Krispy's suit was starting to look a little creased around the elbow and knees, clumps of chocolate icing had smeared onto his lapel, yet Coupland regarded him like a proud father at sports day.

'I checked through the names of onlookers taken by uniform at the scene Sarge and cross checked it with the video footage taken by the CSIs. Bearing in mind it was dark, I've been able to confirm the ID of most of those present from Facebook. None of those I've checked are known to police, a couple had minor traffic violations, nothing to get bent out of shape over. Three youths stood out in the video purely because they kept to themselves. They dressed like they were in a gang, you know, same colour neckerchiefs poking out of the top of their anoraks.'

Coupland nodded, it was the trio that had caught his eye.

'I've not been able to ID them though,' Krispy added. 'They've pulled their hoods up so their faces are partially covered.'

'Get in touch with the security at the hospital,' Coupland instructed, 'I think the same group of lads were hanging about A&E when I got there. Go and check out the CCTV by the main entrance. You might get a better look at them.'

Krispy nodded eagerly.

'You come back here when you're done, you hear? No going all Ray Mears on me.' There'd been a junior DC join Coupland's team a couple of years before. Keen, eager to please. Ambushed during an unofficial stakeout. Coupland blamed himself for the young officer's death.

He wasn't going to make the same mistake again. Krispy smiled and shook his head, making a note on his pad to google Ray Mears as soon as the briefing was over.

Coupland jabbed the whiteboard with his index finger, 'As a result of this attack three kids have lost a mother. Parents have lost a daughter. Relatives are mourning loved ones they thought were somewhere safe.' Several heads nodded around the room. He handed out actions, satisfied the team were doing their best with what little information they had to go on. Investigations like this started frustratingly slow at first, all the necessary fact finding and admin that needed to be carried out before the proper detecting could begin. They had to start somewhere, and inroads were being made.

The phone on Coupland's desk rang. 'Get that for me, Krispy,' he called out. He turned to Alex as the team dispersed. 'We need the information on the other victims pronto. For all we know Harkins could have been having a fling with this Barbara Howe and then broken up with her. She then starts the fire to get back at him.'

'A woman scorned?' Alex asked, eyeing him as she returned to her own desk. 'Speaking from experience?'

'You'd be surprised, me and the missus have been known to create a few sparks over the years.'

'Purleese,' Alex mock groaned, 'Let me keep my breakfast down.'

'Just sayin',' Coupland grinned, although his next conversation had him hot under the collar for an entirely different reason.

Krispy held Coupland's phone out towards him as he returned to his desk. 'It's the manager from Cedar Falls, Sarge, he's in a bit of a state. Reckons there's someone unaccounted for. A patient by the name of Johnny Metcalfe.' Coupland snatched the phone from Krispy and growled into the receiver: 'How come we're only hearing this now?'

The manager's voice was several octaves higher than the last time they'd spoken. '*Johnny's a bit of an evasive chap,*' he explained, '*tends to take himself off when the mood arises, his absence didn't raise any concern at first.*'

Coupland pulled at his ear as though he was hearing things. 'But your staff know how to count, right?' he persisted.

A pause. '*Friday's head count tallied with our patient roll.*'

'Well obviously it didn't,' Coupland barked, 'or else you wouldn't be calling me now. According to the information you supplied the emergency services believe they carried out a full retrieval. Only now you're telling me you forgot someone, that because you needed more than ten fingers to count folk off on there could be a patient lying collapsed out of sight somewhere, suffering from burns or smoke inhalation. They could have regained consciousness disoriented, wandered into traffic, in fact the list of possibilities is bloody endless.' Not to mention the possibility that the death message he and Alex delivered yesterday might have been given to the wrong next of kin. Until each body had been formally identified names couldn't officially be assigned – apart from Ellie Soden's and Catherine Fry's, but Coupland had made an assumption that the three people unaccounted for and the three bodies retrieved from the fire would eventually match up. Another missing patient blew that assumption out of the water. Coupland swallowed at the thought of having to explain this to Superintendent Curtis, or DCI

Mallender for that matter. 'Do you have a photo of this unaccounted for person?'

'*Yes.*'

'And you still have the card I gave you?'

A pause, followed by the sound of paper being shuffled. '*Yes.*'

'Then email the most recent one through to me. Now.' Coupland ended the call. Cursing at the top of his voice he moved round to his computer, drummed his fingers on the desk top until an icon appeared on screen telling him he had mail. He opened Harkins' attachment and pressed 'print.'

'Krispy,' he called out, forwarding the email onto the DC, 'do me the honours and circulate this round the local hospitals to see if he's been brought in.' He moved to the printer to retrieve the photo, glancing at it briefly before folding it and putting it into his pocket. He was heading into the corridor when he stopped in his tracks as though his batteries had suddenly stopped working. He pulled out his phone, tapping into Google until the online newsfeed for Salford Network came up, together with the link to the paused video image he'd seen while waiting in line in the newsagents. He hit the 'Play' button. Once more the naked man came to life on his screen as he ran down the street. A drunken prank or running from a crime scene? 'On second thoughts forget it,' he called out to Krispy, staring at his phone's screen as an Asian man waved his sweeping brush at the camera, right up until a squad car pulled up alongside him on the kerb.

*

'Shame your man didn't get his head count right two

nights ago,' the custody sergeant said when Coupland slipped the printed-out photograph of Cedar Falls' missing patient across the desk to him. 'Poor beggar's had to put up with the usual weekend frequent flyers, can't have been easy.'

Coupland nodded in agreement. 'He was brought in starkers then?'

It was the custody sergeant's turn to nod. 'We've given him some clothes and the duty doc administered diazepam but to be fair we've not had a peep out of him even though it must have worn off hours ago.' He pointed to a line in the custody register, 'Sign there and he's all yours.'

Coupland did the honours, following one of the custody officers through the locked entrance into a corridor of cells. A rhythmic knocking sound came from the cell closest to the entrance. The entry written on the card at the side of the cell door, said *Gobshite*. 'Headbanger too, by the sound of it.' Coupland observed.

The officer nodded. 'You know what they're like; he'll keep doing it until we send him to casualty. He's getting his wish,' he shrugged. 'It's the Sarge's wedding anniversary today, promised his wife he won't be late back on pain of death. He's requested transport to A&E to get him out of his hair.'

They stopped outside Johnny Metcalfe's cell. Mindful not to trigger the panic strip as he leaned against the wall, Coupland watched the uniformed officer unlock the cell door before pushing it open. He stood aside when Coupland stepped forward. Johnny was perched on the edge of his cell bed, a frown on his face like a school child waiting to be picked up by a tardy parent. There were dark crescents under his eyes, the hint of stubble on parts of his chin. Coupland approached him with caution. 'He isn't dangerous,' the officer stated, 'just liable to kick out if he feels cornered.'

'Aren't we all?' Coupland muttered as he stopped in front of the forlorn figure and introduced himself. 'I'm going to escort you upstairs where you can sign out,' he said, his voice measured. He managed a smile, kept it in check. 'Then I'm going to take you back to Mr Harkins.'

The figure dropped his head into his hands and groaned. 'Can you do me a favour and cut out the crazy horse routine,' he said, 'I get enough of that as it is.'

'Sorry,' Coupland replied, 'I didn't want to alarm you.'

Metcalfe pushed himself to his feet and studied Coupland. 'By what? Coming up to me and introducing yourself? I'm hardly Hannibal Lecter. I'm not a danger to the public, nor am I doolally.'

Coupland tilted his head. 'So what was Friday night all about then? Do you often run about starkers? I'm sure we'd have picked it up if you did.'

A pause. 'No. I just wanted to be left alone.'

'Why run down through the city naked if you want to be alone? That's a sure fire way of drawing attention to yourself.'

Metcalfe thought about this. 'Maybe I did lose it a little bit,' he conceded.

'Look,' Coupland said, deciding to strike while the iron was hot. 'You're not under caution,' he added, glancing at the officer in the corridor, 'but given you've been staying at Cedar Falls and your subsequent disappearance the night a fire breaks out I feel obliged to ask if you know anything about it?'

'There was a fire.' It wasn't so much a question, just a statement.

'Yes, a serious one.'

'Did people die?'

'Yes.'

Metcalfe's shoulders slumped. 'Can I go now?'

Coupland pushed on. 'Why did you run away on Friday evening? Did you know about the fire?'

'I can't remember.'

Coupland sighed. He'd need a responsible adult to be present if he was to go any further down that path, and his faith in the care home manager was deteriorating. 'Come on let's go.' He beckoned Metcalfe to follow him. Metcalfe was tall, had to dip his head to leave the cell, but he was wiry. The sweatshirt and jogging bottoms he'd been given swamped him.

'How long have you been at Cedar Falls?' Coupland asked as they walked along the corridor. They were on safe territory with that question, it didn't matter that audio and visual equipment would be recording their conversation, there was no way Metcalfe could incriminate himself by answering.

'I'm twenty-two now; I was twenty when I was sent there.'

'And how is it? I mean you know, all things considered.'

Metcalfe shrugged. 'You mean how would I rate it if I was writing a review on Trip Advisor? How would I know? I'm not an expert on residential institutions, you know. Some people get moved around if they don't settle down and play nice but I've stopped fighting the system a long time ago, no point.'

'What about your family?'

'What about them?' Metcalfe shrugged. 'They come and see me when they can. They make the right noises, to be fair, ask the same questions in bored little voices, I mean, they only really get animated when visiting time is over, it takes a lot of effort to keep the relief from their eyes, but it's there all the same.'

They'd reached the custody desk, waited while the sergeant found the entry on his computer and updated it. He slid the register across the counter top. 'Sign here please, and I'll just get your belongings.'

'I thought he came in starkers?' Coupland asked.

'He was wrapped in a blanket.'

'It isn't mine,' Johnny told them. 'It belongs to the man in the shop.'

Coupland remembered the Asian man wielding a sweeping brush in the video. The off licence was on Pendlebury Road, one of the few remaining open-all-hours shops that hadn't been replaced by a Tesco Metro. He held out his hand to take the plastic bag containing the blanket from the custody sergeant. 'I'll return it, it's on my way home.'

A commotion saw Gobshite being led from the custody suite flanked by two officers, a smile like a coat hanger had been rammed in his mouth. 'Told yer you couldn't keep me here,' he snarled, a bloody gash on his head where he'd hit it against the cell door repeatedly. 'S'against my European rights.'

'Back of the net for Brexit,' the Custody Sergeant muttered as he processed his transfer to Salford Royal. 'Scribble here,' he said, pushing the log book across the counter, his finger pointing to the space where a signature was required. Coupland sneaked a peek at the offence that had brought the boy in. Breach of the Peace. No big deal in the grand scheme of things, yet the kid seemed hell bent on making a drama where none existed. Some thrived on the adrenaline rush from having a run in with the police, didn't matter the reason.

'What you lookin' at?' the gobshite yelled at him. Coupland raised an eyebrow in the boy's direction but said nothing. Being yelled at by angry punters came with the territory; it faded into the background like white noise.

'C'mon,' he said to Metcalfe. 'Let's get you back.'

The wind had picked up, causing Metcalfe to shiver as he followed Coupland to his car. 'Soon have you home,' Coupland said, wincing at his faux pas.

'It's OK,' Metcalfe said, turning to him. 'I know how you meant it.' He climbed into the passenger seat, trying to avoid the empty sandwich cartons and cans of diet coke discarded in the car's footwell. Like its owner, Coupland's Mondeo had seen better days, but it was reliable and he knew it like the back of his hand. It was an extension of himself, a mini office come canteen, even served as an interview room on occasion. He forgot how it must look to regular folk, who used their cars simply to get from one place to another.

'Did you always want to be a policeman?' Metcalfe asked. Coupland's mouth turned down at the corners as he mulled it over. 'Well… United had just signed Giggs so I was all out of options.' He thought some more. 'I suppose I always expected I'd go into the Force. My old man was a cop and I reckoned since they'd let him in it couldn't be that difficult. What about you?'

A shrug. 'In case you hadn't noticed I'm not exactly what you'd call employee of the month material.'

'Why is that?' Coupland had been told what state Metcalfe had been in when he was brought in, and had read the duty doctor's notes, but couldn't see any evidence of the agitated young man he seen on the tabloid newspaper's website. 'What are you like when you're not running about the place stark bollock naked?' he asked, 'The duty doctor's report said something about learning difficulties.'

Metcalfe nodded. 'I have a problem processing things apparently. I mean, I'm oblivious to it, but that's what I've been told. It impacts my reasoning, memory and attention,' he added, counting them off on his fingers. 'Basically, when it all gets too much I tend to lose the plot.'

'That sums up most of my clientele,' Coupland replied.

'You said you expected you'd be a cop because your dad was,' Metcalfe commented, 'but what made you *want* to do it?' Coupland hesitated. To tell this lad the truth would be to admit to his biggest failing, something he hadn't acknowledged, even to himself, in all his years as a serving officer. 'I suppose I like putting things right,' he said, which was as close to the truth as he was prepared to go.

Johnny's attention had moved to the CD cases wedged down the side of the passenger seat. 'I can put some music on if you fancy?' Coupland offered.

The boy leaned forward to flick through the compilations on Coupland's CD multi-changer. The Stone Roses, Oasis, James. 'Don't you have anything more up to date?'

'I've got some Ian Brown stuff in there.'

A tut. 'I mean like Sam Smith and Calvin Harris.'

Coupland sucked air through his teeth. 'You're having a laugh, aren't you?' He chose Noel Gallagher's High

Flying Birds. *Everybody's on the run.* Tapped his fingers on the steering wheel when the track came on. Halfway through he looked across to see Johnny was leaning back in his seat, eyes closing. 'I can take a bloody hint you know,' he said, flicking the radio back on when the track had ended. George Ezra's Shotgun had reached its first chorus. 'I quite like this one,' he admitted.

'Me too.'

Coupland glanced at his companion, clocked the relief now he was listening to someone from his own generation. Grinning, he turned the radio up loud and put his foot down.

*

The care home manager was waiting outside the primary school's entrance as Coupland pulled up to the kerb. 'He doesn't like me,' Johnny muttered.

'How do you know?'

'I just do. You can tell these things can't you? In the pit of your stomach, I mean. Not like I care, though. It's only a problem if you want to be liked. If you keep flogging a dead horse when there's really no point.'

'He treats you OK though?'

A shrug. 'I suppose.'

Coupland climbed out of his car and stepped round to the passenger door to hold it open. 'Best get this over and done with then, eh?'

'You've had us all worried, young man!' Harkins said as soon as Johnny was in earshot. So worried no one noticed he was missing till an hour ago, Coupland thought, making him wonder if Johnny's assessment of Harkins' attitude towards him was spot on, after all. They followed

Harkins into the school, along a corridor towards double doors leading into the dining hall.

Coupland tapped him on the arm as he reached to push open the door. 'If I can have a word...' he said, indicating with a nod of his head that it was to be in private.

'Of course,' Harkins turned to Johnny and ushered him in. 'I'll be with you shortly,' he said, watching as Johnny slouched into the dining hall.

'Can't wait,' Johnny muttered, raising a hand in acknowledgement to a girl with blue hair.

Harkins turned to Coupland, his mouth forming a smile that didn't make it to his eyes. 'I've already had to hot foot it over to the office this morning because two of your officers insisted they wanted to speak with me there, then when I arrive they go on about payments into my bank account and demanding access to files. I've got to say I'm not too happy with what they were inferring.'

'Only doing as they were told,' Coupland replied. 'I'm sure they appreciated your co-operation.'

Harkins didn't look convinced. 'Not sure there's much more I can help you with, to be honest, short of going out and catching whoever did this myself.'

Coupland cocked his head. 'Is that so? How about you start off with an abacus first. Teach yourself how to count.'

Harkins bristled. 'For God's sake these were exceptional circumstances. You have to understand it was chaos that evening. I'm not surprised—'

'—Not surprised someone went off your radar for nearly 48 hours? Or not surprised that a patient can walk out of your building without anyone realising? The log book back at the station shows Johnny was taken into custody half an hour after the fire alarm was sounded. Nobody had missed him at that point, nor when a register was taken during the evacuation. Fire procedures are put in place for that very reason. Procedures you claim you took a lot of time over. You can see why I'm a bit confused, can't you?'

If Harkins had an answer to this he didn't share it. He shifted from one foot to another like a naughty schoolboy, or a schoolboy who needed the toilet.

'How can his absence go unnoticed?' Coupland persisted. Harkins stared at his feet. 'Can you show me a copy of the register you used on the night of the fire?'

Harkins lifted his phone from his pocket, began tapping to locate an electronic file. Satisfied, he handed the phone to Coupland who was already waving his hand away.

'I don't want a generic copy,' Coupland said, barely glancing at it. 'I want to see the one that was used on the night.'

Subdued, Harkins pushed open the dining hall door, beckoning Coupland to follow. He located a canvas holdall that had been placed out of harm's way on the stage. He forced his lips into a smile as he opened the bag, as though being pleasant might make the detective overlook what he was certain he would find. 'I thought I'd bring a few things over for them,' he explained, nodding in at the bored looking patients sitting around on plastic chairs. 'Items which will hopefully make staying here a little more comfortable. At least until we find somewhere suitable.'

Coupland peered over Harkins' shoulder; instead of beer and takeaway menus and a shed load of chocolate there were DVDs, a couple of blankets and own brand toiletries from the local Tesco.

'I'm sure they'll appreciate it,' Harkins muttered when it was clear Coupland wasn't playing ball.

Coupland took the clipboard Harkins lifted from the bag. On it was the list of patients' names typed onto a sheet of A4 paper. He scanned down the list. Most names had a tick against them to show they had been evacuated from the fire. Four names remained unticked:

Sarah Kelsey
Roland Masters
Catherine Fry
Ellie Soden.

Coupland squinted as he read down the register once more. Johnny Metcalfe was not on the list.

Just then Coupland's phone rang, its shrill ring making Harkins practically jump out of his skin. Coupland snatched it from his pocket. Turnbull's name came up on the screen. He hit 'Decline'.

'Hold on.' Coupland nodded in Johnny's direction. Johnny was chatting animatedly to the blue haired woman, who was brushing an older woman's hair. 'Why's his name not here?'

Harkins pulled a face which suggested it was news to him but Coupland shook his head.

'Don't give me some clap trap that it isn't your job – you're in charge, you're responsible.' He waited while Harkins imitated a fish out of water, his mouth opening and closing but nothing of any sense coming out. 'Time's up mate,' he sighed, stomping past Harkins and toward the woman Johnny was talking to, holding the clipboard out to her. With his other hand he pointed to Johnny.

'Why's he not on this register?' he demanded.

Lucy knotted her eyebrows as she glanced at Harkins before looking at the list, 'The boss must have had new ones typed up,' she answered, dropping her gaze. 'I hadn't realised that when I grabbed the sheet from his desk when the fire alarm started. I was following procedure. If the alarm goes off you evacuate the building and carry out a roll call.'

'That doesn't answer my question,' Coupland persisted. 'Why had his name been removed from the list?'

Lucy turned so she was facing away from Johnny. She dropped her voice. 'He's leaving us at the end of the week.'

Johnny's head shot up. 'Am I?'

'We hadn't got round to letting him know,' Lucy sighed. 'Sometimes it's easier that way. Less disruptive.'

Harkins, who'd been lurking in the background while Lucy dropped the bombshell, decided to step forward. 'He's been getting more and more restless. Refusing to engage with staff, getting agitated, causing problems with the other patients.'

'And talking about me like I'm not here really helps,' Johnny said.

Coupland turned to Harkins. 'And that's the reason to send him away, is it? Because he doesn't conform? Doesn't it prove he needs help?'

Lucy wrapped her arms around her middle, 'Look, I just do as I'm told at the end of the day...'

Harkins spoke up once more, his tone suggesting an authority his body language lacked. 'Disruptive behaviour can impact the other patients, unsettle them, then they complain to their families and they in turn complain to us...'

'So he's an inconvenience, then,' Coupland said, his tone making the word seem obscene. 'Just so long as someone deemed less of a handful comes along and you still get your fee, I suppose there's no reason why you'd give a toss. It's all about bums on seats. Or fragile minds on couches, Ka-ching…' There was nothing to be gained hanging around; he'd learned nothing other than Harkins was a mediocre manager with woefully inadequate admin skills. Didn't mean he was guilty of arson.

'Told you he didn't like me…' Johnny mumbled as Coupland turned to leave.

'If it's any consolation I don't think he's that keen on me either,' Coupland replied. 'Besides, you might be better off somewhere else,' he added, throwing a glare in Harkins' direction. 'But in the meantime you need to stay here, where…' He turned to the blue haired woman and the hippy standing beside her.

'Lucy and Bernard,' the woman added for him.

'Yeah.' Coupland nodded his thanks. 'Where Lucy and Bernard can look after you.'

'And me,' added Harkins, a beat too late, 'I'll look after him too.'

'Whatever,' Coupland growled before heading to the door.

*

Shafiq Ahmed was surprised to see a detective from Salford Precinct Murder Squad waiting for him by the off licence counter. 'I thought my son was winding me up,' he panted, 'I was out the back of the shop putting out rubbish, is anything the matter?'

'Not at all,' said Coupland, holding up his warrant

card while introducing himself. He placed the plastic bag containing the blanket Mr Ahmed had given Johnny Metcalfe on the counter top. Mr Ahmed took it, nodding as he did so. Coupland retrieved Johnny's photograph from his pocket, held it up for Mr Ahmed's inspection. 'So, this is the boy that was here?' he asked. Coupland nodded, 'Have you seen him in your shop before?'

'Not that I remember. I mean, you only pay attention to the trouble makers, don't you? And we have plenty of them.' He pointed to a camera mounted on the wall behind him. 'I have CCTV and tapes which I keep for a month before I re-use them, I could look through them if you like, see if he's been here recently.'

'There's no need,' Coupland said. 'I just wondered if there was a reason he ran into your shop, whether you or your son knew him.'

Ahmed shook his head, 'Like I said to the officers who collected him at the time, I hadn't seen him before, or if I had he'd never done anything to draw attention to himself.'

Coupland looked out of the shop window to the street beyond, row upon row of red brick terraced houses interlinked by ginnels. Ahmed's off licence doubled as a grocers, was likely the first shop Metcalfe had come across that was open at that time of night. Coupland placed his card on the counter top before turning to leave. 'If you think of anything later that might be relevant please give me a call.'

'The young man is alright though?' Mr Ahmed asked.

'He's fine,' Coupland said, 'back where he belongs.'

The shopkeeper thought about this, a frown forming on his face. 'Given he ran away from this place without waiting to dress himself, I doubt that's how he sees it, detective sergeant, don't you?'

*

Krispy walked into the CID room to find Turnbull and Robinson elbow deep in case files collected from Cedar Falls. Alan Harkins had baulked at first but they'd convinced him that cooperating with the police in their enquiries looked far better to insurance companies than claimants resisting every step of the way. Harkins had complied, albeit with a face like thunder, allowing them to take what they wanted. Krispy peered at Turnbull over the mountain of files cluttering his desk. 'I can give you a hand if you like,' he offered. 'Create a quick database, put in the information contained in the files and run a few queries to pull out the patient names that match what you're looking for.'

Relief flooded Turnbull's face.

'Nice one,' Robinson said gratefully, 'I'll owe you one, kid.'

'Just need to check something on this CCTV then I'm all yours.' Krispy beamed, referring to the tapes he'd collected from Salford Royal's A&E.

*

Ashcroft rang the doorbell and stood back. It was opened by UB40's father, still wearing yesterday's clothes if the creases and sweat stains were anything to go by. 'Finally!' the man sniped, his lip curling, 'Funny how when the shoe's on the other foot you take your time coming out.'

Ashcroft's brow creased. 'Sorry? I don't get you?'

'I know he's been a thorn in everyone's backsides all

112

these years but he didn't deserve this.'

'What's happened?'

'What do you mean "what's happened?" I got on to you lot when he dragged himself home last night, practically passed out on the doorstep. Beaten up, he was. Jumped on by a couple of lads. I took him down the hospital myself. They said they'd have to report it, that someone would come and speak to him straight away. They're moving him onto a ward this morning, I've only come back to get him some clean clothes. His mother's still down there, going out of her mind, she is.'

'This is the first I've heard about it,' Ashcroft said. 'Does he know who it was?'

'He didn't know what day of the bloody week it was when he fell through the front door last night, let alone anything else.'

Ashcroft scratched his head. 'Look, it's likely being dealt with by uniformed officers, but there's no harm in me paying him a visit. If you're quick about it I can give you a lift.'

*

Ashcroft waited at the reception desk with UB40's father while the A&E receptionist typed in Tyson Gemmell's name. He'd put a call through to the control room but the information mirrored what UB40's father had told him, that the assault had been reported after the casualty had arrived at the hospital, uniformed officers had been dispatched but had been diverted to an incident on the other side of town. A follow up call over the radio confirmed they were now en route.

'They've moved him to the Acute Admissions Ward,'

the receptionist told them, pointing to a lift beyond the nurses' station. Ashcroft made his way towards it, almost colliding with a pitiful figure clutching an arm in a sling.

'Sorry mate,' Ashcroft said, his gaze moving from the arm to a face that even swollen looked familiar. 'Is that you Darren? Christ, what the hell happened to you?'

Special Brew grimaced showing newly broken teeth. 'Got on the wrong side of a baseball bat, didn't I? Wouldn't mind but it was my own,' he lisped.

'Any idea who it was?'

Special Brew moved his head from side to side causing him to flinch. 'No, but it wasn't random.'

'Why do you say that?'

He stared at Ashcroft as though he was being particularly dim. 'They came round to my house, didn't they? In fact, not long after you left.'

Ashcroft turned to UB40's father. 'I'll catch you up, I need to make a phone call.' He pulled out his phone, his finger pausing mid-air as something occurred to him. Two calls would be necessary, he decided. No point ringing the boss without gathering all the facts first. He pulled out his notebook and tapped Warren Douglas's number into his phone. Waited while it was answered.

*

Coupland was mulling over Mr Ahmed's words as he logged into his computer, moving the mouse around with one hand while downing what was left of a takeaway coffee with the other. It was clear Harkins didn't have much time for Johnny Metcalfe, and according to the care assistant he'd spoken to there had been enough incidents to warrant Metcalfe's transfer to another home.

It wasn't beyond the realms of possibility that the dislike was mutual, in which case Metcalfe's whereabouts prior to the fire starting needed to be clarified. He made a note on his pad.

Alex entered the CID room making a beeline for Coupland when she saw him at his desk. 'Turnbull called while you were out,' she told him.

Coupland recalled hitting the 'decline' button when the DC had called him while he'd been speaking to Alan Harkins. 'Did he leave a message?'

A nod. 'He wanted to update you following his visit to Cedar Falls.'

'Whatever he and Robinson said rattled him; when I took the lad who'd absconded back to him he got all defensive, moaning about the level of attention he was getting from us.'

'I've a feeling that attention's going to intensify.'

Coupland glanced up at her sharply, 'How come?'

Alex looked serious. 'When Turnbull asked him about Stannis Holdings he gave them some rubbish about it not being unusual for company owners to use their business accounts to pay for relative's care home fees. Turnbull wasn't buying it, though, said Harkins looked shifty as hell.' Alex pulled her phone from her bag, began tapping and scrolling. The look on her face told him he wasn't going to like what she had to tell him one little bit.

'So?' Coupland leaned towards her so he could take a look at what had caused frown lines to form across her forehead.

'Krispy looked up Stannis Holdings like you asked. The company is owned by Kieran Tunny.'

Coupland felt the familiar tingle when they discovered

a lead, followed by the familiar dread when this particular name was mentioned. 'Oh, you have got to be kidding me,' he said, trying to process the information. 'Nice work,' he called over to Krispy who could barely be seen behind a stack of files.

'I'm helping DC Turnbull,' Krispy informed him when he saw Coupland staring at the papers on his desk.

'I trust you've cleared your own work first,' Coupland checked.

Krispy nodded. 'I've looked through the CCTV footage from the hospital reception, Sarge, although the faces are blurred the youths captured on film are wearing the same clothing worn by the youths in the crowd at Cedar Falls. I've blown up a still from both clips and emailed them to you.'

Coupland nodded his thanks. Kieran Tunny was well known for his army of teenage foot soldiers; he recruited them young, liked to instil his values from an early age. 'What the hell does he have to do with this, though?' he muttered.

Alex pushed her phone towards him to show him a photograph on her screen. 'Turnbull took this while he was waiting for Harkins to arrive. It's a photo of the reception area outside his office.'

Coupland could make out a small table and a couple of chairs, several framed photos on the wall behind them. 'I take it it's the photos on the wall I'm interested in?' He was already enlarging the shot so he could see more.

'Hang on,' said Alex, taking the phone from him so she could do the honours. 'Here.' She handed it back to him. The framed photo at the centre of the wall had been made to fit the size of Alex's screen. Coupland looked at the sea of blurred faces. 'It was taken at a garden party the care home holds every year for its patients and their families,' Alex explained. 'Turnbull recognised Tunny straight away but asked Harkins to name all the people in the photograph to be sure.'

'Christ, without any prompting? What is the world coming to?' Coupland's gaze fell onto a heavy set man with a shaved head. He wore large glasses reminiscent of the eighties, and the kind of suit an investment banker would wear, only this was no investment banker. His face might be blurred but it was easy to make out the gold rings the size of knuckle dusters and heavy bracelets on each wrist. This was Kieran Tunny alright, one of Salford's most notorious crime bosses, and there he was posing for the camera, large as life, his arms snaked protectively around a petite woman with Down's syndrome. The same woman whose beaming smile stared down at them from the incident board. Coupland frowned as he looked from the photo to Alex. 'Catherine Fry is Tunny's sister,' she told him.

CHAPTER SIX

For all the money he turned over from robberies and drugs Kieran Tunny had stuck to his roots, buying up homes on the Salford street he'd grown up in and moving in family members. If he wanted a house and it wasn't for sale he made an offer to the owners they couldn't refuse. His brothers and cousins lived on the same street, his mother and aunties on the one round the corner.

The street Ma Tunny lived on was like any other. Red brick terraced properties with back yards leading onto a ginnel. It was the henchmen that set it apart, wide men in imitation Crombies, hands clasped at their fronts like footballers defending a free kick. They didn't block the road; they didn't need to. No vehicle dared to enter without their say so.

'Do you think this is wise?' Alex asked. 'Coming to see Tunny's mother, I mean?'

'She's entitled to be treated like any other next of kin,' Coupland reminded her. 'Don't want the family accusing us of unfair treatment.'

'You sure you're not looking for any excuse to get into the inner sanctum?'

Coupland thought about this. The relationship between Tunny's family and GMP was acrimonious; dozens of cases taken to the CPS every year were dismissed for lack of evidence, those that made it to trial collapsed as quickly as the witnesses in the run up to it. Coupland didn't like the word untouchable, it implied someone was beyond justice which went against everything he stood for, but he conceded Kieran Tunny was one hell of a lucky bugger.

Coupland acknowledged two men approaching his car and lowered his driver's window. 'Your boss knows why I'm here,' he said, thinking of the hoodies standing in the crowd by the cordon at Cedar Falls, and again later the stand-off with the WPC at the hospital. Small boys kicked a ball up and down the road. The man closest to Coupland nodded before moving towards them, making a shooing motion with his arms. The boys parted, forming a gap just wide enough for Coupland's car to pass through. They were miniatures of the older men, stocky and mean looking. 'It's like going on safari,' Coupland muttered as he kept his speed low. In his rear view mirror he saw one of the men reach for their phone. Coupland didn't need to wonder whether Tunny would be at his mother's home, the three youths perched on the low brick wall in front of the property signalled his presence. Coupland rummaged in his pocket and pulled out the CCTV stills Krispy had emailed him. 'If it isn't them it's their evil twins,' he said, holding the images for Alex to see. They'd been horsing around when Coupland's car approached, pushing and shoving each other, drumming their knuckles into the skinniest boy's scalp. They stopped as Alex climbed out of his car, their attention moving to Coupland when he slammed his driver's door shut. Coupland caught the eye of one of them and stared.

'Do you know 'im?' a fat lad asked, slipping his hand into his joggers to have a good scratch.

'Nah,' the youth replied, 'Maybe he fancies me.'

The youths sniggered as Coupland pushed open the

gate, their attention turning to Alex as she followed close behind.

'Don't even think about it,' warned Coupland, sending a glare in their direction.

'I can speak up for myself you know,' Alex hissed as the front door was opened by a man who wouldn't have looked out of place on the door of a nightclub. They stepped into a small front room made smaller by the number and size of people in it. Two draylon settees arranged around a coffee table covered in cups. Wooden chairs had been carried in from the kitchen beyond. Coupland recognised some of the faces sat around, family members who'd been pulled in over the years; several of the men had served time. They sat grim faced, attention turning to the detectives as they walked into the room. Ma Tunny sat on the smaller of the settees, her eldest son beside her, holding her hand.

'I've been expecting you, Mr Coupland, please, sit down,' Kieran Tunny said, indicating to two men opposite that they give up their seats.

The men jumped to attention. 'Here you go, Sir,' one said.

'Here, Miss,' said the other.

They might be on opposite sides of the fence but Tunny drilled his gang into showing respect. To their elders, to the police, to anyone he deemed necessary. The way the mouthy guy in the front garden spoke to Coupland marked him out as a recent recruit, but then Coupland already knew that. He put out a hand to indicate the men keep their seats, 'I'd rather stand, if it's all the same to you,' he said, keeping his back close to the wall while counting how many folk there were between

120

him and the nearest exit. It was unlikely they'd come to harm while they were useful; still, manners or no manners it was best to have an exit strategy worked out.

'Good of you to come in person, Mr Coupland, thought you might have sent one of your flunkies.'

'I've got no beef with you or your family, Mr Tunny; I'm here the same way I would be for anyone else.'

'She's dead then,' Tunny stated.

Coupland paused, letting his silence be the answer. Tunny's mother started to sob. She was a big woman, round like a Weeble, hefty shoulders heaving up and down. Coupland gave them a moment for the news to sink in, his eyes scanning the room. Several 'Happy Birthday Nanna' cards sat atop a sideboard, photos of little cherubs in school uniform beside them. Little cherubs currently serving time in young offenders' institutions up and down the north of England.

'I'm sorry for your loss,' Coupland began, his gaze resting on a bullet proof vest draped over the arm of a sofa.

'Thank you, Mr Coupland, we'll take it from here,' Tunny said.

''Fraid it doesn't work like that, Kieran, there's a couple of things I need to clarify.' Coupland paused. 'I saw a couple of your wise guys last night, when I was called out to the fire.'

Tunny shrugged, as though he'd been expecting this. 'By the time I heard about it the blaze was well under way. I knew if I turned up you lot would take your eye off the ball and start dancing around me.'

There was a grain of truth in what Tunny was saying, Coupland conceded, his presence caused a commotion wherever he went. Depending where you were in the city the locals either loved him or hated him. He was the human equivalent to Marmite.

'My lads couldn't find out anything from the hospital and the runt who runs the home had his phone switched off.'

Coupland chose his words carefully: 'When something like this happens we have to be sure of the facts before we can divulge them to the families. Due to the extent of the fire some patients remain unaccounted for. At least Catherine was able to be removed before the fire took hold.'

'And that's supposed to bring us comfort?'

'No, but it means she's able to be identified, unlike many of the other victims.'

Tunny clenched his jaw, his grip tightening on his mother's hand. 'I can do that,' he said to her, before turning his attention back to Coupland, 'But right now I want you to leave.'

'Your sister's death is now part of a major investigation,' Coupland cautioned. 'We'll need you to answer a few questions—'

'I don't have to do anything I don't want to, Mr Coupland. The day I come running to you lot will be a dark day indeed.'

Coupland refused to be put off. 'Your cooperation would be appreciated, Mr Tunny, several people have been killed in this fire which we are treating as suspicious.'

'You'll make inspector yet with those powers of deduction,' Tunny said.

Coupland ignored the barb. 'Can you think of anyone who'd want to get back at you like this?'

Tunny's gaze swept over his minders before returning to the detectives in front of him. 'I can think of a dozen men who'd take me out in the blink of an eye if they had the chance, but my harmless little sister? No one would dare.'

'Someone has though,' Coupland reminded him. 'Help me catch them, bring them to justice for you and your family.' His comment brought sniggers from every direction, though one look from Tunny silenced them. Ma Tunny stared at him, trying and failing to process the information.

'I'll be doling out my own form of justice, thank you very much,' Tunny informed him.

Coupland sighed. 'To what end though? So another crime is committed? Where's the sense in that?'

Tunny eyeballed him. 'It's about family, Mr Coupland. Flesh and Blood. Respect. Do you know anything about that?'

Coupland pushed thoughts of Lynn, Amy and the munchkin out of his head. Grief made people say things they didn't mean. He'd lost count of family members hurting over loved ones, threatening to take out whoever had caused their pain. Promises made in the heat of the moment turned out to be wishful thinking at best. Kieran Tunny was a completely different kettle of fish. A stint inside held no fear for him. He would need careful handling. 'I promise you I will do everything within my power to find whoever did this, but you can't get in my way.'

Tunny laughed. 'Do you really think anyone will talk to you? If I put the word out this city will turn deaf and dumb overnight. To you lot, anyway.'

'I mean it, Kieran,' Coupland persisted. 'Leave it to us.'

Tunny ignored him: 'I hope the person whose done this knows what they've started, Mr Coupland,' his voice dripped with venom, 'because the way I'm feeling right now I'm even scaring myself.'

'That seemed to go alright,' Alex said as they walked back down the garden path. Coupland turned in time to see Tunny watching them from the living room window. He pictured the person responsible for the fire looking up at the gangster as they begged for their life. The terror in their face. The slow realisation that it wouldn't change a thing.

'We'll see,' he answered.

CID room, Salford Precinct Station

Coupland pulled a face as he read through his inbox. There was the usual detritus sent out by the social committee: a round of golf followed by drinks at the country club in Worsley, a drinks reception at The Lowry, a pub quiz, venue to be advised. Funny how alcohol seemed to be the common theme. Even so, a room full of cops making small talk was the last thing he needed. Polite chit chat bugged the hell out of him. He much preferred conversations that were recorded on tape, where both parties knew where they stood. He hit delete and moved on.

There was an email from Colin Ross, asking him to prepare a draft response to Austin Smith's allegations. His hearing with Professional Standards was at the end of the month, the date in bold and underlined. Coupland copied the details into his electronic diary. Made a post-it note reminder to check his electronic diary more often. Stuck it at the top of his computer screen.

The email below it was an update from Andy Lewis, the DC working the hit and run case. The forensic investigation on the abandoned Mitsubishi had drawn a blank. The victim, James McMahon, had no gangland connections. He worked the night shift in the warehouse of a local sweet factory, had taken the job as it meant he was around to take the kids to school. His wife worked for an insurance company in Manchester's city centre. Lewis was arranging a press conference for the following day. He'd spoken to McMahon's widow who was keen to participate. Coupland hit the reply button, asked Lewis if he'd checked her out. From Coupland's recollection the news of her husband's death had devastated her, but it didn't pay to be complacent. He thanked Lewis for his update anyway, and remembering the Super's words suggested they meet at the end of the week if there hadn't been any further developments. He pressed 'send.' If the wife was clean then they were looking at an accident, but why the cloak of silence?

Lewis's reply was instant, telling Coupland his comments were noted and reminding him that the updates he'd been sending him were for information only and he didn't intend taking up more of Coupland's valuable time than was necessary. Oh, and of course he'd checked out the widow, but was grateful for his suggestion. Seems Coupland wasn't the only one who took micro-managing personally. Lewis might as well have replied 'Go fuck yourself,' but the difference in rank prevented it.

Coupland's mobile rang. Cursing, he grabbed it, his mood darkening as he listened to what Ashcroft had to say. 'The day just gets better and better,' he sighed, swiping his screen to end the call.

Alex looked up from her computer screen. 'How come?'

'Apparently all three arsonists Ashcroft questioned yesterday have ended up in A&E.'

'What, together? Were they at some sort of Arsonists' Anonymous meeting that went horribly wrong?'

Coupland shook his head. 'Each was paid a visit by two men in black, and I don't mean Will Smith and Tommy Lee Jones.'

'What were they after?'

'To give them a pasting, by all accounts.'

'Why them though?'

Coupland gave her a look that conveyed she was being dim. 'Wakey Wakey, Alex, Tunny's sister is killed in a fire and three local arsonists are battered 24 hours later. Get a grip.'

'Has Ashcroft managed to get anything out of them?'

'I'll give you three guesses.'

'Is there any connection to Tunny though, anything obvious?'

'None that Ashcroft can make out. He reckons he saw a couple of youths lurking while he was doing the rounds.'

'He didn't think anything of it at the time?'

'You start getting twitchy every time you see a kid in a tracksuit, you're in the wrong job.'

Alex frowned. 'True. But how would Tunny have found out about them in the first place?'

'Same as us. We use the Police National Computer but the criminal fraternity have their own database, like Checkatrade only instead of I'm looking for a plumber you type in armed robber or fire starter or whatever else

126

floats your boat.'

'So Tunny sends out two of his finest henchmen?'

'Not quite horsemen of the Apocalypse, but near enough.'

'How serious are the injuries?'

'Enough to warrant a head CT for Tyson Gemmell and they're keeping Warren Douglas in for observation.'

'Do you reckon Tunny thinks all three are involved?'

Coupland shrugged. 'Christ knows, hedging his bets would be my guess. Hoping those who had nothing to do with it will squeal on the other.'

'Assuming they know.'

'Exactly. Ashcroft says they don't even know each other.'

'Nothing you've told me gives us any reason to suggest Tunny's involvement.'

'I know.'

'You go charging round there and he'll squeal harass-ment. You don't want to make newspaper headlines two days in a row.'

'You saw it, then.'

'Everyone's seen it, Kevin. No one is paying it any attention, mind. Timing could have been better though, what with your hearing coming up.'

'Tell me about it.' Coupland hoped his smile was convincing, gave the impression that he couldn't give a toss. Truth was, however hard he tried to kid onto himself it didn't matter, the professional conduct hearing was never far from his mind.

*

He would never admit it but it was comforting to come

home at the end of his shift to the chaos and clutter of a baby. A welcome distraction. Lynn appeared in the kitchen doorway with her fingers crossed. 'Just got him down. Need wine.'

Coupland did as he was told and poured her a glass of red, grabbing a beer from the fridge for himself. 'Where's Her Nibs?'

'Off to the cinema with a pal.'

Coupland tugged the ring pull and lifted the can to his lips. Took a long, hard slug. He regarded Lynn as she took a small sip of her wine before slouching against the kitchen unit.

'You look knackered,' he sympathised. After a day at work then a full on couple of hours with Tonto it was hardly surprising.

'Charming!'

'You know what I mean.' He thought of Donna Chisholm juggling three full time grandkids and a job. 'It takes it out of you. That's all I'm saying. This time around, I mean.'

'Took it out of me the first time around, if I remember it right.'

She had a point there. Chasing after a baby whatever your age was exhausting. 'I'll sort dinner,' he said, guessing with Amy out for the evening they'd have their hands full.

'A kebab and chips from the Turkish it is then,' Lynn smiled.

'I can go to the supermarket if you'd rather,' he offered, 'but the ready meal portions sizes are never enough.'

'True.'

'I'll set the table how you like,' he added. 'Put paper towels out and everything.' He began to set about the task, making a sweeping gesture with his hands when he'd finished.

Lynn raised a brow at him. 'You know how to show a girl a good time, Kev, I'll give you that.' They leaned against the kitchen worktops, facing each other, enjoying their drinks. It was a routine, when their shifts permitted it, that brought Coupland comfort. Like stepping into a decompression chamber before emerging properly into the life they shared.

'Someone left a newspaper in the staffroom,' Lynn said. 'I see that prick has raised his ugly head again.'

Coupland was taken aback to hear Lynn swear, there was certainly no doubting her anger. After all this time together he was touched how quick she was to take his side. Although they rarely spoke about work, it was impossible for individual cases not to seep through the lining of their life. 'It'll sort itself out,' he reassured her, 'Professional Standards have procedures to follow, they are accountable, just like me.'

Lynn thought carefully before she spoke next. 'Do you think it was finding out about the baby, you know, that made you act the way you did?'

'Sorry?'

'Come on Kev, you know what I mean. When you found out Amy was pregnant you were a bit…difficult to live with for a while, that's all I'm saying.'

'"That's all I'm saying,"' he quoted back at her. 'Now's not the time to pull any punches, Light of my life.'

'Fine! You were a twat of the highest order while Amy was pregnant.' She threw him a look. 'Satisfied?'

That she'd sworn twice in as many minutes? A little. In Coupland's view there was nothing like a four-letter word to ease you through the day; whether you'd stubbed your toe or had your parking space stolen, certain words summed up the frustration just right. He flashed her a smile. 'What you mean is I was more of a twat than usual.'

Lynn turned away. 'You said it, tough guy.' There was an edge to her voice. The one that warned him to toe the line, that his jokey banter was beginning to wear thin. Truth was, things had been difficult between them for a while. From the time Amy had announced her pregnancy, right up until the birth, all things considered.

'I was bent out of shape,' Coupland admitted. 'Who wouldn't be? But would I have done things differently?' He replayed the case he'd been working on when Amy had dropped her bombshell. The human trafficking of Albanians into Salford. A little girl's body rammed into a sports bag. Austin 'Reedsy' Smith, a tampon stuck up each nostril after Coupland had broken his nose. He shook his head at the truth of it. 'Nah, don't think I would, love.'

Lynn busied herself pulling salt and a bottle of vinegar from a cupboard above the kettle. He spoke to her back. 'Look, I was heavy handed – I hold my hands up to that.' As a result of his actions he was under the microscope at work; his career was starting to mimic José Mourinho's before he was given the heave-ho by United, but there was no need to worry Lynn about that. The last thing he needed was for Reedsy's complaint to be upheld. It would be just the ammunition needed for his lawyer to unpick his conviction.

Lynn placed the condiments on the table before finishing her wine. She topped up her glass, asked if he wanted another beer. 'If it saves you from drinking alone, my love, it's a sacrifice I'm willing to make,' Coupland smiled, reaching for his mobile, hitting the number programmed into his phone. He ordered two doner kebabs, all the trimmings, chips on the side. Extra chillies on one. Waited while the person on the other end of the phone wrote down his order before reading it back to him. Holding the phone away from his mouth, the look he sent Lynn was sheepish. 'Am I less of a twat tonight?'

The smile she flashed him was crooked. 'You'll find out the answer to that later,' she answered. 'If I can stay awake long enough.'

Coupland grinned as he spoke into the phone once more: 'Hold the extra chillies,' he instructed, not wanting to spoil the mood.

MONDAY

CHAPTER SEVEN

Morning briefing

The CID room was crammed full of people. Uniformed officers, civilians, detectives borrowed from other investigations, all facing Coupland. More photographs had been added to the whiteboard too. The first was a grainy shot of Roland Masters taken from the garden party photo Turnbull had spotted outside Alan Harkins' office. The second was a grinning young woman wearing small round spectacles, placed beside the one of her body retrieved from the fire. Coupland pointed to her name beneath it which had been underlined several times.

'OK, so I'm guessing everyone got the memo that Catherine Fry is Kieran Tunny's sister.' A DC at the back of the room raised his hand, 'I didn't even know he had a sister, Sarge.'

'Neither did I. The family have been protective of her over the years, made sure she didn't get any undue attention. When she was sent to Cedar Falls Tunny had her registered under her mother's maiden name.'

The DC nodded.

Coupland jabbed her name with his finger, 'This changes everything. Whichever way we look at it we now have to consider a gang related motive.' There were several nods and remarks made Coupland couldn't make out. The mood in the room was subdued. The investigation had only just got underway and now they were stepping into a volatile mine field. 160 organised crime gangs operated in Greater Manchester, over 8000 'troublesome' families. Crimes relating to any of them took months, sometimes years, to bring to justice. Coupland dug deep in an attempt to lift the team's spirits. 'Remember, Tunny is on the same side as us this time. He wants justice for his sister, too.' The faces staring back at him gave nothing away. Much like he'd tried not to when the Super had pontificated about the virtue of shoe leather, but he knew what they were thinking. Images of flying pigs and a frozen Hell flashed in front of him.

Through the CID room's internal window a shiny Superintendent Curtis could be seen marching along the corridor, followed by a pack of journalists as they headed towards the multifunction room used for press announcements and visiting dignitaries. Walking at a slower pace a tearful woman held the arm of a plain clothes WPC, behind them a sombre looking DC clasped a manila folder. The appeal for information relating to the killing of Elaine McMahon's husband outside his sons' school would be aired at tea time that night. Coupland wasn't a fan of exposing the grieving to public scrutiny but if it pricked someone's conscience into action maybe it was worth the additional pain.

He turned his attention back to the officers facing him. 'Finding whoever started this fire could rebuild some of the trust broken down over the years in certain parts of the community.' He glanced up at the ceiling. Maybe if he said it loud enough, he'd begin to believe it.

'What about the assaults on the arsonists?' Ashcroft asked. 'How do they fit in?'

'We've no evidence to suggest this is Tunny.' Coupland raised his hand to quell the muttered objections coming from the back of the room. 'Yeah, yeah, I hear what you're saying, but we've three statements telling us the best part of bugger all. Yes, it could be Tunny, but it could be the real arsonist covering their tracks.'

'Or creating a smoke screen,' a DC from the front row quipped, causing a few groans.

Coupland nodded. 'We have to keep an open mind.'

'What's this guy like, Sarge?' Ashcroft asked.

Coupland stared ahead, could feel the anticipation of the officers around him. He tilted his head to one side as he thought about his answer, making eye contact with several DCs dotted around the room, wondering if they'd concur with his description: 'Tunny likes to think of himself as a community fixer. You go to him with a problem, he'll sort it, but you'll owe him. He can be deceptive, not your traditional hard man routine. He acts ever so humble but don't underestimate him for one minute. He's dangerous. Never forget that. We call him Paul Daniels because he makes witnesses disappear.'

Ashcroft nodded. 'Been inside?'

'More than he's been out but that doesn't seem to stop him.' The truth was life on the inside wasn't a deterrent for men like Tunny. Access to mobile phones smuggled into the prison meant business as usual in terms of running their empires and their reputations meant they weren't short of lackeys on the outside to do their bidding.

'He made a fortune last time he was inside,' Turnbull piped up, 'had drones flying drugs over the prison walls right up to his cell window.' Drug use in prison was at an all-time high and it never ceased to amaze Coupland the ease with which gangs skirted the system. 'Drones are quite the accessory for drug smugglers these days, suppose it beats shoving bags of spice up your backside on visiting day.'

'He's got a racket going on in most of the jails around the north of England,' Robinson added. 'Even though the authorities are aware of it there seems bugger all they can do to stop it.'

'What can we do about these attacks though?' Ashcroft persisted.

Coupland considered their options. 'If we find out who the culprits are we can issue them with GANGBOs.' He pulled a face at the groans that went up around the room. Like an ASBO, a GANGBO was a civil injunction but for all the members of a gang, banning subjects from associating with each other or entering certain locations. The truth was they were a pain in the backside to monitor and an ever bigger pain to uphold. 'OK, scrap that,' Coupland conceded. 'Let's just hope Tunny really has decided to play ball.'

He turned his attention back to Turnbull. 'Did you ask Alan Harkins why he failed to mention his connection to Tunny?'

The DC nodded. 'He said he didn't see how it was relevant. That even gangsters are entitled to support their relatives in whichever way they wanted and his money was as good as anyone else's.'

'Well it's certainly fragrant, I'll give him that, the amount of times it's been laundered,' said Coupland. 'No wonder he was cagey with me. He practically jumped out of his skin when you called me earlier. I was tearing him off a strip for not spotting Johnny Metcalfe had gone missing, he must have worked out I hadn't got wind of Tunny's connection.'

'What about this Johnny Metcalfe? Should we be looking at him more closely?'

Coupland puffed out his cheeks as he considered this. 'I don't see him being involved, I'm not sure he'd have the wherewithal.'

'What about Harkins, then, Sarge? His record keeping is lax; he's economical with the truth. Is he just incompetent or is it something more? Do you want us to bring him in?'

Coupland was already shaking his head. 'Not yet, we've got no real grounds to, though he's certainly a person of interest. Think I'll pay him another visit at the home. Alex and I are meeting the fire officer there anyway. See if there's anything else he's been keeping from us.'

'When's the PM due?' Alex asked.

'Professor Benson has emailed to say the forensic anthropologist is arriving today at 3pm. She's here to secure identification on the three bodies that suffered severe burns.' A small but vital difference between the victims' fate being forever unconfirmed and their families being able to lay them to rest.

Coupland's gaze returned to Turnbull, prompting the DC to hold up a printout in front of him. 'I've emailed you all a list of ex-patients who raised complaints against Cedar Falls in the last two years that didn't have their grievances upheld.'

Coupland skim read his copy, gave Krispy a nod of approval. 'I take it this is your work?'

Krispy nodded. 'It's easier extracting information from a database query than searching through a ton of papers.'

'For you maybe,' Coupland countered, wondering once more where the Super's shoe leather factored into this equation. 'Nice work,' he said, his attention turning to Robinson who spoke next.

'Some patients were transferred out of the area, either because facilities became available closer to where they lived or the other way round, they went to wherever a place became available because they were unhappy.'

'Can they be accounted for on the night of the fire?'

Robinson nodded, 'Not all the patients who moved on went into another care home though, some returned home. We're in the process of tracking their whereabouts…'

Coupland caught a look that passed between Robinson and the young DC. 'Anything you want to add?'

'The lad's played a blinder, Sarge. We couldn't have pulled this together so quick without him.'

Coupland regarded Krispy. 'I do believe our baby's all grown up. That said, you've got to walk before you can run, but I reckon we can start putting more, how shall I say it, "Customer facing" actions your way. Leave it with me.'

If Krispy could have wagged his tail and panted he would have done. 'Yes, Sarge.'

*

After a failed attempt at writing his statement for Professional Standards, Coupland slipped out onto the fire escape steps for a sly cigarette. He stared down at the line of patrol cars and police vans, wondering if his days viewing the world from this vantage point were numbered. A white Honda Civic with a broken wing mirror drove into the car park, circling the perimeter before heading towards the exit. The driver slowed, as though consulting something before turning left without indicating.

If Reedsy's complaint was upheld Coupland would be long gone. Curtis wouldn't keep him around if the division had to fork out compensation, he'd be lucky to pull on a uniform, and he didn't fancy his chances much at that, given the plods he'd rubbed up the wrong way over the years. Besides, he wasn't sure he was up to the flexibility expected of today's beat cops. He winced as an athletic looking PC pedalled a police issue BMX into the car park, padlocked it to the bike rack beside the station's back entrance. The PC removed his bike helmet, saw Coupland looking over and waved a hand in greeting before heading in his direction.

'You're only coming over for the nicotine hit, Ronan, admit it,' Coupland scoffed, wafting the smoke downwind.

'You're not wrong, given the bloody day I've had, Sarge,' the officer replied, trudging up the stairs. 'These cycling shorts are chafing the hell out of me.'

'Save that talk for your wife, Ronan, I'm getting an image that'll keep me awake tonight for all the wrong reasons. At least it's keeping you toned.'

'I'll be doing trials for the Olympic team at this rate, given the sodding miles I've done today.'

'Go and get yourself a well-deserved bacon roll, son. There's only room for one Adonis in this station and that place is well and truly taken.'

Ronan looked as though he'd be more at home in a boy band than pounding the beat. He took a pride in his appearance most men didn't bother with once they'd married but Ronan's wife worked at Media City, was surrounded by suave news readers and weathermen, it didn't pay to become complacent.

As he drew level his radio crackled into life with a message from the control room: *There's a man jumping over a fence carrying a machete on Canal Street.'*

Ronan tutted before hitting the reply button. 'Do you have a description?'

'He's carrying a machete, Ronan,' Coupland cut in. 'What more do you want?'

Ronan rolled his eyes to imply Coupland didn't know the half of it. 'This is my fourth machete shout this shift, Sarge,' he said, stomping back to his bike, thoughts of a butty up in smoke. 'A thug on a bike kicking off in all different parts of the city, it isn't the same person, I'm telling you.'

Coupland looked at him. It wasn't unusual for scrotes to use pedal bikes instead of cars to commit serious crimes. It meant there were no registration plates to be picked up by ANPR cameras. Plus, a bike meant they could go off road if police vehicles came in pursuit. Coupland sighed out a lungful of smoke. 'Send your report over to me when you've finished the shout,' he called down as Ronan clambered back on his bike, a thought taking shape in his head. Battered arsonists and thugs with machetes. The incidents might be happening in different parts of the city and carried out by several people, but with everything that had gone on in the last three days it could only be one man pulling their strings.

*

'Are you DS Coupland?' A young woman held a mobile phone towards him as she moved in his direction.

'Who wants to know?'

'I asked at the desk and the officer said you'd be out here.'

'Did he now?' Coupland said, though more to himself, already working out she was one of the journalists who'd attended the press appeal for James McMahon's killer.

'Is it true Kieran Tunny's sister was one of the victims of the fire at the weekend?'

Close up she was older than she looked, tattooed on eyebrows and lash extensions made her resemble a Russian prostitute. A highly surprised one at that. 'All press enquiries should be forwarded to our media department.' Coupland quoted the standard phrase that had been drilled into them following a spate of officers being caught off guard by local journalists.

'I know that, I've just spent the last hour with them.' The reporter sounded tired, as though it had already been a long day but she had to go through the motions. 'But our readers like to hear what's going on from the horse's mouth, so to speak.'

Coupland studied her. 'Do they now? And which arse wipe of a rag have you crawled out from, dare I ask?'

If she was startled by his reply the tattooed eyebrows gave nothing away, instead she fished in a pocket and held up a business card. 'I work for an on-line paper; our articles are updated hourly and we encourage readers to send in their own news.'

Coupland bent down to take the card from her, curiosity getting the better of him. Angelica Heyworth. He stiffened, recognising the reporter's name and the logo on her card. An image of Austin 'Reedsy' Smith with his broken nose. Of Johnny Metcalfe running naked into a corner shop. 'Wow, I can see I'm in the presence of a true professional,' he said. 'Tell me, how long did you have to train to do your job? A week of *Ladybird* How to books or did the *Dummies Guide* do the trick, then you were off, bad-mouthing cops and sympathising with traffickers like you'd been doing it for years?'

A smile tugged at thin lips. 'Ah, I was wondering whether you'd read it.' Her eyes lit up, already formulating her next story.

'Is anything you write remotely connected to the truth?' he asked. 'I mean, come on,' he took in the polyester coat pulled in too tight at the waist, the clunky platform boots scuffed at the heel, 'you're more Angela than Angelica, love, who are you trying to kid?'

Angelica bristled, tugging at the belt on her thin coat. 'At least I don't go round punching people.'

Coupland looked up at the sky. 'It would help if you got your facts right for a start. I didn't punch him, it was a head butt!' he spat, seeing, too late, the recording light glowing red on her phone. He rolled his eyes in frustration, 'For Christ's sake, is that all your job is about?' he snapped as she tapped something into her phone before dropping it into a faux leather shoulder bag. 'Make you proud, does it? Tripping folk up till you get the story you want!' he called after her but she was already walking away.

*

'When's the boss back from his course?' Alex asked Coupland as he returned to his desk.

'Seminar,' he corrected her. 'Any time now. Got a text from him earlier to say he was just leaving Knutsford Services.'

'So, what was the seminar about?'

'Sharing best practice.'

'Christ, and Superintendent Curtis didn't get an invite?'

'He sent the DCI in his place. Apparently delegates were being put up in a Travelodge.'

A ping in Coupland's inbox signified an email. As promised Ronan had sent him a copy of his report. Machete wielding youths had been spotted running out of a dry cleaners on Bolton Street, a hairdressers on Broughton Lane and marauding across an allotment off Mossfield Road. Dressed in dark clothing, the men were described as white, mid-twenties, faces partially obscured by scarves pulled up over their noses. Victims were shaken but otherwise unhurt. None wanted to give a statement. All started off trying to deny anything had taken place at all. The calls had been made by concerned neighbours who now all suffered from amnesia. Coupland wasn't surprised, it was easier that way than saying something that might come back to bite them further down the line. The manager of the dry cleaning firm insisted there had been no disturbance at all until Ronan pointed out a machete blade embedded in the wall.

'Forget Tunny hedging his bets,' Coupland called over to Alex, as he cross checked the victims' names against Turnbull's report. 'He's conducting his version of house to house enquiries.' He forwarded the email to her. 'Take a look for yourself.'

Alex's eyes widened as she read the list of names. 'These are all folk who supply goods and services to Cedar Falls. Where's Tunny getting his information?'

'Think we can take a guess at that, don't you?'

'Time for that briefing?' DCI Mallender popped his head around the CID room door, indicating with his hand that Coupland follow him to his office. Coupland obliged, eyebrows raised at Alex as he passed by her desk.

'Good luck,' she mouthed, referring to the pointless request Coupland would make for the team's overtime to deal with the spike in assaults following Catherine Fry's murder. Pointless because it would never be granted. The mantra from on high was that each station had to do more, with less. Alex knew that Coupland would do right by his team; she also knew that no officer would do any less than was expected to get the job done. The problem was that the powers that be knew this too.

Coupland brought DCI Mallender up to speed with the investigation. There'd been no time for preamble, no making small talk or enquiring how the seminar had gone. They were both still standing in Mallender's office, the DCI had placed his jacket over the back of his chair and on seeing the post piled up on his in tray had moved round to the front of his desk to perch on the edge, as though by keeping it out of sight he could concentrate that little bit harder on the news Coupland was imparting.

'So Tunny's sister is one of the victims?' he winced, hands automatically going to his hair as though he was about to pull out a clump of it. 'That's all we need.'

Coupland made a sound like a toy gun popping. 'You've not heard the half of it yet.'

'I'm sure I haven't,' Mallender grumbled. 'Did you deliver the death message yourself?'

'I wasn't delegating that one.'

'How's he taken it?'

'We've got machete wielding henchmen rampaging through the city; I'll leave you to work it out for yourself.'

'Great.'

Coupland shifted under his gaze. 'Three arsonists we've questioned have ended up in A&E.'

'Nothing to do with you I hope?'

'No, boss, and I've witnesses to prove it.'

'But you're sure it's Tunny?'

'As sure as I can be given there isn't a scrap of evidence.'

'Any link between the arsonists and the fire?'

Coupland shook his head. 'Unlikely.'

'How's he getting his information?'

'The victims of the machete attack are on the care home manager's list of suppliers that he gave to Turnbull. I reckon he's passing the same information he's giving us onto Tunny along with anything else he's damned well asked for.'

Mallender considered this. 'I don't suppose he felt he was in a position he could refuse. Can hardly blame him.'

Coupland grunted in agreement, his body language suggesting he needed to bloody well blame someone.

'Did CCTV capture any of this?'

Coupland blew air out from his cheeks. 'Units were either disabled or non-existent, no forensics either.'

'Sounds to me like he's got the upper hand.' There was a hint of accusation in Mallender's tone.

'I can only work with what I've got,' Coupland said. 'If there was a chance to bring in more officers, have more of a presence on the streets, overtime—'

'—Not happening.' Mallender cut him off. 'We'll need to rope in additional resources as it is, for the funeral.' Funerals of crime bosses or close relatives created a lot of attention; extra police would be brought in from across the division when the time came for Tunny to bury his sister. No one seemed to question that money would be made available for *that*.

'I'm not saying you've made a fist of containing the situation, Kevin, just that whatever you've been doing isn't working.'

Coupland threw his hands in the air. 'We've only just discovered the gang connection, boss, none of this could have been foreseen!' He took a breath, a thought forming in his mind that he couldn't resist saying out loud. 'No pearls of wisdom from your summit, Sir? Any shared best practice from down south that we could benefit from?'

The DCI threw Coupland a look. 'I stopped listening the moment you addressed me as Sir, Kevin, you only ever do that when you're taking the proverbial.'

'Sorry, boss.' Coupland said, but they both knew he didn't mean it. 'Look, the moment I discovered Tunny's connection I asked for his cooperation, I can see now I was wasting my time.'

'Did he give you any names of who he thought might be responsible for the fire?'

'A phone book would be more concise – that's if they still make them.'

'Get in touch with the VIU, they may have something that can prove Tunny's involvement in these disturbances.' The Video Intelligence Unit consisted of plain clothes officers who moved about the city videoing freed high profile prisoners after serving their sentences. The videos were circulated around local stations and uploaded onto You Tube with the intention of providing other officers and the public up to date information on their appearance, although in Tunny's case he was so well known it gave him celebrity status.

'He's the subject of an exclusion zone banning him

from certain streets, isn't he? If there's footage of him breaching that he'd be returned to prison. Job done.'

Coupland pulled a face. 'He's got minions to do his dirty work boss, besides, getting him off the streets doesn't help us find our arsonist.'

'No, but it's a stick to beat him with while we conduct our investigation.'

'You know what happens when you poke a bear, Sir? Or a hornets' nest for that matter?'

Mallender shrugged. 'Best I can come up with, in the circumstances.' He looked thoughtful. 'You haven't said what your take is on this.'

'You mean do I think it's a tit for tat situation initiated by one of Tunny's rivals?' Coupland's mouth turned down at the edges. 'It'd be daft not to explore that angle. I'm not focussing solely on that, though to be truthful we've got bugger all in terms of other leads.'

'What about local intelligence?'

Coupland was already shaking his head. 'I doubt any informers will be willing to put their neck on the line. Besides, I don't want to act on something likely to be thrown out by the CPS later, given the division's recent record.' He was referring to the criticism levelled at GMP by the police watchdog for taking on an informant who had offered his services to three other forces – a rent-a-snitch, for all intents and purposes. The other forces turned him down, yet GMP in its wisdom took him at his word. He went on to commit murder right under their nose. Two officers from another station were currently on leave pending an internal review. Coupland sighed; he had the ability to make things go pear shaped without help from anyone else, let alone working hand in glove with someone already involved in criminality.

'Have you informed Superintendent Curtis about any of this?'

'Thought I'd save that pleasure for you. He's had the honour of my company twice this week already; don't think either of us relish a third time.'

'Cheers for that.' A pause. 'You all set for Judy Grant's trial?'

'All spick and span, boss.'

Mallender eyed him. 'I see what you mean about spending too much time with the Super.'

Coupland was halfway to the door when he remembered. 'How did it go in the end, Sir, your talk I mean, did you get a standing ovation?'

'Keep walking,' Mallender said, pointing towards the door and the corridor beyond.

Coupland's phone pinged just as he returned to his desk. He tapped on the screen to see a notification from the Salford Network news app he'd downloaded a couple of days before. Angelica Heyworth had updated her article. The headline made him wince: *'Cop admits assault on Austin Smith.'* Below it, an image of Coupland standing on the fire exit stairs holding a cigarette loomed large, with the 'Play' icon above it. He hit 'Play'. The clip had been edited so that all Coupland could be heard saying was *'I head-butted him,'* Over and over like an angry rapper. He groaned.

'What is it?' Alex had been watching him since he'd come back from his update with the DCI, saw him glaring at his phone. He told her about his run in with the journalist earlier.

'She'll run the story for a couple of days until something more sensational comes along, like a mugger suing a granny for hitting him with her handbag.'

'You reckon?'

'Course I do. It's rubbish.'

'Yeah, but stories like this aren't tomorrow's fish and chip paper any more, are they? They're there, preserved on the interweb for the rest of eternity.'

Alex's smile slipped. 'Well, there is that,' she conceded. 'But with any luck no-one'll see it,' she soothed. 'Unless it starts trending.'

Coupland threw her a look. 'Cheers for that, you can get back to pulling the legs off spiders or whatever it was you were doing before you pissed in my sandpit.'

She tipped her head. 'Glad to be of service.'

Coupland looked up a number on the division's intranet and telephoned the VIU. The officer he spoke to was helpful enough. Yes, they had footage on Tunny dating back 18 months, none of it incriminated him in terms of breaching his exclusion zone order, nor was he seen fraternising with the heads of other crime families. 'He keeps himself to himself,' the officer said. 'He's a creature of habit too, does the same thing on set days, we're thinking of scaling our obs down to tell you the truth.'

Coupland thanked him and asked him to email footage for the last two weeks over. It'd keep him out of trouble for the rest of the morning, if nothing else.

Two hours in and Coupland could see the VIU officer hadn't been exaggerating. Tunny wasn't so much a creature of habit but painstakingly anal about the places he went to: the same café in the morning for his breakfast, the same pub for his lunch and then home for tea.

Evenings he would be dropped off at a wine bar which he co-owned, and at midnight he'd be driven home. He took his partner out to dinner on Friday, went to football on Saturday, church on Sunday. He had a weekly haircut, went to visit Catherine at Cedar Falls the same day every week, did the school run on a Thursday. Not a single boxing club, drug den or arms cache in sight. Coupland tried not to think of the money spent watching and waiting for these men to commit their next offence, while there was bugger all in the pot for his team to deal with the crimes that had already taken place. He sucked in a breath; someone far higher up the totem pole deemed it money well spent, who was he to argue?

Coupland scraped his chair back as he got to his feet, rubbing the back of his neck as he did so. He'd seen enough.

'Fag break?' Alex asked.

Coupland glanced at his watch. 'Off to the barbers, if you must know.'

Alex cocked her head as she looked him up and down, 'Well, if you are going to become the next media sensation, you might as well look the part, I suppose.'

CHAPTER EIGHT

The barber shop on Bolton Street closed to the public every Monday afternoon, the chair reserved for Kieran Tunny and his crew. It offered only one style – shaved heads. Inside, the seats were taken with big men and skinny youths waiting for a number one cut. One youth sucked on a lolly while he scrolled through his phone, another picked at a spot under his nose. They were the same young guns that'd been lounging on Ma Tunny's garden wall like lazy sentries. The youth picking his nose caught Coupland's eye, flicked him a snot covered finger. The older men sat back in their seats, discussing the result of Saturday's match. All eyes fell onto the interloper, bringing their conversation to an abrupt halt. Tunny, reclining in the barber's chair, sent Coupland a look that would have stopped most men in their tracks.

'So, what are you getting today then?' Coupland asked. 'Hair extensions?' He moved around the salon as though taking an inventory. No Brylcreem on sale here, though there was plenty of beard oil. 'Thought your man here was in the business of removing hair,' Coupland observed.

'There's money to be made grooming beards, not shaving them off,' the barber shrugged. Wearing a faux leather apron over jeans and a white shirt he was a good example of practising what he preached, no hair up top but a thick pirate style beard that glistened under the spotlights.

'Not on my watch,' Tunny said, his eyes running along the line of clean shaven minders until, satisfied, his gaze settled on the gobby detective.

'Can I help you, Mr Coupland?' His tone was pleasant enough. With the muscle sat around him he could afford to be.

Coupland nodded, mirroring Tunny's jovial manner. 'Yeah, you can. I want you to stop leaning on people.'

Tunny settled back while the barber ran clippers over his scalp; the look on his face told Coupland his request came as no surprise. 'Trust me, I haven't even started.'

Coupland eyeballed him in the mirror. 'Several of your goons have been seen running round the city brandishing machetes. That's hardly small beer.'

The barber didn't blink at the mention of machetes; Coupland wondered what other topics of conversation he was privy to.

'Depends where you drink,' Tunny commented. 'Anyway, what makes you think it has anything to do with me?'

'Because of the places the reports are coming in from. The estate beside Cedar Falls where the mobile hairdresser they use lives, the laundry where the bed linen gets washed and the garden maintenance firm they use. It's not rocket science for Christ's sake. And now I'm getting reports of assaults on local balloon heads, I'm starting to think you're reneging on our agreement.'

'So you've got 'em then? Whoever slaughtered my sister? Because that's the only reason you'd want me to call off the hounds, surely?'

Coupland huffed out a breath. 'We're making headway, Kieran.'

'What does that mean exactly? And if your next sentence contains the words lines of enquiry I'm afraid I'm going to have to ask you to leave.' His minders leaned forward in their seats, ready to spring into action if needed.

'My officers are all over this investigation, and yet everywhere they go your henchmen are there, biding their time.'

Kieran sighed. 'If your guys were on top of things you wouldn't be here doing my head in. People talk to us.'

Coupland pulled a face. 'But how reliable is their information? When people are intimidated they'll tell you what they think you want to hear.'

'You included?'

Coupland's brows shot into his hairline. 'Me? I say it as I see it, Sunshine. Too long in the tooth to change that.' His eyes met Tunny's, held his gaze, 'And for the record? You're way too old for the fat head look. Maybe try growing it more round the sides?'

Both men stared at each other. 'I've got no beef with you, Mr Coupland. Some of your colleagues on the other hand…'

Coupland was already shaking his head. 'I can't speak for them. All I know is when I took my oath I swore to serve without fear or favour. Just because you are the scourge of the earth as far as GMP is concerned, doesn't mean your sister deserved to die, and it is my intention to bring the person who did this to justice.'

'And how are you going to go about it? Knock politely on doors holding your shiny warrant card?'

'It lost its shine a long time ago,' Coupland drawled, 'but I have ways of extracting the truth, yes.'

Tunny made a snorting noise.

'Is that not enough?' Coupland demanded. 'You want us to run around with guns?'

Tunny shook his head. 'No need, I've got more ammo than Greater Manchester Police put together.'

Coupland didn't doubt it. He felt the same frustration he had when trying to get his point across to a senior officer. If they started losing the argument they pulled rank. In Tunny's case he pulled out the *My guns are bigger than your guns* speech. 'Is that meant to intimidate or impress me?' He asked.

Tunny shrugged. 'Your choice. Either way the clock is ticking. You carry on with your investigation, Mr Coupland, and we'll try not to get in your way.'

The barber pulled a pair of scissors from the tool belt round around his waist and began to trim stray hairs from Tunny's eyebrows, but not before two henchmen moved either side of him.

'Ken here is the only fella in Salford allowed to come near me with a sharp implement,' Tunny boasted. Even his minders weren't allowed to carry blades.

Once he'd finished, Ken brushed bits of hair from Tunny's shoulders before handing him a mirror. The gangster studied his reflection, turning his head this way and that as he checked out his profile. 'More hair round the sides, you say Mr Coupland?' he asked, running sausage like fingers over his scalp. 'You may be onto something there.'

He nodded, handing the mirror back to the barber before stepping out of the chair. He was fast on his feet for a big man, moved in front of Coupland as though blocking his path. Although the men were of similar height and build there was little muscle in Tunny's bulk. He had men to fight for him, had no need to defend himself if the situation arose. Coupland could hold his own with him, he was sure of it, if the fight was allowed to be fair. He squared his shoulders in readiness.

Tunny laughed, stepping back to show he was no threat. 'I have a good feeling about our collaboration, Mr Coupland. A good feeling indeed.'

'There's no bloody collaboration, Kieran, just an understanding of the rules of engagement.'

'There are restaurants spitting distance from here that call a chip a pomme frite. We both know what to expect when the waiter brings our plate over.'

'I wouldn't know,' Coupland said. 'If it doesn't have a photo of the dish in the window I don't go in.'

'Whatever you choose to call our joint efforts I am confident they will bring about the desired result. Remember, you lot run Salford in the day, Mr Coupland,' Kieran fixed him with a look, 'but at night the city belongs to me.'

*

'So come on then,' Alex kept her smile in check, 'What's it like being a grandad?'

A beat. 'OK, so I'm not his grandad, I'm his Papa.' Another beat. 'Why, do I look like a grandad now?' he asked, lowering the car's sun visor to take a look at his reflection.

'You look no sodding different Kevin! Do I look like a mum?'

He returned the sun visor to its upright position, satisfied. Alex slid a glance in his direction when he didn't reply. 'A bit,' he said, enjoying the moment, 'but in a good way.'

'In a good way how?'

Coupland rolled his eyes to the ceiling. With a wife and daughter to deal with he should know the warning signs by now but sometimes he couldn't help it, ploughed in where wiser men would have taken the Fifth Amendment. Alex was already pulling a make-up compact from her bag to study her profile. Her baby weight had gone, though her waistline would never be the same. Carl mentioned once that her face was fatter; she didn't speak to him for a week. She threw a warning look in Coupland's direction like a boxer defending their title.

He gritted his teeth. 'You weigh things up more.' He raised one hand from the steering wheel in mitigation. 'Look. It's not a criticism, I get it!' he said. 'A good day in this job is when we go home safe. You mean the world to those kids of yours, why would you do anything to risk that?'

Alex folded her arms. 'You saying I haven't got your back?'

'Did I say that?' Coupland asked, 'Did I bloody say that? Having a conversation with a woman is like navigating the Amazon with an egg cup and one spoon.'

Alex huffed out a sigh. With two children on the go she didn't get the time to work out as often as she used to. It didn't matter that many of her male counterparts didn't make the effort; that wasn't the point. The job may not be open combat but it required stamina, and if you didn't have brawn you had to be fast on your feet. She hoped to Christ he didn't think she was holding him back.

'I was trying to say I respect your level headedness,'

Coupland said.

'Why does it sound like an insult coming from you?'

He turned towards her, eyebrow raised, 'Does Carl ever accuse you of overthinking things?'

'Only once…' she said ominously, turning her head so that she was staring through the passenger window, hands clamped beneath her armpits. When her favourite song came on the radio she didn't bother tapping her foot.

Coupland sighed. 'In answer to your question, it's quite nice having a kiddie about the place.'

Alex regarded him out of the corner of her eye. 'Only quite nice?'

Coupland shrugged. 'Like I imagine having a dog would be,' he said. 'When I walk into the room he stares up at me like I know how the world works, plus he never answers back. He isn't shy about crapping everywhere either.' Funny thing was Coupland couldn't remember any more what it had been like before Tonto came along. Quieter, that was for sure, but he had a way of making them all pull together, and if they tried hard enough, they might one day forget about his father.

'How do you think Tunny fits into the picture?' Alex asked. 'I mean, his sister was surely the target of the fire, which alters the direction of the investigation completely.'

Coupland thought about this. 'Possibly. Or it could have still have been a random act.'

'That what you really think?'

Coupland shook his head. 'No, but I'm trying not to run headlong down any rabbit holes without considering all the possibilities. What I do know is that whatever the cause, whoever did this, we've got a potential gang war on our hands if we don't get to them before Tunny does.'

'Is that who you went to see when you disappeared to the barbers earlier?' Alex asked. 'Given you didn't look any different when you returned.' She gave his hair the once over. 'You know, a trim wouldn't do any harm.'

'Lynn likes something she can run her fingers through,' Coupland grinned, his mind wandering to the previous evening. He caught Alex looking at him, remembered she'd asked him a question. 'I wanted to appeal to his better nature. Remind him that we want the same outcome. All I got for my trouble was a "My dad's bigger than yours" speech.'

'Charming.'

'The boss isn't happy with how I'm handling him.'

'Easy to say when you're not the one negotiating with someone who isn't scared of jail.'

'Even so.'

'What other options do we have?'

'We lean on the care home manager, put the fear of God into him if he even considers passing anything else on to Tunny.'

Cedar Falls was a red brick Victorian mill converted into a thirty bedroom residence with a modern glass and concrete extension added a couple of years back, providing office space and staff accommodation. The fire had gutted the residential block, while the office and staff quarters remained intact. Today was the first time anyone from the murder squad had access to the damaged part of the building. Though the fire brigade had certified the residential block was safe to enter, it had done so on the proviso they were accompanied by an officer from the Fire Investigation Unit. Coupland parked as close as the police cordon would allow.

'This job can be a barrel of laughs sometimes,' he said.

'Laugh a minute,' agreed Alex, unclipping her seatbelt. They stepped around a pile of fire damaged items that had been laid out across the pavement, blackened photo frames, melted televisions, singed bedding. Any items of significance had already been bagged and tagged; the items lying here were headed for a skip, unless relatives wanted a single blackened shoe or broken mirror as a keepsake.

*

The fire scene investigator from the FIU waited for them in front of the warped main door. He looked a similar age to Coupland albeit slimmer, though Coupland was pleased to note the flecks of grey in his hair were more noticeable.

'Fire Officer Grayling,' the man barked. Instead of a hand he held out blue forensic suits. 'I can't stay long. Not if you want my report by the end of the day.' He waited as the detectives climbed into them, donning gloves and masks that he pulled from a cardboard box like a magician pulling a rabbit from a top hat.

Coupland shared a look with Alex, deciding to keep his mouth shut. It never paid to wind up folk that could impede an investigation if they chose to.

'If you could stay close to me, that would be helpful,' Grayling added, turning his back on them as he stepped through the splintered and buckled door. Even through their masks the smell was pungent. The interior was still damp from the firefighters' hoses. The flooring in the reception and residents' communal area was sodden underfoot. The walls were black and the high backed chairs dotted about the room were caked in soot. The damage in the dining room was less severe, nothing, on the face of it, a lick of paint and a bit of spit and polish couldn't fix. The same couldn't be said as they approached the stairs.

The bannisters leading to the first floor were charred. The stair carpet burned through to the boards. 'You're fine,' the officer told them, 'it may not look it but the upstairs is structurally sound.'

Despite this, Alex, trod gingerly in his footsteps. When they reached the landing Grayling pointed to several patches of missing carpet. 'We've taken them up to check for accelerant, given the worst hit areas were the bedrooms along this wing.'

Coupland stuck his head into one of the bedrooms; a lone CSI was crouched lifting more of the flooring.

'We're taking samples from all the bedrooms, that way we'll know if one person in particular was targeted.' He turned to look at Coupland. 'That's assuming there's accelerant to find.'

'What do you mean?'

'People are cagey when incidents like this happen. Start covering up anything that might get them into trouble. All of the staff I spoke to who smoke confirm they only ever had a cigarette in the allocated area, but experience tells me when it's cold or raining people huddle by the back door, where in this instance the medical equipment, including flammable gases, are stored.'

'Rule breakers, eh,' Alex said, shooting a glance in Coupland's direction.

'Trust me, this fire is no accident,' Coupland said, ignoring her.

'I'm not saying it is, but it could be down to negligence,' Grayling reiterated.

Coupland watched the CSI place a small patch of carpet into a plastic evidence bag. The mattress on the bed had burned through to the frame, a charred carcass that had once been a wardrobe stood beside the door. A melted television, slick with foam. To Coupland's eye the level of damage in each room seemed the same. 'I don't get it,' he said aloud. 'How come some residents died and others survived?'

'I believe the ones that survived were the night owls, or those in no hurry to turn in at least. Apart from the care assistant our victims were all obediently tucked up in their beds.'

'Sometimes it doesn't pay to be compliant,' Coupland stated, returning the look Alex had sent him earlier. He'd seen enough. There was nothing they'd learn from this exercise that he wouldn't glean from reading the report later. A look from Alex told him she felt the same. They made for the stairs.

Coupland paused to point at the ceiling. 'How come these places get away with not having smoke alarms?'

The officer shrugged. 'Your guess is as good as mine. If it were my business it'd be the first thing I'd do.' If it was down to Coupland he'd reinforce all the doors and windows and cover the place in CCTV. It depended on which angle you were looking from, he supposed. Which level of expertise. Or paranoia.

*

Alan Harkins was waiting for them outside the block that housed the staff quarters. He looked different, a lot more casual than on their previous encounters. 'You'll have to excuse what I'm wearing but I've ended up borrowing a friend's clothes. Though I don't see why I can't move back in since there's nothing wrong with the staff quarters.'

Coupland regarded the too tight sweatshirt and dark jeans. Reckoned this friend was a lot younger than Harkins. More able to carry them off. 'The fire service will be done by the end of the day…' he said, trying to convey a sympathy he didn't feel.

Happy at least with that response Harkins rewarded Coupland with a smile as he showed them through to his office, a pokey room made to look even pokier by its untidiness. 'I often eat in here,' he told them apologetically, eyeing polystyrene takeaway containers and screwed up chip wrappers beside a wicker bin. A TV perched on a filing cabinet, a laptop and mobile phone sat on top of the desk. 'Have you any news on who might have started the fire? Only I've spoken to your colleagues so many times I feel like I'm starting to repeat myself. '

'Funny you should say that,' Coupland drawled. 'Only I'm not aware of you alerting us to the fact that Catherine Fry was the sister of a notorious crime boss. Any reason my colleagues had to find that out by chance?'

Harkins paled. 'I didn't see the relevance—'

Coupland puffed out his cheeks. '—Now I know you're telling me porkies. One of the most feared men in Salford entrusts his sister into your care, a care home that is later burnt to the ground, and you don't think it's worth mentioning?'

'When you say it like that…' Harkins muttered.

'Like what? Like we know you're on a retainer and I'm wondering what other services you provide?'

'It isn't a retainer! Mr Tunny pays fees like everyone else.'

'That isn't quite true, is it? Or do most folk siphon money through dummy companies? Thought not,' Coupland added when Harkins didn't respond. 'How long had Catherine been a resident?'

'A year. Her mother was finding it hard to manage on her own.'

Ma Tunny was as tough as old boots but Coupland guessed caring for a fully grown adult needing support required a different strength.

Harkins read his thoughts. 'It's never an easy decision to make, you know. Deciding someone else can provide better, more consistent care for your loved one than you. Trying to second guess the future is hard. Loving someone and caring for them twenty-four-seven are two different things. We try to make the relatives feel as at ease with their decision as they can be.' Harkins paused. 'Besides, I didn't feel I could turn him down. He can be very persuasive.'

Coupland didn't doubt it. 'Which is why you've been passing on copies of the information we've been asking for onto him.'

'What do you mean?'

Coupland shook his head as he looked up at the ceiling. 'Am I speaking in forked tongue or something?'

Harkins drew back as though trying to widen the gap between them.

'Some of Tunny's boy soldiers were here the night of the fire, the same time as the fire crew, I saw them again at the hospital when I came to speak to you, I know he's been in touch.'

Harkins dropped his gaze. 'He wanted a list of patients'

names and contact details. Staff too.'

'And you gave it to him?'

Harkins stared at the floor.

'I mean, you didn't quote data protection or tell him your memory sticks had melted?'

'I was in shock, I wasn't thinking!'

'You thought about saving your backside more like.' Coupland huffed out a sigh. 'He's had men running round the city waving machetes in people's faces. I could do you for aiding and abetting…'

'I'm sorry!' Harkins stuttered. 'Please, don't ruin my livelihood.'

'Then you need to get your priorities right. I want all the data you gave to Tunny emailed to me now.'

'I can put it on a memory stick for you,' Harkins offered.

'Nah, I like audit trails. I don't want some tosspot lawyer further down the line saying I obtained the data illegally.'

'I wouldn't do that!'

Coupland's mouth formed a grim line. 'Folk act out of character when their bums start to squeak. I think you've already proved that.'

Harkins looked down at his bandaged hands, as though reminding Coupland he was a victim too.

'Have you any idea of the havoc you've caused? The number of folk scared witless on the back of your loose lips?'

Harkins hung his head, the fight drained out of him.

Coupland decided to back track a little. 'Tell me what you remember about the fire.'

'It's all a bit hazy, to tell you the truth. When the alarm went off the staircase was already full of smoke, everywhere you looked on the landing there were flames…I ran to Catherine's room first as it's nearest the stairs. I managed to bring her out but it was too late.'

'When did Tunny call you regarding the fire?'

Harkins didn't need to think about it. 'Not long after the first fire engine arrived. Someone had seen it and told him. He wanted to know that Catherine was safe. I-I couldn't tell him she was dead. Instead I told him not everyone had been evacuated. He went berserk, said we had to find her.' Sighing, he ran his hands through his hair.

Alex regarded him. 'What's happened is tragic for all concerned, but you mustn't give out any more information to anyone that could be relevant to our investigation.'

'How do I know what's relevant?'

'It's our job to work that out. In the meantime I suggest you say nothing, direct relatives and anyone else for that matter to the incident number on the card you were given.'

'Does this include Mr Tunny?'

Coupland's fingers gave an involuntary twitch. 'Especially Mr bloody Tunny.'

'Does he know that?'

'I've spoken to him; he's agreed to cooperate with us fully.' Harkins didn't need to know that wasn't exactly the gist of things, but it'd keep him onside for the time being. 'Any of your other residents have infamous connections?' Coupland asked.

'Absolutely not.'

'Good, if you want my advice you'll keep it that way.'

Alex moved to the doorway and looked out onto the reception area and a set of stairs leading to the floor above. 'Was this extension put on under your ownership,

Mr Harkins?' A nod. 'Can we have a plan of the buildings? I'm guessing you'll have one to hand.'

'Gave a copy to the fire officers when they first arrived,' Harkins told them, moving to the filing cabinet and pulling out a folder. He lifted the flap and pulled out a sheet of paper which he unfolded before handing it to Alex.

Alex spread the drawing out onto Harkins' desk. Cedar Falls was two storeys high but part of the roof space had also been converted into accommodation. 'The top floor, is this for patients too?'

Harkins' nod was slow.

'What's it used for?'

A pause. 'It's a locked ward. We keep our more... challenging patients on that floor.'

Alex raised her eyebrows at Coupland, moved to the side of the desk so he could get a better look. 'It's like something out of Jane Eyre,' she said, 'and didn't that end with a fire?'

Coupland stared at her askance.

'You know...the novel?' she prompted.

'You're looking at me like I know what the hell you're talking about. I was strictly a Beano boy.' He turned to Harkins. 'Was anyone in this locked ward when the fire broke out?' A pause. 'Spit it out man!'

'Johnny Metcalfe.'

Coupland cocked a brow in Alex's direction, 'The young fella I liberated from the cells yesterday.' He addressed his next comment to Harkins. 'So, let me get this right, your head counts don't add up, your fire prevention procedures are abysmal and your security borders on the non-existent. Apart from that you run a tight ship.'

'Easy tiger.' Alex muttered.

'Never mind easy tiger, you any idea how much these places charge? I'm not seeing value for money here.'

Alex stared at him.

'I'm just saying.'

He turned back to Harkins. 'Out of interest, what had Johnny done that required him to be locked up out of the way like that?'

'He can be difficult.'

'If that's the only criterion then make me up a bed.'

Harkins looked as though he'd like nothing better than to lock Coupland in a padded cell, after administering something nasty with a big fat syringe. 'He can upset the other patients when he's a mind to. The other staff as well. Sometimes it's easier to keep him apart from the others.'

'Seems a bit extreme.'

'This isn't the right place for him anymore. Too many people are placed in facilities like ours and many stay for too long.'

'You think that's the case with Johnny?'

'Yes, I do.'

'Look. I'm not the one in the wrong here.' Harkins had gone back to being defensive, his hand hovered in front of his fly as though he needed to go for a pee. 'I've co-operated every step of the way.'

'Not every step,' Alex reminded him. 'I'm still waiting on next of kin details for Barbara Howe.'

Harkins looked sheepish. 'I don't have any. Or emergency contact details either.' Adding, when he saw a look of irritation flash across Coupland's face, 'I asked her for them several times when she first came here but after a while gave up. She was a good worker, never took a day off sick, hardly ever took time due, so it didn't seem important.'

'Doesn't it worry you that every decision you make seems to be the wrong one?'

Harkins said nothing.

Alex tried a different tack. 'Barbara was in the residential block on the night of the fire, yet I understand her shift had ended. Any idea why she'd still be there?'

'Barbara was like that, she'd often stay on. She was always the first to start work and the last to leave.'

'And she lived in the staff quarters?'

'Yes. In this block.'

Coupland caught Alex's eye: on this they were agreed, 'We'll take a look at her room.'

Barbara Howe's room resembled that of a Premier Inn or Travel Lodge. Enough space to swing a cat but not much more. A bed, a set of drawers, a wardrobe on which several photographs had been Blu-tacked. A couple of pot plants sat on a small table beside an uncomfy looking sofa.

'There's a staff kitchen downstairs,' the manager informed them when Coupland's gaze fell upon a kettle plugged in beside the TV, an unused Pot Noodle beside it.

Hands shoved into his pockets, Coupland moved to the window. Not much of a view, unless you got a thrill watching NHS vans pull up outside the loading bay. 'So what can you tell me about her?'

Harkins had been hovering in the doorway. He blushed, his hand moving to his crotch once more. 'I tend not to get too involved with the staff,' he admitted, 'Jobs like these – with live-in accommodation – tend to attract people who are starting again, maybe after a relationship breakdown or a downturn in their finances. It pays not to delve too deep. I'm their boss, not their agony aunt, after all.'

'Surely you want to know they are safe to be let loose on your patients?'

'All the appropriate criminal checks are done; I don't take on anyone who isn't squeaky clean.'

Coupland didn't need to take Harkins' word for this. Turnbull and Robinson had checked out all the staff and nothing untoward had been flagged up.

Alex moved around the room taking photographs on her phone and making notes. They'd removed their CSI suits before walking over to meet Harkins but both had kept their shoe protectors on and stuffed their nitrile gloves into their pockets. Coupland retrieved his and slipped them on. He opened the drawers beside the single bed. Underwear. Paracetamol. A half-eaten Twix.

'Anything in the chest of drawers behind you?' he asked.

Gloved up, Alex was already sifting through the top drawer. She frowned in his direction. 'There's no handbag anywhere, yet I can't see a purse or any personal items like make up or a hairbrush.'

'She may have left them in her locker over in the residential block, saves them having to return to their rooms if they need something while they are working.'

'I'll make a note to check whether the lockers have been damaged,' Alex said, scribbling into her notebook.

Coupland sauntered over to check what else she'd written: 'Electoral roll' and 'DVLA.' 'Did she drive?' Coupland asked.

The manager shrugged.

'Doesn't mean she's never had a car,' Alex reminded him.

'I know.'

'I spoke to Barbara's previous employer – you never followed up her references, did you? She says she's never had that happen before.'

Harkins' hand moved to his crotch once more, a nervous reaction or he had trouble with his waterworks; Coupland couldn't be sure. 'I-I kept meaning to get round to it, but she seemed a decent sort, and once she'd started, her work was a high standard…'

'Yeah, you said.' Coupland's voice was monotone. He eyeballed Alex who was already ahead of him. She turned her pad to show a love heart underlined several times. If Harkins had the hots for this Barbara it would explain his lack of diligence during her recruitment.

'Come to think of it, how come the contents of this room haven't been bagged and tagged?' Coupland asked.

Alex whipped her phone from her bag. 'I'll check with Turnbull.'

'Never mind the reason why, tell him to get his backside over here sharpish.'

Alex nodded, searching for Turnbull on her contacts list before hitting 'dial'. There would be time enough for recriminations but right now this room needed to be treated like a crime scene.

'I need to ask you to step outside,' Coupland told Harkins. 'There's an officer coming to remove the contents of this room.'

Harkins didn't seem bothered. Most people who kept up to date with their favourite crime shows expected it these days. 'I'll be downstairs if you need me,' he said, stepping out onto the landing.

'Hey, not so fast, is this her?' Coupland called out, his finger pointing to a photo of a woman Barbara's age on the wardrobe door. Harkins paused, his gaze following the trajectory of Coupland's finger before nodding.

'We can get a copy of that for the incident board,' Alex said, waiting until she heard Harkins' tread on the stairs. 'He's a lazy so and so with a thing for the hired help. Perhaps you weren't that far off the mark when you said it could be a case of unrequited love.'

Coupland said nothing.

Alex moved towards him, placing a hand on his arm. 'We should leave, too, let Turnbull get on with it.' Still, Coupland didn't move. It was as though he couldn't hear her. He hadn't budged an inch, just stood stock still, staring at the other photographs Blu-Tacked around the one he'd been pointing to. In one a fat kid scowled at the camera. The kid was even fatter in the photograph beside it, a solemn face with join the dot pimples starting to show. Coupland stared at another photo, a younger one of Barbara sat with a group of friends raising a glass to the camera, then back to the kid again.

He pulled out his cigarette pack, looked at it for a minute before putting it away. He shifted his gaze to a photograph of a gap toothed boy grinning up at the camera. The boy looked about six years old, wore corduroy trousers and a jumper with a hole in. Yet it wasn't the boy that held Coupland's attention. It was the Scalextric set beside him, the red car with a broken front light on top of it. Something inside him quickened. 'Help me find more photos of her,' he barked, blood draining from his face. 'Older ones would be better.' He opened drawers hurriedly and searched through the contents.

'What is it?' Alex asked, doing as he'd requested even though she wasn't sure why.

'The fat kid in the photo is me,' he muttered. 'Which unless I'm mistaken means that Barbara Howe is my mother.'

CHAPTER NINE

Alex stopped what she was doing and stared at Coupland for several seconds while she worked out what to say. She was trying to remember if he'd ever spoken of his mother. There was no reason why he should, she supposed, he was so full of Lynn and Amy, though for all she knew they spent every Sunday with her, a roast dinner followed by him doing DIY jobs around the house. Alex wasn't close to her own mother, but still, the shock if anything happened to her. 'Are you sure?' she managed at last, though the look he gave her told her she needn't have bothered.

'Of course I'm not bloody sure!' he spluttered, causing Alex's brows to knit together in confusion. 'She left when I was a kid,' he explained, 'Dropped me at school one morning and never came back.'

'Oh God, Kevin I'm so sorry!' Whether she meant for his mother buggering off or being dead, he wasn't sure.

'It's OK,' he said anyway, his head already working overtime.

'She changed her name then?'

Coupland shrugged, 'Howe could be her maiden name I suppose. Could have remarried for all I know. We need to go through the contents of this room with a fine tooth comb, see if there are more photos, letters even.'

Alex was already shaking her head. 'Kevin you can't work on this case if you're related to a victim.'

'Yeah, but I don't know that yet, do I? But I need to find out, Alex, and I need to find out now.'

*

Coupland was on his third cigarette by the time Turnbull arrived. He watched from the cordon as Alex went over to brief him before he followed her indoors. Her facial expression was neutral, her body language controlled, even though the news about his mother seemed to have shaken her as much as it had him. She'd agreed to keeping quiet about the potential link until he had the chance to show the photos they'd found to his sisters. There'd been no other photographs of him, nor any of the girls for that matter, but they'd come across one of Barbara as a young woman, long haired, slim, with a spark in her eye he didn't remember. He'd taken a picture of it with his phone, along with a couple of the other photos. 'I remember these being taken,' he'd told Alex, his finger jabbing the wardrobe door, 'and I spent hours playing with that car set, drove my folks bloody mad.' Mad enough for his father to smash the red car against the wall when he was late to the table for dinner, but he kept that memory to himself.

'And your mother, though, Kevin?' Alex had persisted. 'Does she look how you remember?'

Coupland closed his eyes. She looked like the woman who'd waved him off to school that morning, but still...

Coupland used to hope that she'd left for a reason. A purpose that justified abandoning a surly kid with a bully. When he got older he wondered if another man had been involved, and if so, whether more children had appeared further down the line, half brothers or sisters that made him redundant, something else to forget about, along with the tosser she'd been married to. His early years in the force brought him into contact with domestic violence and he'd realised for the first time that was the environment he'd grown up in. The treasured quiet nights when his dad was on shift, when his mother would come into his room and read to him, or let him stay up with her to watch her favourite soap. When his father came home Coupland would slope off to his room, develop strategies to keep out of his way like a religious fanatic warding off evil. Yet even that effort couldn't prevent the inevitable. The temperature in the flat dropped the moment his father's key could be heard in the lock. The raised voices, one angry, one trying to placate. The sound of furniture being upended. A thud, followed by silence. On those nights there'd be no story. His mother would walk past his bedroom, pausing briefly behind the door to listen out for him, as though it was possible for him to sleep through the racket they made. He played along though, stayed silent in his bed, tears forming damp patches on his pillow. He understood now the need to escape, the urge to survive. The last thing she probably wanted was another man. Had she planned it? Or had she woken that morning and decided today was the day? His memory of their last morning was etched on his brain. The ruffle of his hair when she came into his room to wake him, the extra-long hug she gave him at the school gates. She'd called after him, he remembered later, but he'd been in a hurry to get a game of football in with the older lads that he hadn't bothered turning round. Would she have stayed if he had? Would she have taken him with her? He'd forgiven her, hoped long ago that her new life had been worth the pain she'd caused. And now, to discover she'd been living a short bus ride away, a humdrum existence working for folk that didn't know what day of the week it was. He'd always though he'd meet her someday, have the chance to ask if she was happy. He'd been prepared to lie if she'd asked him the same thing.

Alex had insisted that he kept his distance while Turnbull did his work, so as not to muddy waters. Coupland had nodded; keen to be amenable if it kept her silence. When she didn't accompany Turnbull as he emerged from the building half an hour later he saw an opportunity too good to miss. Stubbing out his cigarette on the tarmac of the car park, he headed towards the DC as he loaded evidence bags into the boot of his patrol car. 'Let's have a look at the inventory,' he said, taking the clipboard from him and scanning down the list of items removed from Barbara's flat. The items catalogued were hardly substantial. Letters. Bills. Clothing, underwear, toiletries. Not much to show for a life. Jewellery: a thin gold chain, a stainless steel watch with a leather strap and a wedding ring. So, had she married again? Surely she hadn't kept the one that had shackled her to his old man. He handed the inventory back to Turnbull, his gaze falling on an evidence bag crammed with letters. 'Let me take a look,' he said, automatically reaching for them when a voice behind him stopped him in his tracks.

'Let's do that back at the station, eh, Kevin?' Alex asked, her eyes narrowing when he turned to face her. Coupland sighed, his gaze settling on the evidence bag she was carrying. 'Her locker hadn't been damaged,' she told him, 'there's a shoulder bag containing make up and a purse, a couple of bank cards.'

He wondered if she paid her bills on time. Or did she leave things until the last minute like he would if he didn't have Lynn to keep him right?

'Shall we get back then?' Alex asked. 'Harry Benson's office has been on; the colleague he's been waiting for arrived early so they're keen to start.'

Coupland knew that Alex was speaking to him but her words sounded muffled, as though he was listening to her from the bottom of the ship canal.

'Kevin, they're ready to go ahead with the post mortems.' She glanced at Turnbull as he added the new evidence bag to his inventory, unaware of the tension around him. 'You still want to attend?'

'Why wouldn't I?' Coupland's mouth felt dry, making him trip over his words. He could feel Turnbull lift his head to study him, oblivious to the grenade that had been hurled into his life.

'You OK Sarge?' he asked.

'I'm fine,' Coupland growled.

Though in truth he was anything but.

*

'I'm only really here as an extra pair of eyes, a subtle steer at most,' Kate Faraday said as she nodded at the detectives. Medium height with a gaunt face on a skinny frame, she reminded Coupland of the teaching skeleton in Harry Benson's science lab, only with hair, which she had tied back in a ponytail. Professor of Anatomy and Forensic Anthropology based at the University of Exeter, she had shared a flat with Benson during their student days. That alone should have sent her screaming into the light, Coupland thought, but then most people were different away from the day job and maybe Benson made a bit more effort when he wasn't wearing his surgical scrubs.

'Ah, I see you have met,' the brusque pathologist stated as he entered the theatre, tilting his head up to the gallery where Coupland and Alex stood to observe the proceedings. He spoke into the microphone above cutting table 1. 'We're lucky Kate's schedule permitted her to be here.' Benson's mouth turned up at the edges, 'She's a leading force in her field.'

'Charmed, I'm sure,' Coupland said, trying to match Benson's smile but failing.

'I'm here to help Harry reunite each victim with their name,' Professor Faraday explained, 'which shouldn't be too burdensome given we have the same number of unaccounted for patients as we have bodies, though one can never take anything for granted.'

'Patients and *staff*,' Coupland corrected.

'Sorry?'

'One of the victims was a member of staff at the home, not a patient.' His mouth felt dry as he spoke.

'Duly noted, DS Coupland,' Benson acknowledged, muttering something out of earshot once he'd turned away from the microphone. Coupland felt Alex's gaze slide in his direction, settle on him for a moment before returning to the theatre below.

During the introductions a technician with tattoos up each arm wheeled in three trolleys and lined them up against a wall. Despite being sealed in stay fresh bags there was no mistaking the smell of incinerated meat. Each body had been labelled 1 through to 3 with enough space left on the label to write their name once it had been confirmed. The technician wheeled in two more bodies, placing them a short distance from the others. Instead of numerical labels the name of both victims had been written on in ink: Catherine Fry and Ellie Soden.

'I'll carry out the examination of our two named victims as the end of this session; I don't want to keep Professor Faraday longer than absolutely necessary.'

Coupland nudged Alex and rolled his eyes but kept any smart comments to himself. It was safer that way, especially with the complaint hanging over his head. Instead he busied himself picking dirt from under his nails. He watched as the three burned bodies were placed onto cutting tables. Twisted limbs that had fused into blackened torsos. Hideous masks where their faces used to be. He swallowed.

Benson pointed toward the first body. 'My role this afternoon will be to distinguish between the normal effects of fire on a body and evidence that may have a more sinister explanation. As you can see, heat causes the muscles of the body to seize up, the resulting loss of water shortens the limbs and the torso bursts, creating tears.' His hand moved to the solid mass as the centre of the table. If Coupland stared hard enough he could see slits on the surface, like the cuts made into pork skin to give it a crackling effect. Benson continued: 'I need to confirm these are not wounds inflicted prior to death.' His hand hovered over the upper and lower parts of the blackened lump. 'The flesh here, and here, has been burned clean away, leaving bones that have been made brittle by exposure to heat. In the case of badly charred victims, it is often impossible to tell their sex. To establish this with some confidence we will be studying each fragment of bone to be certain of the location in the skeleton they came from.'

Professor Faraday began to nod and stepped towards the mic. 'When fire damages a body to this extent, teeth, DNA and fingerprints are incinerated. Normally the pathologist would rely on dental records that could be sent to local practices to help identify who is who but that's not possible in this case. I will be examining areas of the skeleton that show the largest discrepancies between the sexes. The shape of the greater sciatic nerve in the pelvis, the prominence of the nuchal muscle markings at the back of the neck, the size of the mastoid process behind the ear and the presence of supra-orbital ridging under the eyebrows all hold important clues. Of course any information you can give me would be helpful, whether the women had gone through childbirth, any operations…'

Benson singled out Coupland when he spoke next: 'I'm hoping you lot have pulled your finger out and have something to tell us, or why else would you be here? Not like there's much of a floor show in these cases.' The contents of Coupland's stomach rose as his gaze fell onto the three charred masses.

'We know Roland Masters suffered from Alzheimer's,' Alex offered when Coupland remained silent. 'But there's nothing in his medical history that refers to any operations. Sarah Kelsey had three children. She was only at Cedar Falls for respite care, her medical records are still with her GP but I could give them a call.'

Benson smiled his thanks. 'And the third unidentified victim?'

'Barbara Howe,' Alex informed him.

'She was 65,' Coupland added.

Benson laughed. 'That's the sum total of your detection skills, detective sergeant?'

Coupland turned to see Alex studying him. *Well…?'* she whispered.

He drew spit up into his dry mouth and swallowed. 'Medical details are sketchy…but three children also.'

Satisfied that no other information was forthcoming Benson circled the body on the first cutting table, leaning in to consult with Professor Faraday before selecting a scalpel from a row of instruments on a trolley beside him.

Coupland got to his feet. 'I'll get in touch with Sarah Kelsey's GP,' he said to Alex. 'Not like we both need to be here.'

Alex nodded.

Benson looked up in time to see Coupland make his way towards the gallery's exit. 'Something more pressing you need to attend to?' A mean smile twisted his mouth out of shape.

Coupland slowed his breathing as he turned to answer, trying to keep his stomach contents where they should be. 'Isn't there always,' he grunted, trying hard but failing not to notice the fragment of bone that had come away in Benson's hand.

CHAPTER TEN

Coupland trudged the path to Donna Chisholm's front door, a well-kept terraced house on Eccles Old Road. Her house was walking distance from Buile Hill Park and there was a primary school nearby if he remembered it right. He guessed Donna's job at the supermarket had kept her ticking over financially, paid the bills with a bit left over for smokes or prosecco or a night at the bingo. Bringing up three motherless kids was a whole new ballgame.

Standing opposite her in the small kitchen while she scrolled through her phone for the number of her daughter's medical practice Coupland revised his initial impression of her. On closer inspection there was more grey in her hair than he had first noticed; the makeup she wore failed to disguise the lines around her mouth and the dark circles beneath her eyes. A face changed by tears and guilt.

She found the number she wanted and wrote it down on a scrap of paper. 'I don't know how to use this thing properly,' she said, handing the number to him. 'Sarah kept offering to show me how to work it but I wasn't interested.'

'Paper's fine,' Coupland reassured her.

'The only operation she had was to put pins in her leg after she came off her skateboard when she was a teenager. The GP will tell you more. She was such a tomboy…'

Coupland pocketed the slip of paper, nodding when she pointed to the kettle which had just boiled.

'I'm up to bloody here with everyone's sorrow.' She flattened a hand, held it over the top of her head to emphasise the point. 'The tone of voice they use to say how sorry they are, the way they tilt their head and wring their hands. Makes me want to puke.' Coupland knew what she meant. Folk had been much the same while Lynn had been ill. The number of times he'd had to remind them she wasn't dead yet.

Donna dropped teabags into two cups, adding boiling water into them both and a splash of milk from a carton she sniffed before pouring. She handed Coupland the larger of the two cups, 'I'm out of sugar,' she said.

Coupland reached into his jacket pocket for his sweeteners, clicked the dispenser a couple of times before lifting the cup to his lips.

'I just don't get it,' she said. 'She was only there because I kept telling her to go to the docs. She wasn't coping. Her GP persuaded her she needed to take some time out to get well. Better to go in willingly than have it forced upon her. Hinting, you know, that other measures may need to be taken if she refused. Fat bloody good it's done.'

'Had you been to visit her while she was staying there?'

'With three kids in tow I don't think so! Besides, the docs said it was better she had a complete rest, give her a chance to recharge her batteries….' The lines around Donna's eyes deepened. 'It was only supposed to be for a couple of weeks.'

Coupland nodded, 'I just wondered if she'd made friends with any of the other patients, if she'd mentioned someone in particular.'

Donna was already shaking her head. 'She told me she intended to keep herself to herself. She didn't see much point in bothering with any of the nutters, as she called them. She was deluded like that, couldn't accept there was anything wrong with her own state of mind so there was no way she was going to mix with anyone whose symptoms might be a bit too close to home.'

'And the staff? How did she get on with them?'

Donna shrugged. 'She never said anything, so I'm guessing that's a good thing, right?' Donna studied Coupland. 'When they first go in they're not allowed to ring home for a while, you know that don't you?'

Coupland didn't but nodded anyway.

'It's so they can get acclimatised, I suppose. New surroundings, new routine. It's just that… it meant when she was allowed to phone home she wanted to hear about the kids, wanted me to put Natalie on the phone to her so they could talk. She wasn't interested in telling me about her day.'

Coupland's tea was cool enough for him to take several gulps. He placed his empty cup on the draining board, nodding his thanks. 'What would you want them to do?' he asked. 'The head tilters and hand wringing brigade. What would you rather they did?'

Donna didn't need to think about it. 'Offer to do things for the kids, the odd lift here and there. Practical things. Maybe then they wouldn't be going into care.' Her face hardened then, mouth twisting with the helplessness of it. It took Coupland a second or two to process what she'd said. 'They've been made wards of court,' Donna explained when she saw his confusion. 'I'm not fit enough apparently, to have them in my care.'

A rock formed in Coupland's stomach. Cold and hard. 'I thought it was temporary foster care, while you got sorted?' For the second time that afternoon his mouth ran dry.

Donna gave him a strange look. 'And how do I get sorted? This is my life, how I've lived since Sarah left home. The irony is I've now lost my job. I had to take time off work to wait for the social worker, only the store manager didn't like that one little bit. Apparently I've had too much time off in recent weeks. So here I am rattling around, I could be with them all the time now but it's too bloody late. Anyway, there's a case review next month. Complete strangers will decide on my grandkids' future.' She turned away then, whether to spare him her tears or shield him from her expression he couldn't be sure. 'Thing is, I'm too old to take them on. Who in their right mind would go back to nappies at my age? Probably better I let them go. Easier, you know, in the long run.' Her eyes glistened, making her eyeliner smudge. He could tell she didn't mean it, that it was bravado to mask the pain. He pictured Tonto being driven away in the middle of the night. The image made his throat constrict. 'Probably,' he agreed, not knowing what else to say.

*

The call to Sarah Kelsey's medical centre confirmed she'd fractured her leg in adolescence. Her GP emailed Coupland an x-ray of the repair, highlighting the location of the titanium pins used. Coupland let out a breath as he forwarded the email to Alex. At least he was off the hook having to supply information about Barbara Howe without giving away the fact that she was his mother. He might have swerved that bullet for the time being, though he was under no illusion another would aiming towards him any time soon.

*

Coupland had done a fourteen-hour day by the time he pulled up outside his front door. He couldn't recall the journey. Had no recollection of his nightly commute which normally involved hammering his fist on the car's horn or swearing at tailgaters. Maybe the God of traffic lights had been on his side for once, greenlighting him all the way. His head felt numb, the kind of numbness amputees felt after losing a limb.

An arson attack on this scale was a major inquiry; the gangland connection meant he had to tread with care. Suspects were being hunted down and beaten. And his mother? Where did she fit into all this? He'd spent the day sifting through information, examining evidence, prioritising actions. At least now DCI Mallender was back he didn't have to waste his time briefing Superintendent Curtis. He wasn't paid enough to couch his words, to gloss over specifics in favour of helicopter views. But how could he deal with this? With any of it?

His sisters needed telling that their mother had been found. He wondered if found was even the right word. It wasn't as if they'd been looking for her. Not once the realisation had sunk in that she'd gone of her own accord. That she wanted a future that didn't have them in it. He'd thought knowing she was dead would hurt more. Was it possible to miss what you'd never had?

Coupland looked at the clock on his dashboard radio

and sighed. He was knackered. Didn't have the energy for a barrage of questions he'd be unable to answer. Tomorrow was a rest day. He'd tell his sisters then. Give him a chance to get his head around it.

The clouds moved, covering a half-hearted moon, plunging the street into darkness. He'd have to inform DCI Mallender, too. But the boss would assign the case to someone else and that someone would learn things about his mother that they might not pass on. Foibles, character flaws, likes and dislikes. He'd be robbed of her all over again. And if he didn't tell the boss? Another disciplinary when the truth came out. A pinging noise signalled an incoming email. He reached for his phone, tapped onto the email icon. The fire officer had sent through his report. His message was to the point: "*Although there were no signs of forced entry, thin lines of severe burning were found along the corridor and landing, indicating a trail of accelerant had been laid down. The culprit used lighter fuel, and concentrated their effort on the bedrooms I have indicated in the attached plan. As I feared, any significant forensic evidence regarding the culprit was destroyed in the fire. The team lifted a couple of prints but that's your lot I'm afraid. Your man or woman seemed to know what they were doing.*" Coupland didn't bother opening the attachment, he forwarded it to Krispy to print out and run through the database first thing.

By the time Coupland put his key in the lock the house was cloaked in darkness. They kept baby hours now, sleeping when Tonto slept, that, or the TV would be on low, flickering images that no one paid attention to as they listened out for his lordship to awaken. Lynn was in bed, eyelids heavy; a faint smile told him all was good. He threw his clothes over the chair in the corner, picked up a t-shirt and jersey shorts before heading for the shower. The water felt cold, despite him turning the dial up to scalding. It was the shock, he supposed, that made him shiver. He let the droplets run over him, turning his skin red. Some detective he'd turned out to be. His mother had been living and working right under his nose yet he'd had no idea. No gut instinct alerting him to her presence, or any tingling to warn him she was in danger, that harm had befallen someone he'd loved. Now she lay in the city mortuary, a pile of ash and bone. He closed his eyes. Of all the ways he'd imagined their reunion, seeing her on a pathologist's table hadn't been one of them. He opened them again. Shook his head from side to side. Life had a funny way of taking the piss. Of putting up speed bumps in the road ahead. He should be thankful. He knew that much. He had a wife that loved him most of the time, a daughter not addicted to crack and a grandson that was growing on him daily. So why did it feel like there was a stone in his stomach? A bloody heavy one at that.

He sighed, turning the dial to 'off' before stepping out of the shower to dry himself. He threw on his night clothes before turning to stare in the mirror above the sink, running his hands over the day's stubble. The face staring back at him was older than the one he pictured in his mind's eye when he thought about how he looked to others. He looked worn. In his head he was 25, hard muscle and attitude. The attitude was there still and some of the muscle, but there were lines around his eyes that nothing would erase.

He stepped out onto the landing. Paused. Took a peep inside Tonto's nursery. The baby was asleep in his cot, blanket kicked away, arms and legs akimbo as though he'd spent the evening on jagerbombs before calling it a night. 'Time enough for all that,' Coupland muttered, as he stepped into the room, switching the baby monitor to silent before leaning in close. Babies did have a smell, Lynn was right about that, a smell that was clean and pure, that suggested the future was a bright one. He homed in over the baby's face, inhaling as far as his lungs would allow, taking in the scent of him. If the boy was aware of Coupland's presence he didn't show it. His chest rose and fell to its own rhythm. Had his own mother done this, Coupland wondered, slipped into his childhood bedroom to watch him sleep? She'd have been too tired, he reasoned, three kids to look after and an old man that didn't do a hand's turn. By the time he came along she'd have been worn down, maybe already fantasising about a new life, Reggie Perrin style. 'Come on Tonto,' Coupland whispered, 'help me out here.' He tickled the baby's tummy, making him wriggle, kept on tickling until two sleepy eyes stared up at him. For a split second it looked as though he was going to cry. 'I'm not the Bogey Man,' Coupland said quickly, though in truth folk had called him a lot worse. He pulled a face then; the kind people do when there's a baby about and no one else is looking, making his eyes go wide and sticking his tongue out. Tonto's lip stopped trembling and he made a gurgling sound that resembled a laugh. 'That's more like it,' Coupland acknowledged, scooping the boy up into his arms. Tonto fitted into Coupland's shoulder like he'd been measured for it, and as he held him with one hand, the other stroking the soft down on his head, a thought occurred to him. Amy was their entire world, and now he was holding hers. He held the boy closer, shutting out the kaleidoscope of images that flashed through his mind, different ways one person could inflict harm upon another. All the bastards he'd need protecting from. A nerve in Coupland's neck pulsated. 'You know kid, in the grand scheme of things I'm nothing more than a caretaker. Keeping the world in check till you're ready to navigate it.' He thought of the pain that had leaked into his own childhood. Of the darkness that lay dormant in Tonto's soul. The thought that his grandson's blueprint for life was already mapped out scared the hell out of him. The child was loved; what he did with that love was up to him.

'I didn't hear him wake.' Lynn's voice was sleepy; she pulled her dressing gown around her, tying the belt at her waist. 'Though I did hear your bloody phone bleep.'

'Sorry,' Coupland said, cocking an eyebrow. 'I'd have been through sooner but this one started scrikin' the minute I walked past.'

Lynn glanced at the monitor. 'S'funny, thought Amy would have heard him.'

Coupland stepped in front of it. 'I turned it down once I picked him up, no point disturbing her.'

Lynn nodded. Leaning against the doorjamb she told him about her day; hospital politics, what she'd watched on TV, the broken down bus that had made her journey home a pain in the backside. Coupland joined in here and there, trying to disguise the fact he had other things on his mind.

Lynn held out her arms. 'It's OK, I'll take him, you must be shattered.'

Coupland shook his head. 'Nah, got a bit of shut eye in the canteen, I can stay with this one for a while, you go back to bed.'

'You sure?' she asked, failing to disguise the relief in her voice. Satisfied, she turned to leave, but not before pausing in the doorway. 'He seems to like that.'

Coupland frowned at her. 'What?'

'You, stroking his head like that.'

He looked down at his hand cupping the boy's skull. 'Just checking him for horns,' he shot back, ignoring the look she sent in his direction. 'I did get a smile out of him though,' he said, remembering. 'Just before I picked him up he looked at me and beamed.'

Lynn's brow creased. 'I thought you said he'd been crying.'

'He had, but one look at me and he was smiling, I promise you.'

'It's just wind, Kev,' she laughed, 'seems to be the one trait he's inherited from his grandad.'

Coupland's face dropped. 'Christ, there's a thought,' he said, looking her up and down, 'I'm sleeping with a granny.'

Lynn pursed her lips. 'Only if you're very lucky Kev,' she threw back before returning to their room.

Coupland stared down at Tonto and tutted. 'Wind! What does she know? You inherited a lot more from me than hot air. You've got my scintillating wit and good looks for a start...'

Tonto stared up at Coupland, arching his back in reply before making a fart sound so long and satisfying Coupland knew a nappy change would be essential.

TUESDAY
REST DAY

CHAPTER ELEVEN

The phone on Coupland's bedside table rang causing him to huff out a sigh. He reached out an arm to grab at it, glancing one-eyed at the screen. Alex. Aware that she'd only call him on a rest day if she had a damned good reason, he picked up the phone.

'Sorry for the early call but seeing as you didn't reply to my text last night I wanted to check you'd got my message.'

'What? Oh…' Coupland remembered Lynn grumbling that his mobile had pinged, but by the time he'd changed and settled Tonto he'd fallen into bed exhausted, not bothering to check his phone.

'I thought you'd want to hear this from me. It's about Barbara.'

Coupland slid a sideways long glance at Lynn beside him, was already easing himself out from under the covers when she stirred.

'What time is it?' she mumbled, raising her head off the pillow as she squinted at him.

'Go back to sleep, you've got another hour,' he soothed, stepping back from the bed before heading out onto the landing. He closed the bedroom door quietly, careful to tiptoe past Tonto's room before asking Alex to give him a minute while he padded downstairs.

He stepped out onto the patio while he lit himself a cigarette, moving from one foot to the other in an attempt to keep his feet warm. 'This about yesterday's PM?' he asked, wishing he'd stopped to put socks on. 'Do the IDs not match?'

'It's not that, the info relating to Sarah Kelsey's operation made Professor Faraday's job pretty straightforward, or that's how it looked, anyway. She's confident the right IDs have been assigned. It was something Benson discovered, when he was examining Barbara, that I thought you'd want to know before it comes out in the briefing.'

'Go on.'

'There was very little lung tissue left.' Alex spoke slowly, letting each word sink in. 'However, Benson was unable to find any trace of soot – as you know most fire victims actually die from smoke inhalation but there was no evidence of that with Barbara.' A pause. 'Kevin, she was dead before the fire broke out.'

Coupland leaned back against the patio door, planted both feet flat on the ground as he tried to make sense of what he was hearing. 'How?'

'There was a fracture towards the front of her skull…'

Coupland's cigarette had worn down to its filter, he sucked on it anyway.

'Look, I guess you'll be seeing your sisters today?'

Coupland's shoulders slumped. Telling his sisters wasn't something he relished but they needed to know sooner rather than later.

'Kevin?'

Startled, he looked at his phone. He'd forgotten Alex was on the other end, waiting for a reply. 'Whatever,' he said, ending the call.

*

The woman answering the doorbell widened her eyes in mock surprise. 'Oh my God, look what the cat dragged in. It must be Christmas!'

Coupland forced his mouth into a smile. 'If it was you'd be three sheets to the wind and at each other's throats by now.'

'Hah bloody hah, always the sodding comedian,' she muttered, shaking her head as she looked him up and down.

'Just telling it like it is, Sis,' he said, following her into a tired front room. Scuffed wallpaper and ceilings yellow from chain smoking, it made his place look like a palace. His eldest sister Pat lived two streets away from Coupland, had bought her terrace under the Council's right to buy scheme but she'd spent no money on the interior. She was a saver, not a spender, one of those people who put their faith in tomorrow, holding down a job she hated so she could enjoy a happy old age.

She lifted a packet of Mayfair from beside the ashtray on the coffee table, took out a cigarette and threw him the pack. Coupland took two out and lit them, handing one to a woman already seated, legs tucked beneath her, who nodded her thanks, studying him as he returned the pack to its former position on the coffee table. High days and holidays. That's all their get-togethers amounted to these days, but the rituals remained the same. Pat would have no more thought to offer him a coffee than she would have baked him a cake. It wasn't how they did things. She moved to sit beside a younger woman on the sofa, leaving Coupland to slump into an armchair he'd have to be winched out of later. He regarded his sisters as they sat side by side. You could tell they were siblings, sat in such close proximity they were carbon copies of each other, though with the same wide jaw and heft as Coupland the women had drawn the short straw, as they would never be described as petite. Pat still sported the same Lady Diana haircut cut she'd had from her teens, whereas Val kept hers long and straight, which would be flattering if she didn't frown so much.

'So come on then,' Pat ordered, 'what was so important you had to get us together like the final scene in an episode of Poirot? Are you going to accuse one of us of murder?'

Coupland took a drag on his cigarette, held it there before exhaling a lungful of smoke into the centre of the room. He shook his head in answer to her questions but still, there was something he needed to know. 'When was the last time either of you saw Mam?'

The women looked at one another. 'Seriously?' Pat asked, her voice tinged with relief. 'Why the sudden interest? Christ, you had me going for a minute. I thought it was something important.'

Coupland stared at her. 'This is important.'

Val was already shaking her head. 'It's raking over old coals, that's what it is. Besides, you already know the answer.'

'Humour me.'

His sisters exchanged glances once more but Pat did as he asked. 'I'd come round for tea the night before. Mum'd phoned me at work… I thought it was odd, we normally ate together on a Sunday but Mam said she'd got a cheap piece of beef from the butcher and we could have it that night and give the following Sunday a miss. Said it would be nice to put her feet up for once, with it being a day of rest and everything.'

'Last time we ever had Sunday dinner,' added Val.

'But it wasn't a Sunday,' Pat corrected her. 'I'd just explained.'

A tut. 'Same difference.'

'Anyway,' Pat chided, sending a look in Val's direction, 'you won't have anything to add, you were sulking in your room all evening because you'd fallen out with the lad you were seeing. You came down for your dinner then buggered back upstairs straight after.' She jerked her head in Coupland's direction. 'And soft lad here was playing with his train set.'

'Scalextric,' Coupland corrected her.

'Same difference,' she sniffed.

It was a repeat of the conversation they'd had over many years. In the early days they had gone over their mother's last day with them forensically, each time one of them blaming the other: Pat for not being there having left home six months earlier, Val for not pulling her weight at home, and Kevin for being the 'accident'. 'Don't think Mam wanted a third but Dad was desperate for a boy,' Pat would tell him. Coupland found that hard to believe, unless it was a sparring partner his old man had been looking for.

His voice was low when he spoke next. 'She never said anything, did she? That night, I mean…'

'Kevin, we've been over it a thousand times, she didn't say a word, nothing to make us guess what she had planned—' Pat clocked the look on Coupland's face before raising her hand to silence the question that was coming from Val. She'd clocked it too. 'This isn't a casual enquiry Kevin, is it? Why the urgency, why did you ask to see us both this morning, out of the blue?'

'You sure she never made contact with either of you? Afterwards, I mean.'

Val had been silent long enough, 'Christ Almighty Kevin! Don't you think we'd have told you?'

Coupland studied the cigarette in his hand, wondering if it were possible to slow time down. He didn't want to be the one to tell them. Didn't want anyone else to do it either.

'What is it?' Pat asked.

Coupland sighed as he pulled out his phone and tapped onto the copies of the photos he'd taken the previous day. The one of Barbara Howe as a young woman, then when she was older, laughing with friends. Him and his bloody Scalextric. He held out his phone to them both, swiping between the first two photos. 'Is this her?' he asked, holding his breath as he waited for their reply.

Pat creased her brow in confusion. 'Of course it's her, don't you remember?'

Coupland shrugged. 'I needed to be sure.'

Pat reached for another cigarette, lit it from the dying embers of the one she was still holding, steeling herself. 'Tell us how you got the photos, Kevin.'

'Mam's dead.'

Val let out a gasp before reaching for Pat who was already moving towards her, arms outstretched.

'I'm sorry,' Coupland said, 'I shouldn't have told you like that. I— I'm still trying to process it myself.'

'When?' Pat asked. 'How did you find out?' As the eldest, she'd always been the one to cascade family information; it felt wrong that on this occasion, for something as momentous as this, that Coupland was the one with the answers.

'She was one of the victims in the fire I was called out to at the weekend, the one at Cedar Falls.'

'I heard about that on the radio…' said Val, 'What was she doing there?' A pause. 'Was she a patient?'

Coupland shook his head. 'She worked there,' he answered.

'How long?' Pat's tone was sharp. 'How long had our mother been working down the road from us without bothering to get in touch?'

'Well, it's a bus ride really,' Val pointed out. 'Rather than down the road—'

'—Shut up will you!' Pat turned on her. 'That's not the point and you know it.'

'She might not have had the money for a bus, so it is bloody relevant.'

'For Christ's sake I could have gone and picked her up!' Coupland said. 'Or given her money, if she'd needed it.' Val's reasonableness was starting to grate on him too. 'If she'd bothered to get in touch, that is.'

'How long had she been working there, Kevin?' Pat persisted, her voice low.

'A couple of years, she'd been living in the staff quarters.'

'And before that?'

Coupland shook his head. 'Temporary jobs in other towns, all hand to mouth work really.' 'She'd changed her name,' he added, as though an afterthought, 'The home had her down as Barbara *Howe*.'

'That's her maiden name,' Pat told him.

Val dabbed at her eye with a sleeve. 'Where did you find the photos?'

'She had them pinned up in her room.' He showed

them the one with him in it. 'This was beside them.'

'No surprise there,' Pat grumbled. 'You always were the bloody favourite.'

'I thought I was the accident.'

Pat didn't reply. It was Val who spoke next, touching on the issue they'd always avoided. 'She looked out for you, never let Dad raise his hand to you, even when you were a little shite.'

So, the beatings had been about making up for lost time then. It was no secret that the old man had a temper, that their mother suffered the brunt of it. What they never discussed was the violence, as though keeping quiet about it made it less real. The girls weren't to know how things stepped up when they moved out. No point them hearing it now.

'Were there any photos of us?' asked Val. Coupland glanced at Pat before answering, 'I didn't get the chance to have a proper look. Her belongings have been taken away as evidence.' 'Evidence for what?' Coupland swallowed. 'Murder. The thing is…'

CHAPTER TWELVE

It was a judgement call. The amount of information you released in one go to the victim's loved ones. 'We did everything we could…' was a doctor's stock in trade which readied the recipient for the blow to come, whereas in his line of work there was no crutch to lean on. There was simply no way to soft soap that a loved one had been murdered. Coupland dug deep into his reservoir of platitudes to find something to mitigate his sisters' pain. *The blow to the head meant she was dead before the flames engulfed her.'* Deciding, in the circumstances, to say nothing.

That their mother had died in a fire was bad enough. That she'd been murdered… his sisters were struggling with the concept. Coupland found himself mentally running through the checklist he'd used countless times but the words stuck in his throat. Was there someone he could call? He already knew the answer to that. Pat's husband was a porter at the children's hospital, Val's latest fella would be waving goodbye to his wife and kids before turning up to the office they shared as payroll clerks for a chain of garages. He asked anyway. 'Do you want me to call Jim and Gary?'

Val looked to Pat to answer for them both. 'I think we need time to work this out for ourselves first,' she said.

Coupland nodded.

'Does Dad know?'

'Not yet.'

'I'll tell him,' Pat said, asserting her position as the eldest. Already she was striding into the hall to get her coat.

'No, I have to do it; Mum's murder is part of an ongoing investigation.'

'Christ, you don't think Dad can help you with any of that, surely?'

'No, but he may have information that would help.'

'You mean something that he kept from us?'

Coupland looked at her. 'Would that surprise you?'

'He's not devious, Kevin.'

In Coupland's experience bullies were just that. Manipulative, patient, cruel for the sake of it.

'Mum leaving like that devastated him.'

Not enough, he found himself thinking.

'I didn't think you'd be allowed to get involved, with it being our mam and everything. I mean...' her voice tailed off as his gaze fell on her.

'It's not that easy to reassign cases,' he said, 'we no longer have the resources.'

Pat hadn't yet stood down. She lingered in front of the coat rack defiantly. 'When will you go and see him?'

Coupland blew out his cheeks; decided honesty was the best policy. 'I might wait until tomorrow, not like one more day will make a difference.'

Pat thought about this. 'I suppose it gives us a chance to get our heads around it. You'll let me know when you've been, so I can go round afterwards?'

'We both can,' Val called from the hallway.

Coupland nodded. 'If that's what you want.'

Satisfied, Pat padded back to the living room where she slumped into her seat. She ran her fingers through her hair, sighed as she thought of something. 'He's going a bit deaf, Kevin, it takes him a while to answer the door.'

Coupland nodded, 'I'll wait,' he said.

'I wonder how he'll take it?' Val asked.

Coupland shrugged. 'Like we have, I would imagine, sad, but not entirely sure why. Like when someone famous dies and even if you couldn't stand them you start playing their songs or watching their interviews on TV.'

'It's hardly the same, Kevin, we all remember her.'

'Speak for yourself.'

'Did she still look like our Mam, Kevin?' Val asked. 'Despite everything?'

Coupland knew he'd have to tread carefully; a lie told in kindness could still backfire. If he reassured her too much she'd be demanding to see the body. What was left of it. Coupland blew out a breath. 'Not really.' He tried not to think of the blackened torso on the mortuary cutting table, the piece of bone in Benson's hand. 'Better not to dwell on it,' he added, trying hard to follow his own advice, but failing miserably.

*

He decided the walk would do him good. Clear his head, shake off the mugginess that had descended since he'd discovered his photograph pinned up in Barbara Howe's room. Besides, he'd run out of cigarettes; he could call into his local newsagents, assuming they hadn't barred him. His smoke rate doubled when he was with his sisters. No sooner had one of them finished a cigarette than they were lighting up another, handing their pack around like Nigella handed round canapés at Christmas. His GP, who'd long since given up on getting him to quit, had started on at him recently about exercise. Said he should get one of those gadgets that measured how far he walked. 'Aim for 10,000 steps a day,' he'd said without a trace of humour. He should join forces with Superintendent Curtis, Coupland reckoned. With all that shoe leather being expended Salford's crime solving stats would be top of the division's leader board in no time.

The wind had got up, skittering litter across the pavement. Coupland's jacket blew open, there was a chill in the air but he was oblivious, his mind working overtime. He'd have to let Alex know he'd broken the news. Despite what he'd claimed to his sisters he would be taken off the case, though with any luck his replacement would let him watch from the sidelines, might even throw him a bone if he promised not to get under their feet.

There was no queue in the newsagents this time, no gawpers giving him the evil eye. The owner's wife was behind the counter; without prompting she reached for Coupland's Silk Cut before he had to ask, teamed it with his chewing gum. She was usually a chatty woman, would start a conversation about anything if it saved her from stapling invoices into the inside covers of the pile of newspapers waiting to be delivered. Yet this morning she counted out his change in silence, her gaze shifting to the tabloid on the counter top. Angelica Heyworth's piece had made front page once more. There, in all his glory, was a photo of Coupland, cigarette in hand, glowering at the camera from the top of the station's fire escape steps. The caption beneath it went straight for the jugular. *'I head butted him,' Assault cop confesses all.*

'I-I don't believe everything I read,' the woman stated somewhat nervously, catching the scowl forming on his face. 'There's so much fake news these days it's hard to know who to trust.'

Coupland shrugged. 'Welcome to my world,' he said, stuffing the change she handed him into the plastic charity box beside the till, even though it included a handful of pound coins. She might not blame him for assaulting a human trafficking paedophile; if he baulked at supporting the local greyhound sanctuary she'd think he was a complete twat.

*

Coupland clamped his lips round his cigarette in readiness to light up as he left the shop, nodding to folk as they called in for their papers, receiving a nod in return. Fishing in his pockets for his lighter, he collided with a young man coming from the opposite direction. 'Watch it!' he said, not looking up.

He was ten feet or so away when he heard the boy shout: 'Oi!' Coupland carried on walking. 'Oi!' the lad repeated, 'Are yer deaf, piggy? I'm talking to you.'

Coupland stopped, returning the unlit cigarette to its packet in a bid to buy time. Eyes narrowing he turned in the boy's direction. It was the coat hanger smile he recognised, that and the scab on the boy's forehead that reminded him where he'd seen him last. Fresh from the custody suite where he'd headbutted seven bells out of his cell door.

'You got the all clear at the hospital then?' Coupland observed, 'No lasting damage, I hope?'

The boy widened his shoulders as though mimicking an ape, pushed his feet wide apart. 'You makin' fun o' me?' His face grew dark as he gave Coupland the beady eye. The boy was thin like a reed. His mates, watching from the precinct wall, weren't much bigger. These wannabee gangsters needed a change of career, either that or build some muscle. A smart mouth only got you so far, used unwisely it could bring attention from all the wrong people, and Coupland wasn't thinking of the police. Many of the gangs in Salford were headed up by men Coupland's age or older; there was a hierarchy within them like in any corporate firm, a pecking order to be respected. Young bucks had to be skilled at something or be well connected to be tolerated, and he doubted this kid was either.

Coupland shook his head in answer. 'Wouldn't dream of it sunshine,' he countered. 'You're doing a good job of that all by yourself.' Coupland wasn't intimidated by the boy and his cronies though he couldn't be sure they weren't carrying anything. So much of his job required judgement calls in difficult situations. A daft lad wasn't going to behave well in front of his pals when he was hungry for their approval. If the kid wanted to play cat and mouse with the constabulary today he'd chosen the wrong cop. Besides, it was a rest day, and he couldn't be bothered with the paperwork. 'Go back to your mates,' Coupland told him, turning away.

'I fucked your mum!' the boy called after him.

Coupland stopped. He recalled the times over the years when men that he'd collared – because it was usually men – told him they'd lashed out in anger when provoked, that they hadn't meant any harm but found it impossible to stop. He of all people knew what it was like to have buttons pressed, to react without thought or care for the consequences. A moment of anger that led to a lifetime of regret. When he moved towards the boy he was smiling, but even so a look of alarm flashed across the kid's face. Coupland ground his teeth together. Though keeping gob-shites in check was something he excelled at, on this occasion he couldn't be arsed. If the lad had insulted Lynn or Amy he'd be a skid mark by now but Coupland hadn't worked out his feelings yet for the woman who'd walked away over thirty years before. 'I'm gonna give you that one, kid,' he said amicably, 'on the house, like, if you get what I mean.' He was closing in, his hands deep in his pockets to show he was no threat. Last thing he wanted was the woman in the newsagents to look out and see him bearing down on a kid half his size. Even so the boy swallowed hard. He looked to his mates but they'd lost interest, either that or they didn't fancy their chances. Instead they took turns on a broken scooter one of them had pulled from a skip. 'You know you can't go round throwing insults around the place, don't you?' Coupland told him, 'Unless you're on a death wish?' The boy's shoulder's dipped before he stepped back a few paces. The gap between them restoring his confidence. He threw his head back and grinned at Coupland. 'Right up the bum!' he taunted, but Coupland was already walking away.

WEDNESDAY

CHAPTER THIRTEEN

The Evidence Management Unit was situated in the basement of Salford Precinct. Coupland used to joke it was where all the tainted goods and relics were kept but on this occasion chose to keep his Smart Alec comments to himself, didn't want to rub the duo that worked down there up the wrong way. As it was, he found it hard to act nonchalant. He felt as though his forehead had been stamped with the word LIAR across the front of it. It seemed odd that the officer serving him didn't bat an eyelid at his request, nor did he look at him sideways when his hand shook as he signed his name on the log sheet and again when he picked up the box containing his mother's worldly goods. If they thought he was quieter than usual, or his lack of banter caused them concern, they hid it well.

Despite being desperate for a closer look at his mother's belongings he'd waited until Alex had popped out for some lunch, he didn't want to face her disapproving frown. She'd listened sympathetically while he told her how he'd broken the news to his sisters, and their positive identification that the woman in the photograph he'd shown them was their mother. 'I'm sorry Kevin,' she'd said, and he'd thought for a moment she was offering condolences but the next words out of her mouth included 'Mallender', 'case' and 'reassign'.

'Christ, can I have a bit of time to get my head around

215

it?' he'd asked, promising to keep his direct involvement to the minimum. 'At least for today. I'll observe and direct, nothing more.' Alex had uttered several choice words before agreeing, reminding him that he was putting her neck on the line now, not just his, so he'd better not screw up.

Coupland shrugged her words away now as he scuttled back to his desk, eyes checking out the detectives milling about as he lifted the box's lid and began removing the contents one by one. He didn't want to tamper with the investigation, just do a little personal digging, learn about his mother. Something tangible he could show his sisters, documents that might give some clue to the life she'd been living without any of them in it.

The box was stuffed with envelopes and receipts, a couple of note pads, greetings cards, a shopping list of groceries. Coupland sighed. Tesco receipts and cinema stubs, a life policy that had long since expired. Nothing to suggest a rock and roll lifestyle, something to justify what she'd left behind. He picked up the photo that had originally caught his attention at Cedar Falls. The gap toothed fat kid holding a toy car up to the camera. She'd kept that photo. Placed it on her wall. She must have seen it every day; did she wonder how he'd turned out? Or did she only picture him as a child in her mind's eye? Did his fat face staring down at her bring happy memories or guilty ones? Was he a pleasure or a penance? Maybe it was better that he'd never know the answer.

The phone on his desk buzzed, causing him to jump. He snatched at the receiver, growling his name into it.

'There's someone here asking to speak to Turnbull or Robinson but they passed this desk about half an hour ago. It's about the investigation into the fire.'

Coupland stared at the items on his desk. Thought about the promise he'd made Alex. 'I'll be right down,' he grunted, stuffing the contents back inside the box before sliding his desk drawer shut. He'd signed the chain of evidence log, which meant the clock was ticking. He needed to hand the items back before a flare went up saying they were overdue. First he had to deal with the person in reception. Then he'd come back and look through the evidence box. He'd be fine.

A pink faced man in reception jumped to his feet as Coupland let himself into the public waiting area. 'This is Mark Flint,' said the desk sergeant; the look he sent Coupland conveyed 'this one's all yours.'

'I've been meaning to come in since I heard about the fire on the radio,' the man said, 'then I got a missed call from a DC Turnbull. He left a voicemail on my phone saying he wanted to speak to me, so here I am.'

Coupland nodded, beckoning with his hand that the man follow him into one of the small interview rooms through a door marked 'Authorised Personnel only.'

The man hesitated at the threshold.

'Anything wrong, Mr Flint?' Coupland asked.

Flint paused before shaking his head. 'Can you leave the door open though?' he asked.

Coupland narrowed his eyes, wondering if he'd read Reedsy's tale of police brutality. Coupland had been named and shamed, after all.

In his late thirties, the man was dressed in a short sleeved patterned shirt and chinos. His hand moved to his mouth while he waited for Coupland's answer.

'I could get another officer to sit in if you'd prefer?'

Coupland offered, wondering if he should have someone riding shotgun with him for his own protection.

A look of alarm flashed across Flint's face. 'No!' he said, 'I'd rather just get on with it.'

Doing as Flint asked, Coupland waited while he sat down before introducing himself. He kept his voice low, as everything about Flint's body language suggested he was on high alert, from the way he sat forward in his seat as though ready to run for the hills, to his breathing which was a series of shallow in-breaths followed by an occasional sigh. 'I take it you have information regarding our investigation,' Coupland prompted. 'Is there something you'd like to tell me?'

Flint swiped a hand across his face before taking a breath. 'Is it me or is it warm in here?' he asked.

The corner of Coupland's mouth twitched. 'These rooms have a way of making people feel uncomfortable,' he said, 'though in my line of work I'd call that a bonus.'

Flint said nothing. Back in the day Coupland would have been able to offer him a cigarette to put him at ease, smoke one himself if he thought a touch of camaraderie was required. As it was, the only hospitality he could offer now was coffee from the vending machine in the corridor and the poor sod didn't deserve that. 'Why don't you tell me what's brought you here today?' Coupland prompted, hoping Alex's lunch was a long one and she didn't come back via the EMU. Someone in the team would be assigned the task of going through the items removed from Barbara Howe's room; with Coupland's conflict of interest she may decide to perform that action herself.

'So,' Coupland said, his gaze shifting to the clock above Flint's head. 'Are you here about the fire or your experience of the home?'

Finally, his question drew a response. Flint nodded, before running his hands along the front of his chinos. They hadn't been ironed, Coupland noticed, either that or they'd been worn several times since they'd last been washed. 'I stayed at Cedar Falls once,' he began. 'It – it's not a nice place. In fact, to be quite honest, I'm glad someone set fire to it.'

Coupland's jaw clenched; he pushed the sight of his mother's twisted torso out of his mind. He kept his tone neutral. 'People were killed, patients as well as a member of staff, no one deserves that.'

'Which staff member died?' Flint asked; his breathing came easier now, as though he was past the hard part.

'I can't give out that information yet,' Coupland said. 'Until all the next of kin have been informed.'

'No matter,' Flint replied. 'The name'll come out soon enough.'

'Are you here because there's something you'd like to tell us? I can take a statement from you.'

Flint shook his head. 'Things weren't so bad for me,' he said, 'I was only there for a month, so no lasting damage.'

'What do you mean?' 'The long-term patients got the worst of it. They don't have as many visitors, so there's no one watching over them. The staff could pretty much treat them as they wanted.'

Coupland reached into his pocket and took out his pad and pen. 'Mind if I take a few notes?'

Flint continued to speak, oblivious to Coupland's request. 'I spat out my tea in the dining room on my first day. It had been laced with sugar. What is this thing about making people sweet tea? I hate the stuff. Always have.

No sooner had I wiped my mouth with the back of my hand than a male orderly pulled me out of my seat and pushed me onto the floor. He pinned my arms back and instructed one of the others to pull my trousers down and inject me with a tranquilizer. I don't remember anything after that. I woke up hours later on my bed, shivering. Someone had removed my clothes.'

'Did you report this at the time?'

Flint peered at Coupland. 'And how do you think that would have worked out? I was suffering from depression; I couldn't deal with any more stress. I kept my head down; made sure I didn't rock the boat again.'

Coupland wrote something in his pad, circling it to follow up later. 'What was the orderly's name?'

'I don't know. He never wore a badge. None of them did, it was fairly lax like that.'

'Would you like to make a statement? We may come across other patients with similar allegations. If enough people come forward we'd be able to make a case against the home, or even individual staff members.'

Flint laughed, but there was no mirth in it. 'Good luck with that. Most people won't want to be reminded of being locked away, it's a time in your life you'd rather forget.' He paused, as though something occurred to him. 'Look, there were two patients there the same time as me who had it much worse. We never spoke of it but something or someone had put the fear of God into them. You can sense it in others when you feel it yourself. They were often subdued, like me they preferred to keep their own company. '

'Can you remember their names?' Flint thought for a moment, then nodded, watching while Coupland wrote down what he said.

'I just wanted you to be aware, to have an open mind during the investigation. The fire may not have been started by someone on the outside, that's all I'm meaning. For all you know it might have been one of those poor bastards on the inside, desperate to get out.'

*

Coupland was on his way back to his desk when he collided with DC Ashcroft. 'I've just left a report on your desk, Sarge, I've been out to see UB40, Special Brew and Warren Douglas but none of them are saying anything.'

'How are they?' 'They'll live to set something ablaze another day. They might be tight lipped but there's nothing wrong with their other senses. They've got Tunny's message loud and clear.'

Coupland considered this. 'They've been reminded what happens when something rattles his cage, they'll be in no hurry to be on the receiving end when he really wants to teach someone a lesson. If they don't want to make anything of it there's nothing we can do to force their hand that won't end up with us having egg on our faces when they don't turn up to court.'

Ashcroft shrugged. 'Can't win 'em all…' he said, ready to continue on his way.

'Where you off to now?' Coupland asked.

'DS Moreton wants me to go through the evidence brought in from Barbara Howe's staff quarters, see if anything causes concern.'

Coupland swallowed. 'Look, I've just had an unexpected visit from someone who stayed at Cedar Falls a couple of years back. I want you to find out how these homes are regulated and what kind of training the staff are supposed to have. Disciplinary procedures too.'

Ashcroft nodded but still made as if to go in the direction of stairs leading to the station's basement.

'I need that information sooner rather than later,' Coupland stated.

A pause. 'I'll just get this action done then—'

'—Then I might as well do it myself.' Coupland's tone was sharp. 'I'll square it with DS Moreton,' he added. 'We need to know what we're dealing with here, we might have been looking at this the bloody wrong way round.'

This seemed to garner Ashcroft into action. 'I'll get straight onto the Care Commission,' he said. 'Find who I need to be speaking to…'

'Good man,' Coupland called after him, wondering what the hell he could say to Alex that wouldn't have her seeing through him in five seconds.

He didn't have long to find out. Alex was back at her desk when he returned to the CID room but instead of demanding why he'd assigned Ashcroft to another task she beckoned him over to her desk. 'What was the name of the fella picked up on Friday night after running away from Cedar Falls?'

'Johnny Metcalfe, why?'

'I knew it rang a bell,' she sighed.

Coupland narrowed his eyes, 'How come?'

'I thought it was worth running a check on all the patients at Cedar Falls at the time of the fire. I know the boss wanted histories on the victims but what if they'd just been unlucky, wrong time, wrong part of the building?' Alex had all the right characteristics of a great detective. She never left a stone unturned and kept meticulous notes. Like Coupland she wasn't an order taker, not because she was bolshie, but because she was thorough, doing more than was asked. Yet at this moment she looked less sure of herself. 'I thought it was worth checking the backgrounds of everyone – including the staff,' she looked away quickly, 'just to see if anything stuck out like a sore thumb.'

Coupland kicked himself for the oversight. As designated SIO he should have been all over the case. It should have been *him* asking *her* to widen the scope on background checks. Tunny's sister turning out to be one of the victims had given them a focus, but it had also made him blinkered. And now, with the discovery of his mother, he'd been guilty of a huge blind spot in terms of the investigation. Even now he wanted to ask her what she'd learned about Barbara Howe, but that wasn't what she was animated about. 'So, go on then, what did you find out about Johnny?' he asked instead.

'He was sentenced to three years detention after being convicted of arson.'

Coupland was already at the door, patting his jacket pocket for his car keys.

Alex hurried over to him, mindful not to draw undue attention from the detectives around them. 'It doesn't mean he's guilty of this, Kevin.'

'I know that. But we need to check him out.'

A pause. 'I considered not telling you.'

'Why would you do that?'

'Seriously?' She gestured his stance with her arms. 'Because of your reaction. The one you're trying so hard to hide. This young man might have killed your mother; it's understandable you want to knock seven bells out of him.'

Coupland said nothing. After all, she'd pretty much summed up how he was feeling.

'I'll go and pick him up, Kevin. We need to do this properly. By the book. Do you hear me?'

Now wasn't the time to remind her that his involvement in this case made any book she was referring to well and truly redundant. With the Complaints hearing looming what did one more misdemeanour matter? Then he remembered that foolhardiness was the luxury of the single man. That he had a wife, a daughter and now a grandson to consider. There could be no more boat rocking.

'So,' Alex's voice was uncertain, 'will you cool your heels while I bring him in?'

'Fill your boots,' said Coupland, hurling his car keys onto his desk.

*

For the next hour Coupland read through reports then typed up his notes from his interview with Mark Flint. He sent it to Turnbull, asking him to be added to the matrix Krispy had built for them, along with the two names Flint had provided. Coupland didn't reckon Flint was in the category of bearing a grudge, especially as Johnny Metcalfe was now a person of interest, but it was better to record every incident of abuse as they came across it accurately, in case further complaints came out of the woodwork later on. A thought occurred to him, something that required a call to Turnbull with a polite request. 'Leave it with me, Sarge,' Turnbull said, and Coupland knew it would be as good as done.

An email from DCI Mallender asked him for a status report on the hit and run case so he could update his decision log. Another from his union rep asking to schedule a pre-hearing meeting. Coupland made a note on his desk pad to speak to DC Andy Lewis. He'd need to tread carefully, no one liked to feel their every move was being questioned, especially if they were making headway. He pinged a reply back to Colin Ross suggesting a day the following week. Barring acts of God and the good folk of Salford behaving themselves, preparing the statement for his hearing would be his top priority.

When he looked at the wall clock a second time and found it hadn't moved he pushed his chair back, announcing to anyone who gave a toss he was going for a smoke. It was impossible to concentrate. To breathe. To think of anything other than his mother and the role Johnny Metcalfe might have played in her death. This time he avoided his usual haunt, reckoned HR would already be sending him a reprimand for flouting health and safety regulations after being outed on the fire escape steps. Instead he left the station through the main door and loitered with the other ne'er-do-wells at the smoking shelter, cooling his heels until he heard from Alex.

CHAPTER FOURTEEN

When Alex's text came he stamped out his cigarette, flicking the filter into a bin that clung onto the shelter wall for dear life. She was surprised when he stomped into the interview room. 'I was letting you know we were back as a courtesy, that's all,' she hissed, ushering him back into the corridor. 'I've got this.'

'Let me sit in.'

'No chance.'

Johnny Metcalfe looked marginally more pleased to see him. 'Come to play me some more of your tracks, DS Coupland?' he called out, smiling, 'Even though I've never heard of them.'

Coupland cocked his head in Johnny's direction. 'Does he know why he's here?'

'Of course he does! You're forgetting I'm the only one who knows your connection with the case. He's come here voluntarily to answer questions relating to his conviction, that's all. We're just waiting on his appropriate adult.'

Just then a woman with blue hair walked in their direction behind a uniformed officer. She saw Coupland and raised her hand in greeting. 'Are you sitting in too?' she asked when she drew level. 'Johnny will be glad of a friendly face.'

Coupland kept his smile in check as he turned to Alex. 'What do you reckon?'

Alex tutted, pushing the interview room door wide.

'I reckon I must be bloody well off my rocker,' she muttered, standing back to let him pass.

Once the formalities had been taken care of Alex reminded Johnny that he was free to leave at any time, that this was simply a matter of clearing something up rather than formal questioning, adding that although DS Coupland was present he was there only to observe. He might as well have been the invisible man, seemed to be the message she was conveying.

'DS Coupland stood up for me against Mr Harkins,' Johnny commented when she'd finished.

'Never mind that,' Coupland said. 'How come you failed to mention the real reason you were sent to Cedar Falls?'

He felt Alex's eyes bore into the side of his head. 'I'll take it from here, thanks.' She used the tone she normally reserved for dealing with drunken idiots, kept on staring until Coupland turned in her direction.

'My mistake,' he muttered.

Alex opened the file in front of her, traced her index finger down the centre of the first page as though searching for something in particular. 'It says here you set fire to the flat you'd been renting. Big one by the sounds of it. Caused so much damage the floor couldn't bear the firefighters' weight.'

'They were alright though,' Johnny answered. 'No one was injured…'

'More luck than judgement, I'm reckoning, but why do it in the first place?'

Johnny sat forward in his chair. His hands were splayed flat on the top of the table; he turned them over, inspecting his palms like a fortune teller looking into his future.

A frown formed on Lucy's face. 'Johnny has poor reasoning skills, DS Moreton, he may simply not have an answer for you.'

Alex waited anyway.

'I'd had a row with my girlfriend. She'd gone off in a huff and I... I just wanted to escape the way I was feeling. I felt overwhelmed with everything that was going on around me. I set fire to a pile of clothes. I thought they would smoulder for a while then peter out, that she'd come back and see how upset she'd made me. I promise you I never gave any thought to how quickly it would spread. Yes, the building was badly damaged but as I said, no one else was hurt. That was never the intention. I realise now how stupid I was, it was a reckless act that could have gone horribly wrong.'

'Is there anything you want to add?'

Johnny looked down. 'She's not my girlfriend anymore.'

Alex fished in her pocket for a pen and wrote something down as though Johnny not having a girlfriend was a salient point.

Johnny pointed to the papers in front of Alex as though she should get this down too. 'The judge wanted to send me to jail but my lawyer argued that prison wasn't the right place for me.'

'It wouldn't have been,' added Lucy. 'I've worked with Johnny long enough to know he wouldn't have coped.'

'You're here to observe that Johnny's needs have been met,' Alex said, turning her attention to the care assistant. 'Not to provide a running commentary.' Her tone was polite, but warned she was in no mood to repeat herself a second time.

Coupland gave the tiniest of nods. If he'd suspected Alex wouldn't command the same level of control in the interview room as him he needn't have worried.

'The thing is, Johnny,' Alex coaxed, 'in light of this information we need you to account for your whereabouts prior to the fire being discovered at Cedar Falls.' She was pushing her luck, and PACE guidelines, but Coupland wasn't about to call time. He sat back, decided to see where Metcalfe's answer led them.

Metcalfe was already shaking his head. 'You can't think I had anything to do with that, surely?'

'We want to be able to eliminate you from our enquiries, that's all. I'm sure that's what you want too.'

Johnny slumped back in his chair, slack-faced. 'I don't remember a great deal,' he said.

'Try,' persisted Lucy, 'It's really important.'

Alex nodded, glancing down at her notes. 'I understand from the manager, Alan Harkins, that you'd been moved from your room on the first floor to the second-floor annexe, can you remember why that was?'

'The care home manager doesn't like me. Ask DS Coupland, he'll tell you.'

'I want to hear it in your own words.'

'He said the other residents had been complaining.'

'About what?'

'I get annoyed when Ellie plays her music too loud in her room, and when Roland pushes in front of others in the dinner queue. They said I swore at them... but I wouldn't have done if they didn't keep getting on my nerves.'

'Did you get on with the other residents?'

'Most of the time.'

'And other times?'

'I admit I probably lose my rag a bit with them.'

Lucy had been silent throughout this exchange, head bowed as if in prayer. Alex picked up on her sudden reticence. 'So, we've established you had a run in with two of the victims killed in the fire, what was your relationship like with...'Alex pretended to look for the other names in her file, 'Sarah Kelsey?'

A shrug. 'I don't know her.'

Lucy started tugging at the hem of her tunic, her thumb and forefinger running over the piping edged round it.

'How about Catherine Fry?'

'She accused me of stealing.' Alex stared at him. 'What?'

'It was all a misunderstanding I'm sure,' Lucy piped up, a fray forming on her tunic.

'I won't ask you again,' Alex warned, her attention returning to Johnny. If she was aware that Coupland was starting to fidget as well she didn't show it. Johnny was opening up, but she needed to tread with caution, she'd crossed the line as it was. 'What did Catherine accuse you of taking?'

A sigh. 'Her headphones, but I already have a pair, why would I want hers?'

Alex addressed her next question to Lucy. 'I take it there's a procedure that deals with any allegation of theft?'

Lucy's smile was tight. 'We searched Johnny's room,' she said.

'And?'

'And we found them.'

'I didn't bloody put them there!' Johnny's face was twisted in anger, his hands curled into tight fists.

'Who found them?' Coupland asked, already sensing the answer.

'Barbara,' replied Lucy.

'I think we should stop here,' Alex said, gathering up her notes. Coupland coughed several times but she wouldn't play ball, instead she ushered Johnny and Lucy into the corridor. 'When we reconvene I'd like to have a solicitor present,' she told them, thanking them for their time. She paused at the reception desk to arrange for a patrol car to take them back.

'Seriously?' Coupland spat when she returned to the CID room. 'You uncover a motive then let him go?'

'He's hardly a flight risk, Kevin. We need to tread carefully, kid gloves on right to our armpits with this one.'

'Why? If he's capable of murder...'

'You know as well as I do that's got nothing to do with it. But if some lawyer turns round and says he didn't have enough rest breaks, that we didn't give him time to prepare his answers let alone caution him, then the CPS will throw it out anyway.'

Alex was right, a trial proceeded on the weight of evidence produced, not how much you wanted someone to be guilty. Still... Something didn't sit right. 'I can't see it though...there's nothing about his demeanour that makes me consider him for this,' said Coupland. 'For a start it's in a different league altogether from the offence he was convicted for. That was attention seeking, this was malicious.'

'And he still might not be involved; we're just proceeding with caution, that's all,' Alex reasoned.

'I suppose.' Had his mother really been killed over a set of headphones?

'I get the impression Johnny thinks he shouldn't be in residential care.'

On this Coupland agreed. 'He said as much to me, that he was fed up with the way people spoke to him differently, how he was treated like a second class citizen because he couldn't process things like everyone else.'

'Did he? Well I'm afraid if anything that puts him back on the hook.'

Coupland looked at her quizzically. 'How?'

'Look at the world from his point of view. People might think it's hard getting a place in one of these institutions, Kevin, but try getting out of them when you think you are well but no one agrees with you. To someone desperate enough, burning the place down in order to leave it might seem like the only option.'

*

He'd had better days, Coupland decided as he pulled out into slow moving traffic and pointed the car towards home. Ones that were right up there, as close to good as it got. These days it didn't take much to tick that box. Something decent on the TV. A can of beer. Sex. Sex while watching TV and drinking beer, now *that* was a result…

Today had been the opposite. There was normally a buzz when a case he was working on started to take shape, when suspects began digging holes for themselves and kept on digging. Instead he felt nothing. Just a numbness where elation should have been. He drummed his fingers on the steering wheel as he waited at the traffic lights. Patched a call through to control, asked for a patrol car to stay close to the primary school overnight. It was clear Alan Harkins didn't like Johnny; if he let slip to Kieran

Tunny he'd been helping police with their enquiries he wouldn't put it past the gangster to send his in-house interrogators to speed Johnny's confession up a little.

Coupland was off as soon as the lights turned to amber, the tension leaving him as his house came into sight. He parked up, scrolling through a sea of emails, his shoulders dipping when he saw two reminders from the EMU. Shit. He'd forgotten his mother's belongings were still in his desk drawer. He toyed with turning the car round and returning to the station but he didn't have the appetite, hoped an early morning grovelling session would do the trick. He climbed out of his car, bleeping it locked behind him.

He paused in the kitchen, opened the fridge to check its contents, bottles of baby milk stacked where his beer used to be. A home-made vegetarian dish covered in cling film. He closed the fridge with resignation. Lynn was in the garden deadheading heleniums. Sometimes it worried him, the energy she put into it, there was a fervour about her actions which bordered on demonic. She looked up to catch him watching her. 'What does a fella have to do around here to get a drink?' he sighed.

Lynn paused, secateurs mid-air as though considering a new target. 'Hell, sweetcheeks I don't know, maybe you should phone your 1950s wife and ask her, or failing that get your arse down to Aldi…'

Coupland felt his neck redden. 'I was just asking!'

Lynn turned back to her plants. 'Ask away, but don't be offended if you don't like the answer.'

A smile tugged at the corner of his mouth. 'I remember a time when you'd rush to the door when you heard my car pull up outside…'

'And welcome you with a gin and tonic before I ran you a bath? Dream on sunshine, I was never that girl.'

'A man can but live in hope,' he volleyed.

'That's what wives do, Kev, every day of the week.' A pause. No comeback. Banter was their thing, their way of communicating when it had been a shit storm of a day. She glanced up to check he was still there. 'Tough day?' she asked.

Coupland shrugged. 'I've had worse.'

Lynn's brows knotted as she studied him. 'Want to talk about it?' It was something they never did as a rule, preferring euphemisms and sighs to indicate the depth their day had plummeted to. Being a neo-natal nurse had many downs between the ups, and Coupland's days started with him wading knee deep in someone's sorrow. A look flitted across his face she hadn't seen before. This man of hers was as easy to read as the day was long, he went from gobby to grumpy at the flick of a switch but he always had their back, would sleep with one eye open if it kept them safe. Lynn put the secateurs down and stepped into the kitchen. 'Kev? What's going on? You were odd the other night but I put it down to work. Then you crept outside yesterday to speak to someone on the phone without giving me a running commentary on who it was. I'd be worried you were seeing another woman if it wasn't for the fact you went out this morning wearing the superman underpants Amy bought you last Christmas.'

'Maybe this other woman has a sense of humour.'

'She'd need one.'

Coupland grew serious. 'There is another woman of sorts,' he began, raising his hands in mitigation when Lynn's eyebrows shot into her hairline. 'I've found my mam.'

Lynn's eyebrows stayed in her hairline. 'Christ, Kev!' She searched his face for some indication of how he was feeling; if she was hurt he hadn't told her straight away she didn't show it. 'Is that what you got up to yesterday? Were you meeting her?'

Coupland held her gaze. 'No. I went over to our Pat's, Val was there too. I wanted to tell them in person.'

Lynn looked confused. 'You make it sound like she's dead!' She laughed, but it was laced with caution. He was a joker but she couldn't see the joke and there were shadows under his eyes that she hadn't seen since she'd been ill. Lynn's hands flew to her mouth. 'She's really dead?'

Coupland's nod was slow. 'I wanted to find out what they remembered of her. She was one of the victims of the fire at Cedar Falls.' His voice was flat. As though telling her the full time score of two teams he didn't give a toss about.

Lynn kicked off her wellingtons and hurried into the dining room, returning with a bottle of malt his team had bought him when the baby was born. She poured some into a glass, took a slug before passing it to him. He gulped at it, though his gulps were half hearted. His hand shook as he raised the glass to his mouth a second time. The whisky not tasting quite so good as the first time he'd opened it.

'Was she a patient?' Just as his sisters had, Lynn was trying to find a Pollyanna spin on things. His mother had abandoned him because she'd been institutionalised. The white van spiriting her away to save him the agony of her clinging to the lamp-post, shouting his name.

He shook his head. 'She worked there.'

Disappointment flitted across Lynn's face before she could hide it. 'Oh,' she replied, 'And how long had she been there..?'

Coupland stared into the bottom of his glass, swirling the contents round before swigging them. 'A couple of years,' he said, reading her mind. 'Long enough to make contact if she'd wanted.'

'Assuming she ever left Salford,' Lynn countered.

It wasn't like her to see the bad in folk, but he looked at her with gratitude. Sometimes it was better not to pussy foot around things. His mother had left without a backward glance. 'I've been wondering about that. Whether she gave us any thought, I mean.' Any moments of regret that saw her standing by the school gates to get a glimpse of him? Coupland chided himself. In his line of work he saw the depths people sank to, and even loving mothers could do selfish things. 'Don't get me wrong, I wasn't picturing Davina McCall rocking up to the door with a letter she'd written to us or anything like that, but, I wondered, you know, in time…'

'I know,' Lynn soothed. 'I always wondered if I'd get to meet her one day.'

Coupland looked up at her. 'I told myself she was dead. That seemed preferable in a way, more honourable. Better that than the truth.'

'But what is the truth, Kevin?'

'That's the million dollar question, isn't it? My dad walked round for ages like someone who'd been hit by a truck so I guess her leaving was as big a shock to him as it was to us. Mind you, let's not get too sentimental, he was a shit dad and I know damn well he was a shit husband too.

'After a while any mention of her became taboo. My sisters used to stand in the kitchen whispering but whenever I tried to join in they clammed up. For a while I thought she'd been abducted, it seemed the only sensible option that someone was keeping her against her will, yet no one seemed that worked up about her absence.'

'Your sisters would have been devastated; they were probably just trying to protect you.'

'Yeah, but it would have been better to let me in a bit more, I felt like I was on the outside, missing her but I had no-one to share it with... I promised myself that when I was older I'd join the police so that I could look for her properly. Only as each year passed I realised things I hadn't noticed when I was a kid. Like she'd taken her best coat and bag along with the suitcase we used for family holidays. The girls finally confessed she'd taken the money in the housekeeping jar as well. Looking back her friends never came near the house – not that she had many – so I guess they all knew she was leaving, either that or they just didn't blame her for going.' Coupland paused. 'I told the girls I'd break the news to him.'

Lynn busied herself refilling his glass, rearranging her features into a neutral smile.

'I know,' he said, reading her mind as he took the drink from her, sipping it slower this time, the bitterness matching his mood. 'I don't know which bit freaks me out more, my mam being dead or the prospect of being in the same room as my old man.'

The evening drifted away in a haze of whisky. Sleep came easily enough, overpowering him like an incoming tide, bringing burnt corpses and avenging gangsters with it.

THURSDAY

CHAPTER FIFTEEN

Coupland could sense it coming the moment he stepped into the CID room and saw DCI Mallender perching a buttock on the edge of his desk. Although coming in at this time wasn't unusual for him he normally stayed in his office, dealt with the ever burgeoning paperwork Superintendent Curtis threw in his direction. Despite this break from the Super's spreadsheets he looked far from happy. Coupland cast a guilty glance at the drawer directly below Mallender's backside and readied himself. 'I can explain…' he began, grateful that Alex wasn't in yet, meaning he could throw himself under the bus without her coming to his aid and incriminating herself in the process. Besides, she had no idea he'd been daft enough to take evidence belonging to his mother out of the EMU and then fail to return it. It was standard procedure when an item wasn't returned to escalate it up the ranks if the officer you'd been chasing failed to respond to your reminders.

'Save it Kevin,' Mallender sighed. 'It's bad enough you go about as though the rules don't apply to you but to be caught on camera while flouting said rules is taking the bloody biscuit.'

Coupland frowned. 'Come again, boss? I'm not with you…'

Mallender pulled out his phone, held up Angelica Heyworth's on-line video of Coupland smoking on the fire exit steps. 'Someone brought it to the Super's attention at a function at divisional HQ yesterday evening. To say he's apoplectic is an understatement. You know he hates being on the back foot, so he rang me at home last night to pass it on.' Mallender sighed. 'Why the hell didn't you bring this article to my attention yesterday?'

'For precisely this reason, boss, no one volunteers to have their gonads squeezed. Besides, she shouldn't have been there!'

'No, but then neither should you. It's bad enough that Curtis has asked HR to re-circulate the division handbook on smoking regulations but to top it all Joe Public can now download your confession at the push of a button. It's not going to do your credibility any good come the date of the hearing, is it?'

Coupland's shoulders dipped. 'I'm sorry, boss; I don't know what came over me…'

'And that false piety won't wash either, Kevin. I prefer it when you take the piss; at least I know where I stand.' Mallender got to his feet, nodded at the night shift stragglers on their way out and the day shift early birds on their way in. 'OK, we're done.' His voice was low, he'd come to bollock, not humiliate. 'The Super's pushing for this month's stats, maybe now's the time to pull something good out of the hat.'

'Now who's taking the piss,' Coupland scowled, but only once the DCI had stepped into the corridor and was out of earshot.

*

Coupland ran his fingers over his chin. Close call. Maybe Mallender wasn't as up to date with his emails as he liked to make out. Coupland started slightly at a noise sounding from his jacket pocket. He reached for his phone, barking his name at the caller.

'Ah, you are alive and well,' the droll voice observed, though there seemed little relief in their observation. It was one of the laugh a minute duo from the basement. Coupland went on the defensive; glancing round to check no one was listening he spoke quietly into his phone. 'Yesterday was a bastard, mate, any chance I can keep the evidence a while longer?'

'That's why I was calling, there's another bag here, it wasn't logged properly when it came in which is why it hadn't been put into the box we gave you. I reckoned you'd want to take a look at it while you were wading through the other stuff. Didn't want you going off the deep end if you found out about it later. You can sign an extension request while you're here.'

Coupland was already nodding. 'I'm on my way,' he said, checking the time on his watch. The canteen would just be opening; he decided to call in before heading downstairs, reckoned as long as cholesterol levels weren't taken into account bacon rolls all round would be just what the doctor ordered.

Morning briefing

For some strange reason Superintendent Curtis had insisted on sitting in on the briefing. Whether he wanted an update from the horse's mouth or wanted to make sure Coupland didn't chain-smoke his way through it with his head stuck out of the CID room window he couldn't be sure but he sat beside Mallender, lips pursed, for the duration. As it was, Coupland's gaze kept returning to his own desk drawer where he'd stashed the additional evidence bag following his return visit to the EMU.

'Now the news has had a chance to sink in that Kieran Tunny's sister was one of the victims, what's the general feeling been, from anyone you've spoken to so far?' He looked around the room as he asked this.

Robinson was the first to speak. 'In the main, shock. Wondering how anyone could do something like that.'

'Any comments about Tunny?'

'Folk knew he had a sister, Sarge, and they were sorry she was dead. But not one of them said they knew anything about the fire.' No surprises there.

'Tunny's involvement has swayed the way the investigation's been run, but I had a visit yesterday from a Mark Flint, responding to one of Turnbull's calls to previous patients. Mark was there less than a month a couple of years back, and yesterday made serious allegations about the treatment he'd received. He gave me the names of two patients who were there the same time as him. Said their stories were much worse, though he wouldn't elaborate. Krispy, I want you to trace them ASAP.'

'I'm on it, Sarge.'

Ashcroft had been making notes while Coupland spoke; he now raised his hand: 'What this fella Mark Flint claims ties in with the stuff I've dug up following my call to the Care Quality Commission. At first the switchboard kept referring me to the website for information. All their inspection reports are uploaded onto the site for the public to see but what I wanted was more of a behind the scenes tour. Anyway I got a contact name from Turnbull's missus, someone she used to speak to from her time in social services.' Turnbull beamed, acknowledging the name check with the nod of his head. 'Shola's contact was very helpful. Sent me the unabridged version of the latest report which had flagged up some serious issues. Cedar Falls has been placed under special measures. The reasons listed include poor risk management, over-use of medication and lack of supervision – seems staff are often left working on their own which means that if they have to deal with a patient in difficulty they'd need to leave others with no one to keep an eye on them. There've been several near misses over the last couple of years – people falling, bumping into furniture, avoidable injuries – and a shedload of complaints. Basically the home's in breach of that many regulations if it doesn't adhere to the action plan it's been given it'll be shut down.'

Coupland paused to take this in. 'This action plan, how's it supposed to be monitored?' Ashcroft referred to his notes. 'The plan was put in place two months ago, the follow up review is scheduled for a month's time.'

'Christ Almighty,' Coupland muttered. 'It beggars belief. Unsafe practices, piss poor management, yet patients are still able to be referred there.' He pictured Sarah Kelsey's three motherless children, their fate awaiting them pending a case review.

Ashcroft nodded. 'I've spoken to two members of staff who'd left the previous year, asking them about the training they'd received. One of them mentioned a course he'd attended showing him how to restrain patients using physical force. Seems the course also showed them how to justify any force used in the paperwork they were required to complete.' He lifted his note pad so he could read from the statement he'd taken. '"If we kneed someone in the balls we were told put down on the form that the patient was big and that we thought they were going to strangle us".'

'At least I know now why you weren't able to complete the action I gave you,' Alex muttered, sending a look of disapproval in Ashcroft's direction.

Ashcroft kept his head down, made a point of shuffling the papers on his lap. If he was waiting for Coupland to come to his rescue he'd have a long wait, Alex would smell a rat a mile off. 'Good work,' Coupland mumbled by way of an apology, catching Ashcroft's eye when he looked up.

'This bloody care home gets better and better,' A DC on the front row stated, followed by several grunts of agreement. 'Any one of us could have had a family member there.'

Coupland avoided Alex's eye; instead he wrote the names Mark Flint had given him onto the incident board. Helen Foley and Colin Grantham. He turned to Krispy. 'When you've tracked this pair down I want you and Ashcroft to go and pay them a visit, it's about time we got you out of those training pants and Ashcroft will keep you right. Just remember these are vulnerable people who've possibly been detained against their will. They won't thank you for asking them to drag up the past. Tact, diplomacy, and a great deal of sensitivity is required, which is why I'm giving this task a body swerve,' he added before Curtis, or Mallender for that matter, had a chance to.

The Super nodded his approval as he got to his feet. 'There's certainly a motive here for the fire being started by a disgruntled patient, and given Johnny Metcalfe's history he's looking like our man.'

'He's certainly a contender, Sir,' DCI Mallender concurred.

'We're bringing him back in today,' Alex added.

'Has he an alibi?' Mallender turned to Alex for an answer.

'No Sir, other than he was having a melt-down.'

'He needs to do better than that.'

Coupland felt detached, he shared none of the excitement displayed by his team as Mallender doled out actions relating to Metcalfe in order for them to establish the opportunity he'd had to start the fire. There was no doubt this lead lifted everyone's mood but a pin prick of doubt tickled at the base of Coupland's neck. 'I want us to bring Harkins in before we question Metcalfe again,' he said, causing Curtis to scowl. 'In light of what DC Ashcroft has reported his management goes way beyond that of someone incompetent. Besides, Mark Flint made an allegation of abuse. Even if this was carried out by other parties, Harkins is ultimately responsible. We're duty bound to follow that up… you wouldn't want someone coming at us further down the line asking why we ignored it, would you, Sir?'

Curtis bared his teeth, his head swivelling in Mallender's direction as if to say dealing with Coupland was his responsibility.

Coupland felt the DCI's gaze sweep over him. 'Look, if nothing else, questioning Harkins might help us build a case against Metcalfe, but he should be our focus for the time being.'

DCI Mallender considered Coupland's words before nodding. 'Agreed,' he said, turning to Alex who was trying her best to hide her disappointment. 'We put Metcalfe on the back burner for the time being.' His next words were to appease Superintendent Curtis: 'This may well end up a separate line of enquiry, Sir, but I think DS Coupland has a point,' he said diplomatically. 'The statements DC Ashcroft and DC Timmins take from the ex-patients identified by Mark Flint will determine our direction of travel.' Mallender reverted to management jargon when he spoke to Superintendent Curtis in the same way inner city kids reverted to patois when speaking to their peers. The sanitised words brought the Super comfort, helped distance him from what was really going on. 'It may even be low hanging fruit, Sir, as far as this month's stats are concerned,' he added.

The Super's grimace relaxed, he turned to Coupland with the nearest thing to a smile he could muster. 'Very well,' he said, 'keep me updated with any developments, and get your skates on regarding that progress report on the hit and run,' he added as he headed for the door. Shoe leather. Skates. Coupland began to wonder if Superintendent Curtis didn't have some sort of foot fetish.

DCI Mallender had been about to follow The Super then changed his mind, making his way towards Coupland instead. 'I've ten minutes or so spare if you want to run through the statement you've prepared for Professional Standards.'

Coupland blew air from his cheeks. 'I'd have to write it first, boss... besides, I'm running late,' he said catching Turnbull's eye and nodding.

Mallender spread his arms wide. 'It won't go away, you know. No good burying your head in the sand.'

Coupland held his hands up as he backed away. 'Wouldn't dream of it boss, honestly, I'll email something over to you as soon as I can but right now there's somewhere I need to be.'

'You're the one with his backside in a sling,' Mallender sighed as Coupland gathered up his car keys and phone.

Coupland didn't respond. He asked Krispy to make a call to Alan Harkins as he passed his desk on the way out, thinking that if the DCI found out about his personal connection to Barbara Howe before he had time to own up, his trussed up backside would be the least of his concerns.

*

Considering she'd been sacked from her job as community social worker following a case review of her conduct during a missing person's inquiry, Shola Dube was remarkably chipper when she'd answered Coupland's call, and more than agreeable when he'd suggested they went for a coffee. 'He just wants to pick your brains,' was what Turnbull had said to her the previous evening over dinner when he'd sounded her out about passing her number to the DS, assuming Coupland was looking for advice ahead of his pending Professional Standards hearing.

'I suppose I can tell him what not to do,' Shola had smiled. 'After all, fat lot of good any of the preparation for my hearing did me.' She'd been worried that he'd want to discuss Judy Grant's trial which was scheduled to start the following day. She'd been the duty social worker who had supported one of the young migrants following her sister's murder. It had been the first time she and Coupland had worked together and both were required to give evidence, but even so, meeting him the day before the trial started made her uncomfortable.

Shola was already blowing the steam from the chai latte in front of her when Coupland strode into the café on Barton Road. There was something different about her since they'd last met. The corn rows previously gathered in a bun at the base of her head were worn loose now, framing almond shaped eyes set into dark chocolate skin. She wore a baggy jumper over skinny jeans, though her trademark scarf remained around her neck. Coupland had heard about her scars. Turnbull had told him once, in confidence, that she'd been attacked by the father of a child on her casebook, slashing her neck so deep 'It's a wonder he didn't take her bloody head off.'

Shola raised a hand in greeting as Coupland approached their table, full painted lips smiling at him despite the fact it was Alex Moreton's report that had cost Shola her job. 'No point in holding grudges,' she'd said to Turnbull after her sacking, 'Everything in your colleague's report was true.'

That was the problem with reviews carried out after the fact; Coupland had reiterated at the time, they didn't capture the urgency of any given situation. The fear, the limited choices, the primal instinct to protect. Easy enough to spot mistakes with the benefit of hindsight. He'd never said as much to Alex but if he'd been asked to conduct the case review a lot less information would have made it into that final draft. With Alex there were few grey areas. People's actions were divided into right or wrong. Correct procedures were followed or not. There were no alternatives, and certainly no middle ground. She hadn't wanted Shola to lose her job, but the writing was on the wall as far as the social worker was concerned the moment Alex had hit the 'submit' button and sent her report to Superintendent Curtis. Heads must roll. How Salford gained from the loss of someone with Shola's level of experience Coupland would never know.

'I've ordered you a regular coffee,' Shola told him. 'I have it on good authority you don't hold with all the fancy-pants concoctions folk like me drink.'

Coupland nodded, pulling out the chair opposite her and taking a seat. Shola had been seeing Turnbull for a few months now; so far losing her job hadn't impacted their relationship, though Coupland supposed they were still in the honeymoon phase. He'd heard she was looking for work in the private sector, though the cause of her departure from social services would limit what she could aim for. Coupland waited while a boy about Amy's age brought his coffee over, nodded thank you before pulling sweeteners from his pocket and clicking the dispense button twice. 'So, how's it going?' He felt it was only polite to enquire, though Turnbull gave everyone who would listen a running commentary.

Shola gave him a wry smile. 'Being unemployed has its perks. I no longer listen to voicemails with a sense of dread, and there are no more clients to visit wondering what I'll find behind every locked door. My sleep's better too, though I suppose that could be the company I'm keeping.' She laughed then, making Coupland suppress a shudder, there were some images that should never be conjured up, and his docile DC in the bedroom was one of them.

'I was trying to work out what was different about you,' he said, his frown turning into a hesitant smile. 'And I've worked it out. You don't look harassed anymore.'

Shola picked up her cup, took a sip to gauge the

temperature before taking several larger mouthfuls. 'Blissful ignorance can be a wonderful thing,' she replied, 'because let's face it, the bad stuff is still happening out there. I'm just not involved anymore.'

They drank in silence. Coupland would have preferred an extra shot of espresso but it wasn't worth calling the lad over, dragging him away from the mobile phone he kept tapping onto every time his boss's back was turned.

'How about you?' Shola asked, when it seemed Coupland had nothing more to say on the matter. It occurred to her he might want to talk about the other time they had met, when the issue to be tackled had been much closer to home. 'How is that grandson of yours getting on?' Shola had met with Coupland's daughter before the baby had been born following a referral from a concerned midwife after Amy had confided in her.

'He's champion,' Coupland said. 'Social services have closed his case file so I guess that means I'm not the threat they thought I was going to be.'

'You were never a cause for concern, not really,' Shola said. 'It must have been stressful for you all…'

'We're getting there,' Coupland said, smiling in spite of himself.

'In that case I'm not entirely sure why you wanted to meet with me… did you want to talk about the complaint that's been made against you, though I am not sure my experience will be of any use, especially given the outcome.' Shola was of African origin but Coupland couldn't detect much of an accent to pinpoint where exactly. Her pronunciation was far better than his; reminding him of old film reels where everyone used the Queen's English, back in the day when regional accents were frowned upon.

He looked at her in surprise. 'What? Christ no! Nothing I can say or do will change that outcome, no point in dwelling on it.'

Shola frowned. 'So how can I help?'

'There's a case we're working on, the fire up at Cedar Falls – I know you put DC Ashcroft in the right direction in terms of who to speak to at the Care Commission – turns out the whole place is a dog's breakfast.'

'I remember hearing rumours,' Shola said.

'Such as?'

'Patients being left unattended, over-use of "As and When" medication to keep patients sedated so they don't require assistance, staff handovers not documented… need I go on?' Coupland got the picture. 'You have to bear in mind those rumours were unsubstantiated. The colleagues I overheard talking about the home reported their concerns to the appropriate channels but you and I both know how slow these wheels turn. Nothing more could be done until due diligence had been completed.'

Coupland thought about this. 'Someone came forward yesterday who claims he was mistreated there.'

If Shola had already been appraised of this via Turnbull she knew better than to let on. 'Poor management enables malpractice, but cannot be used as an excuse,' she said.

'It's for that reason we're starting up another line of enquiry – possible abuse – subject to what the officers I've got looking into it uncover.'

Shola regarded him. 'Let's hope it's not another Winterbourne.' Adding, when Coupland frowned, 'Winterbourne View was a private hospital in Gloucester. There was a BBC documentary on it back in 2011, exposing abuse suffered by several patients.'

Coupland recalled the news reports at the time. The arrests made as the scandal broke and the public inquiry that followed. The political posturing as MPs got their teeth into something new.

'The Government promised a dramatic reduction in the number of vulnerable patients sent to this type of institution, but statements like this should never be made without resources to back them up.'

'Tell me something I don't know.' Coupland looked deep in thought.

'Penny for them?'

'It beats me how it can get to this point – does it mean all the staff were as bad as each other?'

Shola was already shaking her head. 'You know as well as I do there'll be people holding that place together, maybe staying rather than jumping ship was the one thing they could do for the people in their care.'

What she said made sense. Though for some it would always be too late. 'One of the victims of the fire was a single mother with three children. Her mother's been looking after the kids but has been struggling to cope so they've been taken into foster care. She's got to apply to the court to show she's capable of looking after them if she wants them back.' He described his encounter with Donna Chisholm. His first impression. The decision by social services to remove the children.

'Sometimes, putting a child into foster care is the right option,' Shola replied. 'It really depends on their physical and emotional welfare.'

'She made a few wrong choices when she first stepped into the breach but she really cares for these kids.'

Shola smiled. 'In all my years on the job and the awful things I have seen I've only once come across a situation where a child wasn't loved, but love alone isn't enough.'

Having worked a murder-suicide case a few years back Coupland understood this only too well.

'We have to dissect the family's life,' Shola continued, automatically switching into professional mode, the use of 'we' a habit she was unlikely to give up, Coupland supposed. 'Which means working out whether the child's needs are being met across a range of requirements.'

'Like what?'

'Are their basic needs being met? Do they have beds? Are they being fed? Are their needs being put ahead of their parents or in this case their carer?' They sat in silence for a moment, Coupland's attention distracted by a group of yummy mummies huddled in a corner booth while their offspring slept in designer buggies a few feet away. He only recognised the pram brands because he and Lynn'd had to fork out on a modest one for Tonto. The women were looking at photographs on each others' iPhones, discussing paint samples for their kitchen extensions, recommending ski chalets in France. First World problems. Money didn't buy happiness, Coupland knew that, but lack of it – or the desire for more – was certainly at the root of a lot of the problems he had to deal with. He took another swig of his coffee, returning his attention to Shola. 'Removing a child from their parent or loved one is never easy,' she continued. 'I once had to peel a four year old child from his mother's hands and trust me that's something that never leaves you. Yet worse than that is when the judge doesn't grant removal, and you go home wondering what the hell is happening to that child every night.'

'So you're saying these kids may be better off in care.'

Shola widened her eyes, 'Not at all! Just that these situations are never prescriptive, that without knowing the circumstances it's hard to make a judgement call. Sometimes it's just a case of the right support being provided.'

Coupland glanced at the well-heeled mothers once more. 'She's broke. I think a lot of the bad decisions she's made are because she's hard up.'

Shola's mouth turned down at the edges. 'It's rarely that simple, and economics alone would not be a reason to remove a child. But I acknowledge it may play a part in the problem and ultimately the possible solution. Either way where the care giver can be supported they will be.'

Coupland placed his empty mug onto the table, wiped his mouth with the back of his hand. 'Failing that she should buy a lottery ticket?'

Shola laughed good-naturedly, but Coupland could see she wouldn't be drawn further. She hadn't offered to put a word in for Donna but then why should she? Coupland reasoned. She'd never met her. Had learned the hard way the consequences of getting it wrong. Besides, despite her use of the term 'we' she was no longer a part of the social work team.

It was as though she could read his mind. 'You're damned if you do, damned if you don't. But then it's no surprise really. Only five per cent of the population ever come into contact with social services, the job we do is mostly hidden from sight so it's no wonder we're misunderstood.'

Coupland knew *that* feeling. Their jobs were both vital, yet unpalatable in so many ways. 'So, what's the worst thing you've had to deal with, then?' he asked, interest piqued. 'Apart from being nearly decapitated, obviously.'

Shola's hand flew to her throat as though checking the scarf was still in place. Satisfied, she placed both hands on the table top.

'I dealt with a young boy in the aftermath of a trauma.' Her voice was low, measured. 'People say kids are resilient but it depends on what it is they have to deal with. His problems took a while to develop, and I'm talking a long time after the incident took place, but there was no doubt in my mind. Mood swings, anger, problems at school although nothing that stood out enough when I tried to get him referred for an assessment. In my view he needed counselling, psychotherapy even, but it wasn't deemed a priority.'

'What happened to him?'

Shola smiled, but it was the kind of smile a gambler might give before he threw in his chips. 'Sometimes this job makes you paranoid. Just because you see an oncoming train it doesn't mean it's going to hit you. What this boy suffered defined him, that's all. Limited his choices. It shaped him in a way that he didn't deserve. I wanted to do more for him but wasn't able to. The could-have-beens, I think, are the worst cases. It's frustrating, you know, when you see wasted potential.'

Coupland wondered how Amy's trauma would define her. She'd refused the counselling she'd been offered following Lee Dawson's attempt to kill them both, had thrown herself into motherhood with a fervour that amazed him considering the dizzy teenager she'd been. Where would this fissure show itself? Would she take Tonto to school one day and not go back for him? He stifled a shudder.

He thanked Shola for her time, reminding her that he'd see her in court. His smile told her it mattered just as much to him that the justice process was respected. As they walked out of the café Shola apologised for not being as helpful as he might have hoped. 'Not at all,' Coupland answered, for something she'd said to him, something he couldn't quite put his finger on but could feel all the same, was already taking shape in his head.

*

Alan Harkins smiled as he walked into reception, made an observation on the weather followed by a prediction on who he reckoned would be lifting the Champions League trophy at the end of the season. He received a curt nod in return, Coupland indicated with his arm that he follow him into one of the interview rooms on the other side of the door marked 'Authorised Personnel'; beneath his other arm was a copy of Mark Flint's statement which he placed on the table.

Harkins paused when he stepped into the crammed room, took one look at the table and four chairs in its centre before turning to Coupland in surprise. 'Seems a bit formal for the couple of things you said you wanted to go over,' he said, trying to keep his tone light.

'I'm looking for a killer, not trying to sell you a timeshare,' Coupland replied, his tone as jovial as an undertaker's.

Harkins kept his smile in place as he lowered himself onto a moulded plastic chair. 'I understand. Please, I want to help in any way I can.'

'Glad to hear it,' Coupland said, plonking himself

down on the chair opposite. Just then the interview room door opened and Alex strode in, though not before sending a glare in his direction.

'It's either me or the boss,' she cut in when Coupland looked as though he was about to object. 'And that might take some explaining.'

Coupland considered her words before pulling out the chair beside him. 'The more the merrier,' he shrugged.

He reiterated to Harkins that he was here voluntarily, and that they appreciated him helping them with their enquiries. He began by asking innocuous questions, things he already knew the answer to. Five minutes in and Harkins leaned back in his chair looking pleased with himself. Coupland decided it was time to crank up the gear a little. 'Seems odd, Alan – Oh, is it OK if I call you Alan?' He made the name sound foetid, but then that's how he was beginning to see the care home manager. A lazy turd. A big one at that.

Harkins nodded. 'Go ahead.'

'Thanks. Seems odd then, given everything you've told us, Alan, that Cedar Falls is failing so miserably.'

Harkins' face fell in on itself. 'I can assure you patient care is at the forefront of everything we do.'

'Going by recent events you might want to rethink that answer. Why didn't you tell us the home has been put into special measures?'

Harkins frowned. 'It's a temporary setback. We're taking remedial action. Yes, there's been sloppiness… I can give you a copy of our revised staff handbook—'

'—Do I look like someone who spends his time reading?' Coupland cut in. 'Give me the abridged version and make it snappy.'

Harkins' face took on a pinched look. 'We've taken the Care Commission's report very seriously—'

'—I don't want the Disney version.' Coupland pulled his phone from his jacket and tapped on his screen. Seconds later he'd found what he was looking for, held up Cedar Falls' Twitter page for Harkins to see. 'Says here,' he turned the phone back round to face him so he could scroll through the tweets, 'residents enjoying music before their tea.' Attached was a photo of a man playing an accordion. In another the tweet said 'a walk around the garden before lunch'; the attached photo showed the same man pointing to a clump of begonias that had seen better days. 'You get my drift?'

Harkins nodded.

'So, edited highlights please...'

A sigh. 'There have been occasions where complaints brought to my attention could have been handled more efficiently.'

'That's better,' Coupland replied. 'It's not that difficult when you try...' Coupland lowered his gaze to Mark Flint's statement then back to Harkins. 'So, let's say you get a complaint about a member of staff who's been a bit heavy handed...what do you do?'

'I would speak to the staff member involved.'

'And?' prompted Coupland. 'What happens then? He says they imagined it and you close the complaint?'

Harkins reddened. 'It's not as cut and dried as you make it sound. Some of our patients can play up; can be violent towards the staff or indeed other patients. Sometimes force may be necessary.'

Coupland considered this. 'I daresay, but if you weren't there how do you know the pressure used was in proportion to the situation?'

Harkins hung his head. 'I don't, but I do trust my staff.'

'Must be hard though, given the numbers that come and go.'

Harkins wafted Coupland's comment away. 'People move around a lot in this industry, it's not unusual.'

Coupland pushed aside thoughts of his mother. 'So in a situation where it's a patient's word against a staff member you'd err on the staff member's side every time?'

Harkins shook his head. 'No. I would instigate an investigation into the allegation, so I could consider all the facts.'

Coupland's mouth turned down at the corners as he nodded along. 'Makes sense,' he agreed. 'And who would carry out this investigation?'

'Well, usually me... but if I felt it needed someone distanced from the situation I would ask a manager from another home to get involved.'

'On a tit-for-tat basis I presume?'

Harkins made a sound like he was deflating. 'If you must insist on using simple terms...'

'Oh I do,' Coupland agreed. 'I find that way nothing is lost in translation.'

Beside him, Alex scribbled into her notepad. She'd underlined something several times and tilted the pad towards him so he could get a better look: 'Was anyone forced to leave???'

Coupland glanced at her and nodded. 'So, assuming for whatever reason the complaint isn't upheld, what happens to the complainant then, do they have to leave?'

'Absolutely not! Although if they feel the situation hasn't been resolved they may prefer to move somewhere else.'

'Are there occasions where you might facilitate that? Where quite frankly them remaining there gets right up your nose?'

'No!'

Coupland waited.

'Obviously there are some folk you're glad to see the back of...' Harkins conceded. 'Just like any job I guess.'

'Not mine,' Coupland informed him. 'In fact the more I start doubting someone the more time I want to spend with them.' He smiled as he said this, causing Harkins to sink down into his seat. 'Johnny Metcalfe reckons you don't like him.'

A tut. 'He's mistaken. I don't like how he makes some of the other residents feel but there's nothing personal about it. Look, is there anything else you want to know or can I go now?'

Coupland rubbed at the base of his back that was starting to ache. He glanced down at his own notes but the questions were already formed in his head. 'I want you to tell me where you were when the fire broke out.'

'I've told your colleagues this already – I was in the office doing paperwork. The alarm sounded in the main building and I rushed over to see what I could do.'

'Where did you go first?'

'Flames had already taken hold on the first floor but I went upstairs anyway. I found Catherine Fry in her room but she was unconscious. I tried to lift her but she was too heavy, so I dragged her downstairs and out to the assembly point at the front of the building. Lucy was looking after some of the patients she'd evacuated and I asked her to stay with Catherine until the emergency services arrived. By then the fire had spread along the landing and there was no way I could go back up for anyone else. I concentrated my efforts removing patients in the communal area on the ground floor.'

Coupland regarded the off-white bandage on Harkins' left hand. 'Can you remember where you were when you sustained your burns?'

'To be honest no, it's all a blur.'

'So you can't be certain whether it was going upstairs when you first heard the alarm or coming downstairs with Catherine?'

'That's what I just said!' Another sigh.

Alex made a point of looking at her watch but Coupland had already decided to wrap it up.

'We'll be in touch if there's anything else,' he said, getting to his feet.

Alex waited until Coupland had despatched Harkins back to reception before summing up the interview as they made their way back to the CID room. 'He's completely inept but he's no arsonist, Kevin. I reckon he's that useless if he did try setting anything alight it would most likely be himself.'

'He did suffer burns though.'

'True, but the type of injuries that arsonists sustain tend to be on their legs where they've spilled accelerant on themselves while splashing it around.'

'He's shifty.'

'No more than anyone else. Look, shall I go ahead with bringing Johnny Metcalfe in? Till we get a proper alibi we can't rule him out.'

Coupland pulled a face. 'Let's see what Ashcroft and Krispy dredge up first, there may still be other contenders.'

'What is it with Metcalfe? Apart from your spider senses telling you he couldn't have done it.'

Coupland smiled but the truth was Alex wasn't far off the mark. Thinking the worst of people was his default setting, and he took no pleasure in being proved right. But finding out someone who'd passed through his filter was guilty was like a sucker punch, made him question his judgement on every level. Still, on this occasion he was certain he was right.

Alex let out a sigh. 'Fine, have it your way. I'll leave Metcalfe alone but this is a postponement, nothing more. Pending Ashcroft and Krispy's report, OK?'

They stopped at the vending machine while Coupland fished in his pocket for the appropriate change. Alex declined his offer of three fifty pences. 'I'm bringing in my own drinks, now, green tea in the morning and kale smoothies during the afternoon.'

Coupland's eyebrows knotted together. 'Why?'

'It's called looking after yourself, Kevin, you should try it sometime.'

Coupland inserted his money and selected an espresso. 'Baby keeping you awake?'

'Hardly. I'm never there when the little bugger's up. He's usually spark out by the time I get home. Not sure he even knows who I am.'

'Then take time to let him get to know you. He's been bonding with Amy from the moment he was born and I bet Lynn was by his incubator every break she got while he was in hospital. Then the poor mite comes home to find you glaring down at him. In fact, come to think of it, it's probably better he is asleep when you're around, you can be abrasive at times.'

264

'Good, it's a skill that's taken me years to fine tune. Would hate to think I was losing my touch. He needs to take me as he finds me.'

'If you say so.' Alex moved to one side to let a DC pass by.

It was Andy Lewis, the detective handling the hit and run case. He caught Coupland's eye and nodded.

'Have you got a minute?' Coupland asked him. 'Only the Super's breathing down my neck for an update.'

Another nod. 'A witness has finally come forward, I'm on my way to interview them – you can ride shotgun if you like.'

*

If DC Andy Lewis was hacked off at Coupland accepting his invitation to tag along he did a good job of hiding it. He'd suffered from alopecia since his police training days, his shiny pink scalp earning him the nickname Cueball the moment he transferred to Salford Precinct. 'I got a call about an hour ago from a woman claiming she's got some information,' Cueball said as he manoeuvred the pool car out of the station car park. 'Says she saw the appeal on TV and couldn't stay quiet any longer. Wouldn't say anything else over the phone.'

'What's her name?'

'Shelley Martin.'

'Have you checked her out?'

'Did a PNC check which drew a blank. Not had time to do anything else, spent most of the day reading through transcripts of the calls that came through to Crimestoppers, what a waste of bloody time that was.'

'Cranks?'

'And not even a full moon in sight.'

'So, where are we meeting her?'

'Beside the burger van off Regent Road.'

'And this is your best lead?'

'By a mile. I'm getting pissed about by everyone I speak to, to be honest. There's nothing coming up on the PNC for the victim, no history however insignificant. If this is gang related I can only think it's a case of mistaken identity.'

'You think this woman's genuine?'

A shrug. 'What have I got to lose?'

It could be a trap, Coupland supposed. It wouldn't be the first time an officer had been lured to an address on the promise of information only to be given a going over by some thug hell bent on revenge. The invitation to tag along made sense now. Safety in numbers and all that.

Cueball steered the car through tea-time traffic, turning into a retail park at the next set of lights, pulling up outside an Argos Superstore. The burger van was open for business. A sign at the side of the road offered a meal deal: a quarter pounder and coke with a Mars bar thrown in for £2. Coupland's stomach rumbled at the smell of fried onions but his kebab the other evening had been his 'sin' for the week. He'd make do with a ham roll and a fag when he got back to the station.

The woman flipping burgers eyed them as they got out of the car. Watched as they'd removed their jackets and lanyards, trying hard not to look like cops waiting to meet an informant. 'That'll be four pounds love,' she said, transferring two burgers onto polystyrene trays before holding them out to the bewildered detectives. 'No one'll bat an eyelid you being here while you're filling your faces.'

'You're Shelley then,' Cueball said, causing the woman to roll her eyes.

'No wonder you've not got a bloody suspect yet,' she said, waiting while they took their burgers and fished about in their pockets for change.

'I'll need a receipt,' Cueball stated, making Coupland groan.

'I'll get 'em,' he sighed, slapping four pound coins on the van's counter, wondering if there was a compensation scheme for officers whose arteries had clogged up in the line of duty. Shelley Martin was stick thin with a drooping jawline. She obviously never ate what she cooked in the van, Coupland thought, nor did she get much daylight, given the pallor of her skin. She wiped her hands down the front of her faded pink tabard, eyes darting left and right while the detectives bit into their grub.

'If you don't want to risk being seen talking to us why did you not tell me what you know over the phone?' Cueball asked between mouthfuls. Coupland stayed silent as he chewed, trying to think of the last time he'd had a burger. This was surprisingly good, all things considered.

'Because I need you to do something for me in return,' Shelley said, 'And I wanted you to hear me out.'

Coupland nearly choked on his mouthful of bun, 'And there was me thinking you were exercising your civic duty.'

'That as well,' Shelley said quickly. 'What happened to that fella was tragic, but at the end of the day it's my own flesh and blood I'm bothered about.'

'You don't say,' Coupland drawled. 'And which of Her Majesty's many undesirable residences is your old man in then? Or is it your son you're wanting to curry favour for?'

Shelley turned to Lewis. 'Is he always so cynical?' she

asked, folding sagging arms across a flat chest.

'Curse of the job,' Lewis answered, picking up a thin serviette from a box on the counter and dabbing his mouth and chin.

'My colleague here is spot on,' Coupland said agreeably, brushing a slice of fried onion from the front of his shirt. 'However, I'm more than happy to stand corrected. Tell us what you know and we'll decide what it's worth.'

Shelley studied Coupland before turning her attention back to Lewis. 'I was there,' she said. 'When it happened, I mean. Outside the school. I've a cleaning job nearby three mornings a week. I was on my way home, had stopped to talk to a couple of young mums that I know, friends of my daughter. There was a car parked outside the school on the zig zag lines – the same car that was mentioned in that press appeal – the Mitsubishi. Folk were muttering and glaring at the driver as they went past but you know what it's like, no one wants to be the person that says anything in case it kicks off. The driver kept revving his engine, and we reckoned he was just having a laugh, trying to get folks' backs up, you know, winding up the pointers and the glarers. We said as much while we were talking, and after a few minutes we lost interest. Then the fella, what's his name again?'

'James McMahon.'

'Yeah, well, he walks out of the school gates and steps onto the crossing, oblivious like. I wasn't really watching, I was just facing that way. I heard an engine revving up, but by the time I realised it was the car outside the school it was already off, racing towards him. The speed it was going and the racket it made had everyone's attention, wondering what the hell the driver was playing at, knowing no good would bloody come of it. He saw the car as it screeched towards him, but there was no time to react, he was only half way across. Didn't stand a chance, poor sod.' She helped herself to a can of Vimto and took a swig, regarded both detectives as they glanced at one another. 'I'm guessing no one else has come forward to say as much, am I right?'

DC Lewis gave a slight shrug of his shoulders.

Shelley gave Coupland a smug smile. 'Thought so.'

'And you felt so outraged by what you saw you thought you'd wait two weeks until his widow was paraded in front of the cameras to see if anyone's conscience was pricked enough into coming forward?'

'Well it worked, didn't it? Here I am.'

A pause. 'You get a good look at the driver?'

'Christ yeah, I tried not to, you know what I mean? No one want's to get caught up in any trouble when it's got nothing to do with them…' She had a point.

'Did you recognise him?'

Shelley narrowed her eyes. 'You think I consort with boy racers?'

'You're a consenting adult, Shelley, what you do in your own time is up to you…'

'Hang on, so the driver was young?' said Cueball, shooting a look at Coupland, who nodded. It was a start, they acknowledged. 'Can you give us a description?'

A pause. 'Maybe.'

'Is this the part where I have to remind you that wasting police time is a serious offence?' Coupland barked.

'Wind your neck in, Columbo, I've spent my life putting up with narky men. Trust me, it's like water off a duck's back,' Shelley sneered.

Coupland pursed his lips. He was right then, though it brought him no pleasure. 'Husband or son?' he asked.

Shelley's gaze never left his. 'Son,' she answered, refusing to blink. 'My old man's old enough and ugly enough to look after himself.'

Coupland sighed, rubbed his hand over his chin as he slid a sidelong glance at Cueball. Dealing with hard men was a walk in the park compared to dealing with their wives and mothers. 'Where is he?'

'Strangeways... six months term, drug related before you ask.'

'So? He's rung home to complain there's no room service or free Wi-Fi? Tell him to try the Travelodge up the road.'

'Look, there's no disputing he's a knobhead. What I don't get is why he's been put in a Category A prison when his cousin's in a Cat C in Warrington for the same thing. I want him moved. He's no threat to anyone, doesn't need to be locked up for hours on bloody end. There's more association time in Warrington, more training opportunities too.'

Coupland listened as Shelley reeled off the pros and cons of jail categories like some parents weighed up universities. It was all about perspective, he supposed.

Cueball sent a look in his direction. 'This is above my pay grade,' he shrugged, 'just as well I brought you along.'

'I can't make any promises,' Coupland told Shelley. 'There's precious little we can do without you giving us something concrete to work with. You've given us an account of what happened but bugger all else. You've already said you don't recognise the driver. '

Shelley's smile couldn't have been more smug if she'd

tried. 'No, but when I told my son what had happened outside the school he mentioned something about the victim that will make you want to look at him a lot bloody closer.'

CHAPTER SIXTEEN

'So let me get this right. McMahon was spending his lunchbreak at the warehouse stuffing packets of sweets with ecstasy tablets.'

'Yup, got it in one, boss. Brings a whole new meaning to '*The happy world of Haribo.*'

They were standing in DCI Mallender's office. The information Shelley Martin had given them would have to be verified, but if correct they would need to act swiftly as the consequences didn't bear thinking about. Mallender walked over to his window, stared out of it in silence. His office was situated at the far end of the station; his view of the neighbouring precinct roof was hardly stimulating, but Coupland knew the DCI wasn't looking for inspiration. 'The Super will go ballistic,' he said, referring to the TV appeal where Curtis had stood side by side with McMahon's widow, assuring the tea time viewers his officers would leave no stone unturned in bringing her husband's killer to justice.

'A crime's still been committed, 'Coupland pointed out.

'You know what I mean.'

Superintendent Curtis came off his perch for heinous crime, the sort of stuff that set the public's teeth on edge and made front page news. Slain boy scouts and brides on their wedding day, not dealers hiding drugs in kids' sweet packets. 'How did we miss this?'

'I don't know. Some people are better than others at

hiding things, I suppose.'

'Have you spoken to his widow?'

'Not yet, DC Lewis is going to speak to Shelley Martin's son first, get the measure of it, before he goes knocking on her door.'

'How does he know McMahon?'

'He doesn't. But prison jungle drums are the same as anywhere else. The word on the inside was McMahon was the victim of a cuckooing sting.' Cuckooing was a method used by organised crime gangs wanting to extend their operations by identifying vulnerable people in their target towns and using the properties they lived in or worked from as a base to deal drugs. 'McMahon had a loan he couldn't pay off – it had been sold onto this gang so he was obliged to play ball. Everything was peachy until he wanted out. His kids had started school and he realised the risk he was putting them under if the bags got into the wrong hands. Only it's never that simple is it? There's no such thing as saying "Thanks very much but I'd like to hand my notice in."'

'Was he working alone?'

'Dunno. Nor do we know the scale of this operation, though there's an easy enough way to find out.'

Mallender sighed. 'I'm guessing whoever he was working for wanted to send a message to anyone else thinking of leaving.'

'Or maybe they were worried he'd grow a conscience and turn himself in.'

'This Shelley Martin's son – what's his name?'

'Danny Martin.'

'Is he prepared to make a statement?'

Coupland nodded. 'DC Lewis is arranging an interview

with him by video link so it'll look to the other inmates like he's having a bog standard meeting with his lawyer, much safer than one of us turning up to interview him at the prison.'

'OK.'

'And the transfer, boss, how likely is it?'

Another sigh. 'I'll see what I can do. The Super won't be ecstatic but if I can persuade him to look at the bigger picture, that we may have unveiled a major drug network on our doorstep, I'm confident he'll authorise the raid on the warehouse as well. I could see that's where you were going,' he said, noting Coupland's mock surprise. 'Though with your track record it's probably better if you stay away from this one.'

'Agreed.'

'Leave it with me while I find a way to sell it to Curtis.'

Coupland clicked his tongue as he shoved his hands into his pockets. 'Just tell him to think of all that shoe leather,' he muttered as he made for the door.

*

If the man staring at Coupland was shocked to see him standing on his doorstep he didn't show it. The face was the same, thinner maybe. Deep lines etched the forehead and skin around the eyes. One corner of the old man's mouth lifted, though Coupland knew of old this was no greeting. 'Jesus Christ.'

'No. Just me. I need to come in.'

The man stood back as he held the door open. 'I'm not stoppin' yer.'

That was the difference between them now, Coupland acknowledged, the old bastard couldn't control him anymore, couldn't make threats he knew damn well he wouldn't be able to follow through. Not yet seventy, yet there was a stoop to his shoulders, a heaviness to his step that shouldn't be there. Ged Coupland had never taken a day's exercise in his life – unless beating seven bells out of his son counted as a sport – and it showed. His lip remained curled as he looked Coupland up and down. 'I hear you're a grandad now.' No smile accompanied the statement, no pat on the back or look of admiration. Coupland strained to hear the snort, the note of derision that followed these observations as sure as night followed day. 'Pff.'

'News travels fast,' he replied.

'I heard the father's done a runner already.'

Coupland had kept the details of Tonto's paternity from his sisters, telling them instead that the low life had buggered off, wasn't worthy of the little boy. Not all untrue. 'Better for all concerned,' he admitted.

'Another mouth to feed though, that'll eat into your police pension.'

'Can think of worse ways to spend it,' Coupland volleyed, eyeing the empty takeaway cartons and ready-meal-for-one wrappers left lying on the counter top in the kitchen, a bottle of Bells whisky open with a half drunk glass beside it. 'Besides, got no intention of handing my stripes in yet.'

'They'll chew you up and spit you out the same way they did me,' Ged grumbled.

Coupland considered this. 'No one's indispensable.' An image of Lynn came into his head reminding him there were exceptions to everything. 'Turning up to the job sober helps,' he added, remembering too late this was no time for a sparring match, his old man deserved to be told the news with professionalism, if not kindness.

'Come and sit in the front room,' Coupland told him, 'bring your drink with you.'

'I'm going out later, though the traffic boys'll not cause me any bother.'

'The boys on traffic weren't born when you were on the job,' Coupland said, 'don't go looking to me to pull any strings.'

That sound again. 'Pff,' and a look that said this wasn't the first time Coupland had come up short.

'I know better than that,' the old man glowered, standing his ground. 'Don't bother giving me the come and sit down crap either, just tell me what's happened? Is it one of the girls?' His voice rose a little, his hand automatically reaching for the whisky glass anyway. He took a swig, wiped his mouth with the back of his hand the way Coupland did, though there was a tremor in his father's hand that hadn't been there before.

Coupland swallowed. 'It's Mum,' he said. 'Her body was discovered in the fire up at the care home at the weekend.'

He watched as his father reached into his trouser pocket for his cigarettes and lighter. One swift movement and he pulled one from the pack and lit it, sucking on it hungrily. Coupland found himself doing the same. It was a reflex action, when the going got tough a smoker reached for a cigarette the same way most folk put their hands out to break a fall. They smoked in silence. Coupland watched his father lift the lid on the kitchen bin so they could use it as an ashtray, and it wasn't lost on him that smoking was the only activity they shared. The old man had never taken him fishing, kicked a ball around with him or cheered him on from the side-lines. The only time he'd had his full attention was when he loomed at him from the doorway, belt in hand. He tried to imagine what his father was feeling. There'd never been a divorce, no formal parting of the ways. Even if he'd stopped caring he must have wondered what had become of her.

Ged stared down at his glass, reaching for the bottle to top it up he paused mid-way. 'You still here?' his tone was sharp. 'You've done your duty now piss off.'

Coupland stared at the pitiful figure in front of him. He wasn't sure what he'd expected, but not this. 'There's going to be an investigation,' he said. 'It's not just a suspicious fire. She…she was dead before it started.'

The old man looked at him. 'How?'

'Head injury. Details are sketchy.'

Ged opened his eyes wide as he poured another glass, 'Too sketchy for an ex-cop – or a suspect?' he asked.

Coupland shook his head, though strictly speaking the old man was right. He wouldn't be the first spurned husband to seek revenge on a prodigal wife. But then he would have had to know she was back in Salford. 'Did you know she was working there?' Coupland blurted the question out. The thought had formed in his mind while they'd been talking and he couldn't get shut of it.

'Are you for real?' his old man sniped. 'It's no wonder you never made it any higher.' 'Is that all you can say? I come with news about your wife and you'd still rather have a go at me? You've not asked about how the girls have taken it.'

'So you told them first?' A shrug. 'No surprise…'

'It's not a competition, Dad.' The word caught in his

throat like stubborn phlegm. 'Look, I'm trying to piece together details of her life after she left us, I wondered if you'd heard anything over the years, anything that could point me in the right direction.'

'Not much of a detective then if I've to do your job for you. Any road, since you're connected you won't be allowed anywhere near the investigation…'

'I haven't told my boss yet.' Coupland paused, ignoring the satisfaction on his father's face before adding, 'She was using a different surname. I didn't know it was her at first.'

Ged's face clouded in confusion.

'I'm sorry if I didn't make it clear, she was badly burned, her remains were unrecognisable. Her ID wasn't confirmed until after the post mortem.'

Coupland saw the shock register on his father's face.

'Do you want me to get the girls to come over?'

'And spend the evening listening to them dredging up memories I'd rather forget?' Shiny eyes stared back at Coupland as he wrestled with his conscience and lost.

'I could stay for a while, I suppose…' he sighed, switching his phone to silent.

FRIDAY

CHAPTER SEVENTEEN

Outside Manchester Crown Court. Judy Grant's trial.

Coupland paced up and down in front of the court house, the tip of his cigarette glowing red before smoke hissed from his nose. He clamped his phone to his ear, listening as Krispy informed him he'd tracked down Helen Foley and Colin Grantham, the patients Mark Flint claimed had been abused at Cedar Falls the same time as him. Both lived a short drive from the home. 'My phone's going to be on silent but message me with how you get on,' Coupland said, ending the call as a cab pulled up at the bottom of the court steps. Two passengers alighted from it, a gaunt young woman and a much older man Coupland recognised as her father. Mariana Gashi and her sister Zamia had been trafficked from Albania before being sent to beg on the streets around Salford. Zamia had died following a bungled attempt to pimp her out to a client who had so far evaded capture. This was the last trial Mariana was required to attend; once it was over she would be deported.

'Though nothing could ever make me want to stay here,' she'd said to Coupland after the trafficking gang's month-long trial had ended. 'And to think my people think this is a civilised country.'

Coupland raised a hand in greeting when Mariana looked over; flicked his cigarette butt into a nearby bin before following them into the building.

*

The youth worker looked at the group of teenagers sitting around her. Most were slouched back in their chairs, baseball caps on their knees where she'd asked them to be placed when they'd first swaggered into the community centre half an hour before. 'I'm here to help you with interview skills,' she'd chided. 'Rule number one is to turn up looking like you've made an effort – not like you're about to hold up a post office – Brad, take that scarf off from round your neck and if you think I'm going to speak while you wear a Jason mask you've got another think coming.'

She waited while the groans and teeth sucking stopped, her attention turning to a girl sat directly in front of her. 'Kelly, if you keep on using your phone I'm going to have to ask you to leave. I need your full attention today.'

The girl's thumbs flew across the phone's keyboard as she finished her message before stuffing her smartphone into the pocket of her shorts. Satisfied, the woman smiled at her audience. She was about to speak but paused; footsteps could be heard in the corridor, purposeful, heading in their direction. The door opened and a young man entered, a blush creeping up his neck as he stepped into the room. Several heads swivelled in his direction as the woman looked him up and down.

'Well, you're certainly dressed for the part,' she said, 'though you need to work on your timekeeping.' She stopped, her attention drawn to the black man entering the room behind him. Mid-thirties, he was far too old to be sent to a youth group, she thought irritably, she really did need to get back onto the job centre. If they didn't send her the right clients how the hell could she help them?

'Miss Foley,' the young man said as they stepped towards her holding up lanyards with the Greater Manchester Police logo on them. 'Is there somewhere we can go for a quiet word?'

Helen Foley's frown deepened when she heard the reason for the detectives turning up unannounced. She'd ended up letting the group finish early. There was no way she could keep an eye on them from the corridor, all the other rooms were taken so she'd stayed put and asked the detectives to give her five minutes while she set the group a task to be done before they came back the next day. 'There's no chance any of them will bother,' she'd muttered when the last one hurried out through the door, 'but I can live in hope.'

Krispy had made the introductions, explaining they were following up an allegation that had been made against staff by an ex-patient at Cedar Falls.

Helen's eyebrows knotted together. 'Oh, I assumed you were here about the fire, checking to see if I thought any of these terrors were up to the job. I mean, it's arson right? That's what it said on the news.'

'The news report said the circumstances were suspicious,' Ashcroft corrected her, 'but I suppose people will draw their own conclusions.'

'You can hardly blame folk,' she said, turning to watch her group heading in the direction of the precinct up the road towards Greggs. A sausage roll and an afternoon of lurking round the shops to look forward to. 'So much for job hunting.'

'We understand you were treated at Cedar Falls a while back,' Krispy stated.

Helen said nothing, although a nerve beneath her eye started to twitch. 'Sorry, is that a question?' she responded, attempting a smile.

Krispy shook his head. 'Not really. We checked the home's records. You were there between January and May 2017.'

Helen blew out a sigh. 'You've got your answer then.'

'True, but someone has come forward who states you and another patient were mistreated there, and we need to ask whether you wish to make a complaint against the home…'

'Or decide whether that makes me a suspect for the fire, given the recent turn of events,' she added for him.

The flush across Krispy's neck deepened, but it didn't stop him from ploughing on. 'Can you tell us why you were sent to Cedar Falls?'

'Why the hell should I? It's got nothing to do with the bloody fire – I've got nothing to do with the bloody fire – so why don't you sod off and leave me to get on with my life.' Her voice had deepened as she spoke to them, became more gutteral, harsher. It was the voice of someone who knew how to handle themself, who could hold their own in a shouting match if needed – and win. Helen folded her arms and turned back to the window as though wishing she could join the stragglers as they traipsed up the road.

'How did you get into youth work?' Ashcroft asked, trying to diffuse the situation.

Helen let out a long sigh as she turned to face him. 'I needed support when I left Cedar Falls – I guess everyone does – and I was assigned a support worker from a local charity. They really helped me regain my confidence, and I decided that was something I could do, a way of giving back I suppose.'

Ashcroft had coached Krispy before they'd met with Helen and told him the best way of getting someone to talk was often to say nothing. Use silence to break down their defences. Krispy glanced at Ashcroft to see if now was one of those moments. Ashcroft nodded. Both detectives waited. Krispy stared at the space above Helen's head, silently counting backwards from twenty. He got as far as seven.

'Fine!' she snapped. 'As long as this doesn't go any further, OK?' Both men nodded. Another sigh. 'I suffered from Anorexia and depression in my early twenties, it got so bad at one point I needed to be watched twenty-four hours a day in case I harmed myself or tried to bring the food they forced me to eat back up, so my GP referred me to Cedar Falls. I was under constant observation, every 15 minutes someone would come into my room and check on me. It felt like I'd lost any right to privacy, as though my life wasn't my own anymore. One day a male member of staff came into my room while I was sleeping, shoved a cloth in my mouth and raped me. I was pinned down on that mattress for 45 minutes. I know that because it had been my birthday the previous day, my parents had bought me a watch. I willed the minute hand to move round that watch face for forty-five minutes. And not once in that time did anyone else come in to do my obs. Why was that? Did they know he was there?' She glared at them. 'It was hours later, I'd fallen back asleep, a female care assistant found me bleeding on the mattress. Turns out my attacker had been rougher than I gave him credit for. She cleaned me up, asked me how in God's name I came to have those injuries, but I said nothing. I knew that it was pointless complaining. I never told anyone, not even after I'd been discharged. I just wanted to bury the whole incident.'

'Who was it who hurt you?' Krispy asked, unable to say the word rape.

A breath. 'I don't know. I didn't want to know either. Afterwards, I mean. When the assault was over I made sure he'd gone before I turned around. In a way I was grateful he'd hidden his face from me. I didn't want to look at him outside of that room and know what he'd done.'

Something occurred to Helen. 'Hang on, I never told anyone about what had happened, so how was this person able to tell you about me?'

Ashcroft shrugged. 'They didn't go into detail. Perhaps they just recognised another victim when they saw one.'

Helen considered this, before nodding. 'It does stay with you, that feeling of helplessness. Perhaps they saw that.'

Krispy looked at Ashcroft before ploughing on. 'I'm sorry, but I need to ask you this. Where were you on the night of the fire?'

A faint smile tugged at the corner of her mouth. 'That's easy. I was at home. Doing what I always do. Heating up a ready meal for one then sitting down in front of the TV to distract myself while I ate it.'

'Can anyone else confirm that?'

'I still don't like people watching me eat, so no.'

'One last thing,' Ashcroft said. 'If we track down the person who did this would you be prepared to make a statement?'

'What? And be their victim for a second time?' Helen shuddered. 'Thanks, but I'll pass.'

*

The riverbank was quiet on a weekday. Best time to come, the weekenders who came with their bottles of beer and banter shattered his precious silence. He'd booked the day off ages ago, had no idea it'd turn out to be so nice. Sheila had sulked during breakfast, had hoped he'd spend the day with her going round garden centres. 'For Christ's sake woman we can do that anytime,' he'd said, but the truth was come the weekend he'd have another excuse at the ready, whether she was angling for a trip to the DIY store or visiting their grandkids for that matter. Give him a sunny afternoon catching trout and he was a happy man.

'Colin Grantham?'

The voice seemed to come from nowhere, but when he turned he saw a boy in a man's suit and a black man resembling that fella off the TV staring at him, holding up IDs that they wore round their necks. He'd peered at the boy's lanyard, saw the words 'Detective Constable' and stopped reading. 'You a detective too?' he said to his companion.

Ashcroft nodded. 'We'd like to ask you a few questions regarding an allegation that's been made against staff at Cedar Falls.'

Ignoring the boy, Colin put down his fishing rod and turned to Ashcroft. 'I thought you might,' he said, sighing.

'The moment I heard about the fire on the news I've been expecting you,' Colin said, zipping up the front of his gilet as though a barrier between them was needed.

'It didn't surprise you then, that someone could have

set fire to the place?'

'So it is arson then?'

'We're making a number of enquiries,' said Ashcroft.

'Which is why you're here.'

Ashcroft nodded. 'We were given your name by a patient who was at Cedar Falls the same time as you. He got in touch following the fire to say he'd been badly treated at the home, he said he thought you had been too.'

A sigh. 'And how would this person know that?' asked Grantham.

'They said you looked guarded a lot of the time, said they recognised the fear.'

'And does this person have a name?' He looked from one detective to the other, 'Oh, don't tell me, you can't divulge that information at the moment, however if I could rip open any wounds that have long since healed and bleed out my life story you'd be really grateful.'

Krispy glanced at Ashcroft.

'A bit harsh,' Ashcroft said, 'but something along those lines, yes.'

Grantham folded his arms. 'It's not something I ever talk about.'

'We appreciate it must be hard,' said Krispy, 'and we wouldn't be here if we didn't think this information was absolutely necessary.'

Grantham moved to sit on a green folding chair, ran stubby fingers through hair that was starting to thin. 'If I'd have known you were coming I'd have brought the rest of the set,' he said, 'there's another three chairs and a picnic hamper in my garage, bought them on the off chance the family decided to spend time outdoors and not traipse the length and breadth of every shopping centre on their time off. Should have kept my receipt,' he sighed.

'We're happy to stand, Mr Grantham, take all the time you need.'

Grantham spread his hands on his lap. 'I had a breakdown a couple of years back,' he began, looking up at them. 'My business had gone belly up and I'd started drinking. My wife threatened to leave and something inside me stopped working. I couldn't get up or dress myself; Anne didn't leave in the end because she couldn't see how I'd pull myself together. I started doing daft things, only eating certain foods, walking on one side of the pavement, next thing I accused her of trying to kill me. I was sectioned. Sent to Cedar Falls when I was assessed as being psychotic.'

'How long were you there for?'

Geoffrey pulled a face. 'It's not something I like to think about let alone talk about,' he said, mentally doing the calculation. 'I was there for two months, one week and three days,' his mouth formed a grim line as he said this.

'And how was your treatment?'

Grantham's face darkened. 'Have you had access to my medical records?'

'Not at all,' replied Ashcroft. 'We're contacting you purely because we've been given your name.'

'Yet you can't share the name of the person who told you about me...'

'We'd prefer not to say at this stage, to protect their identity until we decide how to proceed.'

'Surely that's my decision?'

'That depends on the nature of the allegations,' Krispy added.

'Look, if you can tell us about your time there it'd really help.'

Grantham blew out a breath. 'I couldn't get a place in the local psychiatric hospital as it was full, I was put on a waiting list but in the meantime I needed constant care and Cedar Falls was meant to be a safe place. Only it turned out to be the opposite. There wasn't enough staff, they couldn't spend the time with you that was needed. Everything was rushed. You could see they weren't happy about it either. All it took was one person playing up and that was the day's schedule gone for a Burton. We were constantly threatened with sedation, even when we learned to mind our own business. "Go to your room now or I'll give you the needle." That's what I was told whenever I tried speaking up for myself. I was punched once and kicked, called a dirty bastard because I'd wet myself when I was too drugged to make it to the toilet in time. I told my wife what was happening but the authorities said there were channels she had to go through if we wanted to complain. Then one day when she asked a member of staff to explain why I was losing weight. I'd told her they'd been holding back food as a punishment, you see. She went in all guns blazing; the problem was the person she spoke to was the one giving me all the grief. He cut short her visiting time, forced me back to my room and pinned me down, grinding my face into the floor. He picked on me regularly after that, though I made sure my wife never found out. In the end a space came up in a facility closer to home and she got me transferred. It's a time we prefer not to talk about.'

'And the man that treated you this way? Who was it?'

Grantham closed his eyes and blew out another breath.

Then he gave them a name.

*

Lunchtime recess and Coupland still hadn't been called to give evidence. He'd sat in a side room with Shola Dube alternating between checking his phone and helping himself to the urn of coffee left on a table with sugar coated biscuits he didn't think supermarkets sold any more.

His phone vibrated signalling an incoming text. Krispy advising that Colin Grantham had given them the name of his abuser. Coupland moved to an empty part of the waiting room and dialled Krispy's number. He listened as the DC gave his report.

'Neither Colin Grantham nor Helen Foley want to make a statement, Sarge, both have moved on with their lives.'

'They can give evidence anonymously,' Coupland replied, voice low.

Krispy sounded put out. 'I told them that, but they don't want an investigation or a trial dredging up bad memories.'

'I don't see as we have a choice,' said Coupland. 'We have three allegations of assault and you've just been given the name of Grantham's abuser. Bring him in.'

'Will do, Sarge.'

Coupland thought for a moment. 'Do Foley and Grantham have an alibi for the night of the fire?'

'Grantham's wife was at their daughter's, babysitting, and Helen Foley was watching TV at home alone, so no.'

'OK, so our list of suspected arsonists just got longer.'

'Seriously, Sarge? asked Krispy. 'You can't really think

they had anything to do with the fire?'

'You shouldn't be interested in what I think, Kiddo, just about following due process. Let the facts tell us what to think. And for the record, I have no bloody idea, but I do know that revenge makes folk do unpredictable things, so no; we don't rule anyone out yet. Their names get added to the incident board.'

'Yes, Sarge,' Krispy replied, subdued.

'You're doing well,' Coupland reassured him. 'Ashcroft messaged earlier to say he didn't need to wipe your backside once.'

'Cheers, Sarge.'

'So why do you sound like you've lost a fiver and found fifty pence?'

'The people we spoke to were treated abysmally. I mean, I don't think it could get much worse, could it? What I don't understand is how it was allowed to happen. Is cruelty something you learn, if not to do yourself, at least to tolerate as long as it happens to someone else?'

Something shifted inside Coupland. He'd been mulling over similar thoughts since the accounts of abuse had come to light. Had his mother witnessed this cruelty? God forbid she was part of it…

Coupland sighed. 'Fear makes people complicit to all kind of things they would normally disapprove of.' Even so, had she ignored what was going on under her nose, agreed to keep shtum for the sake of her job? If he closed his eyes he could see her smile, put a plaster on his knee when he'd cut it. She knitted him horrible jumpers and let the hem down on his school trousers when a new pair would have been preferable. She couldn't mop up an anorexic's blood knowing a colleague had raped her.

Could she?

Footsteps could be heard along the corridor. A court clerk appeared behind the door calling Coupland's name. He gave her the thumbs up and ended the call.

SATURDAY

CHAPTER EIGHTEEN

CID room, Salford Precinct Station

Coupland moved towards his desk with a purpose. The incident room was virtually empty, down to civilian staff inputting data and covering the phones. Keeping his eyes peeled for Alex he slid open his desk drawer and removed the box containing the items taken from his mother's room.

He'd been halfway through giving evidence when he'd remembered that it was still in his drawer, that Ashcroft was already in Alex's bad books for not checking through it. He'd fired off an email to the EMU as soon as he'd been able to, explaining the hold-up, but whichever way he dressed it up he was hanging onto property that may be relevant to the case.

Taking a sip of his take away coffee he gingerly lifted the lid. The first item he pulled out was the last thing to be added – the evidence bag he'd picked up from the EMU two days earlier. Inside was a bundle of photographs. Snaps of his mother with people he didn't know. Friends she must have filled her life with after she'd walked out. There were several of her smiling beside the same woman, in pubs, on beaches, in European cities. The photos showed his mother age over time, become heavier, greyer, but there was a confidence in her eyes that hadn't been there during his childhood.

Coupland placed the photographs back in their envelope, returned it to the box. A notepad nestled between a staff handbook and an address book; he reached in to retrieve it.

'Please tell me this isn't what I think.'

Coupland nearly jumped out of his skin at the sound of the voice behind him. He looked round guiltily, caught the disappointment in Alex's face.

'Since Ashcroft didn't follow up the action I gave him I thought I'd go down to the EMU myself only they told me Barbara Howe's evidence had already been signed out. By you.' She moved in close to hiss at him: 'What the hell do you think you are playing at?'

'I wanted to find out more about her, that's all.'

'And in the meantime prevent anyone else from looking through her effects objectively.'

'Hardly, I was going to hand them to Ashcroft when I'd finished.'

'Yeah, after your sticky paws have been all over them.'

'She's a victim in all this too,' he said, swallowing his doubts.

Alex refused to listen. 'I just don't understand why, when you're already being investigated by Complaints, you see fit to flout evidence management regulations as well. They are there for a reason, and we all have to comply. The rules are no bloody different for you, Kevin. Maybe I was wrong when I agreed to give you time to get your head around all this.'

Coupland waited for her to run out of steam. With any luck she wouldn't ask him to come clean to the boss about his conflict of interest, or worse still, drop him in it. One whiff of his mother's connection to the case and he'd be toast. Off the case – off the force even, given his recent track record, and no time for a whip round.

Coupland opened his mouth to say something in the full knowledge he'd be cut off.

'Don't bother making excuses, Kevin, you're abusing my trust and I think it's time you come clean to the boss.' Alex paused to take a breath. 'I'm in your corner, truly, I am, but don't make that job harder than it needs to be.' She had every right to be hacked off; her loyalty to him was putting her career on the line too. 'I need to go through the evidence, Kevin. When the investigation is over you'll be able to go through your mother's belongings to your heart's content but in the meantime let me do the honours. I promise I'll take care of it all.'

She picked up the box, her gaze sweeping over his desk in case he'd kept anything back. A pause, as though she remembered something. 'I nearly forgot, how did it go in court?'

The look he gave her said it all. 'Adjourned, pending a psychiatric report. Her lawyer's claiming she wasn't thinking clearly due to numerous failed attempts at IVF.'

'That's why they earn the big bucks,' Alex sympathised. 'I heard Ashcroft and Krispy got a breakthrough on the abuse investigation.'

Coupland nodded. 'Colin Grantham named Bernard White as the person who assaulted him.'

'He was interviewed by Turnbull,' said Alex. 'He was the member of staff claiming Harkins had something to do with the fire. Made out it was an insurance job.'

'Nice guy.'

Alex hadn't budged from beside his desk. She folded her arms as she regarded him. 'What about the DCI?

When are you going to speak to him?'

It was a prompt, not a question, and Coupland acknowledged the fact by scraping back his chair as he got to his feet. 'No time like the present, I suppose,' he sighed.

*

Coupland was halfway along the corridor leading to DCI Mallender's office when he heard someone call out his name. He turned to see Cueball hurrying towards him. 'I tried calling you but someone said you were in with the boss. Thought you'd want an update following my video call with Danny Martin.'

Coupland nodded. 'I take it he corroborated his mother's claims?'

'Yeah, and more. Says he and McMahon had crossed paths a couple of times, not mates in any sense of the word but they knew the same people.'

'Course they do,' Coupland said amiably. 'Birds of a feather and all that, though not sure what you call a group of drug dealers.'

'He said McMahon hadn't been on the scene that long. He owed money to a loan shark. When he couldn't settle his debt they sold it on to a community fixer who recruited him into their distribution network. His job in the warehouse meant he could keep the doctored sweet bags to one side which were then collected by local dealers for selling on right under everyone's noses.'

'So who was he working for?'

'Danny wasn't playing ball with that one, Sarge, said information like that was worth a damn sight more than a move to a lenient prison.'

'Can't blame the guy for trying,' Coupland said. 'But going by the DCI's demeanour when I spoke to him there's nothing else in the pot negotiation-wise. There's more chance of finding a City supporter in the Stretford End than the Super sanctioning anything else.'

A nod. 'So, we need to take a closer look at McMahon's associates,' said Cueball.

'No names came up when we carried out our initial victimology. These aren't folk he normally fraternises with. If he kept whoever he was dealing with at arm's length, minimising his contact to purely when the pickups were made, there's a chance they'll be captured on the warehouse CCTV – assuming they use it. When's the raid organised for?'

'Monday.'

Coupland nodded. 'I'm guessing you've been told I won't be joining you?'

A pause. 'It may have been brought to my attention, Sarge…'

Coupland puffed out his cheeks. 'Good. I didn't want you thinking I was cherry picking what I got involved in, the orders have come from up high.'

He glanced out of the corridor window as a squad car pulled up in front of the station's main entrance. A uniformed officer was at the wheel but when the passenger door opened DC Ashcroft got out of it before moving to open the rear door for a bemused looking man with a straggly beard. 'Bollocks,' Coupland muttered, backing away from Cueball, requesting that the DC keep him updated before marching down the flight of stairs leading to reception.

Coupland caught up with DC Ashcroft outside the bank of interview rooms. 'Are you out of your mind?' he demanded, waiting while Ashcroft opened the first door he came to and ushered the man inside, telling him he'd be back in a minute before closing it behind him. Coupland recognised him as being one of the members of staff on duty when he'd returned Johnny Metcalfe into Harkins' care after his walk about. 'What the hell were you thinking of, using a patrol car to bring him in?'

Ashcroft frowned. 'We couldn't get hold of him yesterday and the pool cars are being serviced, Sarge, I didn't think it mattered...'

'Other than Tunny has eyes and ears everywhere. If he gets a whiff of our interest in Whyte – and the reason – I doubt he'll make it to trial – assuming we can make a case against him.'

Ashcroft closed his eyes and leaned against the corridor wall. 'Shite.' It was pointless rubbing his nose in it, their energy was better served keeping Bernard Whyte in one piece.

'I'll go and speak to Tunny,' Coupland said. 'Tell him he's helping us with another enquiry, that if he so much as suffers a paper cut when he leaves here I'll be back for Tunny myself.'

*

The sun shone down on Salford beneath a clear blue sky. When the weather was good everything changed. The city glistened and its inhabitants abandoned anoraks and parkas in favour of vest tops and sundresses. Coupland flashed a pizza delivery driver pulling out of a line of parked cars into the traffic, flicking on his indicators before moving into the space he'd vacated. An Indian restaurant, Turkish kebab house, and an all you can eat Chinese buffet restaurant occupied the bulk of the units operating on Tattersall Road. Coupland climbed out of his car, headed in the direction of a wine bar on the corner, signs boasting half priced pitchers of cocktails. A crowd of youths stood outside smoking. Pale skin starting to redden. Flabby backsides strained against jersey shorts. Shaved heads with buzz cut tops. The girls wore traveller style clothing with drag queen make up trowelled onto spray tanned skin. Every conversation was shouted, punctuated by swear words that would have made a docker blush. Coupland caught the eye of a young man on the edge of an all-male group. His eyes widened when he saw Coupland and he began inching away from his cronies before anyone could see what – or who – was making him twitchy. He inclined his head towards the bar's entrance, saying to the others, 'Need to splash my boots.' Wearing jeans and a slim fit tee shirt, he looked different without the uniform of black anorak and neckerchief he'd been wearing when Coupland had last clapped eyes on him.

Coupland followed him into toilets that resembled a Zen spa; marble effect tiles set off white porcelain sinks with contraptions above them that soaped, rinsed and dried hands without the user having to move. 'Classy,' Coupland observed.

He'd no sooner stepped over the threshold than the boy rounded on him. 'What the hell are you doing here Mr Coupland? Don't you lot have your own place to chill out in?'

Coupland shoved his hands in his pockets and tried to

look sorry. 'I know, Liam, three times in one week, folk are going to talk.'

The youth frowned. 'Yeah, that's what worries me, fraternising with the Feds will seriously damage my health.' He glanced at the toilet's entrance as though fearful who may walk in.

Coupland moved so that he was leaning against it, preventing entry – or exit. 'That the reason you acted like a prize prick when I showed up to break the news about Catherine to Tunny and his mam? I mean, it's not as though I was going to come over and bump fists with you.'

'It was the first time I'd been invited over. I didn't want to lose his trust because my mum's friendly with a cop.'

The first time Coupland had met Liam's mother was to break the news that her husband had been gunned down in a supermarket car park. They hadn't kept in touch exactly, but whenever their paths did cross he made a point of asking after her and the boy, the same as he did with any of the families he'd come into contact with over the years. It was impossible to wade in someone's tragedy then walk away after the case had closed without ever looking back.

'You were perched on his garden wall son, hardly an invite for tea and scones.'

Liam's face fell. Shrugging, he turned to use the urinal closest to him. When he was done, he zipped himself up then allowed the chrome contraptions to wash and dry his hands.

'This place used to be a right dive,' Coupland said watching as Liam studied his reflection in the wall length mirror as he ran his hand over his jaw. 'Though I can't say the clientele has improved any.'

A protective plastic sleeve covered Liam's left arm. 'New tattoo?' Coupland enquired.

Liam gave him a sheepish look, 'Had no choice. Had my ex's name on it, didn't I?'

Coupland sucked in a breath as he regarded Liam. 'Big mistake that. What's wrong with mermaids or a picture of your mother? So, go on then, what have you gone for?'

Liam held out his arm for inspection. Coupland could make out a pair of hands clasped in prayer, a set of rosary beads wrapped around them. 'In God's arms,' written inside a scroll. The writing was close together even though Liam's biceps could never be described as weedy.

'Didn't know you were religious.'

'I go to church every Sunday.'

'That's not what I meant.'

Liam dropped his gaze, 'I'm not,' he admitted, 'but it was the only thing the tattooist could come up with that would cover up Gillian's name.'

'Thought you'd have gone for something tribal, what with the amount of time you hang around with that lot.' Coupland jerked his thumb in the direction of the door and the pub's clientele. The punters weren't as random as the management made out, consisting mainly of people on Kieran Tunny's payroll. The bar was run by Aiden Franks, his protégé in the making, one of the new school of gangsters who made his fortune in cyber-crime: dodgy investments, counterfeit goods, an online dating site offering foreign brides who disappeared once they received the airfare for their tickets. Franks dodged arrest because his mentor's loyal henchmen were persuaded to take the blame, confess to crimes they were far too thick to have thought up themselves, in return for a generous lump sum on their release. Tunny could be found there most days, a subtle reminder to all concerned that he was in charge.

Coupland scratched his head. 'I don't see what you get out of all this. Apart from a nice line in knock off designer gear.' He was referring to the oversized watch Liam was wearing, worth more than Coupland earned in a month if it was the real deal.

'I'm earning good money now, I can afford to treat myself every once in a while.'

'There's more to life than money,' Coupland reminded him. 'Your mam dotes on you, do something that makes her proud.'

Liam gave Coupland a funny look. 'She's happy enough,' he shrugged. 'Besides, I have a laugh with the other guys. Nothing wrong with a bit of craic.'

Coupland sighed. 'In the old days we had something similar that bound gangs of people together day in day out…'

'Yeah?'

'It was called work…'

'We all work.'

'Not in the sense I mean. Tunny owns this club, his cousin provides the door men, what is it you do again?'

'I'm a security executive.'

'And what does that mean exactly? You hang about on street corners looking mean? When you're not lurking about here, that is. None of it makes sense. I wouldn't mind but you're a bright lad.'

'Let's not make out that I was destined for NASA.'

'Fair enough, but what was wrong with getting a

normal job?'

'What, work in a call centre? I want more out of life than that.'

'And being Tunny's gopher is living the dream?'

Liam had heard enough. 'You didn't come here to give me careers advice, Mr Coupland, why did you come?' He was already starting to sound like one of Tunny's mini-me's.

Coupland shuddered. 'I want a word with the big man; I take it he's in residence, going by the number of 'executives' lurking round the place.' Liam's dad had been one of Tunny's so called executives, a fat lot of good it had done him. Coupland remembered walking away from the family home a decade ago after delivering the news of his death, a young Liam staring down at him from an upstairs window.

'They're both here, if you must know,' Liam told him now, 'said they weren't to be disturbed.'

'Oh, I think Tunny will make an exception for me.'

Liam pulled out his phone and tapped out a message on the keypad.

'Christ, maybe he is moving you up the ranks,' Coupland muttered, eyeing the adapted smartphone favoured by career criminals. A company in Holland had created software with a 'remote wipe' function, enabling incriminating data to be wiped at the push of a button. The phones didn't come cheap though; at the best part of two grand a time they were given to the gang's movers and shakers at the top of the food chain, not the apprentice.

'There was one going spare now one of Mr Tunny's associates has gone inside. He said we could take turns using it when we had any special jobs to do.'

Coupland's eyes narrowed. 'And what might those special jobs entail?'

'Nice try Mr Coupland but I'm no grass.'

Liam moved towards the door Coupland was blocking. 'Mr Tunny's replied, said I've to take you to him.'

Coupland didn't budge. 'It's not too late to change career you know. You're not so far in they can't afford to let you go. Following in our fathers' footsteps isn't all it's cracked up to be.'

'My dad was a good man.'

Coupland said nothing. Liam's father had thrown his weight around like most men attached to a gang. He'd been aggressive and obnoxious, though that didn't mean he'd been a bad father. Coupland sighed. 'Your mother worries about you.'

'All mothers worry.'

Coupland wasn't so sure. 'When you joined Tunny's crew she phoned me you know. Asked me to have a word. My head was somewhere else at the time and I never got round to it.'

'You needn't worry. She still thinks you're one of the good guys.'

Coupland raised a brow. 'I wouldn't know about that, son, but I know a good kid when I see one. Don't be the reason I have to pay her another visit.'

'You know your problem, Mr Coupland? You worry too much. We need to go.' He held his phone screen towards Coupland so he could see it. 'Mr Tunny's window is a narrow one; the last thing we should do is keep him waiting.'

Coupland stepped to one side. 'Then I guess we're done.'

*

Tunny's protégé was as different from the mean-looking gangster beside him as night was from day. Where Tunny was old school, Aiden Franks was definitely new. Dark hair slicked back into a topknot and dressed in a black silk shirt, he looked like he was about to go on Strictly. Wasn't a stranger to the sunbeds either, no Salford sun ever produced a tan like that.

Both men were seated either side of a Formica desk. It was obvious they'd decided who was going to do the talking. Tunny got to his feet as Coupland walked in. Glitter Ball remained seated, arms folded, brooding.

'What an unexpected surprise Mr Coupland. You here to look around our back room? It's available to hire, you know, weddings, funerals, acquittals…'

'I'll give it a miss if it's all the same to you,' said Coupland. 'Got a lot on my plate at the moment. It's the reason I'm here.'

'And there was me thinking you liked the ambience. Can I get you a drink?'

Coupland turned to Liam who was still hovering in the doorway. 'I'll have a beer, but I'm paying.' He fished a five pound note out of his wallet and handed it over. 'Keep the change.'

He turned back to Tunny. 'You said you'd call your jokers off before things got out of control and I appreciate that. So in return I'm giving you a heads up—'

'—You've got the bastard?'

Coupland held his hands up to quell the barrage of questions Tunny was about to spew in his direction. 'That's my point, a member of staff from Cedar Falls is currently helping with our enquiries and I'm here to make sure he comes to no harm.'

Eyes black like coal stared back at him.

'It's in relation to another matter, Kieran, not the fire,' Coupland explained.

'What then?'

'I can't say, you're going to have to trust me.'

'Not sure that's enough to stop me making my own enquiries, Mr Coupland. After all, you've piqued my curiosity now.'

Coupland sighed. 'Look, there have been allegations of abuse. Not from current patients,' he added hastily. 'But we have brought a member of staff in for questioning, and we may bring in others. Don't read anything into it, Kieran, that's all I'm saying.'

'Do the allegations relate to the period our Catherine was there?'

Coupland hesitated a second too long.

'Are you saying some bastard interfered with her?'

Coupland caught the look Tunny and Glitter Ball exchanged. 'Look, if I'm honest with you I don't know for sure, but I can't have you barging in with your bully boy tactics!'

Tunny lurched forward, slamming his hand onto the top of his desk, his eyes turning to mean little slits. 'You're having a laugh aren't you? If our Catherine was messed with in any way I'll skin the bastard, *and* that streak of piss who calls himself a manager…'

'We need space to carry on with our investigation, work out whether the abuse and the fire are linked. But I can't do that if you're breathing down everyone's necks.'

'Easy for you to say, you haven't just lost a member of your family.'

Coupland could be fast on his feet when he wanted to. He moved towards Tunny's desk and leaned over it, slammed his own fist down inches from the gangster's. 'You know nothing about me, Tunny! Don't start second guessing whether I give a toss about this case or not. Trust me, that won't end well.' Coupland realised he'd said too much the moment the words had left his mouth. He could only hope that Tunny hadn't picked up on it. It never paid to reveal any part of yourself to men like these.

The gangster's eyes flashed, but there was no malice when he spoke to his sidekick. 'Leave us. I want to talk to Mr Coupland alone.'

Glitter Ball threw a sullen look in Coupland's direction as he did as he was told, nearly colliding with Liam carrying Coupland's bottle of beer on a tray, a glass beside it.

Coupland lifted the bottle to his lips, waving the glass away with his other hand.

Tunny waited until they were alone, gesturing that Coupland take a seat, waiting for him to do so before returning to his own chair. 'You know, we're not so different, you and me, crime pays both our mortgages.'

'That'd be right,' Coupland sniped, resting the bottle on his lap. 'Like you've got a bloody mortgage.'

Tunny leaned forward, a smile on his lips. 'The people of this city call me a gangster. It's not a label I asked for, but if that's how they choose to see me I won't argue.'

'How do you see yourself then?'

Tunny thought before he spoke, his face growing serious until he found the right answer. 'I'm more like a social worker; after all, I make decisions that impact people's lives.'

An image of Shola Dube floated into Coupland's

mind. He struggled to find any similarities.

'It's not a position I take lightly,' Tunny added as though reading Coupland's mind. 'The community I grew up in is important to me. The younger generation, mind,' he nodded towards the door, where Glitter Ball and Liam had both made their exit,. 'they have different aspirations. I blame Netflix, to tell you the truth. Young men swaggering about like extras from *Narcos*. High drama but none of the values you and I grew up with.'

Coupland rinsed the beer through his teeth before swallowing. 'What, like *An eye for an eye*? Since when did that solve anything?'

'I'm thinking more of *'If the end justifies the means'*. From what I've heard that's more your style.'

Coupland put the beer bottle down by his feet, his eyes never leaving Tunny's. 'What do you mean?'

'I heard about the complaint that's been made against you.'

Coupland's eyes narrowed. 'Been reading the gutter press? Mind you, it's a step up from Janet and John books I suppose.'

Tunny smiled. 'I get my information from more reliable sources. Trust me, I know everything that goes on in this city, Mr Coupland, I make it my business to.'

'So you knew about the trafficking then?' Coupland challenged, referring to the case that had placed him under the microscope.

Tunny looked startled. 'Not to the extent it was going on. I thought they were bringing over cheap labour. I had no idea about the other stuff, I can assure you. What happened to that little girl was unspeakable. If it's any consolation I can tell you none of them are having an easy time of it inside. Rumour has it that Reedsy fella drove kids like her around the city, I'm not surprised you took a pop at him.'

Coupland said nothing, keen to maintain a degree of distance.

'Look, I just wanted to say I get you, Mr Coupland, I get you because you have a backbone and if there's anyone I trust with catching the bastard who took my sister away from us then it's you. And for the record you're right, I would have had someone pay the fella you're questioning a visit.'

'You know who it is then?'

'I got a call from Harkins minutes after your guys picked him up.'

Coupland's lip curled.

'Don't tell me you're surprised, people like him are only as good as their last conversation.'

'On that we're agreed,' Coupland said. 'Listen,' he added. 'If we're playing it straight you need to know I won't be working on the case much longer.'

'Why the hell not?'

'Personal reasons.'

Tunny regarded him. 'You think that's good enough?'

'Not really but it's the best you're going to get.'

Tunny's eyes grew dark. 'Did you know one of the victims?'

Coupland considered this, felt he was entitled to shake his head.

'Your little hissy fit earlier told me something was wrong…'

'Whatever.'

'…That you're more emotionally invested than you

should be.'

A shrug.

'You don't want to step aside do you, Mr Coupland? I think catching this bastard means more to you that you're letting on. What if I tell your bosses I don't want anyone else taking over? Won't that carry some sway?'

'More like the kiss of death, given the scrutiny I'm under.'

A sigh. 'I trust you, Mr Coupland, I know you'll do right by my family and in return I'll do right by yours.'

Coupland's eyes narrowed. 'What does that mean?'

'It means I'm a man who isn't used to hearing the word no. If you want me to cool my heels then you need to stay on this case – and I don't give a flying fuck whether it's done officially or not…and in return, as God is my witness, when whoever did it gets sent down he's as good as dead. As these young bucks would say, "Hashtag family", Mr Coupland.' He bumped his fist into the centre of his chest like a rapper at an awards ceremony. 'I have no idea what hashtag means, nor what the hundreds of emojis mean that have been posted onto Catherine's Facebook memorial page but I think you get my drift.'

Coupland stood. 'Revenge isn't all it's cracked up to be,' he sighed, picking up the beer bottle by his feet and placing it in the centre of Tunny's desk. 'There's always a price to pay.'

'Maybe it's a price worth paying,' said Tunny.

CHAPTER NINETEEN

Coupland stepped into the station's reception area and through the door marked *Authorised Personnel Only* in time to see Alex heading into interview room 3 carrying a forensic sampling kit. She looked uneasy when she saw Coupland, refusing to meet his gaze. His brow creased as he followed her into the room.

Johnny Metcalfe stared back at them. Apart from a tremor in his jaw his face was expressionless. He looked paler than the last time he'd seen him and Coupland wondered if he was about to be sick. Johnny was flanked by a grim-faced lawyer on one side and the blue haired care assistant who'd previously accompanied him on the other.

'What's going on?'

'I'm flying solo on this, Kevin, so don't bother offering to sit in.'

'I wasn't going to,' he lied. 'I wanted a quick word though.' He moved into the corridor and waited for Alex to join him. 'You know he needs to be declared medically fit before you can question him formally?'

'Already done, I filled out the paperwork last night and the duty doc came over with a colleague an hour ago to corroborate his decision. He's been declared fit.' It was clear Alex wanted to get on with the interview but he hadn't done yet. 'Heard anything from Ashcroft?'

'Bernie Whyte's admitted to being heavy handed at

times and doling out more meds than he should so that he could have a quiet shift – that tallies with a warning on his staff file. But he absolutely denies rape – he claimed a colleague was sacked a while back, only it was all done on the quiet, made to look as though he had left under his own steam. Ashcroft's following it up with Alan Harkins.'

Coupland nodded. Alex kept looking away from Coupland as she spoke, forcing him to move into her line of vision. 'What is it?'

A sigh. 'You said you were going to tell the boss about your mother.'

'Yeah, and I was, only when Ashcroft brought Whyte in he might as well have had a sign on over his head saying "give this guy a kicking". I had to go and see Tunny, to tell him to leave him alone. Turns out I was right to, our trustworthy care home manager had already phoned him with the news.'

'I wish you'd told me.'

'I didn't realise I had to run everything past you.'

'Well maybe you do when you promise to do one thing and then go and do another.'

Coupland sucked air through his teeth. '*Promise*? What am I, six?'

Alex shook her head, not in response to his question but to what she had done. 'The boss called me into his office not long after I thought you'd gone to see him.' Coupland waited. 'He said he wanted me to take over the reins on the Cedar Falls fire for a while and I asked him if I'd be allowed to keep you in the loop given the conflict of interest. "Conflict of interest?" he asked, turns out he was meaning so your time would be freed up to bring the hit and run case to a conclusion and prepare your defence for your Professional Standards hearing. He knew nothing about your personal connection to the case.'

'Which I bet he knows all about now…'

'What was I supposed to say? "Sorry, just disregard everything I've said for the last five minutes, I was having a brain fart?"'

Coupland sucked in a breath. 'Bollocks.'

Alex clearly hadn't finished. 'He wants to see you in his office,' she added.

Coupland looked up at the ceiling, 'I bet he bloody does.'

*

Five minutes into Mallender's tirade and Coupland had compiled a mental list of countries in alphabetical order although O and Q had proved elusive. He'd just made a start on American states but his concentration levels were starting to wear thin. The DCI showed no sign of letting up and his voice had gone up a notch as though he'd sussed Coupland was trying to block him out. 'All this time you've been working on a case that involves a member of your own family. What the hell were you hoping to achieve?'

It was one of those questions that didn't require an answer, but Coupland searched inside himself anyway in an attempt to rationalise his actions. Had he been trying to gain closure? Or Hell bent on a personal mission to avenge his mother's death? Coupland thought of his mother and at that moment he wanted to kick in the interview room door and drag the truth out of Johnny Metcalfe, for wasn't he the reason this woman he would never get to know was dead? And yet he couldn't summon up the rage. Whether it was because he'd never got to really know her, or he couldn't see a kid with limited reasoning turn into a killing machine, he couldn't be sure. 'Look boss, I promise you that I was on my way to tell you but I got side-tracked. I never had any intention of staying on the case once my mother's identity had been confirmed. Though to be fair it hasn't stopped me paying full attention to every aspect of the investigation, although leaving the evidence bag in my drawer was an oversight, a fuck up of the highest order. I just wanted to find out more about her…'

Mallender's expression changed from cloudy to thunderous.

'I take it you didn't know about the evidence bag…' Coupland muttered.

'For Christ's sake, Kevin, you can do without getting on the wrong side of the EMU with everything else that's going on! You leave yourself open to accusations of tampering if a defence lawyer gets wind of it. I'd expect this from a rookie, not someone with your supposed level of experience. You've kept your superiors and your team in the dark over this, which given the complaint from Austin Smith hovering over your head is foolhardy at best, or worst still, professional misconduct.'

'Yeah but we all know that complaint's bollocks.'

'No. It's not bollocks. You've said yourself his allegation is true – your admission is now online thanks to your inability to keep your mouth shut when it comes to handling the press. There's no doubt he'll get compensation and that expense has got to come from somewhere…'

Coupland closed his eyes. 'Once the hearing is out of the way I'll be on top form again boss. I won't have the same level of distractions. It's true this case has knocked me for six but I can still be useful – I can take a back seat, oversee statements, take on a more administrative role, whatever it takes to show I've learned the error of my ways.'

'It's against regulations.'

'Regulations! I've a good mind to go over to HR and ask them how the hell they'd feel if it was a member of their family lying in the mortuary, how inappropriate would it be then for them to want to be involved.' Rules were all very well when there was no chance of you ever breaking them. No cop would stand aside, and yet this was what the DCI was expecting him to do.

'I've built up a rapport with Kieran Tunny that we shouldn't underestimate. He's pretty much told me that if I leave this investigation he'll take matters into his own hands.'

Mallender's face screwed up in confusion. 'Have you been confiding personal information to a gangster?'

'Of course I haven't, I'm not a complete idiot! I told him I was trying to balance caseloads. But it made sense to try and soften the blow that my leaving the case would bring.'

'You shouldn't be telling him anything that could compromise an investigation or how the public view us. They're already twitchy at the number of stations closing down; if they start hearing that we can't manage our workloads we'll end up walking through a shit-storm.'

Coupland swiped a hand over his face as he waited for the inevitable.

'You know I don't have any choice in this. I'm taking you off the case.'

A sigh. 'Fine.'

'Actually it's not fine, you've flouted the rules, Kevin,

potentially put this whole investigation at risk.' Mallender's expression hardened, 'You've let me down, Kevin. Consider yourself lucky I haven't put you on a suspension. Now go home and think about what I've said.'

Coupland's head shot up, but there was no fight left in him. He did as he was told.

*

'How much longer have we got to wait?'

'How the hell do I know? But you know what he said, 'There's no show without Punch.''

'Do you even know what that means?'

A shrug. 'Other than this job isn't done till we've got the lot of 'em.'

'It's alright for him telling us to do these things. The stuff we do for him, if we get caught we get sent down.'

'Yeah, but he looks after our families, make sure they don't go without.' A sideways look. 'You already know that.'

The sound of air being sucked through teeth. 'Wouldn't you rather be there to do that yourself though? Looking after your kids I mean, rather than end up inside?'

'Course. But what else am I good for? Not like there's anyone else beating the door down to give me a job. Legit work, I mean.'

'Even so…' He turned the radio up a couple of notches, didn't want a lecture on how it was harder these days to find an unskilled job now robots and Eastern Europeans were doing all the menial work. Intimidation was all some men were good for.

His companion screwed up his face. 'What's this crap?'

'Stormzy.'

'Christ, he drones on a bit. Anyway, you'd better turn it down.'

A sigh. 'Yeah I know, don't want to draw attention to ourselves.'

The car they'd been waiting for slowed as it passed them, indicator blinking, before pulling into a parking space a few cars down. 'That's him,' he said, as Coupland climbed out of the driver's side and bleeped the car locked before striding to his front door.

SUNDAY

CHAPTER TWENTY

'I've been thinking.' Lynn said as they stood in the kitchen. It wasn't often that they got a chance to enjoy breakfast together. Their line of work meant one or other of them would be heading through the door with the dawn chorus but every once in a while their schedules permitted it. For it to happen on a weekend was a bonus. Lynn spread honey on toast while Coupland stood at the open back door blowing smoke into the garden. He took the mug of coffee she handed him, waving away the offer of toast while not trying to spill the tail of ash that had formed on his cigarette.

'What have you been thinking, my sweet?' he asked, distracted.

'We could invite your dad to dinner.'

Coupland tilted his head as he turned to face her, his eyes screwed up in confusion. 'You know, I could swear there's something wrong with my hearing, I was sure you just said you wanted to invite that miserable old git round for his tea.'

'I think it'd be nice, that's all.'

'Not for me, and by the time he's insulted your cooking, your choice in soft furnishings and the fella you're married to, not for you either.'

'Don't you think it's the right thing to do?'

Coupland took a final drag, stumping the cigarette out on the ashtray Lynn had bought for the patio table the year before. 'What, like putting down lame horses or sacking bent MPs? Sticking pins in my eyes would be the right thing to do just so I don't have to see his sarcastic face ever again.'

'You told me the news had really shaken him.'

'So?'

'Look at it as bridge building.'

'I heard on a quiz show there's a Bridge to Nowhere, did you know that?'

'For crying out loud, Kev!'

Coupland swore quietly. If it kept Lynn happy what harm could it do? He closed his eyes and shuddered. 'Fine, have it your way,' he said, dialling his father and relaying the invitation. Pulling a disappointed face at her when the old bugger said yes. 'Just don't say I didn't warn you,' he said as he plugged his phone into the charger on the kitchen worktop.

The radio was on in the background. Lynn turned up the sound when a duet came on, some actor and a singer famous for wearing a dress made of meat to an awards bash. Lynn loved it, had dragged him to the cinema to see the film that it had come from. Hadn't been nearly as bad as he'd expected, truth be told, though he'd be buggered if he was going to confess *that* guilty little secret.

His phone made a buzzing sound, signalling an incoming text. He moved over to retrieve it, entered his password to unlock the screen. A number he didn't recognise had sent him two photos. Frowning, he tapped to open them. The first image made the breath catch in his throat. A photo of him letting himself into his house the night before. A cold hand slithered round his chest as the second image loaded.

Lynn helping Amy lift Tonto's pram into the hall.

*

Coupland's face was like thunder as he stormed into the CID office. Alex was already at her desk. She looked up as he hurried towards her. 'Thought you weren't in today?' she asked, eyeing his dark jeans and hooded sweatshirt.

'Have you got a minute?' he barked, his expression telling her to make time even if she hadn't.

She followed him through to the canteen, to a table far away from eavesdroppers. He tapped onto his phone, slid it across to her. She stared down at the image of him at his front door, saw the date and time beneath it. 'Someone followed you?'

On this Coupland was emphatic. 'Not last night. I always check who is behind me; never take the same route home twice in a row.'

'But still.'

'I know, I know, if someone wants to find out where you live it's easy enough.'

'If they know you are married they find out where Lynn works and they follow her.'

'That's what I was thinking,' he said, his jaw tightening. After all, hadn't Lee Dawson tracked him down the year before through Amy? The consequences of which none of them could have predicted.

'Any idea who it's from?'

'Course I know who it's bloody from, isn't it obvious? I pay Tunny a visit, give him the heads up I won't be involved in the investigation anymore and lo and behold, he lets me know his men are watching my house.'

'Why, though?'

'That's the bit I'm not sure about. If it was to get me off his back he could have done this earlier.'

'Maybe he knew you wouldn't listen.'

'Wouldn't I? Not like I'm Robocop.'

'You have to report this, you know that don't you?'

'What, and have some overworked plod turn up at his door—'

'It'll be treated as priority Kevin, it's intimidation. They'll bring him in.'

'So what? For Christ's sake, Alex, even if I'd seen him take the photos with my own bloody eyes his lawyer's that good he'd convince me I was seeing things.'

'We can put a trace on the phone it's come from.'

'What? On a cash-bought pay as you go? Come on, let's not piss away more time and money than we have to.'

'You know there's a protocol to follow when a serving officer has been threatened.'

'It's more of a guideline…'

'Whatever you want to call it, Kevin, we're withholding information which may have some bearing on this case.'

'Not my case anymore.'

'Didn't realise you'd taken your bat and ball home,' Alex sighed.

'Don't you think I'm up to dealing with this?' Coupland's hands shook as he raked them through his hair. His body pulsed with a rage he was trying to subdue. Adrenaline was making it impossible for him to sit still, his legs twitched as though he was attached to the mains supply.

'You've done the right thing by coming to me; I'll get Tunny locked up for this. But we have to tell the boss.'

Coupland leaned forward and clasped his hands together, elbows resting on splayed legs. He stared at her and nodded. 'I don't want you putting your job on the line,' he said.

Alex clicked her tongue against her teeth. 'I'd never have guessed.'

They sat in silence, Alex considering her options while Coupland silently considered *his*. When he'd first opened the images he'd told Lynn to telephone in sick. When she'd refused he'd insisted on driving her to work. Said he'd send a car to pick her up if he was unable to.

'Come home safe,' she'd whispered before kissing him goodbye. They'd both agreed Amy needed to know what was happening; he'd gone up to Tonto's nursery where she was changing him, told her about the photo and her need to be extra vigilant.

'Is it happening again, Dad?' she'd asked, her arms circling the infant as she pulled him close. Something cold and heavy formed inside him.

'So what's it to be?' Alex asked eventually. 'Are you going to see the boss?'

Coupland said nothing.

'Look, I get it,' Alex said. 'I don't know what I'd do if I found those scumbags had been waiting outside my door one night. But you have to believe that I, and the rest of the team, will deal with this. I know it's hard to trust others but you're not the only one who's good at their job.'

He and Alex usually operated on the same wavelength but on this she was wide of the mark. It wasn't about having faith in his team or her ability to do her job, it was the need to be involved; about knowing you had done all that you could. It was about something else too.

Something primal.

Coupland picked up his phone, pushed himself to his feet. 'There's someone I *do* need to speak to,' he said.

A sigh. 'Don't tell me. I've got a feeling the less I know the better.' He turned to go. 'But Kevin,' she called after him.

'*What?*' he muttered over his shoulder. Now he'd made up his mind what to do he wasn't stopping for anyone.

'You're on dangerous ground.' Her voice carried over the canteen hum, several heads turned in her direction but she ignored them. 'Don't go throwing your weight around or you could end up losing your job.'

Coupland snorted. Like *that* fucking mattered.

CHAPTER TWENTY-ONE

The front of the wine bar was in darkness but Coupland wasn't taken in by the dreary façade. It wasn't like the main business was actually selling *drinks*. He did a circuit of the building until he found the door used for deliveries and other less salubrious transactions. It was locked when he tried the handle, and banging his fist on the door brought no response. He stepped back to take aim at the handle with his foot. Kept on kicking. Each time his foot made contact with the door it felt good, like he was connecting with the bastard that had invaded his space. He glared at the CCTV camera positioned in the doorway. 'I'm going nowhere, Tunny, I can do this all fucking day if I have to!'

'Is it happening again, Dad?'

'It's just a precaution, love,' he'd told her.

Kick.

'Come home safe.'

There were some promises he couldn't make.

Kick.

'Don't go throwing your weight around.'

What if that was all you had?

Kick.

The door was opened by a wiry youth in a thin cotton tracksuit. 'Mr Tunny wants me to take you through to his office—'

'—I know the way,' Coupland grunted, shoving past

him. The place was empty apart from a couple of cleaners and a barman doing a stock take. Neither paid any attention to the angry man charging upstairs. Coupland barged into Tunny's office, didn't give a toss about the muscle that might be waiting within it. Tunny was on his feet, a smile playing on his lips. Two youths in black trousers and pristine white shirts slouched on a sofa playing on an Xbox. Glitter ball was nowhere to be seen.

Coupland charged towards Tunny, stopping just short of the gangster so his words were understood. Loud and bloody clear. He moved forward so his face was inches away from his. 'You can do what you damn well want to me,' he hissed. 'I don't give a toss. But you send your trolls to sit outside my house, watching my family? That's a game changer.'

Tunny grinned.

'You think this is funny?' Coupland took a step closer, grabbed the gangster by his jacket lapels. The youths appeared either side of him, Xbox controls discarded.

'It's OK boys,' Tunny told them. 'Mr Coupland here was just letting off a bit of steam. He doesn't mean any harm.' He nodded in turn at both of them when they didn't move. 'You can stand down.'

Reluctantly they did as they were told, eyeballing Coupland until he let go of their boss and took a step back.

The gangster regarded him. 'No, I don't think it's funny. But at least you get it now.'

'What?'

'The point I was trying to make. The point you didn't seem to understand the last time you were here. Or weren't willing to understand. That this thing that has happened to my sister affects every member of my family, every single minute, of every single day. I need to do something. I have to respond in some way, for their sake, and Catherine's.'

The need to be involved.

Tunny hadn't finished. 'You've put me in an impossible situation, Mr Coupland.'

'How?'

'One minute you're asking me to call off the hounds because you're all over the investigation and in the next you're telling me you're stepping away from the case. You can't have it both ways. If you want to keep me on a leash you need to find the person responsible for my sister's death.'

Coupland stared at him, incredulous. 'You expect me to help you after sending someone to my home?'

'The instructions I gave them were clear Mr Coupland: stay outside. Do not approach. Don't hurt anyone.'

'Should I be grateful? Is that it?'

Tunny shook his head. 'I promise you. I meant you nor your family any harm. I couldn't see any other way to make you carry on with the investigation.'

'My colleagues are working all hours…'

'I want *you* on it.'

'My hands are tied.'

'Officially, maybe. But we both know you're not someone that lets things go easily.'

Coupland moved to the window, looked out on a city that had a backbone of steel. Crime lords and politicians operating cheek by jowl. Some days it was hard to tell one from the other. What happened in their past to make them turn out the way they did? Made them believe their way was the right one?

'See it as a compliment, Mr Coupland. If I thought you'd take a bung I'd have offered you one.'

Coupland turned from his vantage point to look Tunny up and down.

'I wasn't lying when I told you I treat everyone the same. That goes for those that piss me off too.'

'Are you threatening me?'

'When it comes to my family I don't make threats.'

'We're cut from the same cloth, you know. You and me. Circumstances may have put us on opposite sides of the fence but we're no different.'

'I'm nothing like you.'

'Fine. Tell yourself that if it helps you sleep better at night.'

'I sleep like a baby, thanks very much.'

'A baby with a serial killer for his dad?'

Coupland's stomach clenched. He pointed a finger in Tunny's direction. 'I'm warning you.'

'I'm just saying, it'll be interesting to see, as he gets older, whether there's any truth in all that nature versus nurture crap. His childhood will be the ultimate social experiment.'

Coupland moved closer, bared his teeth. 'Go on, knock yourself out. But remember this. You'll always be a gangster but I won't always be a cop. Know what I'm saying?'

Tunny's face grew serious. 'All I want is justice.'

It was Coupland's turn to smile. 'Folks are clamming up on you aren't they? That's why you want me on the case. Your bullying tactics haven't got you anywhere!'

'I wouldn't say that exactly,' Tunny countered. 'More like whoever did this has been damn good at covering their tracks. People can't tell me what they don't know. You're right about that, and something else too. I'm not going to crack this on my own. I need your help, Mr Coupland.'

'Then the intimidation stops.'

Tunny nodded.

Coupland backed away, satisfied. But not before something on Tunny's desk caught his eye. A printout of the photographs sent to his phone. Tunny followed his gaze. 'I'll have them shredded, Mr Coupland. The SIM card it came from has already been destroyed.'

Seems he really did run his firm like a corporate business. 'He sent you copies for your approval before he sent them to me?' Coupland asked.

'Something like that,' Tunny said, lifting the first printout and feeding it into a shredder by his feet.

Coupland's smile widened. It didn't matter that the original photo had been destroyed. The sight of the printed out images told him two things. That the photo had been taken from the passenger side of a car, and that it had been cropped before it was sent to him.

*

Liam Roberts had the swagger of a cocky sod. A cocky sod who had the ear of one of the most feared men in Salford. Sometimes that association went to their head; sometimes the arrogance was there to start with. Coupland clocked the attitude as he eyeballed Liam coming out of his mother's red brick terrace. The cocksure way he stood his ground even as Coupland thundered towards him, the smirk on his face when he dragged him down a back alley before shoving him against the wall.

'You ungrateful little bastard!' Coupland hissed.

'I don't know what you're talking about, honest, Mr Coupland!' The lie with a smile nailed on added insult to injury.

Coupland thought of the complaint hanging over his head, wondered whether another blot on his copybook would make much difference. 'What you said to me the other day was bang on, wasn't it? That it's not like you were destined for NASA or anything. Only I never had you down as thick as mince. Those photos you took. The ones of me and my family, outside my home. You were dumb enough capture your tattoo in the picture. I reckon it was Tunny who told you to get the photo cropped.'

Liam cocked his head. 'Whatever it is you think I've done, it wasn't me!' Even so, the smile started to slip.

'Don't waste my time kid; I recognised it, clear as day. The prayer beads. The phoney show of holiness. What is it with playing the hard man?'

'I'm not the one cornering some kid in an alley!'

Coupland sighed before releasing him, though stayed close enough to grab him if he made a run for it. 'You parked outside my home and you took a photograph of my wife and daughter.'

Liam's jaw muscles were working overtime, as though practising what he was going to say next. 'Mr Tunny told me to do it.'

'If he'd told you to fire a gun or run me through with a knife would you have done that as well?' Coupland could barely bring himself to think of other scenarios, ones that made the contents of his stomach turn to lead.

Liam said nothing.

'Yeah, well, your silence speaks volumes,' Coupland

muttered as he shook his head, peering at the youth through narrowed eyes. The knock off designer watch. The diamond chip in his ear. So many young men aspiring to be something they didn't need to be. 'I thought you of all people had your head screwed on, that running around with Tunny's gang was some demented phase that would pass. But I was wrong. You're starting to get a kick out of it.' He paused, weighing up whether he should say the thoughts forming in his head. 'Don't end up like your old man.'

'What…Dead?' Liam laughed. 'I'll try not to!'

'No. I mean so far in that there's no escape.' A pause as something occurred to Coupland. 'Is that what this is about? Trying to follow in daddy's footsteps? Isn't that what most boys do?' Coupland thought of his own messed up childhood and hoped to Christ he was wrong. Yet here he was, a bad tempered cop using his bulk to get results. Maybe the apple didn't fall that far from the tree after all.

Liam slumped against the back alley wall but the fight hadn't gone out of him if the glare he gave Coupland was anything to go by. 'It's never anything important is it? The last thing people say to each other? Nothing profound I mean. The last time my dad spoke to me I'd been giving him lip and he called me a waste of space. I watched him leave the house that day thinking at least I wasn't a thug. Not much of a conversation was it? In the grand scheme of things, I mean. Not much to look back on. Draw comfort from. Isn't that what people say to you, afterwards, that at least you have your memories? I was just a kid; I never got to the stage where we did things for each other because we wanted to. He told me to do things and I did them.'

Coupland blew air from his cheeks. 'So, you fell in with Tunny because life's been unfair to you, is that it? Like you're entitled to happiness?' He looked up at a sky full of rain clouds. 'None of us are guaranteed a golden ticket. The world doesn't owe us a living. I've seen kids like you come and go over the years, too many to mention, and it all ends the same way. A one way trip to Crown Court with your toothbrush and soap.' Coupland couldn't believe he was doing this. Being reasonable, when knocking seven bells out of him would feel so much better.

But wouldn't that make him a thug too, like his own old man, and Liam's? He sighed. 'For Christ's sake, do yourself a favour. You're mixing with dangerous people. Get out while you can. Move away; make a fresh start somewhere else.' Coupland took a breath. He leaned in close to Liam and lowered his voice, even though there was no one else around. He was already up to his gonads at work, what was a few more shovelfuls? 'Look, I'm going to give you a one-time only chance. But first I want you to look at me. Really look into this tired, fat face and tell me you'll make this lifeline I'm offering you count.'

Liam stared at him. Nodded. His face now looked as far from cocksure as was possible. 'What do I need to do?' He swallowed. 'He trusts me. He's already moving me up the ranks…'

'You need to leave. Today.' Coupland reached into his back pocket and pulled out his wallet. Pulled out several notes. 'I don't carry a lot of cash,' he said. 'You can never be too bloody careful. But this'll get you a ticket somewhere.'

Liam hesitated before taking Coupland's money. He

glanced up and down the alley before shoving it into his pocket.

'I can't make you leave but I've given you an option. You need to think long and hard about the choice you make.'

Liam nodded, rammed his hands into his anorak pocket in readiness to leave.

Coupland pressed his hand on his shoulder to stop him in his tracks. 'But know this,' he said evenly, his voice dripping with menace. 'You come near my family again and you can forget about Tunny. You're mine.'

*

Coupland's call to Alex was brief. He told her he'd spoken to Kieran Tunny and that the gangster admitted the photographs had been his ham fisted way of keeping Coupland involved in the investigation. He had his word it wouldn't happen again, so no harm done. She asked if he'd found out which of Tunny's cronies had taken the photo and he said no, he hadn't asked. Better he didn't know in case the scrote was fished out of the ship canal the following week and he got the blame.

He'd walked back to his car by the time the call ended. He slipped the phone into his pocket before opening his driver's door. Paused. Sometimes it worried Coupland how easily he got into the mindset of those he consorted with. To understand on some level why they went about their crime. As he climbed into his car he wondered if Alex had picked up on his lie. Whether right this minute she was checking A&E admissions for anyone brought in with unexplained injuries.

Whether her opinion of him had stooped that low.

*

Lynn had made a Lamb Tagine. An online recipe she'd found during her lunch break. She hadn't exactly typed 'What to cook for your estranged father-in-law' into the search engine but she might as well have done. She wanted the evening to go well, especially after the fright they'd had that morning over the photos some thug had taken. Kevin had been subdued when he'd picked her up from work, even though he'd telephoned her at lunchtime to say the matter was sorted, that he'd had a word in the right ear and they wouldn't be bothered again. He'd wanted to call his old man and cancel, said he'd much rather they had a night to themselves, a bit of peace after a calamity of a day. Lynn wouldn't hear of it, said his father had probably been looking forward to a home cooked meal so there was no way they were bailing out on him. She'd asked Amy to give the baby an early bath, put him to bed so they'd have a bit of peace during the awkward first hour or two, though as Kevin pointed out, Tonto starting to scream might be a useful distraction, they could pass him round the table if the conversation was really struggling.

'I've had worse,' the old man said when Amy asked if he was enjoying the meal. Coupland glared at him, made a point of going back for seconds even though his run-in with Tunny earlier had wiped out his appetite. Coupland sighed.

Ignore him, Lynn's eyes pleaded.

'This is the dog's bollocks love,' he said, 'beats cup-a-soup and a whiskey chaser.'

Lynn took the reference to Ged's diet as an opportunity to ask how he was keeping.

'Same as I've always done,' he told her. 'Not like I get any offers of help.'

Coupland put down his fork. 'The girls are always round at yours, fetching and carrying.' He turned to Lynn. 'Pat goes and does his cleaning once a week.'

Lynn giggled nervously. 'She could do with coming here.'

'Well, I didn't like to say,' Ged began, 'but your kitchen units look as though they could do with a wipe down.'

'So, you were in the police, like my Dad then,' Amy said, reaching for a second helping of rice. She wasn't normally a big eater, but sensed a show of solidarity was needed. Her mum had worked hard preparing a special meal for grandad, the least she and Dad could do was polish it off.

'Yeah, mind you, it was different back then. We had to get off our arses and actually chase the bastards. Now it's all CCTV and Crimewatch.'

'It's not like that at all,' Coupland said. 'CCTV helps, but it doesn't tell you where a suspect is hiding out or whether they're dangerous when you do find 'em.'

As for Crimewatch, he had little to say about it. That was pleasant, anyway.

A smile played on the old man's lips. 'Still, some things never change. Like the irresistible urge to give a toerag a pasting if you think they deserve it.'

'You read the article, then.'

Should have been no surprise, Coupland supposed. He dined out on other folks' misery, that it was his son in the firing line all the better. And here he was, reeling him in, just like old times.

Lynn glanced at Coupland before piping up. 'The

internal investigation will give Kevin a chance to have his say. It doesn't matter what the press choose to write.'

'It does if all the attention gives GMP a bad name. He'll be out on his arse then.'

Coupland ignored the jibe. 'Look Dad,' he began, 'I've been thinking, if no one else comes out of the woodwork for Mam we'll need to start making arrangements.'

The old man's head swivelled in his direction. 'What are you talking about?'

Lynn's glance implied she was asking the same question but refused to join in out of loyalty.

Coupland attempted to convey a 'sorry' to her before answering his old man. 'Funeral arrangements, that sort of thing. No one else has come forward so I'm guessing we're her only family.'

That noise again, the one that grated on Coupland, making him want to place his hands around the old bastard's neck and squeeze hard. 'You're on your bloody own with that then, I'll not be wasting a penny of my pension on her, there's precious little enough of it as it is. Have you told your sisters what you're intending?'

Coupland hadn't even had time to think about it himself. The thought had just popped into his head and he'd blurted it out. For all he knew they could be just as appalled. Not as if any of them had much put by. He and Lynn had diverted their rainy day funds in Tonto's direction but he was sure they'd find a way. 'No, but—'

'You never did think anything through, they'll be shocked you've even suggested it. Mind you, you didn't know her like they did.'

'Maybe that's the point,' Amy said, sending a smile in her father's direction. 'I think it's a great idea.'

'Well you would, wouldn't you,' countered the old man. 'You won't be the one paying for it.'

Lynn sighed. For want of something to do she picked up the ladle, asked Ged if he'd like some more.

'No, ta,' he said, 'it'll be a bugger trying to shift this heartburn as it is.'

Lynn's smile was beginning to slip. 'Oh, right,' she said.

'I'll have more,' Coupland said.

'Do you think that's a good idea?' his old man sniped. 'You never were one to leave anything on your plate and it shows.'

'Kev's lost loads of weight,' Lynn protested. 'Not that that he needed to…'

The old man's mouth formed into a cruel smile. 'Your mother used to say carrying you was like carrying a sack of spuds.'

'All babies are like that,' Amy observed. 'When I was pregnant—'

'—Save your breath, Ames,' Coupland cut in. 'He doesn't give a toss.'

Coupland got to his feet, began picking up plates that weren't ready for clearing. 'Might as well make a start on the washing up.' He wondered how much it would cost to put a hit on the old bastard. Worth every penny, he reckoned.

'I'll help you, Dad,' Amy offered, making it clear that, for the time being, she'd spent as much time in the company of her grandfather as she could bear.

Lynn waited while Coupland and Amy left the room. Looked at the miserable old man sat opposite, wondering why the hell she'd bothered.

'Wow,' she said, picking up the paper serviette on her

lap and screwing it into a ball before dropping it onto the table. 'You're a piece of work, aren't you?'

Ged raised his eyebrows at her.

'Don't come over all innocent now. Your jibes, your little one-liners. All the while looking at me for approval as though I'm actually going to join in and laugh with you.' She pointed in the direction of the kitchen then to herself. 'I'm team Kev all the way, me. He warned me about you but I persuaded him to give you a chance. I thought after all these years you'd have mellowed. Maybe regretted even, the way things had turned out.'

Ged leaned back in his chair, a lazy grin forming on his face. 'Come on love, I didn't mean any harm.'

Lynn's face hardened. 'Isn't that what bullies always say, that no offence was intended? That their victim should grow a thicker skin? You know how much of his childhood he's told me about?'

Ged shook his head.

'Nothing. Not one bloody thing. Speaks volumes that, doesn't it? I mean, if it was mildly shit he'd have moaned about it but I'm talking complete radio silence. He's wiped his memory of you like a war veteran might wipe away the memory of the IED that blew off their leg. And there I was, stupid enough to think the two of you round the table would be a good thing.'

Ged studied her. 'You could do better, you know.'

'You think so? He may not be the most demonstrative of blokes but he gave me a piece of him he knew I could break. And believe me, after meeting you I'm amazed he let me in at all.'

'You're as bad as his mother.'

'Why? Because I won't take your bullshit?' She shook

344

her head, 'You know, I'm a nurse, and it's against every bone in my body to give up on someone. But I'm telling you, if you want to be part of this family you need to put some effort into being nice to him or we're done.'

'Who said I did?' he said, getting to his feet.

'Your choice,' Lynn muttered as she reached for her phone.

'No pudding then?' the old man smirked as Coupland returned empty handed.

'Got it in one,' said Lynn.

With Ged dispatched in a taxi they cleared the table, moving into the front room to eat chocolate cheesecake. Amy could be heard via the baby monitor singing nursery rhymes while she changed Tonto for the umpteenth time.

Coupland turned to Lynn, 'So, how was it for you?'

Her spoon paused midway to her mouth while she considered her answer. 'Well, he certainly lived down to your expectations.'

'Trust me; he was on his best behaviour there.'

'Then I'm sorry, I should never have forced you into it.'

Coupland grinned. 'Christ, is this you finally admitting you were wrong about something, and, newsflash, that I was right?'

'Don't push your luck, Kevin Coupland. You're still a prize prick most of the time, you know that?'

'I know only too well,' he muttered, his mouth forming a thin line as he thought of Austin Smith and the flash of anger that may yet cost him his career.

MONDAY

CHAPTER TWENTY-TWO

The station reception was full of reporters vying for information on the hit and run. News of the dawn raid on the warehouse where James McMahon worked had leaked onto social media, the Evening News and local tabloids wanted details confirming before they ran the story. The desk sergeant had a phone clamped to his ear while holding his palm out to stop the deluge of questions coming his way. He eyed Coupland as he headed through the waiting area. 'Trying to get someone from above my pay grade to deal with this but no-one's bloody answering. Don't suppose you can...?'

'What? Say something else that will come back to bite me? Where's Cueball?'

'Processing the drugs that were seized.'

Coupland sighed, 'I suppose I could get an update, run it by the press office to see what we're allowed to say...'

'Good man,' the desk sergeant beamed. He returned the phone to its cradle and swept his extended arm in Coupland's direction. 'Ladies and gentlemen, if you could all take a seat my colleague here will be back with a statement.'

Coupland darted through the Authorised Personnel door before anyone tried to nobble him for a pre-statement sound bite.

Cueball was making his way up the stairs from the EMU. When he clocked Coupland in the corridor he bounded up the remaining steps, his face resembling a cat that had found a large bucket of cream. 'I was coming to look for you Sarge,' he said. 'Just needed to complete the chain of evidence forms first. We've seized just shy of sixty grand's worth of coke and ecstasy tablets, all stuffed into bags of sweets and sherbet dips.'

'Christ.'

'Made two arrests as well. A fella on the packing line plus a security guard.'

'Did you seize the CCTV tapes?'

Cueball nodded. 'The recording system is operated via a network and I've been given the access code so we can view footage from any desktop here. That was going to be my next task. I'm assuming you'll want to do the interviews?'

'And steal your thunder?' Coupland shook his head. 'I'll go through the CCTV footage. I was going to give the press a holding statement to get them off our backs until the interviews have been conducted but I reckon you should do the honours, you've earned it.'

'You sure, Sarge?'

Coupland nodded. 'Enjoy your moment in the sun when it happens. Trust me, there's always a dirty great cloud looming ready to rain on your parade.'

Coupland was happy enough to fob off the journalists with a 'Watch this space' response so that Cueball got his moment of glory, and even more delighted Shelley and Danny Martin's intelligence had resulted in disabling a feral drug operation. He hoped the warehouse security tapes would reveal another link in the chain leading them to McMahon's killer.

There was an awkward atmosphere in the CID room. The briefing on the Cedar Falls fire had finished and detectives moved round Coupland carefully as he sat at his desk, averting their eyes the way people do when passing someone who's been bereaved. Alex had informed them about his mother then, and that from now on he was persona non gratis as far as that particular investigation was concerned. He turned on his computer and typed the log-in details and access code Cueball had emailed him into the prompt that came up when he searched for the warehouse's secure log-in. The site advised that the footage was stored online for 30 days before it was re-used, so there were several files still available that had been recorded in the run up to McMahon's death.

'Christ, Sarge, I'm really sorry,' Ashcroft said, stopping at Coupland's desk. He held a folder in one hand and car keys in the other. 'If there's anything I can do…'

Coupland shrugged without looking up. He didn't know how to respond, hadn't worked out his own feelings, let alone know how to articulate them. 'Just make sure you catch the bastard,' he said, staring at the screen, waiting for the file he'd selected to load.

'Heard there's been a breakthrough with the hit and run case.'

Coupland nodded, pointing to the video that started playing on his screen: 'McMahon's place of work.' The footage was from a camera positioned at the entrance to the warehouse's loading bay, a concrete area separated from the main warehouse by a metal shutter. Coupland peered at the high definition image of a man as he pushed a button to open the shutters, his hand raised in greeting at the driver of a small van that had reversed into the bay.

'That's McMahon,' he said, pointing to another figure as he ducked beneath the shutter before it had fully opened, pulling a pallet of goods towards the vehicle's rear. Coupland looked at the date at the top of the screen. 'Taken two days before he was mowed down.'

They watched McMahon load the goods into the van while his colleague checked the items against an inventory on an electronic device which the recipient signed by dragging his index finger across the screen.

'Looks legit to me,' said Coupland, fast forwarding until another van reversed into the bay and the same process started all over again. 'Guess it's going to be a long day,' he said, reckoning a decent coffee from the café across the precinct might ease the monotony.

Ashcroft seemed in no hurry to be on his way. 'Problem?' Coupland asked.

The DC considered this. 'Not really…just wondering whether you're still involved in the investigation into the care home abuse alleged by Mark Flint…'

Coupland turned to him and sighed. 'Probably not, but that doesn't mean I can't help…'

A nod. 'I went to see the care assistant who'd been sacked from Cedar Falls following complaints of assault. He and Bernie Whyte used to work together. Reckons he was set up.'

'By Whyte?'

'Reckoned so, said he'd not been there long enough to make anything of it though. Harkins told him he wouldn't bring the police in if he went quietly, said it wasn't worth the paperwork.'

'I bet he did,' said Coupland, hitting the play button

then fast forwarding again when McMahon went back inside the warehouse. 'And where was he when these assaults were taking place?'

'That's the thing. I've been working through the scant employment details Harkins keeps and cross matched them against the date and times of the alleged assaults and the same three male members of staff are on duty each time. Harkins, Whyte and this fella, Tim Russell. They're all performing tasks that leave them unaccountable, Harkins is in the office, while the other two alternate between making beds and preparing the day's medication.'

'None of the complaints were reported to the police, so there's no DNA, right?'

'That's about the extent of it, Sarge.'

'Did the complaints stop after this fella was sacked?'

'Seems that way.'

'That's hardly a resounding yes,' Coupland said, hitting the pause button once more. He turned to give Ashcroft his full attention. 'Have you worked your way through the statements that Turnbull and Robinson took from previous patients who'd made complaints?'

'Yeah, and those complaints tie in with when this fella worked there. But what if our perpetrator was clever and deliberately went to ground once he'd been sacked and couldn't take the blame anymore?'

'Come on, we're talking about Harkins or Whyte for this, would you describe either of them as clever? Besides, the urge to abuse someone doesn't disappear for long if that's how you're wired, it may become dormant for a while but it'll raise its head soon enough.'

'That was my thought, only it leads me to the question were any of the current patients abused. I mean, we know

Harkins has had it in for Johnny, though we don't know the extent of it – could be nothing more than a clash of personality. If you ask me we're spending far too long looking at that kid for the fire.'

'Well, I'm with you on that,' Coupland said, pressing the play button once more with his hand hovering over fast forward for when the approaching vehicle had been loaded.

'What if there are current patients being abused but are too frightened to come forward?' Ashcroft asked.

Coupland considered this. 'No DNA was found on Catherine Fry and as for the other victims all the forensic evidence was destroyed. Turnbull questioned everyone on Cedar Falls' register, albeit to a limited extent, and nothing came up.'

'Yeah, but they were questioned with a member of staff from the home present each time. And his questions weren't specifically about abuse, more about trying to identify a patient with an axe to grind. This is different. I'm looking for current patients who *choose* to keep quiet.'

Coupland had reached the end of the file, clicked the 'Next' button to view the following night's footage. 'This'll need careful handling, but you're right,' he said, 'the patients need to be questioned again but with an independent appropriate adult.'

Ashcroft nodded; tucking the file under his arm he thanked Coupland for hearing him out. 'I'd better start making some calls.' He pocketed his car keys and returned to his desk with purpose, a spring in his step that hadn't been there earlier when he felt he was getting nowhere.

'You're going to have to keep Alex in the loop on this as it may flag up further suspects for the arson,' Coupland reminded him.

Ashcroft cleared his throat. 'And your mother's murder, Sarge.'

A pause. 'That too,' said Coupland.

It wasn't the white van reversing into the loading bay on his screen that caught his attention. Or the fact that when McMahon ducked under the metal shutter this time he looked shifty as hell. Coupland watched as he pulled a pallet containing several boxes towards the rear of the van, while the driver walked round to look inside them. There was no electronic docket to sign this time, just a bumping of fists to confirm all was good with the consignment. It was then that he saw it. The name 'Gillian' inked along the driver's forearm. A name that if Coupland wasn't mistaken had been transformed into a script saying 'In God's Arms,' a string of prayer beads beneath it.

Coupland dropped his head into his hands and groaned. 'No wonder he'd been given a bloody company smartphone,' he muttered. He hit rewind and played the footage one more time in the vain hope he'd been hallucinating. That he hadn't really seen Liam Roberts collecting a shed load of drugs from a man killed in a hit and run two days later.

The same Liam Roberts he'd given money to yesterday and told to get out of town.

*

'For crying out loud Kevin, you did WHAT?'

'I thought I was giving him a chance! He'd had a rough time of it growing up, didn't think landing him with a criminal record was going to do him any favours.'

'Seems he's capable of doing that all by himself,' Alex volleyed.

Coupland blew out a long breath. 'I know, I got it wrong. Big time.' They were sat in the canteen. Coupland had asked Alex if he could have a word out of earshot of the team. Didn't see the point of advertising what a knob he'd been. He'd spent the afternoon looking for Liam. A brief word with his mother confirmed he hadn't been back home since Coupland had collared him the previous day, nor was he at Tunny's wine bar. Moving drugs around the city didn't mean he was responsible for the hit and run as well but either way if word got out Coupland had given him money he'd be out of his job faster than it took to say aiding and abetting an offender.

'Have you told the boss yet?'

'Are you serious? He'd have no choice but to flag it up the food chain and that'd be me put on suspension for definite.'

Alex looked thoughtful. 'I suppose it's not as bad as it sounds. You hear about rotten apples who take bungs from gangsters, but I've never come across it happening the other way round.'

'And that's good?'

'Well, it's enough of a grey area for them to scratch their heads over.'

'My cup runneth over,' Coupland drawled, rubbing his hands over his face.

'Have you put out an APB?'

Coupland threw his head back and laughed. 'Christ, I didn't give him enough cash to flee the country. More likely a couple of nights in a B&B in Liverpool than a new life in the sun. I wanted to give him space to think about the choices he was making.'

'Yeah, well we're past that. He's a person of interest in a hit and run, Kevin, we need to find him.'

'I know, and I reckon he spent yesterday dossing on a mate's sofa while he thinks about his next move. Look…I'm pretty sure we can flush him out,' he said, an idea forming in his head.

Alex shook her index finger at him. 'Whoa, for a minute there I thought you said "We".'

'Are you bailing on me?'

Alex threw her hands in the air. 'I've got a fire that's resulted in a multiple homicide to solve, not to mention getting a handle on the abuse allegations that are coming to light.'

'Yeah but they're connected, and Ashcroft knows what he's doing.'

'Still no walk in the park, though. I've had to let Johnny Metcalfe go. He's not able to explain his whereabouts in the lead up to the fire or how he managed to slip out of the isolation room he was in but equally we've no evidence to pin him to a charge of arson.'

'Keep sifting, he's hiding something, but it may not be the thing you're expecting.'

Alex studied him, 'Abuse?'

'Starting to sound like it. Get Ashcroft onto it. Alan Harkins or Bernard Whyte are the most likely suspects and I know who my money's on.'

'Metcalfe reckons Harkins hates him.'

'So maybe there's more to it.' Coupland paused. 'Look, this has the potential to turn into a career defining case for you. Are you really prepared to stand back and watch mine get flushed down the pan?'

Alex threw him the look she gave tradesmen who wolf whistled when she walked past a building site. The look that stopped their cat-calls mid track. Coupland shifted under her gaze. Wondered if he'd called it wrong.

'Let's not forget Liam works for Kieran Tunny; whatever he's done he's done on the gangster's say so. We go after him, we end up going after Tunny. We'll need back up for that.'

'Agreed…' said Coupland. 'So are you in?'

'You're a piece of work, you know that?' she sighed. 'What in God's name do you want me to do?'

*

The tweet she sent out was short and to the point. In some ways it was no different to the communications the press office had sent out during Operation Sabre, when GMP named and shamed Salford's top criminals, asking for the public's help to get them off the streets. A grainy photo of Liam Roberts taken from the warehouse CCTV footage was embedded into the tweet, the message below it read:

Wanted in connection with a serious crime – police are appealing for help to stop this man peddling toxic children's sweets across the city.

The only real difference, if someone wanted to be pedantic, was that the message hadn't been distributed with The Super's blessing, which was career Russian Roulette if Coupland's plan backfired. Within seconds the post was being retweeted and commented on by members of the public, with names being tagged of people that might know Liam Roberts or his associates.

Thirty minutes later Alex sidled up to Coupland's desk. 'The retweets are going off the radar, people who don't normally engage with us are indignant that their kids could be targeted by dealers.'

'It's working, then,' said Coupland. 'By the time he wakes from whatever sofa he's been dossing on there'll be half a dozen messages from his mates warning him to keep a low profile. Best thing he can do is turn up to work as normal – one of the benefits of being in tow with a gangster is the protection that brings – no one'll have a pop at him without Tunny's permission.'

*

Krispy returned from lunch chomping on a donut, oblivious to the clumps of chocolate icing dropping onto his trousers. He caught Coupland staring at him and his face paled. 'Shit, Sarge, I forgot to pass on a message. Your Federation Rep called. He said you'd arranged a meeting with him for today. He didn't seem best pleased when I told him you were out.'

'That's all I need,' Coupland muttered. 'Did he leave a message?'

Krispy began stabbing at a brown stain that had formed around his crotch, anything that prevented him seeing Coupland's displeasure. 'Said he'd see you at the Professional Standards hearing. If you can be bothered to turn up, that is.' Krispy's cheeks flooded as he looked up at Coupland. 'His words, Sarge, not mine,' he added hastily.

'Forget it,' Coupland sighed. 'I've got bigger fish to fry.' He was looking through the Facebook memorial page created for Catherine Fry by her family. Close to two hundred people had already posted their condolences, many of them strangers. 'I don't get it,' he muttered, summoning Krispy over to take a look. A variety of images had been posted to convey the depth of emotion felt following Catherine's death. 'What is it with these bloody emojis?'

'It's just a form of shorthand, Sarge. A way for people to express how they're feeling.'

'Yeah, 'cos nothing conveys sorrow like a row of crying faces.' There were sad faces. Loudly crying faces. Faces that resembled something from The Scream. A broken heart. Rosary Beads. Hands clasped in prayer.

Coupland let out a slow breath. 'Jesus wept.' He didn't need to look at the profile of the person who'd posted the last emoji. Instead he put a call through to Shola Dube. Let it ring several times. Nor did he bother with niceties when she answered; instead he asked her for the name of the boy that she'd worked with. The one she'd told him about, who'd suffered a trauma but whose lack of symptoms meant he'd slipped through support service cracks. Shola didn't hesitate, gave him none of the bollocks about data protection, just came right out and told him the name. A name he should bloody well have suspected.

He was on his feet, reaching for his car keys. 'Liam Roberts started the fire!' he shouted over to Alex.

Alex blinked in confusion. 'I thought we were after him for the hit and run?'

Coupland screwed up his face. 'Yeah, I dunno, that too maybe. But he started the fire, I'm sure of it.'

Alex was halfway to his desk but was he already at the door. 'You're off the case remember, you need to tell me

360

what's going on and I'll deal with it.'

'I don't have time.'

'Then I'm coming with you.'

'You need to arrange back up, tactical unit, the full shebang. If my hunch is right then we're going to bloody need it.'

'Do you know where he is then?' Coupland glanced at his watch. 'I do now,' he said, giving her the address.

Not every crime could be solved using the PACE handbook, sometimes it really was just about keeping your eyes open, paying attention to the detail most folk didn't give a toss about. Habits and haunts. In the end, when it came down to it, most folk were predictable. Coupland flicked the windscreen wipers on to clear the rain spatters that were blighting his view. In contrast, the thoughts jumbling for space in his head became suddenly clear. He pulled out his phone and jabbed at the Google icon, typing in the details of what he was looking for where prompted. He hit the search button, plugging his phone into the hands free system before dialling the number that came up.

The drive would take ten minutes with his foot down.

*

Tunny was already seated in the barber's chair, passing the time of day with Ken while he shaved his scalp. 'Thought you were going for a change of style,' Coupland commented as he entered the shop, careful to keep things casual while he got the lay of the land.

'Perhaps you can't teach old dogs new tricks after all,' Tunny replied.

Liam glared at Coupland from beside Tunny's chair.

'What are you even doing here?' he hissed.

'Same as I've always done, Son, keeping the good people of Salford out of harm's way.'

'Is that right?' The young man's weight shifted from one foot to another. 'This is harassment, this is, and you're bang out of order.'

'Wind your neck in, knob end. Did I give you permission to speak?' Tunny turned in his seat as much as was possible while the barber ran the shaver over the back of his head, the skin around his mouth tight. 'Liam showed me what you've posted on social media. Whatever happened to innocent until proven guilty? You've practically hung him out to dry.'

'That was my intention,' Coupland said, his eyes seeking Liam's, 'Wasn't it?'

Liam dropped his head, compliant once more. Satisfied, Coupland turned his attention back to Tunny. 'I promised you I'd keep you updated with any news,' he said, 'And I can finally say that I have some.' He turned to look out of the shop window as a van pulled up across the road, ignoring the yellow lines and the sign that said 'Loading Only'.

'Thinking of dobbing them in to the traffic cops?' Tunny asked.

Coupland shook his head. 'If I called in every violation I saw we'd be tied up in paperwork. Sometimes you need to choose your battles.'

The gangster's eyebrow raised a fraction. 'Sounds interesting. Go on.'

'I always thought the culprit behind the fire was bound to be close to home. An act of intimidation gone wrong, and we know how irritating Harkins can be. Now hear me out,' he said, raising his hand to silence any objections. 'I know it cuts both ways, it could have been a rival trying to hit you where it hurts. Either way I fully expected a route back to you. The abuse allegations that came to light provided us with a motive – the culprit could have been a patient seeking revenge. But the callousness of the act, the disregard for the lives lost made me realise my initial suspicion wasn't that wide of the mark after all.'

'You got a death wish, Mr Coupland? There was no reason for me to intimidate Alan Harkins; he's like putty in my hands. I thought you and me had an understanding yet you march in here accusing me of killing my sister?'

Coupland turned to Tunny. 'I wasn't talking to you, I was talking to Liam.'

Liam's cheeks flooded with colour. He leaped towards the barber's apron and pulled out a flash of steel. He was faster on his feet than the men standing beside him; side-stepping their lunges he slashed it against Tunny's neck. Only the razor had been replaced with something blunt.

Coupland charged forward and put Liam into an arm lock. 'There's an armed unit outside, keep back!' he yelled at the henchmen moving towards them, keeping as much distance as he could between Tunny and his would-be assassin. He'd put Liam's bitterness down to youthful rebellion, but now he understood it had hidden some-thing much darker.

'I may not have got to you but at least I got your sister!' Liam spat at Tunny. 'Now you know what it feels like to lose someone you love! All those years you said you knew how I felt, but how could you? The only way you'd truly understand was if I took something away from you that you cared about.'

Tunny's hand shook as he rubbed his neck. 'Why you little—'

A red dot appeared on his forehead, several more appeared on his henchmen.

'I told you to keep back!' Coupland warned. 'Put your hands above your head. Let my officers take him away.'

The gangsters stayed still while armed officers jumped out of the unmarked van and stormed into the shop. Tunny was still cursing, his arms beginning to lower. Coupland glared at him. 'No sudden movements man, for Christ's sake don't give them the excuse they've been looking for.'

It was as if the occupants of the room were playing a game of statues. Coupland waited while the Tactical Unit Manager gave the signal that the room was secure before handing Liam over. Once he had been taken away, and the officers stood down, he let out a long sigh. 'Elvis has left the building,' he said, moving towards Tunny who had slumped in the barber's chair. He was breathing heavily, his minions stood around him unsure what to do.

'So that's the reason you were here!' Tunny gasped, staring at Coupland, his face clouding with anger. 'I was like a father to that boy!' he snarled.

'You wouldn't have had to be if his old man hadn't died on the job. A job you'd orchestrated.'

'Why the hell didn't you warn me?' He turned to his barber, 'And you for that matter.'

'I told him it would most likely save your life,' Coupland said, 'and because you'd have made Liam disappear, and I need him to stand trial.'

'Why does it matter?'

Coupland took a breath. 'Because my mother was in

the fire. She worked there.' Coupland said her name.

Tunny nodded in recognition. 'My condolences. My sister liked her. One of the good ones, in my view.' He stared as Coupland moved suddenly and walked to the other side of the room, a noise coming from low down in his throat, but when he turned his face gave nothing away.

'There'll be questions to answer, Tunny, like your involvement in that hit and run last month, but there's something more pressing I need to attend to.'

Tunny tilted his head as he regarded Coupland. Waited until the detective had reached the shop door before speaking next. 'Something else we have in common, Mr Coupland,' Tunny observed.

'What's that then?' Coupland asked, pausing in the doorway.

'Grief.'

*

The custody sergeant stared back at Coupland, refusing to play ball. Word had gone round about Coupland's mother; there was no way he was going to let the moody detective anywhere near Liam Roberts.

'If I was going to do anything to him I'd have done it by now!' Coupland reasoned but his words fell on deaf ears.

'The only person I'm letting in that cell is DS Moreton or the DCI himself and if you've a problem with that take it up with them. I'm doing you a favour, man,' he said quietly.

Deflated, Coupland headed to the incident room to bargain with Alex who wasn't as polite as the custody sergeant, giving Coupland two words in reply.

DCI Mallender was more restrained: 'Zip it Kevin,' he said, when Coupland turned up at his door. 'It's for your own good.'

To make matters worse the CID room resembled the Marie Celeste. Only Turnbull could be seen at his desk, tapping on his computer keyboard.

'Where is everyone?'

'Krispy and Ashcroft are interviewing Alan Harkins and Bernie Whyte regarding the abuse allegations. DS Moreton's just headed downstairs to interview Liam Roberts while Robinson oversees a search on his home.'

Everyone bar Coupland had a purpose. Seeing as he was surplus to requirements he moved to his desk and logged onto his PC. He scrolled through his emails until he found the report Krispy had produced listing Cedar Falls' patients in chronological order, cross checking it against patients who'd admitted they'd suffered abuse. An hour later and he was convinced of one thing: His mother hadn't worked there when Mark Flint, Helen Foy or Colin Grantham were patients, but if Harkins or Whyte turned out to be the abuser she had certainly worked alongside them. Had she known what was going on?

'Kevin!'

Coupland looked up to see Alex hurrying into the CID room and making a beeline straight towards him.

'You really are on a fast track to inspector if you've charged him already.'

Alex's smile was fleeting. 'Let's not get ahead of ourselves, though it does feel as though the case is finally coming together. Robinson's found a pair of gloves at Liam's home with lighter fuel residue on them.'

Yet instead of doing a jig she perched on the edge of Coupland's desk and picked at a nail. He put her reticence down to caution. An unwillingness to count chickens until they'd been cracked open with a mighty sledgehammer. 'Can't beat a good honest to God confession,' he said.

Alex nodded, 'Turns out he's been supplying Bernie Whyte with cannabis. Their paths crossed one visiting time when Liam accompanied Kieran during a visit to his sister. Said he took one look at Whyte and recognised a stoner when he saw one. He approached him and offered him a regular supply at a discount. Off the books, so to speak. Bernie worked the night shift; most evenings would nip out through the fire exit for a sly smoke in the garden. Liam knew Whyte's pattern, knew he left the door ajar so he could slip back in without being seen. On the night of the fire he waited while Whyte slipped out and he slunk in with a couple of cans of lighter fluid.'

'Is Krispy still interviewing Whyte?'

Alex nodded. 'I've just spoken to him, for obvious reasons Whyte isn't admitting to smoking dope at work but it explains his absences during each shift.'

Coupland sat back in his chair. 'There's every chance Harkins knew what he was up to and used the time Whyte went AWOL to his advantage.'

'That's what I was thinking. All he had to do was wait for Bernie to slip outside before picking a patient and subjecting them to all kinds of hell – if they did complain Whyte wouldn't have an alibi, one that he'd be happy to own up to, anyway. I'm on my way to sit in while Ashcroft interviews Harkins. Today's events have been a game changer as far as he's concerned.'

Alex looked into the middle distance as though, like

for Coupland earlier, she was seeing things more clearly. 'Now Liam's opened up he can't stop. He's confessed to soaking several of the bedroom carpets with fuel as he couldn't be sure which one was Catherine's. He knew the place would go up like a tinder box but once he'd got the idea he didn't care about the consequences. He's given me a full account – he wants the glory of being the person who hit Tunny where it hurts.'

Coupland ran his forefinger and thumb over his chin. 'Why now, though? He's been working for Tunny for a while.'

'He said it was the hit and run that tipped him over the edge.'

Coupland frowned. 'I don't get it. You're telling me Liam had been working with McMahon but he wasn't involved in the hit and run?'

Alex nodded. 'He said he was there when Tunny ordered McMahon's execution. He said it was the last straw, made him realise that as far as Tunny was concerned everyone was disposable. Two more kids had lost their dad because of him. He wanted to put a stop to it.'

And in the process rob three infants of their mother, not to mention the hell he'd jettisoned the other victims' families into. That was the problem with revenge; it removed any semblance of logic.

'Does he know who carried out the hit and run?'

'No.'

Coupland was already shaking his head. 'He's lying!'

'He's come clean about everything else, Kevin. Besides, he says he's willing to give evidence that Tunny sanctioned McMahon's murder.'

'He really is on a death wish,' Coupland muttered. It

was as well to be hung for a sheep as a lamb, he supposed.

Alex looked as though she'd taken root on his desk; she seemed in no hurry to join Ashcroft in the interview room. She was building up to something, though he had no idea what. 'There's something else, though. He swears he didn't kill your mother. He says he didn't even see her.'

Coupland's head snapped up, 'Where is he now?'

'He's been taken back down to the cells.'

'I need to speak to him.'

'I believe him, Kevin. He's got no reason to lie. Besides, it's my case now.'

Coupland looked away, took a breath as he processed this. *Come on man, stay focussed. Bloody well think.* He fixed Alex with his full beam stare. 'He's the closest we've come to finding out who rammed that car into James McMahon, leaving him for dead. And that's *my* case, if you recall.'

CHAPTER TWENTY-THREE

DCI Mallender sanctioned that Coupland could interview Liam Roberts on two conditions: that Cueball would partner him in the interview room, and that Coupland would remain seated throughout the duration. Coupland was more than happy to comply, and equally happy for Roberts' solicitor to accompany his client, even though in this instance Roberts was merely helping them with their enquiries.

'Just for the record my client is here to assist with your investigation into the murder of James McMahon, he is doing so voluntarily. He has been advised to seek advice where an answer may incriminate him in any other ongoing investigation.'

'I'm sure he has,' Coupland replied, 'those school fees won't pay themselves.'

He put the folder he'd been holding onto the table. It contained a copy of Roberts' confession that he'd started the fire at Cedar Falls. Coupland had read it but had no intention of referring to it in relation to this investigation. 'I understand you have denied having anything to do with Barbara Howe's murder, Liam,' he began, 'so I'm going to park any questions relating to that right there,' he said. His eyes fixed on the solicitor to show he knew how to play nice when he had to. 'What I want to know is who killed James McMahon.'

'I already told the other detective I don't know.'

'But it *was* Kieran Tunny who ordered it?'

'I already told her that, too.'

'Yeah, but what I want to know is if he'd asked you instead would you have done it?'

'There's no relevance to this question!' the solicitor barked, but the look Liam shot in Coupland's direction told him his words had hit home.

'I know you want to point the finger at Tunny, Liam, but others are complicit. Murders like this will keep happening if we don't put away every link in the chain.'

'He's hardly a link,' Liam told him, 'he's barely out of nappies let alone school.'

Coupland felt something inside him quicken. 'So you do know who drove the car?'

Liam shook his head. 'No but I know plenty like him. So desperate to impress they'll steal a car to order and mow down a stranger.' Liam paused, enjoying the attention. 'Do you know how much Tunny paid him to kill McMahon?'

Coupland shook his head.

'£500,' Liam replied. '500 quid to decimate a family. Life really is cheap, Mr Coupland, isn't it?'

Coupland let out a long slow breath. 'Can you give me a description, Liam?'

Liam shook his head.

'Come on; help me get him off the street.'

Liam shrugged. 'Not sure I can. He's nothing special, just a short arse wannabee with a daft grin. 'fraid that's the best I can do—'

Coupland was already on his feet, ignoring the worried glance from Cueball. 'We're done,' he barked at him, picking up his folder before heading for the door. 'I'll leave you to thank our guests for coming.'

*

It was easy enough to track him down due to his previous arrest. Sean Bell lived with his parents in a mid-terraced house close to the crematorium. They were at work given the decibel level of the music blaring out of an upstairs window. Coupland stood at the garden gate while uniformed officers banged on the front door before using their big red key to open it. He was brought out in handcuffs, bare chested, manky joggers over top of the range trainers. 'Glad to see you put your blood money to good use,' Coupland said as the boy was taken to the cage at the rear of the police van.

The boy stared at him, his coat hanger grin forming in recognition. 'I fucked your mum…'

'In terms of icebreakers I've heard better,' Coupland replied, shaking his head. 'Save it for when you get to Strangeways, see what your cell mate thinks. Might make for an interesting time come check-in.'

*

The custody sergeant regarded Coupland as he walked up to the desk. 'You on commission?' He asked, eyeing the gob-shite being escorted in behind him.

'All in a day's work,' Coupland answered. 'Has Alan Harkins been brought back down yet?'

The sergeant checked his computer, scrolling and clicking on several buttons. 'Still being interviewed by DC Ashcroft,' he said, turning to greet his latest guest. 'Back so soon..?'

Leaving the uniforms who'd brought Sean Bell in to

do the honours Coupland made his way to the bank of interview rooms in time to see DC Ashcroft coming out of the gents toilets.

'How are you getting on with Harkins?'

'His solicitor asked for a break to confer with his client. DS Moreton's given him ten minutes.'

'Making headway though?'

'We've told him Bernie Whyte's been charged with assaulting Colin Grantham, and that he's admitted to sloping off when he should have been working. It means there's only Harkins left in the frame for abusing the other patients. Just a matter of time I reckon.'

'Where's Alex?'

'Said she wanted to check something in the EMU.'

They turned at the sound of purposeful steps behind them. In her hand Alex held two evidence bags. 'I've just taken these from Barbara Howe's personal effects,' she told them, holding one up to show them what was inside. A copy of Cedar Falls' staff handbook. She turned it over so she could point something out on the back. 'In the spirit of "Transparency,"' she said this making quote marks with her fingers, 'Harkins had the Care Commission's contact details printed on the reverse. I noticed the other day that it had been circled in ink.'

'You reckon Barbara could have been onto him?'

'We can't know for certain, but I remembered there was a note book beside it in the box of personal effects that we collected, in fact it was the notebook I wanted to check.' She showed them a second evidence bag containing a slim jotter, similar to an exercise book a child would use at school. The book had been placed into the evidence bag in such a way that two pages that had been written on were on display.

Coupland took it from her, held it so that the scrawled handwriting became easier to see. A series of random dates had been written down the left hand side of the page. 'Any idea what they refer to?' he asked, glancing at Alex as she shook her head.

Ashcroft held out his hand to take a look. Took a photograph of the pages with his phone before handing the notebook back to Alex. Both Coupland and Alex frowned.

'When I spoke to Shola's contact at the Care Commission, I never asked where they got their information relating to the near miss incidents that had occurred at the home over the previous two years. What if they'd got their information from Barbara? I'll phone them, see if these dates match…' He was already backing away.

Coupland felt a weight begin to lift from his shoulders. The look he gave Alex was hopeful. 'Meanwhile, I'll come in the interview with you…'

'Kevin, if Ashcroft's hunch is right then this gives Harkins one hell of a motive to kill your mother.'

'I know, but I need to hear him say it.'

Alex had moved so her body blocked his entry into the room. She folded her arms as though stressing the point she was making. 'I can't let that happen, Kevin. You do this and he as good as walks away from any conviction and you'll likely be out on your ear. You know that.'

Coupland slumped against the corridor wall. Alex was right but it didn't make it any more palatable. It would mean putting his faith in a justice system he'd spent his whole life upholding. A justice system that didn't always get it right. He shook his head as he walked away.

CHAPTER TWENTY-FOUR

L ynn had sent him a text reminding him she had Zumba after work. She'd uploaded a photo of four bottles of beer she'd left in the fridge for him along with a smiley face. Coupland took one out gratefully before making his way through to the front room. He'd think about sorting dinner later; right now he had neither the appetite nor the inclination for food. The DCI had sent him home, told him he was neither use nor ornament brooding at his desk.

'We'll keep you posted regarding any developments,' he'd promised as he walked with him to his car, as though making sure he was no longer on the premises.

Ashcroft had telephoned him not long after. His contact at the Care Commission confirmed that Barbara Howe had alerted them to concerns relating to the welfare of patients at Cedar Falls, which sparked their initial inspection. He'd re-interviewed Johnny Metcalfe with an independent appropriate adult and he'd admitted to being abused by Alan Harkins. The care home manager had sworn him into silence by threatening him with a transfer to prison to complete his sentence – all he had to do was say he was well enough to serve time.

'Make sure DS Moreton is brought up to speed,' Coupland demanded.

'Already done,' Ashcroft told him.

The doorbell rang. Coupland cursed as he made his

way into the hall, frowning as he eyeballed the figure on the doorstep. 'Christ, shouldn't you be at home watching Pointless?'

'I can go if you like.'

'You're here now.' Coupland stood aside to let him pass. Indicating they go through to the front room where his tell-tale beer bottle awaited him. Amy was having a nap upstairs while Tonto slept; he made a mental note to show his old man the door if he started to get on his nerves. Coupland waited for him to sit down before choosing the seat furthest away from him.

'There's no easy way to say this,' his father began.

'You're dying?' The words came out without thinking; Coupland felt his neck go red. He'd meant it, just not meant to say it aloud.

'We're all dying, Son,' Ged said evenly, 'but no, I'm sorry to disappoint you, it's not that.'

'Okaaay....'

'Suppose I might as well come out and say it.'

'Fill your boots.'

'Your mum kept in touch with me...Not often,' he said quickly, registering the look on Coupland's face. 'Once a year maybe at first, slowing to every couple of years as you got older.'

Coupland struggled to take in his next breath. He opened his mouth but the air wouldn't come. He stood, tried pacing the room, willing himself to stay calm. The room began to tilt and he bent forward, hands on hips like a marathon runner after crossing the finish line. He made a gasping sound, like a fish out of water. He tried to make sense of the thoughts jostling for attention in his head. 'Why didn't you tell us?'

'What good would it have done? Anyway, you never spoke about her.'

'I was scared of you...' His honesty shocked them both, though it was his old man who recovered first.

'Not when you were older,' he said. 'By the time you left home you knew how to stand up for yourself.'

'I left home because I was frightened of what I might do to you.'

A sneer. 'Save your hard man act for the locker room. You were a soft lad. I toughened you up.'

'You were a bully. A nasty, foul mouthed drunken bully, I'm not surprised she left you.'

'So what was her excuse for not taking you, then, if you were so perfect?'

He had him there. 'Why didn't you tell us she'd kept in touch? Why the hell didn't she want to keep in touch with her kids?'

A sigh. Ged eyed Coupland's beer. 'You got anything to drink?'

It had taken all of Coupland's energy to drag himself over to the seat beside his father. He slumped into it, his head falling back until he was staring at the ceiling, 'I'm not budging until you tell me everything.'

'And then we'll share a drink?'

Coupland grunted a yes.

'Your mother had been restless for a long time, Kevin. I knew she was unhappy, I just didn't know the reason why.'

'You didn't look in the mirror then.'

Ged carried on as though he hadn't spoken. 'The day she upped and left I was distraught. She'd packed a bag and left me the briefest of notes. She'd written down your schedule beneath it, what day you had swimming, when I needed to get your games kit ready. She'd bought school trousers in larger sizes for when you grew out of the ones you had. School shirts too. Gifts she asked me to wrap up and give you at Christmas. There was nothing in there about me. It was all about you and how she didn't want your life disrupted because she wouldn't be there.'

Coupland swallowed.

'I didn't hear anything for six months, in that time I threw out most of her stuff. In a way I suppose it was like she'd died. She was dead to me, at least. Then a letter came out of the blue. No address on it, which I don't blame her for. Not now, anyway. She finally told me the reason why.'

Coupland lifted his head and turned to face him. 'You used to bloody hit her, what other reason did she need?'

'It's never as simple as that, Son, you should know that. Turns out there *was* someone else.'

Coupland furrowed his brow, waiting for his father to continue.

'A woman. I know your generation reckon it's no big deal these days, fashionable even, but you need to think about what it was like back then, me a serving officer too. She knew I wouldn't be able to cope with the shame of it. Besides, I had loved her.'

Coupland regarded his father and sighed. If Lynn ever left him, whether for another man or woman it wouldn't matter, it would break him.

'The woman's name was Lillian. They'd met at work. She never said anything else, but I could tell she was happy. Her letters always arrived on your birthday. She asked after you and the girls but it was you she worried about. She thought her being in your life would be a complication. I suppose she thought I'd meet someone, someone else you'd start to call mam, but who'd have me? By then I'd pretty much let myself go. She started using a PO Box address, so I could reply. My letters were short and to the point, answering the questions she asked, nothing more. I suppose it was one of the reasons I didn't move on, I got caught up in the past every time I replied to her and I took it out on you. She didn't write so much once you'd left home. I think she wanted the peace of mind knowing you'd turned out alright. I told her you'd married, and sent her a photo Pat had given me when Amy came along.'

Coupland felt as though his insides had been wrung out. 'What did she say?' he managed.

'She said you deserved to be happy.'

'Did you ever meet up with her?'

Ged shook his head. 'No. Remember she never gave me her proper address. She was right not to. I would have gone over, tried to make her see sense.'

'Like love is something you can switch on and off,' Coupland found himself saying. 'So why did she get a job that required her to live in if she was so loved up?' He couldn't fathom it.

'Lillian got dementia,' Ged explained. 'She died several years back. I reckon that's how your mum got into health care, daresay the live-in arrangements would have helped. Stopped her feeling so alone.'

'Did you hear from her when she moved to Cedar Falls?'
'No.'

'Do you think she was planning to get in touch?'

'Who knows? I suppose it's possible.'

Coupland ran his hands over his face. He felt as though

he'd been hit by a wrecking ball.

'About that drink...'

Coupland pointed to the dining room and several bottles Lynn had bought for their ill-fated dinner. 'Take your pick, just so long as you bring two glasses.'

*

The call he'd been waiting for came just after 9pm. He woke with a start, eyeing the empty gin bottle opened once the wine had run out. There was no sign of his father. In the kitchen, Lynn was talking in hushed tones to Amy. He heard the words, 'rat-arsed' and 'ungrateful sod' though he wasn't sure whether she was referring to him or his old man.

He stared as Alex's name flashed up on the screen. 'Yes?' His voice came out as a whisper.

'Alan Harkins has admitted the charge of murder. He's also admitted to one count of rape and sexually abusing several unnamed patients at Cedar Falls during his time as manager.'

Coupland swallowed.

'Are you still there?'

'Yes,' seemed all he was able to say.

'Barbara wasn't on shift on the night of the fire. Harkins hadn't expected to be interrupted when he made his way up to the isolation room where he'd sent Johnny. Bernie Whyte was off his face in the garden so he thought the coast was clear. He'd drugged Johnny to disorientate him, removed his clothes...'

'Then in walked my mother...'

'Yes. She accused him of hiding Catherine's head-phones in Johnny's room just so he had an excuse to isolate him from the others. She told him she'd been keeping tabs on him; said he wasn't fit to run a home. There was a struggle and Harkins shoved her. She hit her head as she fell backwards against a table. He knew straight away she was dead. Johnny must have run out while they were fighting, Harkins doesn't remember him going as all he could think of by then was getting rid of her body.' Alex stopped. 'We don't need to do this now.'

'Yes we do.'

A pause. 'The drugs had disorientated Johnny; we already have on record he didn't know what day of the week it was. Harkins later threatened him to keep silent.'

'What did Harkins do with my mother?'

Alex cleared her throat. Made a swallowing noise. 'The fire alarm going off was the answer to Harkins' prayers. He saw smoke coming out of Catherine Fry's bedroom and saw his chance.'

'Let me guess. A chance to literally burn the evidence?'

'He carried Barbara into Catherine's room and left her there. Catherine was already unconscious, yet he had the presence of mind to drag her outside in case anyone came looking for her and found Barbara instead.'

'Bastard wasn't as stupid as he looked.'

'Kevin, I'm so, so—'

'—Don't be,' he said, ending the call.

TWO WEEKS LATER

CHAPTER TWENTY-FIVE

It was the day of the Professional Standards hearing. One month since his mother's death at the hands of Alan Harkins. One month since four vulnerable patients became victims of Liam Roberts' arson attack. Two weeks since James McMahon's killer, Sean Bell, began his stint at Strangeways, pending his trial.

One week since Tonto had started teething, and they were all suffering the consequences.

Coupland had arranged to meet his union rep at the station. With time to kill he'd popped out to buy a sandwich that didn't taste as though it had been made a week ago. Besides, he'd needed to stretch his legs, he was getting on everyone's nerves pacing round the CID room though they'd been too good natured to say it. Walking back to the station Coupland froze. Kieran Tunny's car couldn't have been parked closer to the entrance if he'd tried. The vehicle wasn't causing an obstruction but it was turning heads. Coupland sucked in a breath as he moved towards it. The rear window slid down as he drew level.

Tunny eyeballed him. 'I am in your debt, Mr Coupland. Is there anything I can do for you?'

'All part of the job, Kieran, let's leave it at that.'

'I hear you're still getting grief from Reedsy. I can take care of him if you like, make him withdraw his complaint.'

'Like I said before. I can fight my own battles.'

'If you change your mind.'

'I won't.'

Coupland stepped back from the window to indicate the conversation was over, clocking, too late, the Super observing him from an upstairs window, Sergeant Ross, his federation rep, beside him.

*

The mood was sombre in the CID room. 'I've just heard from Donna Chisholm,' Alex muttered. 'Sarah Kelsey's kids are going into care.'

Coupland looked up at the ceiling and swore. 'Seems bloody wrong when it's down to lack of money rather than love.'

'There's always crowdfunding, Sarge,' Krispy piped up, causing both of them to turn in his direction. 'Sorry,' he reddened, 'I didn't mean to eavesdrop.'

Coupland had never heard of crowdfunding. 'Go on lad,' he prompted.

'Well, it's a way of raising money from a large number of people via the internet.'

Alex nodded. 'There was a fella in Newcastle, he was homeless I think. Anyway, he'd been mugged, or assaulted, can't remember which but anyway this girl took pity on him, set up a web page and so much money was raised he was able to move into his own place.'

Coupland looked from her to Krispy. 'Seriously?'

'It would be a way for Donna to be with her grandkids.'

Coupland regarded his eager DC. Had he ever been so keen, he wondered. So desperate for things to turn out right in the end? 'If you're going to get on in this job you're going to have to toughen up, Son. When a job's finished you move on, no matter what the debris looks like in your rear view mirror.' He rifled through the in-tray on top of his desk, pulled out Angelica Heyworth's crumpled business card. 'Call this journalist and tell her she owes me a favour. If she's finished hanging me out to dry maybe she'd consider doing something worthwhile with her time.'

'You might want to consider re-phrasing that,' Alex suggested, widening her eyes at Krispy.

'The lad knows what I mean,' said Coupland, 'She could help start up the bloody campaign.'

Alex grinned at him, 'Deep down under that sullen exterior you're a big softie, aren't you?'

'Breathe a word to anyone and I'll deny it,' he warned.

*

Coupland arrived at HQ an hour early; it didn't pay to piss Professional Standards off. As it was he was made to wait until his allotted time in a waiting room that stank of air freshener. A framed poster on the wall showed off bright eyed officers with shiny teeth and every skin tone imaginable. They all looked happy, as though unpaid overtime and abuse from gob-shites were perks of the job. Coupland scowled. Wondered which of his many misdemeanours would be thrown in his face today. He pulled out his phone and turned it to silent, moved over to the window. The traffic below crawled by. A dog walker inspected the contents of his nose while his dog squatted on the kerb.

'Think there's something wrong with my prostate,' Colin Ross said as he returned from his second trip to the gents since they'd arrived.

Coupland turned to look at his union rep. 'Could be all the tea you've been drinking,' he replied, indicating the empty vending machine cups on the table in front of him.

*

A woman wearing full dress uniform opened the meeting room door. She had more make-up on than was right for her age and eyebrows that looked like glued-on liquorice sticks. 'We're ready to see you now,' she said, standing back to let Coupland, followed by Colin Ross, enter.

She pointed at two chairs opposite a mean looking man with a goitre the size of a grapefruit. He wore standard issue uniform with an inspector's pips on his epaulettes. His colleague took her seat beside him. Coupland whistled inwardly. Two inspectors for the price of one, they were pulling out all the stops, then.

'Sit,' Inspector Goitre demanded, as though Coupland was a wayward dog that needed reminding who his master was.

Coupland's jaw clenched but he did as he was told, eyeballing his federation rep as if to say *See, I can play ball when I need to.* The officers introduced themselves, Inspectors David McAndrew and Sarah Smedley, rearranging their faces into serious frowns as they explained what was going to happen.

'I get it,' Coupland butted in. 'You're going to hang me up by my testicles and I'm going to squirm.'

Liquorice Eyebrows sat bolt upright in her chair, yet neither brow moved, making Coupland wonder if Botox was involved. Inspector Goitre flared his nostrils, 'If you don't treat this process seriously I will have no option but to suspend you pending further investigation.'

The Federation Rep swore under his breath before turning to Coupland. 'Remember what we discussed, Kevin? About you following the advice I give you? Well shut it until I say so.' His voice was neutral but his eyes bore into him. He'd been cool during the journey across the city. Courteous, but nothing more. He didn't bring up that he'd seen Coupland talking to a notorious gangster so Coupland decided not to bring it up either. Even so, something hung in the air, unsaid.

Inspector Goitre shuffled the papers in front of him and began to read. 'Seems you've been excelling yourself, DS Coupland,' he observed. 'I understand you were taken off a case recently.'

Coupland gripped the armrest on his chair but said nothing. 'I would ask that we focus our attention on the current complaint, Sir,' his rep piped up. 'DS Coupland has been asked here to answer to the allegation made against him by Mr Austin Smith, nothing more.'

'As if that wasn't enough,' Inspector Goitre observed, shuffling his papers some more before dropping them onto the desk as though they were contaminated. 'We've read the complaint Mr Smith has made against you, and we've watched the footage of you bringing him out of the premises on Bury New Road where you arrested him. I don't think the injury he sustained is in any doubt here.'

Coupland shook his head. 'I never said it was.'

'So what do you have to say, DS Coupland? How do you intend to answer his allegation that you brutally assaulted him while discharging your duty as an officer of GMP?'

Coupland stared at him, his gaze moving to liquorice

brows then over to Colin Ross. He made a sound that resembled a slow puncture. 'What do you want me to say? That I didn't mean it?' Before his rep had a chance to reply Coupland whipped his head round to give both inspectors his full beam glare. 'Of course I didn't mean it! I was trying to apprehend someone who was trying to get away, how many times…?'

Inspector Goitre's mouth twitched. 'Indeed, DS Coupland, but this isn't the first time you've gone gung-ho into a situation, regardless of the risk to the people about you, is it?'

Coupland's brow creased. 'I don't know what you're talking about.' Confused, he looked to his rep but he just shrugged, as if to say *New one on me…*

'Correct me if I'm wrong but weren't you involved in an incident last year, apprehending a suspect who fell to his death from the top of a multi-story car park?'

Coupland stared at him askance. 'Are you for real?' Coupland asked.

'This has nothing to do with the current complaint,' his rep cut in.

'No, but it sets the scene doesn't it? Paints a picture of the type of man you are representing.'

Coupland's expression darkened. In his mind's eye he saw the response they were looking for. More conciliatory. Agreeable. A wringing of hands before bending over and letting them do the honours. He swallowed down bile threatening to rise in his mouth. Coupland had never taken the easy option in his life, and he wasn't going to start now.

'Have you ever walked up and down the streets of this city?' he asked.

'I'm sorry?'

'Time for me to confer with my client I think,' interrupted his rep.

Coupland ignored him, his hand raised palm outwards warning the officer to butt out. He turned his attention to the two inspectors opposite. 'Ever put yourself in a situation where you think your number's up? Where you wish you hadn't been narky at home the night before, so your Missus has something good to cling onto when she gets the knock?'

The federation rep looked up at the ceiling. Inspector Goitre glared. 'My career isn't the one under scrutiny DS Coupland.'

'Nor mine,' chunnered liquorice brows, sitting forward in her chair.

'Twenty-four years.'

Inspector Goitre knotted his eyebrows. Coupland stole a glance over to Liquorice Brows but they hadn't budged. 'Sorry, I don't follow.'

'That's how long I've served on the force,' Coupland said. 'Twenty-four years chasing arseholes, putting my life on the line so the people of this city can go about without fear. Have I made a difference? I doubt it,' he shrugged. 'Every day I make choices that'd make you piss in your pants. Up there on your high moral ground you can't taste the fear of two dozen refugees as they're led away to safety, the smell of their shit in your nostrils while you square up to the tough guy that drove a child to her death. You don't see the husk of her body crammed into a bag when you sleep. I deal with dangerous men, Sir, Ma'am. Men that kill as soon as look at you, and you know what? I'm proud to defend this city and the people in it, yet sitting here in front of you I'm made to feel ashamed. Austin Smith had access to weapons, you know that don't you? It says so in your *report*.' Coupland's mouth twisted as he said this, as though he'd tasted something foul. 'If he'd been able to reach them he could have shot a civilian, a serving officer, that or been taken out by the tactical unit and not able to give evidence in the trafficking trial. At least I brought him out alive.'

'So we should be grateful. Is that what you're suggesting?'

'I don't want gratitude,' Coupland sighed. 'A bit of respect might be nice though.' He shuddered involuntarily. Christ, he was beginning to sound like Tunny.

'DS Coupland has had to deal with some very difficult circumstances,' his rep piped up. 'I am sure he would be responsive to training, or undergo counselling, if you saw fit.'

Coupland spun round in his chair so quickly his rep blanched. 'What? So some shrink can point to a moment in time and say that's the cause? Jesus wept, man, that'd be some list. Look, I get it, we all have shit to deal with, but we have to live within the rules. If I don't believe that then I'm in the wrong job.' He threw his hands in the air. 'I was out of order, I overstepped the mark…if you want to suspend me or put me back in uniform for Christ's sake, put me out of my misery and get on with it.' He pushed himself to his feet, ignoring the glare from the officer meant to represent him.

Inspector McAndrew lay down his pen and leaned back in his chair. He glanced at his colleague; a nod told him to continue. 'We'll make our decision known to your superintendent, DS Coupland. I've no doubt he'll be in touch.'

Coupland stared at him. Was that it? His career was in the balance but time for a commercial break? He was about to say something else when he caught Colin Ross's eye. If a look ever conveyed, 'Shut the fuck up,' that was it. Besides, both inspectors had shuffled their papers away into shiny briefcases, were already discussing the menu of the gastropub off the slip road of the M62.

He'd been dismissed.

＊

There was a bottle of something fizzy on the table. Three glasses beside it. He'd phoned Lynn and told her how the hearing had gone the moment he'd got into his car. Nothing about his version of events suggested a celebration was in order. 'We won on the lottery or something?' He could but live in hope.

'Better than that. Amy's decided on a name.'

'I'm sticking with Jaxxon,' she said, looking up at him. Lynn was already tearing the foil off the prosecco.

'You know I'll call him Jack,' Coupland warned, 'Or Jacko even, that has a ring to it…'

'I know, Dad!' Amy groaned, but her eyes were smiling the way they used to, back when he'd been the most important man in her life. He looked down at baby Jaxxon and supressed a smile. In terms of relegations it wasn't all bad, he supposed. He didn't mind playing second fiddle to this bruiser one little bit. The sound of a cork popping made him look up; Lynn filled a glass and passed it to Amy, the second glass she handed to him before pouring her own drink.

'We can start planning a naming ceremony,' Lynn began, heading into the kitchen for a notepad and pen.

'While we're on the subject,' Coupland said, moving to sit beside Amy on the sofa where she leaned back, exhausted, 'I think we should speak to a lawyer, get some papers drawn up so that if anything happened, you could be sure Jack would come to us.'

'You're a ray of sunshine, Dad!'

'I'm serious, Ames, you never know, further down the line, if something were to happen to you, his other relatives might crawl out of the woodwork, lay claims you might not have wanted.'

Amy stared at him.

'Besides, I guess this is my ham fisted way of saying to you that he's one of us, and for as long as I'm around I'll do all I can to make sure it stays that way.'

'You're not ill are you?'

'No love,' he smiled. 'I'm going nowhere, just trying to make amends.'

'Then that's champion,' she smiled, digging the remote from between the sofa cushions and flicking on the nightly round up of Strictly, though she was asleep on his shoulder before the celebrity massacring the foxtrot had finished.

Lynn had taken Jaxxon upstairs, was elbow deep in Sudocrem when the doorbell rang. Coupland cursed, propping Amy up with cushions as he got to his feet. They weren't expecting visitors. Whoever was at the door could bugger off.

He could tell they were cops the moment he clapped eyes on them, yet there was an awkwardness about them, in the way they cleared their throats and failed to meet his gaze that put him on alert. He didn't take in their names; they were from Eccles, that's all he registered. He'd played five-a-side footie with a DC from there back in the days when following an exercise regime meant more than watching it on the TV. He stared at their heads while he tried to compute why there were on his doorstep, their features set to neutral.

'DS Coupland, we'd like you to accompany us to the station.'

Coupland's face grew serious. 'What the hell for? I've not long finished my shift.' They exchanged glances, and he felt almost sorry for them as he sensed their reluctance to be there.

'Austin Smith was found dead in his cell this afternoon. An anonymous call has been made, implicating you as a result of the complaint he made about you following his arrest.'

'Is this some sort of sick joke?'

'I'm sorry, Sarge, no.'

He pictured Tunny sitting in the back of his car, window wound down. He recalled their conversation. *I hear you're still getting grief from Reedsy. I can take care of him if you like…'* Hadn't he been clear enough in his refusal? Had Tunny arranged this as the payback he'd promised. Or to stir things up? Either way Austin Smith's death was down to him… Coupland was sure the tightness across his chest was all that prevented the contents of his stomach from rising into his mouth. He heard Lynn's footsteps hurry down the stairs. She'd have seen the patrol car from the baby's room. She paused in the hallway, as though sensing the tension, calling out 'Is everything OK?'

Coupland felt like he'd forgotten how to breathe. He turned, nodding slowly before following the officers to their car.

He heard, from the bedroom upstairs, the sound of Tonto crying.

THE END

ABOUT THE AUTHOR

Emma writes full time from her home in East Lothian. When she isn't writing she can be seen walking her rescue dog Star along the beach or frequenting bars of ill repute where many a loose lip has provided the nugget of a storyline. Find out more about the author and her other books at: https://www.emmasalisbury.com

Read on for the first chapter in the next book of the DS Coupland series:
Sticks and Stones

CHAPTER ONE

The sign above the main entrance said 'Visitor Centre,' though it was unlike any tourist attraction she'd ever been to before. There would be a certain amount of sitting and gawping involved, she supposed…and a hell of a lot of relief when it was time to go home. She presented the ID she'd been asked to bring to the woman behind the reception desk. A passport and utility bill. The passport had been easy. Finding a paper bill had proved a lot more troublesome. In the end she'd had to go online and download a statement from her energy supplier, she couldn't think of the last time she'd been sent a bill in the post. The receptionist tapped on the keyboard in front of her before pointing to a wall of lockers. The woman opened her purse and fished out the pound coin the website had warned her to bring before placing her bag and phone inside one of them and making sure it was secure.

The queue wasn't as long as she'd expected. Mainly women chatting in groups or clutching onto small children. A teenage girl waiting in front of her carried a baby asleep in a car seat. A little girl with a woman too old to be her mother stood patiently, chewing on a finger nail as they waited to go through security. It was a bit like going on holiday, she supposed, as she placed her jacket into an oblong tray then lifted it onto the x-ray machine's conveyor belt before stepping through the security scanner. The rub down was more than she'd had to endure at any airport though, as she followed instructions to lift her hair and open her mouth so they could look under her tongue. Security checks completed, they were ushered into a small room, the rear door of which was closed before the one at the front opened.

She gave her name to the uniformed man behind the desk. He consulted a list in front of him, his finger tracing down the page until he found what he was looking for, then told her which table she'd been allocated. She was the only person who went straight to her seat. The other women, and they were mainly women, headed to a kiosk in the corner manned by volunteers, before traipsing back with drinks and snacks which they laid out in front of the empty place on their table. One by one the visitors took their seats until the room resembled a speed dating venue where only half of the prospective partners had bothered turning up. In the minutes that followed, the woman sitting at the table beside her repositioned the crisps, chocolate and juice she'd bought so that they faced the same way round, like a market trader setting out her stall. Satisfied, she sipped at the drink she'd bought for herself, hands circling the paper cup as she blew across the top of it.

She found it hard not to stare, yet the last thing she wanted was to catch someone's eye. To actually be seen here. To have someone look at her quizzically because she didn't fit in. Or worse still, nod and smile at her because she did. *That* would make it real.

A door at the far side of the room opened and a line of men filed in. Some cocksure, others bewildered, they moved towards the women, returning their waves with raised hands or a nod, their steps measured but purposeful until they'd reached the designated table. Smiles broke onto their faces as they stooped to hug and kiss their partners, careful to keep hands in view at all times. A sign on each table stated drinks and snacks could not be shared.

Two small children ran past her table to get to the play area. She was distracted for a moment, surprised at how normal they found their surroundings, but then children were resilient. It was adults who struggled to accept change when it came. She saw him then. Standing back from the others. Eyes scanning the room as though doubtful she'd show. She raised her hand to wave. He nodded, moving in her direction slowly as though fearful he'd be called back. She wondered if onlookers could see this was the first time they'd found themselves in a place like this. That this was the first time she'd seen him since his incarceration. She rose from her seat as he leaned in to peck her on her cheek; touched her face where his stubble had grazed her. He stood awkwardly in front of her before dropping onto the seat opposite, as though self-conscious of his dishevelled state.

Prisoners weren't allowed out of their chairs once seated and she realised too late that he might have enjoyed a hot drink and a biscuit. If she went to the kiosk now she'd have less time to spend with him. They stared at each other. Even though his lawyer had moved heaven and earth to get her on today's visit list the relief she'd previously felt turned to anger. 'For Christ's sake,' she spat. 'How the hell did this happen?'

Book 6, Sticks and Stones, is available now

400

Printed in Great Britain
by Amazon